Becoming

JANICE

Becoming

JANICE

Ragini Werner

IGUANA

Published by Iguana Books
720 Bathurst Street
Toronto, ON M5S 2R4

Cover design: Jonathan Relph
Author photograph: Leonie Kuizenga

ISBN 978-1-77180-690-9 (paperback)
ISBN 978-1-77180-689-3 (epub)

This is an original print edition of *Becoming Janice*.

For Thea and Fay

One is not born, but rather becomes, a woman.
— Simone de Beauvoir

Part 1: Kobus

London, July 1979

Chapter 1

Janice had no bedtime music of her own. Last night she'd fallen asleep without switching off her transistor and the batteries were flat. No matter. Upstairs man had his radio on loud, and through the ceiling, she could hear Michael Jackson urging her not to stop till she'd had enough. She smiled at the thought. She liked the song, liked the rhythm—it made her want to dance. She pointed her toes under the raw blanket. It was itchy. She'd have to invest in some sheets. Soon.

The front doorbell rang twice, and the song cut off in mid-beat. Upstairs man hauled open a window and called in a guttural accent, "Is that you, Paul?"

A deep voice concurred from below, "Yes, it's me."

The tinkle of falling keys. The front door slammed, and someone trudged heavily up two flights of stairs. Two sets of footsteps shuffled over her ceiling.

Janice waited for the music to start again but it didn't. She turned back to the book she was reading by candlelight because she didn't have a bedside lamp. Yet. A chink in the curtain behind her head let in the glare of a streetlamp, adding its ugly light to the candle stub burning unsteadily on the saucer beside her. The flame flared and died and then it was too dark to read. Janice flicked the curtain shut and put away the book.

Curling into a cocoon, Janice wished she could switch on her transistor and listen to the late-night arts program she always enjoyed. Abruptly, her bedsit door crashed open, shattering her thoughts. A huge man swayed in the doorway, silhouetted by the hall light. Janice clutched the blanket to her naked chest. In an instant, fear turned to fury.

"What the fuck do you think you're doing?"

"Looking for the toilet," slurred the man, backing out fast. "Wrong door."

The bathroom was next to her room. Janice scrambled out of bed and set the lock on her door. Stupid, she hadn't locked it. She would never forget it again. She stomped back to bed. That's all she needed, a stranger bursting into her bedsit.

Janice waited impatiently for her heart to stop its frantic hammering. She had to distract herself from the fright. That bloke must be the visitor. Unlike upstairs man, she didn't get visitors. No matter. She liked being on her own. She quickly had enough of people, having to deal with them at work, and needed time to recover from hours filled with socializing.

Janice sighed, hugging the hollow that settled in her stomach. Why did she feel so empty? Still, dare she say it, so desolate? Four whole years after Ariel. She shook her head to dispel the pain. It had been hard at first, but she'd gotten over losing her first real friend. Hadn't she? And she would make new friends, wouldn't she? So, okay, here she was, a stranger in London. She knew no one. It would take time to make new friends. Janice sighed. A friend, not even a girlfriend, just one friend would do. But now was no time to be maudlin. Trying to stay positive, she thought about her assets.

First, she had the job. A fortnight ago, she'd walked into the Willing Workers Agency under the misconception that she would have to pay them to find her a job. After a cursory chat with Tracy, who looked after the temps, Janice met Mrs. Brockett, the manager, and was surprised to be offered a job on the spot. Now she was looking after people seeking a permanent position. The irony of being new and clueless yet helping Londoners find work in their own city did not escape her.

Second, she had this bedsit, even if it was only a barren room with a bay window on the first floor of a house in Tufnell Park. She'd used her brand-new guide to find it, around the corner from the tube station. Mrs. Palmer lived downstairs and rented out the rooms on the two floors above. She seemed satisfied with Janice. It helped that she had the job. A month's rent in advance, a promise not to keep pets or bring men home (as if she ever would) and she was in. Not bad going for a twenty-two-year-old on her own in a foreign country. She didn't need help, least of all from parents. She stifled a pang of guilt. She owed hers a postcard at least. But knowing them, they would not be worried about their big baby. She might be big, Janice grinned, but she wasn't a baby. Her parents could wait.

Next morning, Janice huddled in the bath as close as her long legs would let her get to the taps. She rinsed her armpits, hoping there was enough of someone else's fifty pence in the meter to keep the tepid water going. She'd put her own piece in tomorrow. Promise. Today she was lucky and finished before the flame died in the geyser. Obeying the sign by the door exhorting occupants to leave the bathroom clean, she dried herself, then swilled a corner of her towel around the grimy bath and returned to her room.

Later, on her way out, Janice noticed an envelope on the hall table addressed to "The Lady in Room Two." Hang on, that was her. She withdrew a pencil drawing of a one-eyed man captioned "No one's perfect." Underneath, in a looping scrawl, was "Sorry. My visitor mistaked your door for the WC." It was signed "Jacobus Boer (Kobus)."

Janice admired the drawing. It was clever, economical, not a single line out of place. Whoever had made it could draw. She was amused by the spelling error (was it intentional?) and touched by the thoughtful note. Upstairs man, his name was Kobus. She'd come across him the day she moved in. He'd offered to carry her rucksack up to her room, but she'd turned him down. Better to keep people at a distance. Better not get involved, especially with straight men.

She dropped the note in the first bin she passed. It was a kind gesture. Kobus seemed okay. Pity he was a bloke.

Chapter 2

Saturday morning and the high street was crowded with shoppers. Squeezing past a mother and pram blocking the entrance of the cake shop, Janice confronted her tall reflection in the glass door. How horrible. Cursed with her father's long bones, narrow hips, and strong, square shoulders that made her look like a man from behind, she felt like a cart horse and didn't need reminding.

In the corner of her bedsit hung a small mirror above the kitchenette sink and that was enough reflection for Janice. She'd had to reposition the mirror higher so that she could see more of herself. The eyes were okay. Top lip could be fuller, if she could change anything, but she liked her sharp cheekbones and soft hair. It was brown, so deep and dark it often looked black, like her eyes, and it framed her face in a natural wave. She felt safe hiding behind her hair.

Janice went in and waited in the queue. The scent of warm bread wreathed around her. She was hungry. When it was her turn, she chose two cream buns and two steak and kidney pies. She always bought two of any takeaway food. Partly out of greed, but more to conceal that she was shopping for one. It didn't pay to advertise that you were alone.

Back on the street she wriggled open a bag and dabbed a finger into the squishy center of a bun. She sucked the cream off her finger, checking to see if anyone noticed. At Tufnell Park tube station, she turned right, hurrying home. When she unlocked the front door, the net curtain twitched in the bay window. Mrs. Palmer, spying again.

In her room, Janice found her place in her book, tore open a bag, and began to eat a pie. The first mouthful was delicious. Savory gravy oozed down her chin. Sunlight hit the prism she'd hung in the window, zapping cheerful rainbows onto the walls. Oh bliss. This was her haven. A place where a person could read and eat in peace.

A knock. What now? Janice hid the food in the kitchenette and opened her door.

A beaming Mrs. Palmer trilled, "Hello, dear, saw you come in. It's time for your rent." She pushed into the room and gave a sniff, discerning a waft of pie. Her beady eye fell on the candle by the bed. "You be careful, won't you? Wouldn't do to burn my lovely house down."

"That won't happen." Janice could see the crown of the landlady's head. She imagined tapping that head like a rubber ball and bouncing the woman out of her room. She shook her hair in front of her face, trying to hide a smile.

Mrs. Palmer tilted her head, detecting the smile, then leaned over and pulled back the blanket on the unmade bed. Janice slept on her unzipped sleeping bag, with only the blanket to cover her. "No sheets. No pillowcase. That's not nice, is it?" Turning, she indicated the paperbacks toppled on the fireside table. "Like to read, don't you, dear? I like Barbara Cartland. Do you too?"

Janice couldn't find a polite reply. Undaunted, Mrs. Palmer continued her inspection. "Besides that glass thingy in the window, you haven't put up the bibs and bobs people do to make themselves at home. I suppose you're taking your time to settle in."

Mrs. Palmer was like that stickybeak who lived down the road from her parents in Auckland, a nosy homemaker with nothing better to do all day than spy on the neighbors and gossip. Janice pressed her lips together, fumbled in her satchel for her rent booklet and wallet, and counted out the ten pounds she owed for this week's rent.

Mrs. Palmer took the money, scrawled the date and her initials in the booklet, and handed it back. "Dearie me. Your room could do with some cheering up. Please make yourself at home. I like my tenants to feel at home. Now I must love you and leave you. It's time for *Tomorrow's World* on the BBC. I do like that program, don't you, dear?" She made a last show of surveying the room. "How silly of me. You haven't got a television set. Never mind, I'm sure you'll be able to afford one soon."

Janice fetched the food from its hiding place. The pies were cold, congealed and unappetizing. She set them aside and crammed the buns down instead, relishing the squishy cream. She tried to read but her focus was ruined. Damn Mrs. Palmer for interrupting her.

Janice unhooked her coat from behind the door. She hadn't explored past the shops yet. She'd go for a walk, run away from the irritation.

Grabbing her satchel, checking she had her keys, Janice slammed her door and rushed downstairs. Mrs. Palmer and that Kobus chap were by the hall table, watching her approach. He was small for a man and made himself look smaller by the way he hunched his shoulders. She could see a bald spot forming in his mousy-brown hair. Hangdog eyes were looking up at her. It would be rude to pass without a word. Janice forced herself to stop. "Got your note."

Kobus rubbed his chin, seeming to register how tall Janice was. "I want to say sorry about last night. Hope you didn't get a fright."

Aware of Mrs. Palmer's curious glance, Janice interrupted. "Please forget it, it's okay." Like a Wimbledon spectator, Mrs. Palmer looked from Kobus up to Janice, and back at Kobus again. Noticing this made Janice shy and want to escape. "Must dash, I'm late." She slipped outside, hearing Kobus answer Mrs. Palmer's question. The woman replied and, funnily enough, it sounded as if they were both speaking Dutch.

It was July, well into the northern summer. In New Zealand, this was no time to be going to the beach. At home, the days would be short and cold. Opening her coat to the warm wind, Janice felt a pang of regret that she'd left New Zealand far behind. July should be cold, not warm like this. She strode past the tube station, jaywalked across the busy high street, and continued uphill, heading for Hampstead Heath. This neighborhood was long past its sell-by date. Most houses needed a new coat of paint. Tiny gardens in the gap between front door and footpath struggled in a battle with weeds. She turned on impulse down a side street.

Shoppers laden with groceries were straggling home. Janice overheard their north London accents and marveled at how foreign English could sound. These people belonged to this neighborhood. *And so will I*, she thought. *I might be new, but I won't be a tourist.* She wasn't like the acquaintances who had made the trip to London before her, traveling all this way and returning with shallow impressions of Buckingham Palace and Earl's Court. Kangaroo Valley, they called it, as too many Aussies and Kiwis gravitated there. But not Janice. No way would she become one of the cud-chewing roos living there. She wasn't like the rest of them up from Down Under, boomeranging here for the overseas experience and going back home straight after. She'd come to London on a one-way ticket. She was twenty-two, all grown up. She could stand on her own feet. Not looking where she was going, Janice stumbled over an uneven tile in the pavement. Regaining her balance, she smiled at the irony.

Looking ahead, she saw that her random march had brought her nowhere near Hampstead Heath. Instead, she was back on the high street. She smiled. She couldn't get lost if she tried. She waited at the pedestrian crossing and followed a mother hauling a flighty toddler by the hand. Leaning back from her mother, the little girl spied Janice and pulled an impudent face. Janice stuck out her tongue in return and was amused by the surprise on the child's face. She could see her thinking, *Big people aren't supposed to act like this.* Janice had to laugh. The naughty little girl reminded her of how Ariel had looked when they had met at school.

The garden gate scraped. Upstairs man was clutching a carton of milk and loaf of bread to his chest. He'd followed Janice home from the shops, and she hadn't even noticed.

Kobus broke the awkward silence. "It is a nice day to be out, isn't it?"

"Yes, it is." Janice had a limited supply of small talk. She shivered. If only Ariel were here to deal with this stranger. Not for the last time Janice wished she could follow Ariel's lead.

Kobus continued, "But the wind is cold, yes? I am putting the kettle on to warm up. Do you join me for tea? Or coffee? I have both. If you like."

The man looked harmless, hunched into his tatty bomber jacket. It was a kind offer. It would be rude to turn him down. There was no escape. "Okay, but I can't stay long."

"That is not a problem. A brief but powerful stay is nice."

What's with this "brief but powerful"? Sounded like a literal translation of a Dutch expression. Janice sifted through her limited vocabulary, what she remembered from hearing her parents speak Dutch. Ha. She had it: *kort maar krachtig.* He meant "short but sweet."

Kobus may be short but was he going to be sweet? There was only one way to find out. Janice crossed her arms over her misgivings and followed him inside.

Chapter 3

They walked to the second floor in silence. Kobus shoved open his door and waved Janice inside. "Sorry it is a mess. Please sit. I bring tea, okay?"

Instead of having a kitchenette tucked into the corner, Kobus had a proper kitchen next door. He ducked in there and put on the kettle. This room was nearly the same as her own, except it had no bay window, and the bed was lined up along the front wall. A table was where her bed stood, with a sideboard beside it. The wardrobe had a long mirror on its door. The low table and armchairs on either side of the fireplace were the same.

But unlike her own barren space, this room was cozy. Huge travel posters showing a field of tulips, the Eiffel Tower, and an azure sea patched the faded wallpaper. They were corny but brightened the place up. Every surface was cluttered, from the ashtray overflowing with smelly stubs of cigar to the floppy coil of white rope on the low table to the sideboard buried under mounds of junk. The mantelpiece was crammed with paper. Janice leaned over to see piles of old betting slips, coupons for football pools, and lottery tickets. Why would Kobus want to keep these reminders of what must add up to a lot of losses?

Pinned above the mantelpiece was a sketch of a triumphant dog holding what must have been a winning ticket in his paw. Janice recognized the looping scrawl of the caption: "What a lotto luck." The drawing was a clever self-portrait. Somehow, in the lines defining the shape of the dog's head, he had managed to suggest his receding hairline and sad cast of his eyes. So Kobus saw himself as a hound dog. Funnily enough, so did she, what with those hangdog eyes he fixed on her. Then Janice noticed the sketch pad and jar of sharp pencils on the sideboard. Well, well, well. Drawing cartoons must be Kobus's hobby. That, and having the odd bet. Oh well, there were worse addictions in life.

Janice eased into the armchair with its back to the bed, rearranging a lumpy cushion behind her, and stifled a shot of irritation. She could see her reflection in the wardrobe mirror and angled herself in the chair to avoid it.

If Kobus noticed her tension, he ignored it. Returning, he handed Janice a mug of tea and sat in the other chair. The tea was strong and milky, the way she liked it. He offered to fetch sugar and when she refused, he laughed. "Just as well you don't take it. I've run out."

Janice shook her hair over her eyes, regretting having come. She took a large swallow to speed her escape. The scalding tea went down the wrong way. She coughed. Kobus leaned over to pat her shoulder, but Janice waved him away. "No panic." She didn't want him touching her.

He slurped his tea. Then he said, "You know my name is Kobus Boer. What's yours?"

"You mean Mrs. Palmer hasn't told you?" Kobus shook his head. "I suppose we haven't been properly introduced. I'm Janneke de Vetter, but you can call me Janice."

"Welcome, Janneke de Vetter." Kobus's eyes shone. He said her name the Dutch way, making the hard *J* sound like a soft *Y*, just like her mother did.

"Janneke is such a mouthful. Please, Janice will do."

"So you are Dutch. You sound like you are from Australia or New Zealand."

"Drat. My accent gives me away." To his encouraging nod she continued. "I was born in Amsterdam but grew up in Auckland. We moved to New Zealand when I was five."

Kobus smiled. "That explains it. *Spreek jij Nederlands?*"

"Nope, it's all double Dutch to me. I can understand some because my parents still use it, but I grew up speaking English. My parents wanted me to become a proper Kiwi."

"Have you been here long?"

"I landed at Heathrow on May 28, 1979. That makes it six weeks next Monday."

"Is that all? I thought you been here for years."

Janice ignored the mistake. She was secretly pleased. "I'm not a real Londoner yet."

"Why did you come here?" When Janice hesitated, Kobus rushed on. "*Ach*, I am sorry. I want you to feel comfortable." His eyes twinkled. "But you cannot when I give you, how you say? The third degree. Forgive my curiosity. None of my business, isn't it?"

Janice hid her embarrassment by draining her mug.

Kobus took her rigid silence in his stride. Finishing his tea with a smack of the lips, he said, "Time for a refill. Are you ready?"

Janice didn't want more but felt it would be impolite to refuse. She handed over her mug and sat in silence as Kobus left the room.

He called from the kitchen, "You know, I am Dutch also."

Janice called back, "I thought you might be German, but I recognize your accent now. My mother sounds like you and she's lived in Auckland for nearly twenty years." Like her mother still did, Kobus placed the emphasis on the wrong syllable of words that must be the same in English and Dutch. The way he'd said "comfortable," for instance, with the accent on "table" and not on "comf" was how her mother said it. The similarity put Janice at ease.

Kobus returned and handed over the tea. Settling in his chair, he asked, "Have you been to Amsterdam?" Janice shook her head. "Don't you want to see your place of birth?"

"Well, yes, I do. It's definitely on my list, but I don't want to go yet. I want to stick around in London first. I came here for the West End." Kobus raised an inquiring eyebrow. "I'm mad about the theater. I love good acting. And English actors are the best in the world. I want to see as many live plays in the West End as I can, when I can afford the ticket."

Kobus agreed. "I like it very well. English acting is best. English actors speak so I can understand every word. Do you have television?" Again, Janice shook her head. Pointing to his own small set, he added, "Every time I watch the BBC program, *Play for Today*. For my English, to improve me. Do you want to watch it with me?"

Janice automatically shook her head. "No, sorry. I have an appointment." She glanced ostentatiously at her watch. "Which reminds me, I have to go now."

Kobus seemed unfazed by the rejection. "*Ach*, well, *Nederland* will be there waiting for you. Like it is waiting for me to come back. We have that in common, *toch*?"

Janice shook her head. What on earth could she have in common with this strange wee man? And hiding her sigh of relief, she escaped downstairs.

Chapter 4

Next morning, it wasn't easy for Janice to escape Kobus. He waylaid her in the corridor, blocking the bathroom door as she appeared with her towel draped around her neck. Leaning back on the banister to give her the space to pass, he began, "Hello, Janneke. How nice—"

"Janice! Call me Janice!"

"*Ach*, sorry. I forget myself. Janneke is such a pretty Dutch name."

"Pretty or not, I prefer Janice."

Kobus hung his head, looking up at her with mournful eyes. "Janice." He paused. "Please let me make up for my mistake. Let me make you a cup of real Dutch coffee."

Janice dithered. It was another long, empty Sunday and she had nothing better to do but keep reading through her pile of paperbacks. She was bored. She was lonely. He was only being nice. She couldn't fault him for that. "Oh, all right. But let me get dressed first."

Thirty minutes later, Janice and Kobus were sitting opposite each other in front of the unlit fire. Janice put her empty cup down on the low table. "That was delicious. Thanks."

Kobus smiled. "I knew you would like it. Douwe Egberts coffee tastes much nicer than the drink the English call coffee."

Janice had to agree. "Do you get it sent over?" Kobus looked blank. "Does your mother or father send you coffee from Holland?"

Kobus gave a one-sided shrug, scratching his nose. He avoided the question. Instead, he said, "I come from a family of fishers of the Ijsselmeer, what used to be called the Zuiderzee before they raised the land around it. Do you know it?"

At Janice's nod, he rose out of his chair and fumbled through the rubble on the mantelpiece. He found the cigar stub he was looking for and lit it. "Do you mind?" When Janice shook her head, he added, "They are so expensive, I ration myself to half at a time. Disgusting habit, isn't it?"

"Doesn't bother me." Janice smiled despite herself. She liked the aroma.

Kobus reached over again and withdrew a postcard. "This is where I come from."

Janice looked at the card and dismissed it. "Very pretty." It was an aerial shot of a quaint village, backed by a lighthouse, with a small curve of beach and bobbing lines of fishing boats in the harbor. She could see nothing remarkable in the card.

"Yes, this is Urk. It was an island in the Zuiderzee until they built the dike that connected it to the mainland. That was in 1939." Kobus smiled. "Long before I was born."

Restraining the urge to giggle (Urk), Janice went to hand the card back. But Kobus refused it. "No," he persisted. "Take another look. I keep it because it is special." He sat with his hand covering his chin, eyes twinkling. "Look at who is walking in the harbor."

She made out the tiny form of a striding boy. Another look revealed the tinier form of a white dog running toward a line of fishing nets hung out to dry in the sun. "That's not you?"

Kobus gave a bow. "Me and my little dog, Kuifje. This card is to buy in the local tourist office."

Janice compared the picture of the boy frozen forever in the card with Kobus before her. She could see no resemblance, apart from the hunch of the shoulders. The figure was too small to recognize. "How do you know it is you?"

"See the hat? I always wore a red woolly hat. And that's my Kuifje, pure white. I took him every day for a walk along the harbor and back along the beach. It has to be us."

Janice made out a red dot on the boy's head and conceded that it could be a hat. It was Kobus. "How incredible. I've never met anyone in a postcard before."

Kobus smiled. "A souvenir of my youth."

Janice returned the card. "How old were you then?"

"I was nine when Papa died. He was a fisher of the Ijsselmeer, fell off the boat in a storm. After he drowned, Mama and I moved to Amsterdam."

Janice didn't know what to say about Kobus's father so ignored the information. He still called his parents Papa and Mama. A grown man. How pitiful.

Kobus touched his scalp. "I have few hairs, but only that change in twenty-four years."

Janice did the arithmetic. Nine plus twenty-four. Kobus must be in his early thirties, far younger than he looked. She'd thought he was fifty at least. Way too old for her. Huh? What was she thinking? She dipped her head, hiding her eyes. "You're from Amsterdam too? I was born near the Albert Cuyp market. Do you know it?"

"I know the market. We be neighbors. Mama and I live on the other side of the canal, the little part called Devil's Island. Mama still lives there, but without me, she is all alone."

Kobus's voice trailed off at the mention of his mother, and Janice wondered why. It would be unkind to dig for an explanation, so she changed the subject. "Do you like London? Have you seen the sights yet? How do you like Mrs. Palmer? I find her tough going, to tell the truth." Janice heard herself rambling on and snapped her mouth shut.

Kobus seemed unaffected by the sudden stop. He took a last drag of his cigar and stubbed it in the ashtray. "Corrie Palmer is my *tante*. The sister of my mother. Tante Corrie married Tommy Palmer after the war and moved here with him." He gave a little laugh. "It is funny his name was Tommy because he was an English soldier. He was stationed in Amsterdam when they met. You know they used to call English soldiers Tommy in the war."

Janice knew that. "He was an English Tommy called Tommy." She tittered a bit, not wanting to be rude. "Where is Tommy-Tommy now? I haven't seen Mr. Palmer around."

Kobus shrugged. "He died of cancer five years ago."

"Oh." Janice didn't know what to say. "Mrs. Palmer is your auntie, and she's Dutch too. I'd never have guessed. She doesn't sound it. She speaks perfect English. Like you do."

Kobus smiled. "Thank you, but my English is no good. Tante Corrie is living here ever since the war, and I'm here only a few months. When I am here longer, it gets better."

Waving at the mess in the room, Janice went on. "You look pretty settled. Like you've been here longer than a few months. I suppose you've got a job."

"Tante Corrie, her son has a shop near the station. Paul, my nephew, lets me help in the shop. No, sorry—my cousin. I am mixed because nephew and cousin is one word in Dutch. My cousin takes me to the pub, the Ship's Bell. It has a cozy 'sphere. You come with?"

Janice was in a quandary. She understood what prompted the invitation. Kobus wanted to be friends, maybe something more. "Look," she said, "I have to tell you something."

Kobus didn't respond, just looked at her.

"I'd rather get things straight." Janice smiled at the irony of her word choice. "I'm one of those strange sisters who prefers girls." Kobus frowned in confusion. "I'm a lesbian."

"*Ach*, so what? I do not want to get in your pants. I just ask you out for a drink."

Janice snapped her surprised mouth shut. "As long as you understand, I don't like men in that way, and I don't want any hassle."

"I respect that. Okay? We will be, how you say, *platonische* friends? All right?"

"Platonic friends? I don't believe that ever works with straight men."

"I make it work." Kobus gave that hangdog smile. "We will be platonic friends."

Chapter 5

Kobus left her alone at first. Janice was relieved that he wasn't being pushy about friendship, platonic or otherwise. He must have received the message loud and clear. But even though he never tried engaging her in casual chat, she couldn't help noticing his entreating looks when she came in after work. Some days it was like running the gauntlet, really, what with Mrs. Palmer twitching the curtain at her unlocking the front door and Kobus stationed in the hallway, waiting for her to come in. She'd brush past with only the slightest nod, run upstairs, and escape into her room.

One day Kobus was on the hall phone when Janice arrived home from work. He didn't notice her taking her time tiptoeing up the stairs, blatantly eavesdropping on him gabbling a torrent of mostly incomprehensible Dutch. Janice could guess whom Kobus was talking to because every other word was "Mama" spoken in an increasingly plaintive bleat. What was this fully grown man doing? Begging his mother for something? What a desperate weirdo.

Up in her room, Janice draped the satchel over a dining chair and withdrew her sketch pad and pencil case. Sitting down at the table, pushing last night's dinner plate out of the way, she fished out her favorite pencil, opened the pad to a blank sheet, and with swift, deft strokes, began blocking in a head. She drew Kobus, captured as she'd seen him from the top of the stairs. Pausing a moment, she held out the pad, squinting to see if she'd got the perspective right, then shaded in some of the space she'd left blank to depict his bald spot. That was better, kinder, but more correct too.

A while later, Janice closed the pad on the finished drawing. She would never show him this portrait. Not that it wasn't any good. Janice was good at drawing, she knew that. She always found it easy to catch a likeness on paper. It was just something she could do. Nothing to show off about. Must be all the practice she'd had drawing Ariel when she was a kid. But this talent, if she could even call it a talent, was definitely not for sharing. Janice had never shown her portraits to anyone. She kept her skill to herself.

Putting pad and pencil case back in her satchel, Janice couldn't help noting that Kobus also liked drawing. And he was good at it too, in his own way. Silly man. Remembering what he'd said about them both coming to live in London, Janice realized that their love of drawing was something else they had in common. But he would never know that, not if Janice could help it. Some things were just too private to share.

* * *

Despite Janice's studied distance, Kobus must have sensed her interest in his drawings. He began leaving his little cartoons for Janice to find on the hall table, always addressed to "The Lady in Room Two." She ignored the first, on principle, but looked at the next out of curiosity. The drawing was charming. It showed a long-legged horse nimbly avoiding a stream of urine produced by a sad hound dog. The dog was saying to the horse: "Sorry, my piss-take."

Janice was surprised and amused. Kobus was making a pun in English, although on the rude side. With his poor English, who would believe he could do that? But he definitely could draw. This was real talent. She began looking out for his cartoons and soon gathered a small collection, each one depicting a funny moment between the horse and hound. She liked his cartoons, but the symbolism wasn't lost on her either. Looking down at her thin legs and long feet, she sighed. She felt like a clomping cart horse, but Kobus saw her as a sleek racehorse, with delicate hooves and a mane she was always tossing about. Interesting. Kobus found her attractive, but it didn't change the way she felt about herself. She knew she was large, lumpy, and ugly. That was that. Still, she found his cartoons clever and, a few mornings later, bumping into him in the hallway on her way to work, she told him so.

Face lit by a huge smile, Kobus stuttered his thanks for the compliment. "I have far more drawings upstairs. If you like—" He paused. "Come up and see them sometime."

Janice restrained a guffaw. "Come up and see your etchings? You'll be telling me that's a gun in your pocket, next." Noticing Kobus's confusion, Janice realized he didn't know that he'd quoted Mae West, the famous Hollywood star who always wrote her own scripts filled with innuendo. It was a cultural difference, she supposed. She couldn't expect him to know of the notorious sex symbol and couldn't be bothered explaining her own suggestive reply. "Sorry, that was a bad joke. Not like your cartoons. They're really good."

Kobus recovered quickly and repeated the invitation, adding, "*Play for Today* is on tonight. Perhaps you watch it with me? If you like." Looking as mournful as his cartoon dog, he waggled his eyebrows at her endearingly.

Oh god, this man was weird, but harmless. Janice gave in. "Okay, I do like."

Chapter 6

Through the rest of summer and well into autumn, their encounters were limited to an occasional cup of coffee in Kobus's room, sitting in front of the hissing gas fire because London summers could be chilly in the evenings. They spent the time together going through his cartoons or watching television. *Play for Today* became a regular fixture. Kobus pretended to watch the play, but Janice could see that he often found the complex plots hard to follow. No Dutch subtitles to rely on. Instead, he played with his soft white rope, practicing the sailor's knots that his father had taught him. "Before he died," Kobus explained helpfully.

To please him, in return, Janice watched the Saturday afternoon sports program *Grandstand*, but after sitting through a couple of tedious football matches and enduring Kobus's attempts to explain the illogical offside rule, she'd had more than enough.

But not Kobus. Switching the set off after the thrilling (to him) conclusion of a match between two First Division teams, he was jubilant. He sprang out of his armchair and grabbed a pools coupon from the pile on his mantlepiece. "Look, Janice." He waved the coupon at her. "This match is a draw. I predicted that score, and that means I win a prize in the pools this week. Just one more match to go and then I know how much I win."

Janice was bemused. What a huge fuss Kobus was making over something so precarious, so beyond his control. She wasn't a gambler, and she wasn't risking her hard-earned pence on the price of a weekly pools coupon. She guessed the chance of his winning anything worth the investment was about one in a gazillion.

But Kobus couldn't be dissuaded. He just knew he would win this week's pools because, he said, "You are my luck. You bring me all the luck in the world."

"Rubbish." Janice was curt. "If you do win something, and I'm putting the accent on *if*, it will have nothing to do with me. It will be the luck of the draw, nothing more."

"*Ik bedoel, je maakt me gelukkig dus breng je me geluk.*"

"That's gobbledygook to me. You know I don't speak Dutch."

Kobus gave a mournful smile, thinking hard. Finally, he said, "What I mean is a *woordspel*, a play with words in Dutch. *Gelukkig* means happy and *geluk* means luck. They are nearly exactly the same. You make me happy, so you bring me luck. Understand?"

Janice stood and stretched uneasily. "I don't mean to be rude, but you're freaking me out." Going to his door, she said, "I'll leave you to it. Good luck."

* * *

It was a long way from Tufnell Park to Chelsea, but that wasn't a problem. Janice had looked up the route on the Underground map and knew how to get there. Emerging from the Sloane Square tube station in the dark of the November evening, it took her a while to find the right bus stop, and she had to wait ages in the cold for the bus to arrive. But it did at last, and five stops later, she got off at Carlyle Square on King's Road. There, around the corner, was the discreet green door of her destination: Gateways, the longest-surviving women-only nightclub in the world, established in the early 1930s and still going strong even now in 1979.

Now Janice had to see this famous lesbian haven alone, to pay homage to her cultural history. Ha. Who was she fooling? Janice had to admit that she hoped to meet someone new, someone alive and well and living in London who would fill this Ariel-shaped hole in her heart and lead her out of this misery. A Wonder Woman.

Nervously, she negotiated the dark flight of stairs down to the cloakroom of the club. After handing over the entrance fee to the scary woman on guard duty, Janice entered a windowless cellar packed with women of all ages and sizes and nearly choked on the haze of cigarette smoke enveloping her head. She weaved her way to the bar at the front of the room, squeezing in beside the wall, and took her bearings. The walls were painted with colorful murals, some more accomplished than others. There was a jukebox opposite the bar. The atmosphere was electric. Couples were swaying to the soft disco beat, and those who weren't dancing were chatting and laughing in closed ranks. Everyone knew one another. No one else seemed to be alone. Or looking for love, the way she was. Janice felt myriad darting eyes sizing her up. She felt like a pound of flesh in a lesbian meat market. She turned her back on the crowd, waiting with simmering nerves to be noticed by the woman serving behind the bar.

A warm body shoved in beside her and instantly attracted the bartender's attention. "Gin and double tonic, love," the woman ordered, smiling up at Janice. "What'll you have?"

Janice couldn't resist noting the order. "Don't you mean double gin and tonic?"

The woman laughed, flicking her head dismissively. She was wearing a yellow cotton blazer and a leopard-print jumpsuit, cinched tight at the waist with a wide leather belt. The latest in King's Road fashion. Janice felt frumpy in comparison and self-consciously undid the top button of her flannel shirt.

The woman noticed. "That's better. Nothing like a spot of cleavage." She gave a knowing grin. "But no, sweetie, I don't mean double gin. I like tonic, so there you have it." She leaned on Janice's arm. "So are we drinking or not?"

Janice wanted to turn down the offer but thought, *Come on!* She asked for a shandy.

The woman crowed, "That's a baby drink. Here, have a gin and tonic on me."

Janice didn't like gin. The one time she'd tried it, she'd found its aroma sickly, but she didn't know how to insist on having the light beer and lemonade she preferred. She accepted the glass and pretended to take a sip.

"Cheers," said the woman, taking a good pull of her own drink. "My name's Jan, what's yours?" Janice gave her name, and the woman drew back in exaggerated shock. "No, really? We have nearly the same name. Big Jan and Little Jan. It must be destiny." She leaned on Janice again and took a deep sniff of her shoulder. "Oh," she sighed. "You smell nice."

Janice tried to pull away but jammed against the wall, she couldn't move. Smell nice, my foot. She'd used up the last of her duty-free Rive Gauche and wasn't wearing perfume tonight. Little Jan was blatant as hell, trying to pick her up like this. Her moves were way too cheap for her taste. No way was this pushy person her Wonder Woman.

Janice had to escape. She put her full glass down on the bar. "Excuse me, just going to the loo." And thrusting a rude path through the dancers, she headed for the stairs.

At the top she exhaled noisily, closed the door, and leaned against it for a long moment. What an awful disappointment. She felt far removed from this tawdry scene at Gateways, and such a long, long way from home. She was very much on her own. Out of nowhere, the title of an Alan Sillitoe story popped into her mind: "The Loneliness of the Long-Distance Runner." Janice gave a wry smile. That could be the title of her life in London. The loneliness of the long-distance lesbian.

Chapter 7

Kobus began repeating his invitation to come with him to the local pub. Janice avoided answering, not wanting the declaration of going out with him. But he was persistent. If she were busy reading, he would wait, try again another day, or slide one of his cartoons under her door. Horse and hound always made her laugh. He never imposed, never took offense at her consistent rejection of his amiable offer of friendship. He just wore her resistance down. Finally, Janice gave in to the quiet barrage of offers and followed Kobus down the hill to the Ship's Bell on Brecknock Road.

The woman rinsing glasses behind the bar smiled up at Janice. "Tall for a girl, aren't you?"

Janice stiffened, drawing herself up to her full height. "Don't English schools teach you not to make personal comments about people you don't know?"

"You're new here, I know that," said the woman mildly, unconcerned by the sharp retort. Leaning forward, she placed her manicured hands on the bar. Dark magenta nail polish. "Don't be a stranger. I'm Isabelle. Call me Belle. What can I get you?"

Janice held her head up high. "Pint of bitter and a shandy, please."

"That's better." Belle uncapped a bottle of lemonade, poured some into a small beer glass and started to draw dark beer into the pint glass she had lined up. "You don't have to be defensive about being tall, you know. You look great, girl, really striking, standing up straight like that. Just relax and enjoy your height."

Janice stiffened. "That's the second personal remark you've made in two seconds."

"So? What are you going to do, sue me?" Belle was laughing, the dimples around her mouth creasing in a way Janice found secretively attractive.

Belle had short black curls, tinged with gray at the temples, piercing blue eyes, and a wide mouth lined with luscious red lipstick. She was wearing a black leather waistcoat that revealed a lavish view of lightly freckled breasts. Janice quickly averted her eyes. She couldn't tell whether Belle was wearing heels or not, but if the woman stood before Janice, her face would be at a comfy height for kissing. How yummy it would be to kiss the seductive Belle. Janice quickly dismissed the idea. *Come on now, be sensible.* She was imagining things. Belle couldn't be flirting. Not with her, not in this pub full of hooligans. And definitely not with Kobus waiting for her over there in the alcove. Belle must have seen them arrive together.

Finished pulling the beers, Belle set the brimming glasses on the counter and made a show of admiring Janice's hands. "You won't need a tray, not with those lovely long fingers."

"That's the third personal comment." Janice shook her hair over her face, unsure whether she felt annoyed or amused by the audacity of the woman.

"Third time lucky, I hope." And Belle turned to serve the next customer.

Kobus noticed Janice frowning when she handed over his pint. "What is wrong?"

"Nothing really. Just that Belle behind the bar was a bit forward, that's all."

"*Ach*, Belle. Is she making eyes at you?"

Janice bowed her head, unable to look at Kobus, not wanting to reveal how sexy she found the woman. "Just a bit."

"Don't take it serious. Belle is a lippy, no, how you say? A cheeky sexpot. She plays with everyone, man, woman, no matter. Even me, the first time I am here."

"Even you? Oh, sorry, I didn't mean to sound surprised."

"It's how she keeps her clientele." He waved a hand at the crowd. "And it works, you see? People like the Ship's Bell. It is nice here. Belle is nice. She makes people come."

I bet she does. Janice quickly hid a wry smile because she was not sure if Kobus was aware of his double entendre. Whatever. Looking around the pub, Janice had to agree. The Ship's Bell was a cheerful pub, one spacious room and a smaller alcove in the back, with the tall wooden paneling around the walls painted a soft peachy cream. It was brightly lit in the crowded space by the bar, but there were shaded lamps on the tables in the back corners and this alcove. The seats were comfortable too. Padded bar stools in the large room and armchairs around the tables, so deep and soft and accommodating Janice almost felt like staying all night. Belle had created a cozy sitting-room atmosphere that would have made Janice feel right at home, if not for the clamor of blokes at the bar and the stink of beer.

Their glasses were empty. Janice had had enough of conviviality and wanted to go home. Before she could suggest leaving, someone rang a bell. The crowd fell silent, and she heard Belle. "Put your money where your mouth is. Come on folks, be in to win."

"What's this?" Janice asked.

Kobus gave an eager grin. "Raffle time. On Friday nights Belle holds a raffle for charity. The money she collects always goes to a noble cause. And the prize is always good."

I bet, thought Janice. *The only cause is Belle herself.* But she kept her doubts to herself as Kobus was already pulling out his wallet in anticipation of buying a ticket. When Belle came around with the raffle tickets and a bowler hat, he waved at Janice. "Here, you choose one for me. You know you bring me luck."

Janice frowned but didn't want to embarrass him in front of Belle and didn't protest. Belle was fanning the tickets out like a hand of cards. Without looking, Janice picked one at random. Number twenty-two. Her age, funnily enough. She saw Kobus registering the coincidence and giving a surprised look. Belle handed Kobus the ticket in exchange for a crisp five-pound note, put the matching stub in her bowler hat, and continued her circuit of the bar.

A while later the bell rang again, and the crowd waited in excited silence. Belle called out from behind the bar. "Will our newest guest do the honors, please?"

All the regulars turned their heads, scanning the crowd for an unfamiliar face, and not finding one, began an uneasy muttering. Before the tension could escalate, Kobus hauled Janice to her feet and dragged her to the bar. "Here, Belle. Let Janice draw the raffle. Janice is here for the first time."

Janice hunched down on herself, trying to make herself disappear. She pressed her lips together. She was furious with Kobus for putting her in this embarrassing position. It was even worse when, following Belle's instructions, she closed her eyes, plunged her fingers into the bowler hat, and plucked the winning ticket.

Number twenty-two.

Kobus couldn't believe he had won. "That's my ticket. No, it's your ticket, Janice. You chose it for me." He looked at her with eyes so vulnerable, she had to turn away.

Belle handed her the prize, an expensive bottle of golden whiskey, single-malt, fifteen-year-old Glenfiddich. "Congratulations, girl. Don't be a stranger. Do come again."

Janice couldn't pass the bottle to Kobus fast enough. He took it carefully, gazing up at her with awful adoration in his eyes. "I told you. You are lucky for me."

Chapter 8

Early next Wednesday morning, Janice stood in the gloomy hall of the bedsit, holding the pay phone receiver in a clammy hand. Her head was throbbing, and she startled painfully when she heard the high beeps that told her the call had been answered. She inserted a two-pence coin in the slot and pressed button A. As the coin clattered down, she heard Mrs. Brockett saying, "Willing Workers Agency. How may I help you?"

Janice hesitated, massaging her brow with her free hand. This hangover was killing her. There was no way she could go to work today. Not after spending what felt like half the night helping Kobus celebrate his win—no, *their* win—of that damn bottle of Glenfiddich. He'd left her in peace on Monday, but yesterday when she'd arrived home from work, he'd invited her up for what was supposed to be only a quick drink, just the one toast to his—no, *her*—good luck. Seeing the avid hope in his eyes, Janice couldn't refuse. It would be rude. Ariel would have had no compunction at being rude, but Janice didn't feel strong enough. So she followed him into his room and had a drink. Neat. But the whiskey was so smooth, so delicious, the first glass led to another, and now here she was, in the middle of the working week and in no state to work. They'd drained the bottle. Damn whiskey. Damn Kobus.

"Are you there?" said Mrs. Brockett into the silence. "Who's calling, please?"

"Hello, Mrs. B, it's me, Janice. I can't come in to work today." She hesitated. She couldn't admit the truth and fell back on the easiest excuse. "My period started this morning. It's really heavy, the cramps are killing me. I'm sorry. It's so bad, I can hardly stand."

"Oh, my dear, how awful for you." Mrs. Brockett sounded genuinely concerned. Not at all annoyed, as Janice had half expected. "We can manage very well without you for the day. Now, I want you to take two aspirin and go straight back to bed. Do you have a nice hottie?"

"A nice what?"

"Hot water bottle. Fill it to the brim with boiling water and hold it against your tummy. You'll find the warmth quite soothing."

"Thank you for understanding, Mrs. B. You're so kind. No worries, I'll be better tomorrow. I'm sure about that. See you then." Janice hung up, jumping again as the receiver clattered into its cradle. *Boozing like this had better not become a habit*, she thought as she dragged herself upstairs and back into bed. *I just can't take it.*

* * *

But now, in the middle of November, here she was yet again, sitting in the cozy alcove at the Ship's Bell. "Here." Kobus thrust a wineglass in her direction. "I got you a double. Neat. How you like it."

"Gracious. What have you won now to be able to afford this lovely Glenfiddich?" Janice savored the aroma as she swirled the amber fluid. "I'll never get used to how Belle serves spirits in wineglasses. Stupid habit if you ask me." Kobus gave a noncommittal shrug, as if to say the English are mad anyway, so why worry? He was grinning, seething with excitement. "What's up with you? Don't tell me you've won on the races again."

"The three thirty at Ascot came in big for me." His voice dropped to a confiding whisper, forcing Janice to bend down to hear him. "I won two hundred pounds."

"Two hundred quid. Why, that's a fortune." She couldn't resist a little dig. "That should make up for all the money you lost last week."

Kobus agreed with a happy nod. "*Ach*, I can clear my losses in, how you say, one fell sweep. And it's all because of you. You made me win."

"Rubbish. Your gambling's a nasty habit. It's got nothing to do with me."

"*Ach*, but there you are wrong," he crowed. "The horse I bet on was called Jan's Delight. You bring me luck, you do."

"Stop spouting rubbish." Janice was annoyed even if his adoration was flattering in a puppy-like way. She exhaled noisily to loosen the sudden tension in her chest. Kobus was incorrigible. But seeing how glad he was, she had to relent. He was harmless, really, and always generous to her, no matter whether he won or lost.

Kobus slurped the last of his pint and gave a satisfied burp. "You are still not convinced. I will prove that you bring me luck."

"More rubbish."

"*Ach*, I will show you. When were you born?"

"You know I'm twenty-two."

"Not your age." Kobus's eyes twinkled. "The date of your birth."

"Oh, all right. If you must know, the date of my birth is October first."

"But that is just two weeks ago. Why didn't you tell me it was your birthday? I could have—no! We could have—"

Janice interrupted, "No way. I never celebrate my birthday." She gave Kobus a fierce look, discouraging him from asking why.

He shook his head and continued. "*Ach, ja*, October first is the first day of the tenth month. One and one is two. Or zero one plus one zero. Like an eleven." Kobus grinned as if he'd just invented the art of addition. "It has a nice symmetry, this number. It will do."

"What are you going to do with it?"

"You'll see. Just you wait and see."

Janice shrugged, not caring much for his air of mystery, as Kobus turned to fetch refills from the bar. What the hell. That lovely smooth whiskey was doing wonders. *Who gives a damn what Kobus gets up to*, she thought. *His gambling's got nothing to do with me.*

Chapter 9

The raucous ring of the office phone tore Janice away from the sketch she was doing in secret. Before she could answer it, her colleague had picked up her own receiver and was parroting, "Willing Workers Agency. Tracy Dixon speaking, how may I help you?"

Imitating Tracy behind her back, Janice mouthed, "Oh, shut your trap, woman."

She wasn't in the mood for Tracy. Or for work, for that matter. It had all seemed so easy her first day on the job. All she had to do was find out what function people were looking for and match them with the vacancies on offer. But in practice it turned out to be hard. She rarely placed anyone or uncovered new vacancies in making those dreadful cold calls to corporate personnel departments that formed such a big part of her job.

Talking to strangers on the phone did not come easy. Janice hated having to beg those snooty personnel managers for their vacancies, and when they said they had none for her, in their awful posh accents, as they inevitably did, Janice had to remind them not to forget Willing Workers Agency if and when a vacancy did arise. More often than not, the person she was trying to charm hung up before she could finish her spiel. Constant rejection was getting her down. Janice took it personally and couldn't cope.

Now, glancing across the room to check that Mrs. Brockett wasn't watching, Janice went on stealthily sketching a portrait of Tracy on the back of a worksheet.

Tracy had chubby cheeks and chubby arms and legs, squinty eyes, and a snout of a nose. If Kobus drew her, he'd probably turn her into a cartoon pig. But not Janice. Her drawing of Tracy was a fair likeness, straightforward and accurate, as always. Even so—Janice crumpled the finished drawing and stuffed it into her satchel instead of the bin (no way could she risk having Tracy discover her portrait)—she hadn't been able to resist exaggerating the piggy slant of that little inquisitive nose. It was always prying into her business.

Tracy was always chatting about her boyfriend—no, fiancé—Bruce. They were getting married in August and, as Tracy had said when she'd told Janice about her wedding, "I can't wait for the big day to arrive. Just imagine, it's going to be grand. And you're invited, you and your plus one."

"Plus, what?"

"Your Kobus, silly. He's your plus one, of course."

Tracy had met Kobus that very morning. She had been unlocking the office door when Janice arrived, panting after galloping through the crowd streaming from Mornington Crescent tube station.

Smiling a curt hello, catching her breath, Janice spotted Kobus coming after her with a huge grin on his face. "What are you doing here?" Her face flushed with anger.

Kobus ignored the question. "What luck bumping into you. Is this where you work? It looks nice." He smiled at Tracy, who was hovering by the door. She was hanging on to his words, charmed by his foreign accent.

But Janice was suspicious. "Shouldn't you be at the shop?"

"Not today. Paul has given me a free day."

"What are you doing here? Did you follow me down on the tube?"

Kobus hung his head in admission, but before he could speak to defend himself, Tracy smiled at him. "I'm Tracy, Janny's colleague. You sound Dutch. Are you the boyfriend?"

Kobus nodded and gave his name. "Enchanted to meet you, Tracy."

"He's my upstairs neighbor," growled Janice. "Not my boyfriend."

Tracy was flattered. "Don't just stand there. Come in and see where your Janice works."

"I'm not his." Janice stamped her foot, furious at Tracy for ignoring her correction.

Tracy ushered Kobus inside and showed him around their small office. "See, this is where Janice sits and looks after the people looking for a permanent job. Mrs. Brockett sits there in the back. She's our manager and will be here in a minute. She's never late. And that's me over there by the window. I look after our temps."

"Temps?" asked Kobus.

Tracy was glad to explain and prattled on. "People working in temporary jobs. Short-term contracts. You wouldn't be looking for temporary work, now, would you?"

"*Ach*, no, I already have a job in my cousin's charity shop."

"His shop's on the high street up in Tufnell Park, nowhere near here." Janice interrupted their cozy chat. She could see that Kobus was charming Tracy. He was trying to win her over and she was lapping it up. If he had a tail, it would be wagging hard enough to knock all the ornaments off her desk. Tracy was falling for his shy smile, tittering, and praising his English.

Tracy went off at last to put the kettle on for their usual morning tea. The moment she was gone, Janice seethed at Kobus. "Get out now and don't ever follow me to work again."

When he'd gone, with a last mournful look over his shoulder, Janice sat at her desk, clenching and unclenching her fists, horribly aware of her pounding heart. Why was she furious? Wasn't she overreacting? Kobus had followed her to work on his day off. So what? It wasn't as if he was stalking her, now, was it? But even if he wasn't, he had already invaded her private life. She didn't want him encroaching on her working life as well. She had to watch out because he was forever pushing at her boundaries.

Mrs. Brockett arrived and Tracy came out of the back with a tray holding four teas.

"Four cups?" Mrs. Brockett looked around for a fourth person. "Who's that one for?"

"Kobus," said Tracy. "Her boyfriend popped in to say hello. Oh, where's he gone?"

Before Mrs. Brockett could respond, Janice said, "Kobus is my upstairs neighbor, not my boyfriend, and anyway he's gone now. Had to get to work." She ignored Tracy's quizzical look, realizing that Tracy had heard Kobus saying that he had the day off.

"Talking of work, ladies," Mrs. Brockett said, putting her coat on a hanger in the back room and returning to sit at her desk, "let us get on with our own work."

Chapter 10

Work. God, her head hurt. Janice had to stop going down to the Ship's Bell on weeknights. It had become too much of a good thing. Tuning out Tracy, who was still nattering away on the phone to one of her temps, no doubt, Janice made a pretense of sorting through the cards in her Rolodex. She was supposed to be calling personnel officers again but with this hangover couldn't summon up the energy. Oh, she wasn't particularly good at this.

Luckily, Mrs. Brockett was lenient with her. Repeatedly she told Janice that it always took a while before you got the hang of things. But even now, months later, she was still hopeless at this job. Really, the woman was too kind for the good of the business, letting Janice off the hook when she didn't deserve it. Janice could never understand why Mrs. Brockett was always unreasonably kind to her, until one lunchtime she found out.

Tracy had gone grocery shopping, flipping the sign on the agency door to "Closed for Lunch" on her way out, leaving Mrs. Brockett and Janice alone in the back room. Janice made the tea as she always did when it was just the two of them.

Accepting her cup (strong, no milk, two sugars), Mrs. Brockett smiled at Janice. "Thank you, dear. You really know how to make a good cup of tea."

"Well, I should know how you like it by now."

Mrs. Brockett took a sip. "Believe it or not, after all the time Tracy's been working here, she can still forget I don't take milk. But you don't. You're attentive, just like my Eileen." Janice gave a questioning look. "My daughter, Eileen. You remind me of her."

"Oh, that's nice, thanks."

Janice wanted to read her book and switch off for a while but then Mrs. Brockett added sadly, "She would have been your age by now."

Janice set down the book, intrigued. "Would have been?"

Mrs. Brockett put on a brave smile. "A drunk driver hit my Eileen when she was only fourteen. She was using the pedestrian crossing when he hit her. And she died."

"I'm sorry." Janice didn't know what else to say.

"It's a long time ago, nearly a decade now, but you know, the pain never really goes away. That's why it's nice to have you around, Janice. Eileen had chocolate-brown hair, just like yours, and she had lovely long legs, just like yours. I'm sure she would have grown as tall as you are."

Janice nodded. What could she say to such an admission? She didn't know Eileen and didn't know Mrs. Brockett that well. She hoped that her resemblance to a dead daughter would not become burdensome. Coping with Kobus was enough of a burden.

Indicating Janice's paperback, Mrs. Brockett said, "But I doubt she would have been as big a reader as you are."

Janice was grateful for the diversion. "Yes, I love reading. Hope you don't mind." And taking the broad hint, kind Mrs. Brockett let her get on with her book in peace.

* * *

Janice was sitting at her desk, clutching her hungover head. Slowly she became aware that Tracy was trying to attract her attention. Tracy was holding out the phone and saying, "Line three, for you. Personal. It's your boyfriend."

"I haven't got a boyfriend." She was about to add, I don't go out with men, but stopped.

"It's your Kobus, silly. Go on, take it." Tracy gave an annoying titter.

Janice picked up her phone. "Yes, what is it?" The hangover made her more abrupt than usual. "Why are you phoning me at work? I've told you not to."

Kobus laughed on the line, unperturbed by her sharp tone. "I have good news."

She was in no mood for fun. "Spare me, I'm busy."

"Okay, I be quick."

But instead of continuing, he paused a long moment, building the suspense until Janice could bear it no more. "What is it?" she barked.

"I win the National Lottery. Fifty thousand. Because of you." Janice's mouth dropped open as Kobus went on. "I told you I would prove you bring me luck."

Janice was unable to take it in. Her chest tightened. Fifty thousand pounds? Because of her? No way. No one she knew could ever win that much money, not on the lottery.

"I used your lucky numbers. Your month, October, your room number, my birthday, my room number, and the number of our house. And your lucky eleven for the bonus."

"That's impossible. The lottery is not like the pools. You can't choose your numbers, they come printed on the ticket. You have to take what you get." She couldn't breathe.

"Yes, that's true, to a point. But you don't have to take what you get. I wanted my lucky Janice numbers, so I look for the right ticket. I go to twenty, fifty outlets all over London to find the right ones. I don't stop. I don't give up. And last week I found the right one. I knew it would be a winner. See, Janice, you do bring me luck. I told you so. This win is the proof."

Janice could feel the blood pounding in her ears. This was wrong. She hadn't realized just how obsessive Kobus was about her bringing him luck. Her chest spiraled in tight panic.

"We got four out of six, including the bonus eleven. Not the jackpot, you understand, you need all six numbers for that. But—"

Janice slammed down the phone. It was too much. Maybe it was the hangover, maybe it was fear, but she didn't want to take on the obligation of being Kobus's lucky charm.

"What's the matter?" Tracy was looking worried. "Bad news, is it?"

Janice shook her head, stunned. Tracy looked concerned. Finally, Janice could speak. "No, the contrary. Kobus had a bit of luck—" Before she could finish, the phone rang again.

Tracy snatched it up. "Willing Workers Agency. Oh, hello, it's you again. Did you get cut off? Janice was just telling me you've had some luck." She paused to listen, then burst into a squeal. "No, you never, you haven't gone and won the lottery!" She paused to listen. "Fifty. Grand. Well, I never. And you're taking our Janice on a weekend to Paris to celebrate."

Tracy turned to beam at a stunned Janice. How dare he tell Tracy, a virtual stranger, about his plans? A weekend in Paris? How dare he assume she would go. Fury was gripping so hard it froze her to the spot. She clenched her fists so fiercely her nails dug into her palms.

"Paris, oh, how romantic," Tracy gushed. "Aren't you the lucky one. Oh, it's Janice who's the lucky one?" She gave one of her inane titters, waving at Janice to pick up her receiver. "I see, yes, the luck of the lotto. Shall I pass you back to Janice? She's dying to talk to you."

Talking to Kobus was the last thing Janice wanted. Knocking her hip on her desk in her rush to escape, she ran to the door. "No. Hang up. I need air."

"You can't go. Kobus is waiting for you. He's going to take you to Paris. Paris in the fall, how romantic." Tracy held out the phone to no avail. Janice was gone.

Chapter 11

Kobus begged her, teased her, did anything he could to please her, anything that would make her change her mind and come with him to Paris. The bribery began when he took her to a fancy French restaurant on Fortress Road, about a mile away from the Ship's Bell. It took longer to get there than their usual quick stroll to the pub, but as Kobus said when the host took their coats, "The walk is worth it."

"Good exercise, anyway." Janice sniffed. She needed to hide the fact that she'd never been to such a chic restaurant before. She felt intimidated by the expensive surroundings, the deep-brown walls, big flower arrangements, dimmed overhead lighting, and dinky little candles on tables laid with huge glasses, rows of chunky cutlery, and enormous octagonal plates on creamy tablecloths. And to top it all, there were real cloth napkins rolled up in silver holders.

Janice was more used to paper plates and serviettes than all this posh carry-on. She shuffled uneasily, slouching behind Kobus as the snooty maître d' led them to a table close to the kitchen door. It was okay because it meant they were out of sight of other diners.

And thank the goddess they weren't in view. Janice sat with her back to the kitchen wall and peeped around Kobus to spy on the diners. Straight couples, long married, judging by the bored glares they were giving each other. Everyone was dressed smartly, unlike Janice and Kobus. She had put on her best flannel shirt, the only one without stains, and Kobus had on his usual checkered shirt without a tie. Compared to these diners, Janice felt out of place.

If only Ariel were here to help her be assertive. Why didn't she have the courage to say no to Kobus taking her here, of all fancy places? Kobus said it nearly had a Michelin star and he'd had to book weeks ahead to get in. He was trying to impress, taking her to a place that scared her. There, she'd admit it. She was scared of doing the wrong thing, and promptly knocked her fork off the table to prove it.

One of the waiters swooped in, picked up the fallen fork, replaced it with a fork from the nearest table, and unceremoniously dropped two oversized menus on their plates. He took off before Kobus could wave him back to take their drinks order.

After a long wait, the sommelier arrived, even snootier than the maître d', and handed Kobus the wine card. Smiling greasily at Janice, he said in what sounded like a phony accent, "*Bonsoir messieurs*. Oh, pardon. *Madame et m'sieur*. What may I serve you for an *apéritif*?"

Janice's mind went blank, too nervous to respond to the waiter's mistake. He'd thought she was a man. *What else is new? And what do you drink before food in a posh restaurant?* Before she could stutter the only thing she could think of, a whiskey, Kobus thrust the wine menu into the sommelier's hands and said grandly, "Bring us your best champagne."

"The best for an *apéritif*?" The sommelier stared down his nose. "That would be the Lanson Black Label, the Brut, *m'sieur*."

"Bring us that."

"As you wish, *m'sieur*, two glasses of the Lanson. A classic *apéritif* if I may say so."

"No, no, not two glasses. Bring the whole bottle."

"As you wish, *m'sieur*." The sommelier hid his sneer behind the menu, spun on his heel, and returned with an ice bucket, the champagne, and two huge coupes. He withdrew the cork without a pop and carefully poured the fizzy wine. Kobus waved the waiter away and handed Janice her glass himself. Raising his glass to touch hers, Kobus said, "Here's to you."

Janice took her first-ever sip of real champagne and loved it. The way the tiny bubbles of liquid broke on her tongue and slid down her throat was delightful. She loved the taste, not too acidic, not sickly sweet, just tart enough to be refreshing. In New Zealand, she'd had what they called champagne at New Year's Eve, but it was sour stuff that produced an instant hangover. Hellish, nothing compared to this hedonism.

Sitting with his back to the room, Kobus was in shadow. The flickering light of the candle played across his face, glinting in his eyes and making his teeth gleam. He looked damn happy. Janice couldn't begrudge him that. Happy that he'd had the huge win, happy that she'd come here with him. Surveying the room, Janice sat up. An old Beatles song popped into her head. "Can't buy me love," she sang under her breath. She stopped. Taking a mouthful of sumptuous champagne, she thought, *I could get used to this.*

Kobus smiled from behind his glass. "Here's to my luck."

Janice raised her glass again. "And here's to my winner."

That first restaurant outing was pure decadence. Kobus made sure they ordered the most expensive items on the menu. Itty-bitty avocado-prawn cocktails for starters, followed by thin slices of rib eye (vampire rare for Janice, done to death for Kobus), and teensy slabs of chocolate cake slathered with dots of whipped cream for dessert. And don't forget the full cheeseboard as well, but that wasn't greed. They were still hungry, unaccustomed to the minuscule helpings of nouvelle cuisine. And not one, but two lethal Drambuies with coffee.

But first they'd emptied the bottle of champagne with the prawns, and in the endless wait for their main course, they'd gone on to drink an incredible cabernet sauvignon.

With each perfect bite of beautifully cooked food, each perfect sip of deliciously smooth wine, Janice slouched deeper and deeper into her seat and forgot about not putting her elbows on the table. While she ate, she listened to Kobus prattling, waving his knife in her face, so tipsy he didn't realize he was speaking Dutch. Although she understood only one word in ten, she let him talk, content to look as if she were listening. Content to eat. And drink. And eat and drink again. Kobus was happy with her. He was making her happy, with this. They had it all.

She wasn't protesting but couldn't help feeling that she didn't deserve this extravagance. Really, she'd had nothing to do with Kobus's win. That was a fact. But Kobus wouldn't accept this reality. He kept on saying it was due to her. She brought him luck and he would never win anything without her. The way he put it, his winning the lottery was all her fault. Forgetting his own obsessive search for the right ticket, he blamed her for the win, and as suitable punishment, she had to let him spend, spend, and spend on her. Janice swallowed her guilt and let him indulge her.

As they weaved their way back to the bedsit, he slurred, "I do not win without you."

"Aren't I the lucky one," she slurred back at him, thinking of the old 10cc song "The Things We Do for Love." *Who me?*

Chapter 12

The bribery continued. Kobus began taking her shopping in the boutiques of Oxford Street. He wanted to buy her a jacket made in Milan from the softest of soft black lambskin. It was supposed to be a belated present for her birthday, even if that had been well and truly celebrated last month, and he wouldn't let her know the price.

They had to go to the men's section of the boutique to find a jacket that would fit, but Janice was used to having to shop for men's clothes. Women's jeans were never long enough, and with her broad shoulders and long arms, women's sleeves barely reached her wrists.

Trying on the chosen jacket in the privacy of a cubicle, Janice stifled a sharp pang of guilt. This was too much already. In the past fortnight, Kobus had bought her an entirely new wardrobe: two pairs of jeans, the one deep black, the other stonewashed blue, a smart pair of chocolate-brown pants to wear to chic restaurants (ha!), and a couple of soft flannel shirts she really wanted, one red-checked, the other a gorgeous shade of violet. He'd only bought these favorites after she'd let him buy more feminine tops as well, and she'd given in without too much persuasion. The best of the bunch was a long-sleeved tunic in deep crimson. The front was too low, and the soft material clung to her breasts. But the color went well with the brown pants, so she couldn't complain.

Janice had never been placed in this position before. It was a cliché, Kobus playing sugar daddy to her gold digger. But had she asked to play this part? Was she truly a gold digger when the role had been forced upon her? If only Kobus weren't so dependent, insistently begging her for company. If only she weren't so lonely, desperate to find a Wonder Woman who clearly didn't exist. If only Ariel were around to protect her from herself, from giving in to all this indulgence. If only Kobus weren't so hopeless. If only he didn't believe he was offering friendship when, deep in her heart, she knew he was trying to buy her affection. Was she this helpless, so desperate for attention, even from a person she didn't find attractive?

Oh, come on, maybe Kobus was nothing to look at, but he did have his good side. He was kind and nice to be with most of the time. He knew interesting things. She liked his enthusiasm, his sense of humor, his irreverent take on life. She liked watching him play with his sailor's rope. He was dexterous and could tie clever knots, and yes, he really could draw. But his gambling on horse races, the weekly football pools, not to mention the damn lottery was starting to scare her. On this scale his gambling was an addiction. Add to that his obsessive need for her to make him happy. That was terrifying. Being forced to be his lucky charm was a trap she could not avoid.

As Janice pulled on the new jacket, relishing the luxurious leather and the fact that the sleeves were long enough for her arms, she forgot all about man-shaped traps. She could get used to this indulgence. Kobus was harmless. Generous and harmless. And what harm could it do to let him indulge his generosity on her? No, don't answer that.

Leaving the cubicle and parading in front of a full-length mirror, Janice focused on this perfect choice of a jacket, at the way its tailored lines hugged her slender waist and molded her small breasts. She caught a glimpse of rampant lust in Kobus's eyes reflected in the mirror and realized, not without a small shock, that her lissome figure looked stunning to him. Standing tall, like Belle said she should, swirling around like a sexy model on a catwalk, Janice was fully aware of his admiration and enjoyed it. She liked being adored, even by Kobus. She wasn't leading him on, now was she? No, don't answer that.

Through the rest of November the spree continued. There were cowboy boots from Brazil, crafted from red embroidered leather with chunky heels that made her even taller; luxurious bath towels and sheets for her bed, made from the softest of light Egyptian cotton; expensive picture books on British actors and Hollywood stars; everything she needed and a lot more she did not, including, of all things, a stupid golden toothbrush from Harrods.

All Janice had to do now was glance covetously at an object and Kobus would buy it. She made sure he spent on himself as well (lots of new drawing stuff), tried to fight any traces of guilt, and took everything he gave her. What would Ariel think of her now?

Chapter 13

"Please fly with me to Paris. I can't do it without you. Please, Janice, pretty please, say yes."

Kobus and Janice had gone for a chilly walk on Hampstead Heath. Now, to warm themselves up, they were having a cup of tea in the corner café opposite Tufnell Park station. Squished on the vinyl seat, sipping tentatively at their strong tea, Janice could not resist his constant blandishments.

"Oh, stop it, you fool. I'll come along to Paris if only to shut you up."

Kobus rewarded this statement with a grin so huge she was frightened his face would crack in half. He clapped his hands in delight. "Thank you so much. You make me happy. I have never been on an airplane. The idea is exciting, but it scares me also."

Having flown the long haul from Auckland, Janice was blasé about flying. She couldn't believe he'd never flown. "It's no big deal. Anyway, what about when you came here?"

"I didn't fly. I took the Magic Bus. Far more economic."

"Economical." Janice corrected his English for a change. "What's a Magic Bus?"

"Cheap bus rides in Europe. You catch the Magic Bus in London and get out in Athens. It leaves from Victoria Station and stops in Amsterdam, West Berlin, Milan, all the big cities. Soon I hear they take you all the way to India. The hippies like that."

"But you're not a hippie. What were you doing on the Magic Bus?"

Kobus wasn't offended. "You don't have to be hippie for the bus. Just poor, like me."

And me, thought Janice, filing away the information. Hoping to distract Kobus from his constant raving about Paris, she asked, "What brought you to London anyway?"

"I just told you, Magic Bus."

Janice hid a quick smile. "Not that kind of bring. I mean, you know I came here for the theater, not that I've seen anything yet, but you haven't told me why *you* came to London."

"Oh." Kobus was silent. He leaned back in his chair and rubbed his chin, the way he did when he was thinking. Finally, he said, "Mama said I must leave home and learn to live without her, and she sent me to stay with her sister, my Tante Corrie, for this whole year."

"Leave home? But you're thirty-five, aren't you? What on earth were you doing still living with your mother, at your age?" Kobus's face fell and Janice realized she had been too blunt. "Sorry, I don't mean to hurt your feelings. I was just surprised."

Kobus wouldn't look at her. "I have no reason to leave. I stay with Mama at home."

Janice realized she couldn't pry. Ariel would have gone on, demanding an honest answer, but Janice couldn't. They took one last sip of their teas and stood to go home. On the way down their street, Janice said, "I've never been to Paris. Have you?"

"No, not yet." Kobus's eyes shone with gratitude. "We discover our place together."

* * *

That first weekend of December, they flew to Paris, and Kobus wasn't at all scared. He pretended to be, though, using it as an excuse to hold Janice's hand throughout the short flight. Compared to what she was used to, this hop was peanuts.

"Straight up and straight down," she complained as they waited for their bags to appear on the carousel at Charles de Gaulle. "We've spent more time hanging about airports than in the air."

Kobus paid a ludicrous amount for a ride into town. As their taxi inched its way between the Gare du Nord and Gare de l'Est, swung around Les Halles, and crawled down the Rue Saint-Honoré, Janice kept noticing how fast the meter was ticking and thought, *What a waste of good money. It would have been cheaper and faster to take the Métro.* Finally, they arrived at their hotel on the Rue de Rivoli, down the road from the Louvre and Tuileries Garden. The clerk in reception assumed they were a couple and brandished a key to a double room.

Summoning Ariel's strength, Janice protested. "Oh no," she cried, embarrassing all three of them. "We can't have a double bed. You must give us a twin, two beds at least."

The clerk and Kobus exchanged a look, which Janice pretended she didn't see.

Paris was wonderful, to begin with. In new clothes, creaking shoes, and reeking of duty-free perfume and aftershave, they played with the city like children, tap-dancing up the Champs Élysées, waltzing under the barren chestnuts in the Tuileries, skating through the Louvre (the *Mona Lisa* was a crowded disappointment), and springing down the iron steps of the Eiffel Tower. And on both evenings, they shared leisurely meals in nearby brasseries on the Île de la Cité, where Kobus wouldn't let her check the prices before ordering. Despite this, Janice had to fight against pangs of guilt at his generosity.

On their last night, there was a full moon. After another decadent dinner, they walked back to the hotel across the Pont Notre-Dame, swaying from all the wine they had drunk. Janice felt caught in a spell. The neon moonshine on the cobblestones and glinting off the Seine, the novelty of this foreign city, the utter luxury—it was like living a dream. She owed Kobus all of this.

Halfway across the bridge, Kobus grabbed her shoulders, pulling her off balance. "Please, you are so beautiful. Let me kiss you."

Janice tried to step out of his grasp. "Come off it. You're not seeing straight." She had to laugh. "Or rather, you're seeing too straight. I'm a lesbian, remember?"

"That doesn't matter. Kiss me. You have to let me kiss you."

Janice tried to shrug him off, but Kobus only stepped in closer. "I cannot live without your love. If you don't love me, I jump off the bridge. Now. I drown in this river. Kiss me."

"Seriously? If you did that, then you'd really be insane." Kobus stared, not understanding the pun. "In Seine?" Janice gave up and pecked his cheek. "Can we go now?"

But later in their room, when he grabbed her again and said he loved her, she didn't protest. Drunk, moon-mad, and weighed down by all the money he had spent on her, Janice had only herself to give in return. And why not? Kobus loved her, wanted her. What was so bad about that? If she couldn't find Wonder Woman, wouldn't a mortal man do?

Lying back on her bed, she invited his embrace. She expected to feel Ariel's soft smooth cheek against hers and tried not to recoil from the stubble rasping her face. She expected Ariel's tender kiss, but Kobus mashed his lips on hers and plugged his tongue into her throat, choking her. She slid her mouth out of reach. He eased alongside her on the bed. She expected to feel the soft swell of Ariel's breasts against her chest, but his body was bony and hard. He took her hand, but she couldn't, wouldn't touch him where he wanted. She didn't want to look at his ugly body and buried her face in a pillow. Kobus took this as an invitation to take her from behind. And she let him, ready to feel a man inside. He pushed into her. Oh. Okay. The wine had made her wet and it didn't hurt, not like she'd heard it would. Losing your cherry was supposed to hurt. Offering no resistance, but not helping, she knelt with her face in the pillow while he huffed and puffed, and when he blew on her rump, the musty smell of semen was sickening. Stifling an urge to vomit, she ordered him back to his single bed. He gave her a sloppy kiss and complied.

Chapter 14

On their return to London, Janice fought with herself and with Kobus. Sober again, she felt she'd crossed a boundary, degrading herself. She'd let herself down. How could she welcome Kobus into her body when she was not straight? She'd let him take her hetero virginity. But so what? She'd been curious and she'd survived. It hadn't been an ordeal. She hadn't minded the feeling of him inside her. But she hadn't liked the feel of his bony body and couldn't like the smell of his come. A gentle Wonder Woman could fill her just as well as a man without subjecting her to that off-putting stink at the end.

As for Kobus? How dare he fall in love with her? He wasn't supposed to. That wasn't the deal. It wasn't as if she'd encouraged his lust. Then, recalling how seductively she had posed for him in her new leather jacket, she reconsidered. Hadn't she led him on, just a tiny bit? Deep in her heart she knew she had sent out confusing signals but, unfairly or not, she was still angry with him for breaking his unspoken promise.

Down in the hallway one evening after work, she rounded on Kobus. "Why did you let yourself fall for me? You knew about me. I should never have let us be friends. I knew this platonic bullshit would never work. I told you that up front."

"Don't blame me, please. You're so beautiful, I can't help me. Please, Janice, pretty please. You bring good luck. You make me *gelukkig*. I love you, I really do. Let me make love to you, please, just one last time."

Kobus had spent too much on her. She owed him too much. She had no choice. But wasn't that rationalization? Wouldn't she rather check if she truly did not like the smell of men? To find out, wasn't she prepared to give him another go? Kobus was shuffling from foot to foot, waiting for her to relent. She kept him in suspense, then held out her hand.

He took it in a sweaty palm and led her up to his room. He pushed her down on his bed and undid her belt buckle. Janice lay there, eyes half closed, making no move to help him pull off her boots, strip off her socks, and ease her jeans and underpants off. One by one, Kobus dropped the discarded items onto the floor.

Janice closed her eyes, hearing his rasping breath, feeling his cold hands lift her legs onto his shoulders. She felt him run his fingers up her legs, his touch light and deft. It felt fine. He leaned over and took something out of the drawer of his nightstand. Janice saw him rip open a small foil package and closed her eyes again. Good. A moment later he gripped her ankles, holding her legs up and out of the way, and pried her open, thrusting in hard without warning. Ah. This time it hurt. The bed creaked and would have gone on creaking when there was an abrupt knock.

Kobus froze. Janice froze. Someone banged on his door again. Kobus sprang from the bed, pulling up his jeans, fumbling with the zipper. Janice wrapped the bedspread over herself and turned to face the window, jamming her nose against the plastic sheet he used as double glazing against the damp. Let him deal with this intrusion.

Kobus held the door closed. "Who is it?"

"It's me. Open up. Now!"

Janice sat up with a shock. It was Mrs. Palmer. Checking on Kobus. Checking on her. Had she heard them talking in the hall, outside the door to her lounge? Had she spied them going up to his room? Had she guessed what they were about to do? Did she know she was catching them in the act? In panic, Janice pulled on her jeans and boots. She threw herself into an armchair, sat on her socks and underpants, and mussed her hair over her face.

Kobus gave Janice a scared look of warning and opened the door. Mrs. Palmer stormed in, registered Janice and, ignoring her, harangued her nephew in Dutch. Facing the angry onslaught, Kobus slumped into himself, hanging his head and refusing to look at his aunt.

Finally, Mrs. Palmer wound down her tirade and turned her beady eye on Janice. "As for you, you big *slet*, what did I tell you? No pets, no men in your room."

Janice could guess what *slet* meant. A sudden image of herself standing up to the boys attacking Ariel in the playground flashed into her mind. She felt her face flush with anger. She wasn't going to stand for this insult. "I know the rules. I've never let a man into my room— apart from Kobus, and he doesn't count. Anyway, we're in *his* room, so what are you on about?"

"Don't you play little Miss Innocent with me. I know what sexy tricks you've been playing with my nephew. Flirting. Making him fall in love with you. Seducing him."

Janice felt a rush of fury spiral through her. It was constricting her chest, squeezing her throat so that she could not speak. She exhaled noisily and stood, jamming her undies and socks in her back pocket. Drawing herself up to her full height, feeling for once as assertive as Ariel would have been in this unjust situation, she towered over Mrs. Palmer and Kobus. "Perhaps you should ask your nephew to explain what is happening." Janice shoved past them onto the landing, turned on her heel, and with head held high, went down to her room.

Chapter 15

Janice never found out what Kobus told his aunt about their relationship. Whatever. She didn't care. Following the scene in his room, the only difference she noticed in the way Mrs. Palmer acted with her was that she stopped being nice. Oh, she still kept a nosy eye on her comings and goings, twitching the curtain whenever Janice unlocked the front door, but there were no more smiles, no more friendly invitations to drop in for a cup of tea, and no more intrusions into her room. In her heart, Janice was glad that the landlady had disrupted the fuck. Coitus interruptus. Saved by the knock. Ha. Well, she had satisfied her curiosity. Used Kobus as much as he'd used her. He knew she preferred women.

She only wished she could keep on opposing Kobus. But once her fury had dissipated, that Ariel-imbued strength faded away. She'd had enough of him trying to touch her. She tried to stop him, but he increased the pressure. He wouldn't leave her alone. Passing her in the hallway, he had to grope her. He'd pinch her bottom or reach out for her breast and laughed when she slapped his hand away. Whenever he could, he pushed her for the touch she didn't want to give.

Guilt made her compromise. He had spent too much on her. She owed him in return. One evening on her landing, she said, "You can have one kiss if you leave me alone after."

Kobus reached up eagerly, gripping her shoulders too hard. He squeezed her face too tightly, bit her lip too hard. He scratched her cheek with the bristles of his beard.

Janice turned away, despising his strength. And his weakness. He was a contradiction. He was macho and bold, assertive in taking what he wanted. But at the same time, he was soft and needy. A submissive puppy begging for love. "You should never have let yourself fall in love with me. You know I'm a lesbian. I was honest. I told you that at the start."

Kobus hung his head. His puppy-dog eyes were brimming with tears. "Yes, I know you did, and I hate me for breaking my promise.

But I didn't mean to fall in love with you. I need you. I can't live without you."

Janice erupted. "I don't want you to need me. And you don't need me to stay alive. You're lonely, I'm lonely, okay. We're two lonely neighbors in this dreadful bedsit. There should be no harm in us being friends. But friends only, damn it."

Kobus had an evil glint in his eye. "You benefit from my lottery money."

Janice closed her mouth with a snap. "Touché, Kobus. Well played. You couldn't resist making me feel indebted to you again. But don't forget, I didn't ask to share your win. You forced your money on me. I shouldn't have let you into my life."

* * *

Kobus left her alone again, for a couple of days at least, but in the run up to Christmas, he began showering her with little gifts. He shoved his inane cartoons under her door and left gaudily wrapped bars of her favorite Cadbury's Fruit & Nut chocolate on the hall table or propped up against her door for her to find after work. She threw out the cartoons straight away but ate the chocolate, filled with guilt, hating herself for succumbing to temptation, despising herself for crossing her own boundaries.

Christmas came and went. Predictably, Tracy had put up tatty decorations in the agency and, to Janice's annoyance, kept the office radio tuned to Radio One. In between a flood of Christmas carols, the station played Pink Floyd's new hit nonstop. If Janice heard that maudlin song one more time, it wouldn't be just another brick she'd throw but the whole damn wall. At Tracy.

The Willing Workers Agency was crowded with job seekers at this time of the year, far more than usual it seemed, and during office hours, Janice was kept too busy to think of the predicament she found herself in with Kobus.

The evenings were different. That dull ache had come back again, and one lonely night in her bed, Janice realized she was homesick. Not for her parents, no way. She'd left home years ago and was used to spending holidays alone rather than with her parents. As far as Janice was concerned, they were a couple of sad narcissists more interested in each other than in their only, lonely daughter. No, she was homesick for New Zealand. This was her first-ever Christmas away. No barbecue on the beach for her this year. Here in London, it was always cold and drizzly, and despite Tracy's fervent wishes, there would be no snow to make it a white Christmas.

On Christmas Eve she made a duty call to her parents on the pay phone in the bedsit hallway, paying a fortune in coins for the privilege. The call woke her mother.

Janice raised her voice over the clattering coins. "Hello, it's me. Merry Christmas."

"What, who? Oh, Janneke." Her mother sounded sleepy. "How late is it? Only five thirty. *Godverdomme*. Why are you calling so early? What's wrong? Do you want money?"

"No, Mum, it's Christmas. Just calling to wish you a Merry Christmas. How are you?"

There was a long pause. Janice could hear the silence stretch through all the long-distance telephone exchanges connecting her to her mother, 11,386 miles away as the crow flies, twenty-six nonstop hours away by plane. Her mother didn't bother to fill the silence, so Janice went on. "Nothing's wrong. And no, I don't need money. How are you? And Dad?"

Another long silence. "Your father's still asleep. And so he should be at this hour. Really, Janneke, you shouldn't have called this early. Gave me the fright of my life."

"I'm sorry, Mum. I'm not used to the time difference. It's only Christmas Eve here."

"I should think you could remember the time difference. Inconsiderate as usual."

Janice's heart sank. Her mother was running true to form, always finding fault, criticizing instead of being glad Janice had taken the trouble to get in touch. And at Christmastime too. She gave up. "Look, I'm on a pay phone. Got to go. Just wanted to wish you and

Dad all the best. Don't worry about me." As if her parents ever would. "I'll write soon, and that's a promise. Bye." Without waiting for her mother to respond, she hung up.

That was a promise Janice would never keep, if she knew herself. Her mother wasn't worried. Her parents weren't ever concerned about her. And that was fine with Janice. She'd done without their approval for years. She could stand on her own feet. Couldn't she?

Chapter 16

Janice spent New Year's Eve on her own. She ignored Kobus's pleas to help him celebrate the arrival of 1980, the start of a whole new decade, down in the Ship's Bell. And as for the invitation to bring her "plus one" to Tracy's party, she'd had no qualms about turning that down. Nothing worse than sharing the hysteria of a new year with hysterical people.

Janice wanted to be alone. She was happiest on her own. Preparing for bed that night, ignoring the crackling fireworks outside her window, she reflected on her lack of what people called friends. After losing Ariel, she found making friends a challenge. She knew people found her standoffish, and they were right. Something always held her back from making easy contact. Yes, she could put on a good front at times and seem confident and at ease with strangers. But really she was intensely shy and didn't think much of herself. Belle had seen through that in a trice. Janice found being social simply exhausting. Look how drained she was in the evenings, after a day at work, being social with irritating Tracy and kind Mrs. Brockett and all those job seekers. She needed time to recover.

But didn't her distance also stem from a sense of self-protection? That was a good thing, surely? She didn't want to have her heart broken as much as it had been when Ariel died. But if that was true—and deep in her fragile heart, Janice knew it was true—why was she always on the lookout for Wonder Woman? Why did she put herself through the aggravation of seeking an updated version of Ariel? Someone who could lead Janice out of this misery. Okay, "aggravation" was a bit strong, given that she'd gone out on the scene only once, to Gateways, and what a sordid disappointment that had turned out to be. If only she had the confidence to try again. Ariel wouldn't hesitate, Janice knew, but she wasn't Ariel. Still, wherever she was, out on the street, on the tube, in the office, Janice couldn't help scanning the women she passed, hoping for a spark of recognition. Yes, this other one would signal, I'm lesbian too and here I am, your Wonder Woman.

If only. Janice sighed, feeling the hollow of contradiction in her heart. Since she'd arrived in London, only Kobus had managed to break through her protective guard. And look what a disaster that turned out to be.

* * *

By the middle of February, Janice had well and truly become a hermit, only going out to work or to fetch books or groceries and refusing all unnecessary contact with people. But there was no avoiding Kobus the night he knocked on her door. Janice opened it with a jerk. Before she could tell him to go away, he handed over a small white envelope.

"Open it," he urged, smiling up at her with a huge grin.

Janice thought it was another cartoon and went to give it back, but Kobus refused to take it. "No, open it, you love what is inside. I promise."

Janice pried the envelope open with her thumbnail and withdrew two tickets. Her heart fell, her stomach lurched. She gripped the tickets in a slippery hand.

Unbelieving, she stared down at Kobus. "Are these for real?"

"Yes, yes, they are real, really real, very extremely real. Two tickets for opening night. I've booked row E, seats ten and eleven, downstairs. They are the best seats in the house."

"But they're for *Rose*. Glenda Jackson at the Duke of York's." Janice's breath caught in her throat. "You really mean it? You've got tickets to a Glenda Jackson play?"

"That's what I said." Kobus was complacent. "Look at them. For opening night, next Wednesday. February twenty-eight."

Janice looked blank. "What's the date got to do with it?"

"It is one of your lucky numbers! You arrived in London on a twenty-eight. Last May, yes?"

"So what?"

"Twenty-eight is two times fourteen. February fourteen is Saint Valentine's Day!"

"Rubbish, I'm not into this contrived numerology nonsense."

Kobus was undeterred. "I give you Glenda Jackson as a lucky Valentine's Day present. A bit late, but from me to you. She is your favorite actor, *toch?*"

"You know she is, ever since I saw her in the film *Women in Love.*"

"Now you see her in real life." Kobus looked up at her, eyes wide with hope.

Janice turned from his entreating gaze, her heart thudding madly. She desperately wanted to see the brilliant Glenda Jackson, an actor she'd always dreamed of seeing on stage. Kobus was going to make this dream come true. She couldn't refuse this chance, because, let's face it, with her salary she'd never be able to afford such a good seat in the stalls of a West End play, let alone any seat, only standing room at the back.

Janice clenched the tickets in a trembling hand. She was eager to go but, reality check, these tickets were another bribe. Kobus knew full well how much she wanted to see West End plays. He knew how tempted she'd be to accept this wonderful opportunity. Such a nice gesture to give what she'd always wanted. Deep in her heart, she knew it was just another ploy to win her over. He was still trying to buy her love. It was a blatant attempt to pressure her, yet again.

What would Ariel do in this situation? Janice knew the answer. If Ariel had allowed herself to be put in this position (which she wouldn't, not in a million years), she'd find a way to reject the kind offer. She'd probably make a joke of it, so as not to hurt Kobus's feelings. Bottom line: Despite the pain in her heart, Janice had to refuse. But she couldn't copy Ariel and be kind about it. "Can't go. Sorry, I've got something planned for next Thursday."

Janice slammed the door in Kobus's face. She set the lock with a loud click and waited with hammering heart for him to give up pounding on her door and leave her in peace.

Chapter 17

Halfway through a wet and miserable March, Janice arrived home depressed after another fruitless search for Wonder Woman on the London scene. Calling on Ariel for help, she'd plucked up her courage and tried a trendy new club on Tottenham Road. It was no good. Just another lesbian meat market, tackier than Gateways, filled with a younger, more energetic crowd, who were just as unfriendly as the Gateways crowd to lonely lesbians out on their own. Standing in a dark corner, as far away as possible from the raucous dance floor, Janice had looked over the dancers. Everyone was coupled, and if a woman happened to catch her eye, instead of smiling a friendly hello, she looked away quickly. It didn't occur to Janice that the frown on her face could be off-putting to anybody willing to strike up a conversation. She'd gone home after barely one drink.

Kobus was lurking behind the front door when she arrived. He leered at her, caught in a shaft of weak light, muttering guttural curses she hadn't heard her parents use. He must have been out too, down at the Ship's Bell, drowning another one of his gambling losses. He was drunk. As she passed him to go up to her bedsit, Kobus reached up and slapped her cheek. Hard. Vicious waves of anger and misery swept over his face.

Janice stood in shocked silence. She had earned that slap. She was to blame for how Kobus felt. The slap triggered the same guilt she had felt when Ariel had died. Janice had been driving that scooter. She shouldn't have braked to avoid that bus. Then Ariel wouldn't have flown over her shoulder and been run over. It wasn't the bus driver's fault. He couldn't help hitting Ariel, because Janice had been in the way. It had been Janice's job to protect Ariel, to keep her alive. Instead, Janice had caused her death.

Caught in the maelstrom of old emotion, she felt powerless to escape the hold Kobus had over her. It was her fault for making him miserable. She had to forgive him for hitting her. She hated the pressure he put on her. But it was her fault, wasn't it? She'd accepted every one of his presents. Who could blame him now for wanting more than she wanted to give? Their battle of wills had reached an impasse and Janice realized only she could break the stalemate.

Next morning, sitting at her desk at Willing Workers, she made up her mind. She would leave Kobus to it in his wretched bedsit, run away, and leave all of London behind. She'd go to see her birthplace, Amsterdam. The Magic Bus would be a long ride, but it'd be cheap and get her there in one piece. She called the Magic Bus office. When at last someone answered, she learned that an overnight trip was due to leave for Amsterdam from Victoria Station that very evening. She booked a one-way ticket. Filled with resolve, she stormed over to the manager, Mrs. Brockett.

"Sorry to spring this on you, but I have to quit work. Now. Right away. Today."

Mrs. Brockett looked up from a ledger, her eyes widening in surprise. "But Janice, dear, why? You can't leave just like this. You've got to hand in four weeks' notice."

Janice was obdurate. The strain of trying to be assertive made her aggressive. "Yes, I know, I'm leaving you in the lurch. But it's an emergency. I have to go. Now. I'll give up my pay to make up for the lack of notice." She ignored Tracy tittering in the background. "Thanks for putting up with me. You know I was hopeless at this job. Good-bye."

And grabbing her jacket and bag, Janice stormed out the agency door before either Tracy or Mrs. Brockett could hold her back. She went straight home, scribbled an explanatory note to the landlady, and ran downstairs to slide it under her door. She'd paid the rent up to the end of March but didn't want a refund. Keep the change, Mrs. Palmer.

In her bedsit, she took down her prism, the only personal decoration she'd put up in the grim space, and tucked it safely in the pocket of her new leather jacket. She rolled up her new clothes and packed them on top of the sheets, towels, and books in the bottom of her rucksack. She left a pile of secondhand paperbacks on the fireside table, along with the key to her room. Janice did not want to meet Kobus on her way out. She owed him too much. He needed her too much. She didn't dare face him to say good-bye.

He arrived home when she was about to go downstairs to call for a taxi on the hall phone. Her rucksack was waiting beside the front door. He glanced at the heavy bag and up at her. He knew. She stood transfixed at the top of the stairs. He blocked her escape, his face distorted with pleading. "You must not be leaving me. Do not do it. I forbid it."

"You can't forbid me anything. I've got to go."

"*Ach*, Janice, I won't let you go. You have to stay." His voice was gentle with menace. He hovered a couple of steps below her, repeating her name.

Scared he would hit her again, Janice tried to keep the fear from her voice. "Leave me alone. You're pushing me for something I cannot give."

"Janice, you know I love you." He reached out. "I know you love me. You do."

"No, I don't, Kobus. Stay back. Stop pushing me."

Kobus stumbled up another step. That broken smile on his face, his hangdog eyes, they terrified Janice. He wouldn't listen, wouldn't let her go. He wouldn't stop pushing her. It was unbearable. He left her no choice. She raised her hand and pushed back. At the end of her fingertips, Kobus teetered off balance. Then with a long moan, hands grasping at air, he tumbled down the dusty flight of thirteen steps, heels thudding all the way. At the bottom, he lay on his back with his limbs splayed and head resting at an awful angle.

Ariel had looked like that when she died. Janice should have looked after her, not driven her to death. It had been her job to protect her, and she had failed. Why hadn't she saved Ariel? Why did she have to die?

Had Kobus broken his back, like Ariel? Or was it his neck? Why did he have to die? Janice couldn't stay vacillating at the top of the stairs. She couldn't cope—causing another death. She couldn't stay—be sensible and call for help. Breathless, she bolted downstairs, hurdled over Kobus's dead body, and grabbed her rucksack. With the load slung over her shoulder, she ran all the way to the phone box on Tufnell Park Road. The taxi took ages to arrive, even longer to drive her to Victoria Station until, finally, after waiting what felt like hours for departure, she claimed her seat on the Magic Bus.

Part 2: Hannah

Amsterdam, March 1980

Chapter 18

Sunlight dappled the trees flanking the Keizersgracht. A thin breeze, speared with ice, ruffled the sprigs of new leaves. Stumbling over uneven cobbles, Janice turned her face to the slight warmth of the sun. The rucksack was pulling at her back. She hunched her shoulders and moved on.

A small dog flopped down on the deck of a gaudy houseboat tethered to the canal wall and leaned against a flower box crammed with daffodils and pansies. Janice caught its eye and it yawned. The mongrel's eyes reminded her of Kobus. That mournful way he always looked at her. But now he was dead and wouldn't look at her again. Ever. Janice took a deep breath and exhaled noisily, blasting the awful guilt away. This was Amsterdam, the start of a new life, minus Kobus. She had no time for scary reminders now.

The journey from London had lasted all night. She'd hardly slept on the boat, on the reclining seat she'd claimed as far away from the rowdy bar as she could get, and not at all on the bus, forced to bend her knees for hours at an angle too cramped for comfort. Now, still stiff, it was an effort to walk. But the youth hostel couldn't be far away. She took a last glance at her map, tracing the route she was following from the Marnixstraat bus station, and stuffed the map in her pocket.

At last. Four steep steps led up to the hostel entrance. Janice eased off the rucksack and pressed the brass doorbell. A metallic buzz came from the door. She listened a moment before realizing the lock was electrically operated and pushed open the door. Dragging the rucksack behind her, she entered. Sunlight swirling with dust cast through a huge plant-crowded window, cutting a swath across a gloomy foyer and onto a thickset man stationed behind the reception counter. Ignoring Janice, he was sorting a pile of receipts.

Janice stood at the head of a long marble-floored hallway. The décor screamed faded kitsch. A vinyl sofa squatted beneath the window. An elaborate chandelier hung above her head. The hostel looked cheap enough for her budget. She cleared her throat and the man looked up, his eyes taking in her height. Janice hoped he spoke English. "I'd like a bed in the dormitory for the night."

The man grunted, producing a form from a drawer under the counter. "Just one night? With breakfast in the morning?"

He didn't sound Dutch, like Kobus did, but his English was accented. With that coloring, he looked Mediterranean, Greek or Spanish maybe. Janice nodded agreement. She wanted to stay just the one night, for starters, in case she didn't like it here. But yes to breakfast, thanks.

"Full name?"

"Janneke de Vetter. Janice."

The man scribbled on the form. "Passport? You pay now."

The tariffs were printed on a poster mounted behind the counter. Janice searched in the inner pocket of her jacket for passport and wallet. She withdrew a blue ten-guilder note and handed it with the passport to the man. Colorful Dutch money was prettier than sterling.

As the man flicked through her passport, his brows lifted in surprise. "You Dutch?"

Janice smiled. "Yes, I am. But not really. This is my first time back."

The man looked at her blankly. "In Amsterdam?"

"In Holland." Janice was too tired to go into the whole story. "My parents were Dutch. We went to New Zealand when I was five. I was born here but grew up there."

The man wasn't interested. Smiling briefly, he returned her passport and gave her the top copy of the registration form as well as a brochure about the hostel that listed the facilities and rules of the house. "I am Negy. The owner. No funny business, understand?" Janice nodded. "Bed fifteen in the dorm, straight ahead. Showers up on the first floor. Breakfast room down in basement. Check out tomorrow by ten o'clock. No later." He fiddled with his receipts, dismissing her.

Janice went down the long hallway. It ended at the top of a shallow flight of stairs, covered in faded red carpet. She looked over a long, high-ceilinged room. This must have been the ballroom in the building's heyday. Now it was filled with regimented rows of numbered bunks, most single-tiered, a few at the far end double-tiered. Each bunk held a thin kapok mattress, worn blanket, and dirty-looking pillow. No bed linen. No need for sheets, Janice figured, as people would have sleeping bags. In the center of the room was a long wooden table surrounded by a jumble of folding chairs. Milky light streamed in from the fourth wall, beside Janice. An enormous window went up to the ceiling from a low shelf that ran along the width of the wall. Shadows skittered across the opaque glass, vague suggestions of the branches of shrubs growing in what must have been a courtyard. Janice wondered if guests were allowed out there.

The empty dormitory beckoned. Any other guests must either have checked out or were doing the tourist thing. *No wonder*, thought Janice, glancing at her watch. It was past ten o'clock and at this hour she'd want to be exploring the city too. Her boots clomping on the bare wooden floor, Janice found her bed and didn't like it. It was in the center of the room, hemmed in on all sides by other bunks. No personal space, absolutely no privacy. Turning, she noticed a mirror-clad cabinet in the top corner of the room, set on the wall beside the big window. The bunk in front of the cabinet seemed vacant. No belongings on or beside it claiming possession.

Janice went over and opened the cabinet. Inside were two shallow glass shelves, also backed by a mirror. *That will be a handy space for my stuff*, she thought, shutting the cabinet. She prodded the bunk, sat on it, and the mesh base sagged deeply under her weight. Could be firmer but it would do, and tucked away in this corner, she need suffer only one neighbor. She set her rucksack in the gap between hers and the bunk next door, pushing it a scant distance farther away. She took off her leather jacket, draped it protectively behind her rucksack, and unrolled her sleeping bag. She pulled off her boots, parked them under the bunk for safety, and loosened her belt. With relief she fell onto her sleeping bag and closed her eyes, dimly aware of the comfortable sag of the mattress and a ripple of light washing over her eyes.

This bunk sagged as deeply as the bed in Paris had done. With an effort Janice thrust away a sharp memory of that weekend with

Kobus. She was done with him. He couldn't get at her here. Forcing herself to unclench her hands and calm her breathing, Janice sat up to rummage in her rucksack for her tiny transistor radio. Lying down again, she twiddled the tuning knob and stopped at the first station she found. It was a talk program with heated voices constantly interrupting one another. She thought, *I can't be Dutch, because I can't understand a single word you're saying. Yet.* Her faithful transistor was doing the trick, as always, distracting her from the awful, tight feeling in her chest.

Chapter 19

Diffused by the opaque windowpane, the light in the dormitory was too muted to create shadows. As the day progressed, the light thickened, and when Janice opened her eyes, woken by the shrill ring of the doorbell and heavy footsteps treading the marble hall, the dormitory seemed jelled in palpable light. She felt rested after her sleep. The cramped weariness of the overnight trip was eased from her bones. She watched a group of tourists disperse to bunks and unfold chairs to sit at the table, their loud voices destroying all traces of tranquility.

Following the group, but not one of them, a young man entered, carrying a commodious travel bag. His wispy strawberry-blond hair was vivid against his pale skin. He was skinny, not as tall as she was, but about her own age. With those fine even features, he was good-looking, for a bloke. Dumping his bag beside him, he nodded at the tourists, hitched the knees of his jeans, and sat on the last empty chair at the table. Taking a paperback out of the bag, he began to read, head tilted back, one raised eyebrow, ignoring the rest. Janice noted how fastidiously he turned the pages. His pinkie finger was sticking out as he read, and that amused her. There was something fey about him, otherworldly, as if he didn't belong in the midst of this tribe of tourists. Like her. She wondered idly if he was gay.

The noise of the tourists was annoying. They were loud Americans, too jocular, too ebullient, and too disturbing after the peace of the empty dormitory. It would be hard to adjust to public living. Sleeping and sharing space in this large room filled with strangers. So different from the grim haven of her bedsit in London. How would she cope? How could that good-looking boy switch off to focus on his book? He seemed unperturbed by the babble around him as members of the group compared their impressions of Amsterdam. It was as if these people didn't matter. He wasn't listening. And, as Janice realized, these tourists would be gone tomorrow, to be replaced by a new crowd making similar observations, perhaps in other languages, perhaps in different accents.

A cascade of giggling disturbed the boy. Janice half noticed him raise his head, but she was more focused on glaring at the maker of the idiotic noise. A young brunette, pretty in a Barbie sort of way, was hanging off the arm of her adoring Ken. Janice felt the boy regard her and nodded carefully in return. He winked at her, a small smile of recognition forming on his lips, then nodded back, as briefly as he had done to the Americans. He darted back to the safety of his book.

Janice hugged herself, aware of the chill emanating from the huge window beside her. She was alone in a crowd of strangers. So what else was new?

That first afternoon Janice kept to herself, as usual. First, she explored the hostel and found the shower room on the floor above, at the end of a long corridor. She passed several rooms on the way up. Those with open doors showed four, five, even six beds inside, all neatly made with blankets and sheets, unlike the bunks in the dorm downstairs, but with the same Formica table and wooden chairs. The hostel was a maze of corridors that wound around corners and up and down short flights of stairs for no clear reason. Janice realized the place was far bigger than it appeared from outside. Finding her way back to the main stairwell, she saw that it went to the second floor. There were many rooms for groups but just one small double on the first landing. There was only one shower room for the whole hostel, with a block of four toilets beside it. No his or hers, communal, like the showers.

She went back down to the dorm to fetch her towel, soap, and a change of clothes and felt refreshed after a lukewarm shower. Then, dressed in her favorite flannel shirt and jeans, she went out. Her exit went unacknowledged by Negy, who was stationed in reception, sorting pieces of paper. She ignored him happily. Two can play that game.

Letting the front door heave shut behind her, she meandered down the Keizersgracht, one of the half-circle canals in the center of Amsterdam. She zipped up her leather jacket, for though the sun was out, any warmth it held was blown away by the cold breeze.

Janice kept pace with two black swans drifting down the canal, stopping occasionally to pet the friendly cats she found sheltering on the stone steps of houses. The steep-gabled buildings were five or six stories high, jammed together like a giant set of badly shuffled cards. Their façades seemed to tilt forward, as if they might fall over. Parked cars filled every space between the lime trees lining the canal, their bumpers jutting out and further narrowing the cobbled road. A footpath running alongside the houses, defined by a row of rounded iron palings, was merely a token gesture for pedestrians. It was too narrow and uneven for Janice to negotiate comfortably. She sauntered down the middle of the road, stepping aside when necessary for passing cars or cyclists.

It was peaceful on the canal. No other tourists around to spoil things. She knew she looked like a tourist. She was strolling too slowly, looking up too often to gaze at the crazy angles of houses propping each other up. She was lingering too long on the bridges to watch the flow of murky water and inhale the stale scent, so different from the crystal-clean blue of the Clutha River in New Zealand. And she stopped too often to read graffiti too carefully to be a blasé Amsterdammer. It was smeared wherever there was space enough to use a spray can. Someone had gone mad spraying *Liever Lesbisch* all over the place. Janice could guess what *lesbisch* meant but wasn't sure about *liever*. She knew the word *lief*. It meant sweet or dear. Her mother used to call her *lief* on the rare occasion she'd been a good girl. But *liever*? She'd have to look that up. At any rate, she liked *Liever Lesbisch*, sprayed on the canal wall in bold lavender paint. Something lesbian. Whatever *liever* meant, the graffiti made her feel rather welcome in Amsterdam.

Chapter 20

Janice stopped in front of a tall house built in 1642, going by the iron date mounted on the gable. Gosh. This house had been built the year Abel Tasman sailed the ocean blue, as her old school rhyme would have it. Amsterdam had been a sophisticated city long before Tasman sailed out and discovered New Zealand, claiming it for the Dutch and naming it after the old province of Zeeland. Europeans were arrogant like that, always believing they were the first to discover anything, when in fact the Maōri had migrated to mainland New Zealand many centuries before, well before Tasman had even been born in the northern province of Groningen.

Senses heightened by the irony of being a foreigner in her own birthplace, Janice drew her first impressions of this brave old world. On the Magic Bus ride into Amsterdam early this morning, she had been struck by the number of black sheep grazing alongside their white cousins. In New Zealand, black sheep were rare, as their wool had no commercial value. Most black lambs were killed for meat soon after they were born. Here they let the blackies live. A thrill buzzed through her. She was the black sheep of her family, the one who wanted to leave Godzone, good old New Zealand. The Dutch would let her live here in peace. She would come alive in Amsterdam. She looked forward to that happy moment, but meanwhile, Janice found the Dutch people sweeping past her daunting. When they went past, prattling in their throaty language, she imagined they rated her just another tourist and felt what she thought was their disdain. But she consoled herself. It would only take time to assimilate. Soon she would speak the lingo as easily as she had done when she was little. Dutch had been her first language. And after she'd lived a while in Amsterdam, she hoped she would be as Dutch as her passport said she was.

Janice continued down the canal toward the open square at its end, the Leidseplein. She passed several cafés with tangles of tables and chairs spilling onto the road. Crowds sprawled across the terraces, soaking up the spring sunshine, gulping the light beer the Dutch called "pils," sipping wine or stirring cups of frothy coffee. Janice didn't want to sit by herself in front of a bunch of strangers. She walked on until she found a corner café deserted enough to enter. She took a chair with its back to the wall. Facing the door and glancing at her watch as if she were expecting someone, she settled down to wait for service.

Two bartenders continued their conversation, ignoring Janice, the only customer seated inside. It was a repetition of the moment with Negy this morning when she was checking into the hostel. Janice wondered if it was a cultural trait of the Dutch, or maybe just Amsterdammers, to always keep people waiting. This attitude was different from the service mentality she was used to in Auckland and London. She felt affronted. It wasn't as if these blokes were too busy to serve her. But she shouldn't be jumping to conclusions. It was too soon for generalizations. Giving up the wait, Janice approached the counter. Now the men were laughing at what sounded like the punchline of a story.

Unsure of the pronunciation, she asked, "*Mag ik een kop koffie?*"

The shorter of the two deigned to turn. "Yes, sir. Cappuccino or espresso? With milk?"

He spoke in English, making Janice feel stupid for trying to speak Dutch. She drew herself up to her full height "Yes, milk," adding defiantly, "and I'm not a sir, I'm a madam."

The bartenders gave each other a knowing look, shaming Janice into shaking her hair across her face to hide her angry blush. She staggered back to her seat. Sipping the strong, freshly made brew, delicious after the weak stuff they called coffee in London, Janice peered through the café window, watching gaggles of tourists clogging the shop windows.

At regular intervals, a glass-canopied, tourist-filled barge floated past on the Prinsengracht, heralded by a squawk of historical highlights broadcast by a host at the helm, before disappearing under the bridge. Janice instantly dubbed these boats Tourist Tubs and vowed never to ride on one until she was a real Amsterdammer. She knew she was overreacting. What better way to see a foreign city than from the padded comfort of a canal boat? But Janice didn't want to just see the city. She wasn't just a visitor, with time only to gain the gist of a place before having to move on to the next stop on the itinerary. She'd come here for a good reason.

In a jagged flash of memory, she saw Kobus, desperately begging her to be kind to him. She clenched her fists. Oh no, this was not about him and having to escape the impossible pressure he had put on her. She hadn't run away from the responsibility for his death (was he dead?), she'd run toward life, to a clean start in Amsterdam, a fresh attempt at independence. Janice promised herself she would make it here, reclaim her birthplace, no doubt about it.

Janice put down the empty cup and slid a five-guilder note under the saucer. That should be enough to pay for the coffee, plus an undeserved tip. On her way back to the hostel, the coffee jiggled comfortably in her stomach. With surprise she realized that she had not eaten that day, but that didn't bother her. She wasn't hungry. Anyway, it was cheaper not to eat.

Chapter 21

When the hostel buzzer sounded, Janice pushed the door open. Negy glanced up as she entered, his hand coming away from the door switch. Janice smiled a hello, but he averted his face. Containing a shrug, she continued down the hall to the dormitory. Crossing to her bunk, she stopped. Blast. The blond-haired boy she'd seen before was curled asleep on the bunk next to hers, his hands tucked neatly between his knees. He looked angelic, his fine features relaxed as he breathed gently in and out. Janice knew it was irrational to expect privacy in the dormitory, but she had hoped not to be bothered by a neighbor on this first night, at least. Stifling annoyance, she took a book from her rucksack and lay on her sleeping bag with her back to the room, hugging her shoulder.

It was impossible to read. The dormitory was filling up. The atmosphere was electric, the hubbub of conversation too loud, too distracting for retreat behind a book. She gave up the pretense and turned to face the room. She looked straight into a pair of friendly eyes.

"Just arrived?" The boy spoke in a soft Scottish accent.

"Yes, this morning, but I'm not just a tourist. I'm here for the duration, I think."

"Me too. I'm staying a while too."

"That's nice." There was something mild and unthreatening about the boy that made it easy for Janice to discard her normal standoffishness with strangers. She was glad that he was her neighbor. She sat up and swung her legs into the gap between their bunks.

The boy flapped his wrist at her. "I'm Colin Campbell, with the emphasis on 'camp,' not 'bell,' but you can call me Colin. What's yours?"

She flapped her wrist back with a grin. "Janneke de Vetter, but you can call me—"

"Madam."

"—Janice. Pleased to meet you, Mister Camp Bell."

"Welcome to the lower depths."

Janice chuckled, glad that she understood the allusion. *The Lower Depths* was a famous play by Gorky. Not that she'd read it, of course, but she wanted Colin to know that she'd heard of it. "Are you saying this place is an old flophouse filled with the outcasts of society?"

"Yes, I am." Colin gave a wicked smile. "We're a couple of outcasts, you and me both, I'd say. And more out than in, I'd say, if not the most raging outré of all *The Lower Depths* cast."

"Where are you from? Hope you don't mind me saying you sound like a Scot."

"Och aye, lassie," replied Colin, exaggerating his accent outrageously. "You're not half right. I hail from downtown Edinburgh, a tawdry tenement in Marchmont, to be precise. Not that you'd ever have heard of that undesirable residential suburb, I suppose."

"What's a good Scot doing in a bad place like this? Come for the fun, have you?"

Colin gave a grin. "Bang on, you blethering hen. I'm here for all the gay old time I can get, believe me." Serious for a moment, he added, "I'm on an adventure, doing the Grand Tour before I head back and do my art history degree at St. Andrews. I'm beginning here and hope to get a wee job to fund my ticket to the next stop, West Berlin, on the Magic Bus."

"Snap. I caught the Magic Bus from London. What a coincidence."

Colin was dismissive. "Everyone takes the bus today. Your name sounds Dutch, but by the sound of you, you're an Ozzie? Doing the usual trip overseas before settling down?"

"No way. I'm here for the duration. And I'm a Kiwi, in fact, not an Ozzie." Janice couldn't be bothered doing the birthplace spiel. "I come from Auckland and I'm not, repeat *not*, hurrying back after my OE." Colin looked confused by the abbreviation.

"It's our school exam system," Janice explained. "Kiwis get their school certificate, then pass the university entrance exam, then take off to get some overseas experience before going back to do their degree or score a decent job. School C, UE, OE. Get it? But not me. I dropped out of university and I'm here to stay. I've been living in London."

"Oh, swinging London and all that. What made you leave the wild West End?"

Janice stifled a rush of memory, shaking her head to dispel the image of Kobus lying broken at the foot of the stairs. Had she murdered him? She didn't dare buy the English papers to find out if his death had been reported. Janice turned to hide the guilt in her eyes. Her lips tightened. She wasn't ready to tell anyone that she'd run away from Kobus.

Colin waited for an answer, but when the silence stretched too long, he simply shrugged.

Watching him go to the table and greet the tourists sitting there, Janice gave a great sigh. How kind of Colin not to press for an answer. He seemed okay. Camp as a row of tents, of course, but how good was that? She hugged herself. At last. It looked like she was making a friend. With Colin she could have a proper platonic friendship, no sexual strings attached. Maybe settling in Amsterdam wasn't going to be as hard as she'd feared. Good.

* * *

Janice didn't have much money but didn't want to carry it around with her. She didn't trust leaving it behind, secreted in the cabinet behind her bunk. She had to open a bank account. Intimidated by the imposing head offices of banks on the Rokin, she went into the smallest, darkest branch she could find, farther down the Rokin, near the Munt.

The one clerk in attendance kept her waiting in the empty office for the usual long while before finally deigning to help her. But first he looked her up and down, making Janice feel like a slob. Having checked her passport and trying to disguise his surprise at discovering she was Dutch, the clerk said in accented English, "What is your address?"

Janice said, "I live on the Keizersgracht," and gave the number of the hostel.

"*Welke verdieping?*" Janice looked puzzled so the clerk translated. "What floor?"

Janice didn't want to reveal that she was living in the hostel dormitory. She stuck to an edited version of the truth. "It's three floors. Kitchen's in the basement, we live on the ground floor and the bathroom's up on the floor above."

"*Ach zo,*" said the clerk. "*Souterrain, begane grond en de eerste verdieping.*"

"Um, yes, whatever that is. On the Keizersgracht." And she repeated the number.

At once the old man was all fawning smiles. "I'll just put HS beside the number. That means house. Is fine, madam."

Janice shrugged, mystified by his complete change of attitude. How weird were the Dutch if they were impressed by a canal-side address? If only this clerk knew the reality of her life.

Chapter 22

"Come on, you two. You're not working."

Janice and Colin jumped in their seats, startled by the silent arrival of the trainer in the data entry unit. Hannah Remkes stood behind their desks in their cluster, waiting for Janice to put away her book, Colin his magazine, and for them to start typing again. The afternoon tea break had finished ten minutes ago. Like the other trainees, they had piles of insurance claims stacked behind their keyboards. They were supposed to be entering the numbers written on the forms into the vacant data fields on their computer screens.

Hannah spoke with what sounded to Janice's untrained ear like the slight burr of a transatlantic accent. Janice had assumed the trainer was American until she overheard her nattering to a colleague in fast, unintelligible Dutch. Small and sinuous, with a cap of silver-blonde hair and hooded green eyes, she looked about forty, in her prime. Janice found her secretly exciting, as thrilling as the radiant smile she'd shone on Janice the day they'd met. Janice had felt bathed in Hannah's exhilarating appraisal and loved it. Hannah reminded Janice of Ariel, even if Ariel would never have worn as many bangles as Hannah did. A collection of seven or eight armbands made of silver, beads, or wood jostled and jangled on both wrists, adding a shimmering soundtrack to her every move.

Now the trainer leaned over Janice's chair, standing so close Janice could nearly taste her perfume. Something soft and expensive, it wreathed around Janice, making her hands shake. She froze, scared of revealing how intoxicating she found the scent, how heady she found the proximity of the enticing woman. Oh Hannah.

Hissing tunelessly under her breath, Hannah watched Janice and Colin complete their next few forms and then, without comment, slithered off to leave them to work on alone.

"The bitch," seethed Colin in mock umbrage when she'd gone. "If she rattles her wrists at me one more time, I'm off."

"You fool, you." Janice couldn't help smiling. "You wouldn't quit this job, not in a million years. We've only just begun—"

"Cue the Carpenters."

"Where else would you find a sit-down job in Amsterdam when you don't speak—"

"Dutch," Colin interrupted. "But typing all day long ain't my idea of a good time."

"Don't be such a drama queen. Who said life for outcasts is supposed to be easy? Or fun. Anyway, you're the one who got us this job, so count your blessings, bonny laddie. Even if it doesn't pay that much, we're lucky to have it."

Colin had no reply to that, merely shrugged and went back to typing. Janice glanced over at the others in the training cluster, English-speaking foreigners, like Colin and herself, but lacking his wicked sense of humor, they could not join in their banter, and she found them tedious. Straight. One typist glanced up and hurriedly went back to work when he caught her dispassionate stare. *No fun at all*, thought Janice, stretching her fingers and typing again.

* * *

It was true, without Colin she wouldn't have this job, and for that she was grateful, even if it meant she'd only had a fortnight's holiday between jobs. On April first (and no it wasn't a joke), two weeks after she'd met Colin, the fool had been walking down the main shopping lane and happened to see the call for data entry typists posted in the window of an employment agency. Unusually, the vacancy was written in English as well as Dutch. An insurance company was advertising for typists to enter numerical data in their computer system. Foreign nationals from the European Community who didn't need a work permit were welcome to apply, no Dutch needed. Recognizing the opportunity, Colin had rushed to sign up for the job.

That evening Colin celebrated getting the job by taking Janice out to an affordable pizzeria he'd found near the main post office. They sat at a table in the corner of the window, scarfing slices. Colin told her about the job and offhandedly suggested that she might try it too.

"Can you use a calculator?" he asked. Janice nodded. "Then you can do this job. It's just punching numbers on the keyboard, entering stuff you read off these insurance claims into a database. It can't be hard. They train you first, teach you what to look for on the forms and which fields to enter on the screen. Come on, let's do it together. It'll be a piece of cake."

Janice chewed on an olive. "Pizza cake, you mean."

"Ha-ha, you've missed your calling, wee lassie. You should be doing stand-up, but"—Colin waited a moment—"at your great height you're better off doing sit-down comedy." He was teasing.

Janice wasn't offended. She could take it from him. She felt comfortable with Colin. Safe, drawn to him because of their common bond. Back on that first evening in the dorm, Janice had joined him at the table where that ridiculous brunette was yakking nonstop to her beefy boyfriend. Colin and Janice exchanged looks of recognition. Janice realized he was secretly admiring Mr. Beefcake while she was secretly admiring Ms. Brunette. They gave each other a complicit smile.

Chapter 23

The following Monday, Hannah was flicking through computer printouts in her corner office in the training unit when Janice arrived at work. She was early. The other trainees weren't in yet and Colin was messing about in the men's room, probably smearing gel in his hair. Pretending not to notice Hannah, she switched on her computer monitor, picked the top batch of forms from the stack in the center of the cluster, and settled down to work. She could feel Hannah's hooded eyes resting on her and typed extra fast to impress her, hoping she wasn't making too many mistakes. She'd have to go back later to fix any errors, otherwise she'd be in for a proper scolding. *Oh Hannah. If only.*

That afternoon Hannah came over to the training cluster. One by one, the typists hit enter as they finished their forms, forcing her to wait patiently for their attention.

"Thank you," she said blithely, totally ignoring the typists' power play. "Now then, I've been checking your worksheets. Only one of you is up to speed and already on quota, but don't worry, you'll all get there in the end. Any questions?"

The trainees shook their heads. No one dared ask who was hitting the quota, but Janice guessed she was. She'd taught herself to type on an ancient typewriter that she'd bought for only five New Zealand dollars off one of her old roommates. She'd used it to type her essays at university and had grown quite proficient. Hoping to impress Hannah, now she tried hard to be the best typist in this bunch of new recruits. And comparing herself to the others, she'd noticed how good she was, faster and more accurate than nimble-fingered Colin.

Hannah was standing near her, as always. Janice felt the magnetism between them, an unspoken allure drawing them together. She sensed the attraction was mutual but, frustratingly, it was untapped. Hannah was about to say something to the trainees, perhaps only to Janice, but changed her mind. Bestowing her warm smile on the cluster, she retreated to her office.

Janice thought, *She could have told us who was best. She could have said my name. She doesn't like me. If she did, she'd be giving me praise. Why doesn't she come out of her office? She could pull up a chair and chat, not about work but all sorts of fun things besides.*

Janice found Hannah confusing. The first morning on the job, Hannah had patiently explained the routine to the nervous trainees. Janice had been unusually bold that day, clowning for Hannah's approval, excited by the approval she saw glowing in Hannah's eyes. She'd performed for that heavenly glow, hoping Hannah would do more than smile, not just at all the trainees in the group but at her alone. She wished Hannah would come out and bestow that radiant smile on her now. If only Hannah would be her Wonder Woman.

Hannah was the first woman Janice had found attractive since she'd lost Ariel. There had been no one else since then. No, wait, what about Belle, the sexy bartender who'd flirted with her that first night in the London pub? Oh, Belle didn't count. She'd flirt with a doorpost, anyone and anything, just for show. Hannah was not like that. Janice longed to have more with her than this fruitless crush.

It was nearly four o'clock. Enough already. Janice was done with work. She hit enter on her last form, put the completed batch away in the right spot on the shelf behind the cluster, switched off the monitor, and stood clumsily to stretch her legs.

"I'm off," she murmured to Colin, who was typing frantically, too busy to notice. Passing Hannah's office she said, "Bye-bye. See you tomorrow."

Hannah checked her watch, rattling her bangles. Janice was leaving early. "Wait a moment. How do you think you're getting on?"

Hannah seemed interested in hearing an honest answer but, Janice wondered, did she genuinely want to know? "I'm getting there, I think."

"Excellent," said Hannah warmly, underlining the superlative. "I think you are too. In fact, you're doing so well I don't think you need to spend the full two weeks in training. Tomorrow you can check in with Mrs. Bekkema, next door. She'll be your new supervisor."

Janice didn't want to leave the training cluster. She wanted to stay with Hannah. For. Ever. She wanted to say sorry. For what? She wanted too much. Silence stretched between them. Hannah just stood there, looking up at Janice with a light smile curling her lips.

"Okay, thanks. See you," mumbled Janice, stumbling out the training-room door.

* * *

Easter came and went, unmarked by either Janice or Colin. The following Friday afternoon, long after working hours, Janice was hanging about the edge of the flower market on the Singel Canal. At her great height, she stood head and shoulders above the throng of tourists crammed around her. On the opposite wall of the canal was the insurance office. Without needing to stand on tiptoes, Janice could look into the windows of the training unit, up on the first floor. Now she was spying on Hannah, standing there alone. Why had Hannah stayed after the shift had ended and all the trainees were gone? Was no one waiting for her at home? Or was she waiting in the office until it was time to meet up with friends in a café? To celebrate "thank god it's Friday" and all that?

A forcefield of trepidation held Janice from looking across the water. Instead, she pretended to admire the packets of tulip bulbs filling the racks of the canvas walls of the stall, along with a host of tatty tourist souvenirs. Porcelain knick-knacks in Delft blue. Tiny clogs and teensy his-and-her Dutch dolls. Her mother liked tulips. She would love to get these bulbs. Janice could buy a packet for her, draw a fat kiss on the back, and label it "Two Lips from Amsterdam." Hardy-ha-ha. She still hadn't written. That long-promised letter home had never happened. And it probably never would. Her parents still thought she was in London. She should tell them she'd moved over here, and perhaps she would. One day.

It was getting chilly. Time to go. She'd arranged to meet Colin at the pizzeria on the Nieuwezijds Voorburgwal to eat together, before he went out on the gay beat and she went back home, alone, to the hostel. Janice was about to leave the market when she spotted Hannah ahead of her, crossing the tramlines on the Koningsplein. How had she left the office without Janice noticing?

Hannah stopped and checked her pocket. Janice's heart jolted and she hid behind the nearest stall. The trainer moved on. She was getting away. "Yoo-hoo."

Hannah looked around. Seeing it was Janice, she gave a little wave and kept walking.

Janice strode fast to catch up. Hannah stopped, turned to face Janice, and smiled politely. To Janice that impartial smile felt like indifference.

"Hi." Janice gulped. "Finished for the week?" God, what a stupid thing to say.

Ignoring the inane comment, Hannah nodded politely, then turned and headed up the canal. Janice followed, a beat later, relieved to have left the hectic crush of tourists behind in the flower market. It was quieter here, just the rustling leaves of the tall lime trees.

"Isn't it nice out on the canal today?" Janice wasn't sure if she was welcome to walk with Hannah. She shortened her stride to meet Hannah's pace.

Hannah gave a dry look. "This early in spring it can be a bit bleak on the edges." She gave a slow smile, waiting until Janice realized she was being teased.

Hot panic rushed to Janice's face. Of course, she'd been spotted hanging about the office after work. Hannah wasn't stupid. "Please don't think I'm stalking you."

"Now why would I think that?" Hannah reached up to pat Janice's shoulder, rattling her bangles. "Never mind, I would be flattered if you were stalking me, but you're not, of course, are you? See you, Janice." She flashed a smile, eyes glinting, and escaped inside a building, one of those magnificent merchant's mansions that lined the inner-city canals, before Janice could close her surprised mouth.

Ducks milled around in the water below, begging to be fed. Hannah had left her dangling like a duck, angling for bread, but that was okay. She'd smiled at Janice, for Janice alone, a wonderful smile that was full of promise, an intimate smile that made her heart race, her knees quiver, and her tummy melt into jelly. Janice was floating, soaring, flying high.

Oh Hannah—oh Wonder Woman. Janice knew she was the one for her.

"Quack," said a duck at her feet.

Chapter 24

While other tourists came and went, Janice and Colin stayed in the hostel. Negy saw them coming and going together and assumed they were a straight couple. Neither Janice nor Colin disabused him of this impression.

Janice told Negy that she would be staying indefinitely, and by the end of April she was paying for her bunk and breakfast a week in advance. Holed up in the best corner of the dorm, Janice had commandeered the cabinet for her underwear and shirts. She let Colin park his books next to hers on the low shelf running underneath the big window, beside her bunk. The ragged line of his paperbacks and her picture books made the space look lived in. They used his bag and her rucksack to barricade their nest against invasion from adjacent bunks but needn't have worried. Any newcomer to the dorm recognized their territorial claim and left them alone.

Life in the dorm became routine. As there were no cooking facilities, they fetched takeaways from snack bars (Janice's choice) or went out for a pizza (Colin's choice) or bought fresh salad stuff and prepared a meal at the dorm table (Colin's healthier choice). After dinner, Colin usually went out cruising on one of his gay sorties, but Janice curled up on her bunk, ignoring the babble in the dorm, reading Colin's novels by the thin light of a flashlight taped to the wall above her head. She liked his taste. Lots of spies and detectives. And to her astonishment, between all the Rendells and le Carrés, she found a collection of Noel Coward plays. Colin was as much a theater buff as she was. Heaven on a stick.

During the week they rose early, before the horde. Always the first in the showers and early for breakfast. The breakfast room was presided over by a thin woman in a burqa who turned out to be Dalida, Negy's wife. She stood in attendance behind the counter, ready to replenish the trays of sliced cheese and cold cuts or refill the bread baskets. She kept her eyes down and never started a conversation, only answering when spoken to by dozy Americans wondering where the butter was when the mini-tubs were under their noses.

Janice caught her eye one morning, wanting to thank her, but Dalida turned away.

Colin noticed. "Don't bother Dalida," he whispered as they crossed to their usual table near the coffee machine. "Negy has probably ordered her not to speak to the guests."

So Janice left Dalida alone.

* * *

Now Janice waited on autopilot behind Colin in the breakfast queue. She didn't have to think, because they chose the same menu every day: coffee and orange juice and a hard-boiled egg each, margarine on a slice of whole grain bread for Colin, and for Janice, a thickly buttered cheese-and-apricot-jam sandwich and a roll smeared with peanut butter and chocolate sprinkles.

They ate in silence, needing this time to wake properly. But that Friday morning, Colin couldn't resist a comment. Brushing crumbs off the Formica table, he said, "You always eat three times as much as I do. You'll get fat."

Janice was unconcerned. "Fat, my foot," she said with her mouth full. Colin could be blunt with her at times, but his acidic humor never bothered her. He didn't have a mean bone in his body. The bitch. "I'm three times as tall as you and need to eat well for energy."

"Well, use that well-fed energy to fetch our refills. And don't forget my sweetener."

"Sweets for my sweet." Janice headed to the coffee machine on the counter. "No wait"—she turned—"I've no time for another cup. I want to be early today."

Colin raised an imperious eyebrow. "Don't tell me you're trying to score brownie points with Mrs. Bekkema by turning up early. I've heard she's strict with the new recruits."

"No, silly. I just want to get in—"

"Into the pants of a certain sexy someone."

Janice shook hair over her face to hide the sudden heat in her cheeks. Colin sussed her out too easily, even if they'd only known each other a little more than a couple of weeks. This was his last day in training. On Monday he'd join her in Mrs. Bekkema's room, and then she'd have no excuse to visit the training unit, hoping to see Hannah.

"Oh, shut up, you eejit," she muttered and left Colin to clear their table. "Later."

Chapter 25

Janice lingered in the corridor outside the training unit, pretending to read the notices on the bulletin board but waiting for a glimpse of Hannah through the glass door of her office. The trainer wasn't in. Apart from the concierge downstairs, whose job was to guard the front door because tourists sometimes confused it with the entrance to the coffee shop next door, no one else had arrived this early to work. Janice enjoyed having the place to herself.

Living in the noisy dormitory, working in the keyboard clatter of data entry, having to share her personal space night and day, Janice found it a rare luxury to be somewhere quiet alone. She raised her arms slowly, reaching up higher and higher, trying vainly to touch the lofty ceiling, then flopped over with a deep groan and walked her fingertips along the carpet-tiled floor. Wearing her chunky Brazilian boots made it an extra-long way down, and she could feel the muscles in the back of her thighs and calves stretching, right to the brink of discomfort. Slowly she unwound to her full height and stretched her back up the wall, eyes closed, breathing gently, totally relaxed.

The faintest jingle of bangles intruded on her. She opened her eyes to spot Hannah standing at the corner of the corridor with that familiar smile teasing her lips. She had a rolled-up poster tucked under her arm. Janice straightened with a jerk. Her heart was sprinting, taking her breath away.

"Well, well, well. What a workout," said Hannah, casting a languid gaze up and down the length of Janice's slender body. "Aren't you the fit one." It wasn't a question.

Janice gulped, clenching her fist. "I was just having a stretch."

Hannah could throw Janice off kilter with just one look. And right now she was doing it: gazing up at her through hooded eyes with that incredibly charismatic smile, half frivolous, half serious, playing over her face. Was she teasing Janice? Flirting with her, or not?

Hannah ignored Janice's unspoken question. "Would you stretch yourself out of the way?"

Janice stepped aside so that Hannah could pin the poster onto the board. Janice bent down to read an advertisement for a play: *Dusa, Fish, Stas and Vi* by Pam Gems. Thalia Thespians were putting it on at Café Suikerhof on the Prinsengracht. *Hey*, thought Janice, *I know where that is. It's on the next canal along from the hostel.* Janice admired the bold red artwork on the glossy black background. Under the banner headline and dates of the run was a confident line drawing of the differently shaped faces of four women, all melded perfectly.

"Like the artwork?" Janice nodded, but before she could speak, Hannah continued. "Do you know the play? It's a terrific piece about female friendship. Very feminist, very funny." She gave Janice a look. "And I'm the director."

Janice tore her eyes away from the poster. Hannah was smiling with genuine warmth.

"You're a director? Really? A real theater director?"

"Not just a pretty face," Hannah said glibly, adding with a laugh, "or just your data entry trainer. I really am the director of TT and I produce all our shows."

"TT?" repeated Janice dumbly, her racing heart keeping her from making sense.

"Thalia Thespians, TT for short. Named after Thalia, the Greek goddess of comedy. One of the muses. We do feminist theater, acting in English. I founded the group a couple of years ago and we're still going strong. I may not be a full-time professional, but I do manage to put on one or two shows a year." Hannah indicated the poster. "Are you interested in women's theater? Come to the play. It's a real gem," she said lightly. "Believe me, it's good."

Janice was struck dumb. How could she say that she wanted nothing more than to come to this play? How amazing that Hannah was the director of her own theater group.

The heavy fire door at the end of the corridor banged open. Colin swung around the corner and stopped abruptly when he saw Janice and Hannah standing too close together. "Oops, sorry, lassies. Am I disturbing a private *tête-à-tête*?" His face broke into a wicked grin. "Or do I mean, tit-à-tit?"

Only Colin could get away with a crack like that and not cause offense. Hannah gave him a conspiratorial wink. Janice glared but he blithely ignored her and approached the notice board. "What's this? Oh, look, it's a Pam Gems play. *Dusa, Fish*, et cetera. Would you believe I went to see this when it was on at the Fringe." He paused to think. "Must have been 1976. But back then it was called *Dead Fish*. They changed the name when it transferred to the West End."

"Fringe? What's a fringe? And how do you know all this stuff?"

"The Edinburgh Fringe Festival, eejit. Why wouldn't I know? Because A, it was only four years ago and two, I've got a memory like a magpie, never forget a thing." He paused. "Or do I mean elephant? Anyway, it's a bit women's libby, but I liked it. Where's it on?"

"Café Suikerhof."

Janice and Hannah spoke in unison. Janice stopped instantly, mortified to see Hannah smiling up at her again. Hannah seemed unconcerned, winked again at Colin, and turned to enter her office. Looking over her shoulder, she fired a parting shot. "Do come to opening night, Janice—the eighth of May, next Thursday, if you want to mark your calendar. You'll love what you see, I promise." And with a soft rattle of her bracelets, Hannah was gone.

At tea break that afternoon, Janice couldn't resist popping into the training unit, supposedly to see Colin. He wasn't fooled. "Get away with you, you brazen eejit. Hannah's onto you."

"What do you mean? I've only come to see how you're getting on, considering this is your last day in training." Janice gave him a look that said butter wouldn't melt in her mouth.

But Colin wasn't fooled. "You've got the hots for Hannah, and doesn't she know it."

Janice was aghast. "Do you think she knows I like her?"

"Oh, girl, don't be naive. The way you drool every time you see her, she's bound to know. Anyway"—Colin gave an evil grin—"if you ask me, she's got the hots for you too, so don't you worry 'bout a thing, to quote the fabulous Stevie Wonder."

Janice pulled over an empty chair, sat heavily, and huddled close to Colin. "No, really? Do you think she likes me? I'm not sure. What do you think? Does she really or not?"

Colin raised a supercilious eyebrow and tilted his head in the direction of Hannah's office. "Don't look now, but she is totally aware of your presence, lassie." Janice went to look but he put out an arm. "I said don't. She's pretending to check the printouts but if you ask me, she's giving you a good going over." Colin giggled wickedly. "With her eyes, at least."

Chapter 26

Janice went out looking for Wonder Woman again. It was ladies' night in Club Homolulu, and Colin wasn't allowed in. No problem. He was cruising the other clubs in the nearby gay quarter and, with his luck, wouldn't sleep in the dorm tonight. At least one of them was having the gay time Amsterdam promised.

The babble of voices, strident over the dull thud of disco, enveloped Janice. She squeezed between two women and waited to catch the barman's eye. He gave a perfunctory smile when Janice paid for her Ballantine's. She grimaced back and, pocketing the change, leaned on the bar. Concealing anxiety behind a mask of indifference, she faced the room, tapping her foot to the relentless music. Her glance dwelled briefly on attractive faces. She was not the only observer. If glances were lasers, they'd weave an intricate web of light.

Catching Janice's eye, a woman protectively clutched at her partner. Janice felt revealed in that hard instant. She was a lesbian alone and looking, implication desperate, while the other was safely coupled. Singles are a threat on the lesbian scene. Pity the unpartnered, but take care, beware. She might steal your lover. *If only I had one*, thought Janice. Unbidden again, a memory of Kobus crossed her mind, of how tenderly he had stroked her legs the night Mrs. Palmer had caught them at it. He really did love her. Oh shit. She thrust the thought away.

The music pulsated, blurred by volume. The dance floor was packed with hot bodies crammed in somnambulant stomping. Janice felt like dancing. The whiskey had hit the spot. She wanted to feel this hypnotic music throb through her. Two more whiskeys and she might.

Holding a fresh drink aloft like a torch, she strode through the crowd and drifted to a stop in front of the dance floor. She leaned against a rough wall. Here she felt safe, like a crab peering out from its cave. A mirror globe revolved slowly above the dancers, glinting fragments of light. An ultraviolet lamp tanned their skin and ruthlessly exposed flecks of dandruff on their clothes.

She sensed somebody stop beside her and carefully made no sign she had noticed. Surreptitiously, she swiveled to take in the shadowy form. The stranger was at least a head and shoulders shorter than Janice. Her T-shirt strained over pendulous breasts and a bulging stomach. Her solid figure didn't matter to Janice, but the anxious smile the woman flashed in her direction felt threatening. She didn't want to meet someone as needy as herself. The wall no longer felt like a refuge. Retrieving her jacket and slinking out the door, she castigated herself. Why put herself through all this aggravation? But as she finished the stairs and emerged into the brisk air of the cobblestoned lane, she couldn't deny the truth. She despaired of ever developing anything serious with Hannah. And if she couldn't have tantalizing Hannah, where else could she go to find Wonder Woman on a lonely Friday night?

* * *

The first Sunday in May, Janice decided to visit Café Saarein, hoping to blend in with the crowd. But as she walked down a silent lane, where pansies and wan daffodils poking their heads out of window boxes were the only sign of life, she knew she'd find the café empty, especially this early. Never mind. She had enjoyed the walk from the hostel, taking the long way, weaving a path through the Brouwersgracht to admire the ancient warehouses, then over to Prinsengracht and down to the Westerkerk. Spotting the Anne Frank House just around the corner from this Protestant church, she made a note to visit the museum if and when it wasn't chock-a-block full of tourists. She took care crossing the busy Rozengracht, watching out for those treacherous trams that gave way to no one, especially not ignorant tourists dithering on the rails, and then continued strolling down the canal.

These inner-city canals glowed in the soft spring sunlight. Taking the time to have a good look around, Janice vowed never to stop appreciating her surroundings. No matter how long she ended up living here, she would never stop registering how beautiful Amsterdam was. Pausing on a bridge, she reconsidered. The city was beautiful, yes, but only if you could ignore the ubiquitous graffiti and deposits of grubby dog poo that made walking the streets such a hazard.

Would Café Saarein be a hazard? It was famous, a proper haven for women libbers and lesbians, no men allowed. Surely she would be welcome. She found the café on a corner of the Jordaan. Janice had read somewhere that this quiet neighborhood on the edge of the inner city dated back to Abel Tasman's time, the seventeenth century. It had been built as a ghetto for immigrants, and some renowned artists had lived there, like Rembrandt had at the end of his career. She'd heard that the women's collective who ran the place now had taken it over only a couple of years ago. They'd named it Saarein in honor of the previous owners, a woman called Saar and her husband, Rein.

Peering in through one of the huge windows, Janice could see why the Dutch called places like this brown cafés. Brown was the color throughout. The bar was highly varnished chestnut, the walls and furniture were chocolate, and the ceiling was tar brown, darkened by decades of smoke. The inside could have looked dark and dingy, but the lofty space and two airy windows put paid to that. Kobus would've liked it here. Janice squashed the thought before it could take hold.

Set in a shallow triangular porch, the door to Saarein was propped open with a wooden peg. Janice went in. A woman appeared from the back, wrestling a keg of beer behind the bar. Waiting in silence until the woman had finished hooking the keg to the beer tap, Janice ordered a tea. It turned out to be a glass of lukewarm water and a dusty tea bag. Unwilling to try making conversation, she took the tea downstairs to a small pool room. She hovered over the pool table, running her fingers over the balls, wanting to but not daring to pick up a cue and try potting a few shots. Nothing could be worse than proving how single she was by playing pool alone.

She returned to the bar and went up a precariously steep flight of stairs to the mezzanine. The confined space was nearly filled by a huge round table. She squeezed behind it and perched on a chair facing the stairs. A pile of magazines lay on the table, nothing in English except an old copy of *Spare Rib*. She flipped through the pages of a *Lover*. She thought it might be lesbian porn, but it turned out to be earnestly feminist. Keeping her head down as if she were reading, she pretended she wasn't waiting for other lesbians to arrive.

Chapter 27

It didn't take long. They entered in dribs and drabs, always in pairs, greeting friends with loud hails of recognition. The first couples claimed seats on the window benches alongside and opposite the bar. Other couples stood before the bar or trickled downstairs. Soon Janice could hear the click of pool cues glancing off balls under the increasingly loud buzz of women in conversation.

The mezzanine was left unoccupied, and Janice sat there, still pretending to read and, with her hair mussed over her face, still pretending not to watch the action below. Her tea was long gone when she looked up from a magazine and, to her astonishment, saw the one she'd been waiting for climbing the steep stairs. Miracle of miracles. Deep in her secret heart, Janice had hoped for this and look, it was happening.

Half concealed behind Hannah on the Café Saarein stairs was a well-groomed woman, judging by the neatly manicured hand gripping the banister. Both women paused at the top. The stranger had tawny-green eyes, a mane of golden hair, and a well-defined mouth. She was taller than Hannah but not as tall as Janice. *Her eyes would come up to my chin*, estimated Janice, thinking irreverently as she usually did whenever she rated an attractive woman. *Good height for a kiss.* The woman was slender, definitely not ugly, and not as old as Hannah. Still in her thirties, guessed Janice, but not half as gorgeous as Hannah.

Both nodding at Janice, Hannah and the woman sat on the opposite side of the table. The stranger gave Janice a polite smile. Hannah tilted her head and subjected her to a long calculating look, the usual smile teasing her lips.

"Well, well, well," said Hannah at last. "Fancy meeting you in this den of iniquity."

Janice didn't know what to say. Feeling the heat rise in her cheeks and quickly hiding her eyes, she pushed the magazines into a pile in the center of the table.

"Puss got your tongue? That must be an occupational hazard." Hannah chuckled, at the stranger, not Janice. "For a lesbian, at least."

"Okay," Janice said firmly, finding strength from goodness knows where. "I'm gay, so what? We're all gay here, all lesbians. What of it?"

"Good. That's out of the way." Hannah was unperturbed by the outburst. Turning to the stranger, she said, "This is Janice, the amazing *pot* at work I was telling you about."

Janice blushed deeper. Hannah had called her amazing. But "pot"? What was that all about? Janice quickly considered asking for a translation but just as fast thought, she'd better not. So Hannah was talking about her after work. Oh Hannah. Even in her embarrassment she felt a wild spark of hope. Did this mean Hannah liked her? Was she interested in her? Miracle of miracles, did she want Janice as much as Janice wanted her? Janice looked away, terrified her spark of hope would be apparent.

The woman ran her fingers through her glossy hair, sweeping it off her forehead. "Hi, I'm Kate. Hannah's been raving about you for weeks. Now I can see why. Been here long?"

Janice liked the way Kate's smile made her eyes crease. Kate sounded English. Going by the accent, Janice guessed she came from the Midlands or somewhere farther north. She pushed her empty tea glass aside, hoping that Kate wouldn't think it was hers. "Only about a minute before you two got here."

Kate smiled, not taken in. "No, sorry," she added kindly. "Not Saarein, I meant Amsterdam."

"Oh, sorry." Janice felt like an idiot for misunderstanding. "I've only been here a month. I got the job more or less straight after I arrived."

"The only straight thing about you," said Hannah, with a sidelong glance at Kate.

Janice drew herself up. She decided to ignore Hannah's teasing and addressed Kate. "You sound English. When did you come to Amsterdam, if you don't mind me asking?"

"Oh, I don't mind. I love talking about myself." Kate laughed in such a way Janice knew she was making fun of herself. "Hannah can tell you that and will if I know her. And I do." Kate shot a glance at Hannah, who merely smiled back.

It was clear that these two knew each other well, if not intimately. Oh god, they were together, they were a couple. How could Janice be so stupid not to realize that straight away. How moronic to imagine that Hannah was single, ready, willing and able to be with her. What a naive fool—no, what an utter idiot she was for hoping in miracles. But then Kate surprised her.

"She's my ex."

Janice stared without understanding, her heart hammering nineteen to the dozen.

"We met in Leeds, oh—how long ago, Han? Six or seven years. At work."

Hannah said, "I went on a course at our head office, to learn how to become a data entry trainer. Kate was working in the personnel department and processed my application."

"Yes, we met on the job, fell madly in love, and I arranged a transfer to Amsterdam."

Janice's eyes flashed from Hannah to Kate and back again. She couldn't believe it. Was history repeating itself? Had Hannah fallen in love with her at work? The way Janice had fallen for her? She didn't dare ask when they'd broken up, but Kate saved her the trouble.

"We split more than three years ago now."

"Three years, two-and-a-half weeks and an hour, but who's counting?" said Hannah.

"But," Janice said, trying to be sensible despite her hammering heart, "you're still friends." When Kate nodded, she went on. "How come I've never seen you at work?"

"Oh, you won't ever find me down in data entry."

Hannah took over, first checking that Kate had finished. "She's staff, assistant to the head of P and O, personnel and organization. Sits with the managers up on the fifth floor. Never goes slumming down with us in production."

Kate gave a catlike smile. "Not that I'm a snob or anything. I just haven't got time to socialize at work."

"With the plebs. That's your story and you're sticking with it." Hannah was teasing.

Kate stood. "Enough of this idle chitchat, pleasant though it is. I need a drink. Pils, Han? What about you, Janice? Your tea glass is empty. Can I get you another?"

Janice didn't feel like another cup of lukewarm tea-flavored water. If that's how the Dutch drank tea, forget it. In New Zealand that sort of muck was called pig's piss. She knew pils was light ale. But she didn't like beer, found the taste of hops soapy, and could only take it if it were sweetened in the form of a shandy. She wasn't really a wine drinker, because the stuff you got in New Zealand was so rough it was simply undrinkable. At least the beer was cheap. What she really wanted was a shot of whiskey, but she didn't dare ask for a decent one. It would cost too much. And anyway, it was too early in the day for hard liquor. Kate waited for Janice to make up her mind. She couldn't. In desperation, she waved at Hannah. "I'll have what she's having. That'll be good."

Kate smiled briefly and went downstairs. Hannah reached across the table to take Janice by the hand. Lightly stroking her long fingers, she said, "We'll have to see about that."

Janice felt a frisson of electricity in the light touch. "What do you mean?" she stammered, not pulling her fingers away but fiercely aware of her thundering pulse.

"You're having what I'm having? Well"—Hannah paused—"we're having a ball."

Mesmerized by Hannah's gaze, Janice repeated inanely, "Oh, we're having a ball."

"Yes, isn't this a ball, flirting like this? You do flirt very well, I must say."

Janice couldn't breathe. Hannah must be pretending. She couldn't mean that she found Janice, of all dull people, truly attractive.

But Hannah went on. "I do enjoy flirting, don't you? But just as well"—Hannah batted her eyelids—"this is just a flirt, because I'm not into anything serious."

The electricity pulsing from her fingers belied the woman's words. Now Janice did a complete irrational turn and refused to believe that Hannah wasn't seriously attracted to her. Body language told the truth, even if Hannah's words didn't.

Kate returned with three beers and broke the spell. Hannah released her hand. Janice's fingers kept tingling even after the electric touch was gone.

"Aren't the others coming?" Kate handed around the beers.

"Nope," said Hannah, "not this time. They have better things to do." Explaining to Janice, she added, "Usually we all have a quick drink after rehearsal, but not today."

Janice sat up, quivering. The tingling had run up her arm and encircled her heart. She was thrumming with excitement. "Oh. You've been rehearsing your play."

"I'm playing Stas." Kate laughed. "Tell her how good I am."

"All four of you are excellent," said Hannah evenly. Tilting her head to give Janice that hooded-eye look, she added, "The whole play is excellent. You'll like it, I know." Then she reached over and, in front of Kate, took Janice's hand again, sending another shock wave into her heart and paralyzing her fingers. Janice could not pull away. Looking her in the eye, Hannah lowered her voice and said slowly, "You must come."

Kate burst out in a huge guffaw, seeing Janice quivering. "Come off it, Han, you big tease. By the looks of it she already has."

Caught in the light of Hannah's gaze, Janice could only breathe, "Already what?"

"Come." Kate gave another deep roar of laughter. She took Janice's other hand. "Do come," she said, laying corny emphasis on the word, "and see our play. Hannah's a brilliant director, and in her talented hands"—she gave Janice a quick squeeze—"we all put on a good show. You'll see."

Janice pulled back, reclaiming her sweaty palms. What was she getting into now?

Chapter 28

From the outside, Café Suikerhof looked like any other cozy brown café. From the street, no one could tell that it harbored a small fully equipped theater in the back, which many amateur theater clubs in Amsterdam, not just Thalia Thespians, hired for their shows. In the front was a brightly lit bar. A long galley with a row of small tables was lined up against the opposite wall.

The opening-night crowd milled in the space between tables and bar. Standing by the door with Colin, Janice was glad she was tall and could see over the heads of the throng. While she waited for Colin to finish buying their tickets, she scanned the crowd for Hannah. Not here. At the end of the bar was a wood-paneled wall broken by two doors, one labeled "Heren," the other "Dames." The restrooms blocked off a wide aisle to the theater auditorium. "Come on," she said, pulling at Colin's arm. "Let's go in and find our seats."

Colin drew back. "It's too early. Don't you want a drink first?"

"No, not now. I want to have a clear head tonight."

"Oh dearie me. Did you just say, 'I want to give head tonight'? One wonders to whom." He smacked his lips on the "m."

"Colin!" Janice smiled, despite herself. Given a choice between crass and class, he would always go for the obvious. But no matter how rude or contrived his jokes were, they were always funny. Even now, when she was full of nervous anticipation, she had to laugh. "Oh, all right, let's have a drink first. Are you buying? Then do me a whiskey please."

Colin squeezed a path through the crowd, smiling at the men he passed, and propped himself in front of the bar. Watching him wait for service, Janice was glad he was with her tonight. She hadn't wanted to come here alone. Although he had seen the play in Edinburgh, Colin said he would give it another go because, as he told her on the stroll here from the hostel, "You need handholding, lassie. Otherwise, you'll never pluck up the courage to do some Han ... holding. Never fear, I am here."

"*Han ... holding.*" How on earth did he do it? Colin had the instincts of Miss Marple for what Janice was truly feeling. She couldn't help thinking of the agonizing handholding she had endured in Saarein. She could never tell Colin about that.

Now she was blocking the doorway to De Suikerhof and stumbled aside so that a couple of women could pass. Hugging the window, Janice searched the room again. Still no Hannah. Well, she would be busy backstage. She wouldn't have time for Janice now. But after the show. The cold hand of anxiety gripped Janice's heart. *Don't get your hopes up. You're tempting fate.*

She watched Colin pay for their drinks—rosé for him, the whiskey for her—and when he was accepting his change, she was not surprised to see the bartender scribble something on a beer mat and hand that over as well. No doubt a telephone number. Every time Colin set his eyes on someone, he scored, or so it seemed. Janice recalled their conversation about this last night. Slicing tomatoes in the dorm, helping Colin prepare a salad for their meal, she'd asked him how he hooked up with strangers so easily.

Colin had given her a hard look, checking to see if she genuinely wanted to know, then relented with a grin. "I smile at people, for starters. I never stand glowering like you do."

Janice felt her hackles rise. "Glower? I don't glower. How can you say I glower?"

Tossing cucumber slices on the greens, Colin said, "You tend to frown in company, Janice, you do. People can find that off-putting. You've got to do nice to get nice."

"But if I pasted a nice smile on my face, I'd be putting on an act. It'd be fake."

"Not if you mean it. I don't put on an act. I like people, especially good-looking men."

Janice was still offended by that "glowering." Thinking of Hannah, she said, "When I see a good-looking woman, I don't glower."

"No, you drool," said Colin quickly. "But seriously, lassie, on the whole, people are nice. If you treat them nicely, they'll treat you well. That's my philosophy. What's yours?"

Oh, that "good things happen to good people" crap. What a load of rubbish. Janice wasn't having any of that. *On the whole, people aren't nice,* she thought, *no matter how well you treat them.* There was always someone mean out there ready to take advantage. Besides, being nice to people always put you in a subservient position. It made you the underdog, begging to be liked. Janice thought of Kobus begging her to be nice to him. "It doesn't work like that," she said. "Being nice to someone because you want something from them."

Trying to sound like Mick Jagger, Colin sang, "You can't always get what you want."

Colin was smiling but Janice didn't smile back. She was still thinking of Kobus. He had wanted—no, needed—her to be nice to him, and see what had happened (was he dead?). Especially by the end, it'd been too great an effort to even pretend she could be nice. She couldn't give him what he wanted. She wasn't nice and never would be for the sake of it. For the fake of it.

Colin handed her the Ballantine's. "Here, enjoy." He took a sip of his wine. "But there you go, glowering again." Janice shot him a warning look. "Oops, I mean, glowing." He turned his back on her frown, adding, "There's the bell. Look, people are going in. The seats aren't numbered. There'll be a rush for the best. Come on, let's join the free-for-all."

They knocked back their drinks and, once they had shown their tickets to the usher and received a free program, they joined the throng inside the dimly lit auditorium. It was not large, the same width as the bar in front, and crammed full of the hard wooden chairs found in all brown cafés. The uncurtained set was in darkness. Beyond the rows of seats was a booth, separated from the audience by a low barrier. With a start, Janice saw Hannah in the booth with a mannish-looking woman, all square shoulders and crew cut. Both faced the stage, ready to do the lights and sound.

Janice dithered. She didn't want to sit in the front, where the actors and director could see her when the stage lights came up. But she wanted an unobstructed view, so didn't want to sit too far back either. Colin made up her mind for her. Grabbing her hand, he pushed her into the nearest empty chairs in the middle of the audience. In a normal theater they would have been the best house seats. Lucky. Shuffling his chair to the left so that he could see between the shoulders of the people in front, he said, "This'll do. Give me a look at the program."

"In a minute." Janice had gripped the folded sheet of paper so tightly it had crumpled. She smoothed it out on her leg. The front page showed the same illustration as the poster, a clever line drawing of four women above the banner headline: "Thalia Thespians present *Dusa, Fish, Stas and Vi* by Pam Gems." Inside were the usual listings of cast and crew. All women. Janice didn't know any of the names apart from Hannah's and Kate's. She read on and saw that Kate had a double credit, first as Stas in the play and then as the program/set designer. She must have drawn the line drawing on the poster, repeated here on the program. So Kate was a talented artist. Like Kobus.

Wiping her palms on her jeans, Janice handed the crumpled page to Colin. As the light faded, Janice trembled with anticipation. Let the show begin.

Chapter 29

Janice clapped until her palms hurt. With Colin and the rest of the audience, she was giving the cast a standing ovation. As the four actors took their bows, Janice stood there, moved by the sad ending of the play. But, oh, there'd been funny bits. She'd remember Vi's line to Stas to tease Colin with: "Every time you bite into that lettuce it screams." And what about the way Kate, as Stas, had transformed herself onstage from a dowdy, unremarkable person into an elegant Poiret model, um … prostitute, um … top-class escort. Come to think of it, Kate wasn't all that bad looking. Nowhere near as gorgeous as Hannah, of course, but she did have a trim figure. Looked after herself.

Now the actors were pulling Hannah out of the lighting booth and onto the stage. Hannah stretched her arms, making her bracelets gleam and glitter, and turned her head from side to side, regally accepting the wave of applause as her due. Then her eyes locked on Janice, standing taller in the dark than anyone near, and she smiled, the radiance of her smile amplified by the dazzling light. She smiled for Janice, standing out in the crowd. Outstanding for Hannah, alone.

After the show, the bar was packed. Using the crowd as an excuse, Hannah maneuvered Janice onto a bar stool and pressed her body lightly against her while they waited for their champagne. Hannah's bracelets tumbled down her arm as she rested a hand on Janice's thigh. It was a possessive gesture, full of promise. Janice was quivering, doing her best to restrain her racing heart and not reveal how intoxicating she found the proximity. Such intimacy. In public. She inhaled Hannah's scent, something warm and woody and oh so seductive. It was all Janice could do not to grab Hannah and bury her face in her neck to absorb all the molecules of that heady scent.

Hannah could tell the effect she was having. With her standing and Janice seated, their eyes were level. She parted Janice's legs, inched slowly between them, and blew lightly on her mouth. "Later," she whispered and disengaged herself to accept another compliment from a playgoer.

Colin was just down the bar, deep in conversation with a new bloke. The harried bartender, kept busy serving the crowd on his own, was shooting evil glances at him to no avail. Colin spotted Janice. Raising his hand at her, he crossed his fingers, gave a huge smile, and mouthed, "See you tomorrow." Then he and the bloke took off, followed by the redhead who'd played Fish, the upper-crust activist. Janice wondered why she was leaving early.

Hannah was still doing the rounds, accepting praise from audience members, and passing it on to her cast. The other actors and the butch woman who'd done the sound were bunched at the end of the bar, enjoying the high of their performance. Janice watched them, stabbed by loneliness. How she longed to be one of their company, to be in Thalia Thespians, to belong. If only she dared get off this damn stool and join them for a cozy chat. Kate would welcome her kindly, she knew.

Instead, she took a nervous sip of champagne from the glass the bartender deposited before her. Then Hannah was back, smiling at Janice and lifting her glass in a toast. "Here's to the ladies Dusa, Fish, Stas, and Vi." She leaned in and ran her fingers down the length of Janice's thigh. "And you."

Janice felt her cheeks flush. Giving in to her hopeful heart, she said, "You too."

* * *

Hannah lived on her own on the top two floors of a grand mansion. It was the same building that Janice had seen her duck into the day she'd met up with her by the Singel flower market.

"Come in, come in," Hannah said, opening her front door and ushering Janice inside. Hannah sprang onto the third step of the staircase, making Janice wait where she was so that she could look her in the eye. "Come up to my cozy little nest," she murmured. "I can't wait for you to see it." And taking Janice by the hand, she led her up two steep flights of stairs.

Lofty ceilings, marble floor tiles, and waxed parquet throughout. Janice looked around, trying to disguise how stunned she felt by this spacious apartment. There was loads of real art on the walls. She watched Hannah switch on and dim the spotlights and twirl flirtatiously between the sliding doors decorated with panels of leadlight glass. She beckoned Janice to follow her into the dining room. "How do you like my massive dining table? That's real cherry wood. And there's seating for ten, twelve in a pinch. Very handy for play readings."

Hannah didn't wait for Janice to answer, just waved her back into the salon, with its three tall windows overlooking the canal. "You like my taste in furniture?" Janice could only nod. There was a four-seater in mahogany leather and two modern chairs, one rocker and one ordinary with matching footstool, both in golden birch and forest-green leather.

Taking Janice by the hand, Hannah pulled her into the kitchen. She waved airily at the equipment crowding the polished granite counters. "The latest mod cons, not that I ever use them all." She smiled deprecatingly. "I can work the cappuccino machine but that's about it."

Hannah must be stinking rich. Janice had never been in such a lavish home. She loved Hannah's good taste. How she hoped Hannah would have the good taste to love her.

Chapter 30

Hannah led the way along the marble-tiled hall and up the stairs. In the bedroom she made Janice sit on a king-sized bed. Perched on its end, Janice slid a hand over the duvet. It was lush silk. Hannah wormed her way between her long legs. Holding Janice by the shoulders, she bent forward inch by breathy inch, all the while gazing into her eyes. Then they kissed.

At last. Janice let out a great sigh of relief, closed her eyes, and gave in to the kiss. Hannah's lips were light on her own, soft, smooth, and gentle. This delicate kiss was different from the way Kobus used to kiss her, devouring her mouth and scraping his bristles all over her face. The tip of Hannah's tongue ran over the contours of Janice's lips, unintrusive, unlike Kobus choking her with his thrusting tongue. Janice stiffened, not wanting to think of him while this was happening. She exhaled noisily, expelling Kobus from her mind, drew Hannah in close, and kissed her back, longer and harder. The tips of her fingers explored Hannah's face, found the little creases in her cheeks, the little lines at the corners of her eyes, the sexy little dip in her chin. *This is how it feels to kiss an older woman.* It felt good, it felt right. Kissing Hannah was all she wanted, all she ever needed.

Hannah stepped away. Subjecting Janice to a mischievous look, she rattled her bracelets down to her wrists then stripped them off, letting them fall one by one on the bedside table. Leaning back on outstretched arms, Janice watched as Hannah came to the foot of the bed and unbuttoned her blouse. Hannah's eyes glinted in the pastel light, compelling Janice to watch her undo the next button. Her fingers teased at the third button, strayed over it, circled it once, twice and again, slower and slower, making mesmerized Janice long to feel those fingers circling her.

Then the blouse was open, and Hannah wasn't wearing a bra. Her breasts were fuller, hung lower than Ariel's had. Quickly banishing the comparison, Janice couldn't resist drawing Hannah's breasts together and burying her nose in the cleavage. But she couldn't help noticing the difference in skin tone. Hannah's skin felt rougher, more spongy than Ariel's had ever been. *Stop comparing.*

Janice succumbed to the sensation of Hannah, here and now. She felt the woman arch her back as she veered from one breast to the other, nibbling the nipples till she heard a gasp.

* * *

A while later, Hannah froze a tense moment, then gave a deep shuddering moan. "Enough! she cried. Stretching languorously, she took hold of Janice's hair and pulled her up beside her.

They lay in each other's arms, heads on the same pillow, Hannah still catching her breath, Janice watching and waiting. She loved the flavor of Hannah. She loved her sweet scent. She savored her compact body, lying vulnerable in her arms. She felt protective, she felt complete. "I've found you at last," she whispered. "My Wonder—"

Janice would have gone on, but Hannah placed a finger over her mouth. "Shush, don't speak. It only spoils things." She placed her palm against Janice's chest and pushed her away.

Janice complied with a generous smile, allowing herself to be shoved onto the cold side of the bed, a good arm's length away. She didn't mind giving Hannah the space to recover if that was what she wanted. It was her turn now, but she could wait.

And she did wait. And wait. For Hannah to make a move. But there was no move until finally the woman reached over and stroked Janice's cheek. "*Welterusten*, nighty-night." Hannah turned over, tucked the duvet into her neck, yawned deeply, and fell straight asleep.

Janice lay there stunned, clutching herself to restrain the furious hormones raging through her veins. Had Hannah gone off to sleep, leaving her high and wet like this? It wasn't fair. She'd done Hannah, how could Hannah not do her? Was she so bad a lover that she'd bored Hannah to the little death of sleep? Inconsequently, a song from Stephen Sondheim's *A Little Night Music* flashed through her mind: "Every Day a Little Death."

No, she couldn't have bored her. She'd felt how eagerly the woman had responded to her touch. Janice knew how to please a woman. Ariel had taught her that. But since she'd lost Ariel, she hadn't been to bed with anyone besides Kobus and he didn't count. Had she lost her touch in the four years since Ariel? Janice felt hollow, caught in the cold spiral encircling her heart. She slid her hand down to comfort herself, holding her breath, holding the duvet away from her questing fingers so that the slight movement would not disturb Hannah. She thought of Hannah, of keeping her trembling in the agony of anticipation. Of Hannah thrumming under her tongue, heaving under her hip, bucking as wildly under her hand as she was bucking now.

Looking over her shoulder, Hannah spoke in a cold voice. "Are you done?"

Chapter 31

Too early next morning, Hannah served Janice in bed. Coffee. Janice was sprawled across her side of the bed when Hannah's bracelets woke her. They rattled sharply, chasing away the quiet pull of sleep. Why on earth did Hannah have to wear so many bracelets? Sitting up to receive a fine-porcelain bowl, filled to the brim with milky coffee, Janice tugged at the duvet to cover her naked chest. Hannah took a sip of her own bowl and set it down by the digital clock on the bedside table. The clock announced the date in livid neon red: Friday, May 9, 1980. Of course, a working day for them both. Hannah was already dressed in neat pants and a soft mohair jumper. Janice wouldn't have time to go back to the hostel and change before she was due to start. Just as well, the clothes she'd worn to the play were the ordinary ones she wore to work.

Janice rubbed the nape of her neck, avoiding looking Hannah in the eye. Recalling what had happened last night, she felt close to tears and mussed her hair in front of her face in case it showed. But she needn't have worried. Hannah pretended that she hadn't caught Janice masturbating. She was acting as if she hadn't taken anything from Janice and given nothing in return. Even so, Hannah wasn't selfish. Oh no, she couldn't be, reasoned Janice. Hannah had just been tired. After the exhausting buildup to the opening of the play, she'd been too tired to give Janice a warm hand on her own opening. Ha. Colin would love this twist on the old theatrical saying. Pity she'd never share the joke with him. She wouldn't tell him what had (not) happened last night.

"Hurry up," ordered Hannah. "Get dressed. I need to get my head together for work."

What else could Janice do but obey? Soon after, shrugging into her jacket by the apartment door, she turned to say, "See you later." She expected only a good-bye, but Hannah held out her arms. Bending down to accept the embrace, Janice felt better after Hannah's kiss.

Hannah stepped back a pace so that she could see Janice more easily. "You were luscious last night. Do come again."

Janice staggered. Had Hannah intended the cruel innuendo behind this remark? Was she being ironic, or sarcastic? Janice searched the woman's face to see if she were acknowledging what had happened but couldn't see past the teasing expression. Hannah was playing, as usual.

"See you," said Janice curtly, close to tears again.

"No wait." Hannah surprised her again by handing over some printed pages bound together with string. "This is my new play for Thalia Thespians. We're putting it on next, and you might be good in the part of Jools. Give it a read."

Janice couldn't stop her heart from making a juddering leap. Was this her chance to become one of the Thespians? To belong? Was this a chance to get to know Hannah better, learn to understand her and earn her trust? Eagerly she took the script, noting the title *Romy & Jools—Do or Dyke* on the cover, followed by Hannah's name. "Did you write this?"

Hannah nodded, adding with radiance, "You'll never guess what play it's based on."

"Well, I doubt it's the Scottish one. But seriously, are you sure about me doing the part? I haven't been on stage since school, and that doesn't count."

Hannah gave her the long calculating look that was becoming familiar. "Judging by your little solo act last night, you should do well as the love-stricken Jools. But you'll have to do an audition first."

"What kind of audition?"

Hannah refused to be drawn. "You'll see."

Chapter 32

Later that Friday, Colin nabbed her in the stairwell outside the lunchroom. Where they stood on the landing, they could see down into the foyer. Janice stiffened. Kate, Hannah's ex, was by the front desk, greeting a motherly woman. Released from a warm hug, the woman handed Kate a cloth shoulder bag holding something bulky, a book perhaps. Kate took it with a grateful smile.

"Thank you, Coby!" she roared, so loudly they could hear her from up here.

The woman replied in Dutch and went on talking. Nonstop. Kate listened attentively at first, but after a while, looked away, glanced upstairs, and noticed Janice and Colin on the landing. She gave them a little wave and turned back to the woman. There was something about this little chatterbox and the way she was claiming Kate's attention. She looked like someone Janice knew. But who? She couldn't put her finger on it and dismissed the thought.

Kate shrugged the bag onto her shoulder and half turned away, making it clear that she wanted the woman to go. Poor Kate. She must want to get back to work. Janice knew the feeling of being trapped in trivial conversation.

Janice hadn't had a chance to catch up with Colin yet. He no longer sat beside her. The cozy bubble they'd shared in training was no more. When he'd graduated from training, Mrs. Bekkema kept them apart, seeing how they were always chatting, always giggling and pushing the limits of breaks.

Now Colin said, "So, lassie, how did it go with the luscious Hannah last night? You did get off with her, I suppose. And did you have as good a gay old time as I did?"

Janice hid behind her hair while she considered what to tell Colin. He waited for her answer. It was one of the things she liked about him. He could be rude, crude, and crass, but he was never pushy. He never put her under pressure. She ticked a finger against her teeth, thinking hard. She really didn't know what to say. The truth about Hannah in bed was the last thing she could admit. She merely told him about the script Hannah had given her.

"Hannah's written a play for Thalia Thespians."

"Labia Lesbians."

Janice ignored the crack. "And she wants me to audition for one of the main parts."

"You. But you can't act. Oh, sorry, don't mean to hurt your feelings. That one just popped out." Colin laughed. "As the actress said to the bishop."

Janice had to smile. "I don't know what she sees in me either. I told her I haven't acted since we did a reading of *The Tempest* at school."

"Oh, brave new … you. You've not been in a play since school? Never acted at all?"

"Not on or off stage. I'm happy to stay in the audience, watching real actors at work," said Janice, tapping Colin on the shoulder for emphasis.

"Ouch," he squealed. "You're bashing me. Bruise me and I won't be able to work."

"Oh, stop it. You're such a big drama queen."

"And you're not?"

"I may be big, but I'm not into drama or a queen like you, Your Royal Bitchness."

Colin held out an imperious hand. "Then bow before a real one, you dreary old dyke."

Before Janice could protest at being called "dreary," Colin blew a quick kiss, mouthed, "Beg your forgiveness, lassie," and darted into the men's toilet opposite the lunchroom. Hoping for a glimpse of Hannah, wondering what she would say if Hannah stopped to speak, Janice leaned against the wall and stared grimly at the stream of people trickling past on their way to their offices. Someone stopped right in front of her. It wasn't Hannah.

"Well, hello," said Kate. "We've got to stop meeting like this."

"What?" It took Janice a moment to realize that Kate was joking. After Colin's repartee, she wasn't in the mood for clichéd levity.

Kate was unfazed by Janice's scowling silence. "Did you have a fun time last night?"

Janice was thrown. Was Kate referring to the show or her after-show party with Hannah? Had Kate seen Janice leaving with Hannah? Whatever, it was none of her business.

Kate went on. "We were bowled over by the ovation. You were a fabulous audience."

Janice summoned her manners. "You were all fabulous. I enjoyed the show, thanks."

"Glad to hear it. And what about the show downstairs just now? Did you like that?"

"What are you on about? We weren't spying on you."

"Oh no, that's not what I meant. Sorry. I just happened to notice you while I was stuck in the foyer with my nice neighbor, Coby. Talks her head off, but she's ever so kind. Always looking after me now that her son's left home. Needs someone to care for, I suppose. She came all the way into town to bring me my lunch box. Silly me, I slept in this morning after all the excitement last night and left in a rush. Put my lunch box on the windowsill when I unlocked my bike and forgot all about it. Just as well Coby spotted it, good old Coby."

Kate was babbling. Why on earth was she telling her all this? Janice interrupted. "Glad to hear you've got a nice neighbor. Coby reminds me of someone, but don't ask who." Enough already. She made a show of looking at her watch. "Time to get back to the chain gang."

Damn Kate for getting in the way of her catching sight of Hannah. Come to think of it, what should she do when she did see Hannah? Their paths would cross, inevitably. Could she pretend nothing was wrong? Would she have to put on an act?

Chapter 33

On the third Sunday in May, they were all up in the huge attic that Hannah used for TT rehearsals. It was right under the slanting rafters of the roof, the same length and width as her apartment below. One section was curtained off to hide a store of discarded furniture and household junk. The rest of the space was open and held nothing besides an old table, a sagging sofa, a few chairs, including an ancient wooden rocker, and a single bed pushed into the far corner. A narrow staircase led down to the apartment. Two skylights bathed the room in sunlight. It was an airy, friendly place, painted creamy off-white, flaking in patches, with the wooden beams of the rafters left untouched.

This had been Hannah's room when she was a teenager. The apartment was her family home. She'd been born downstairs in what used to be her parents' bedroom and grew up in the small room beside it that she'd turned into her walk-in wardrobe. She'd taken over the apartment when her parents moved to a geriatric nursing home years before.

Before Alzheimer's hit him, her dad had been a reputable criminal justice lawyer who, Hannah said, had represented some pretty shady characters in his lengthy career. Her mum had been no slouch either. Before the Alzheimer's hit her, she'd been a psychotherapist, an expert in treating addicts in the Jellinek Clinic.

"Chances are, I'll end up with Alzheimer's too," Hannah told Janice while they were waiting for the others to arrive. "Apparently it's genetic, runs in the family."

"You've got years of good health ahead." Janice was sitting in the old rocking chair beside the sofa. She wanted to get up and give Hannah a kiss, but the woman looked too formidable for Janice to dare. So she swung back and forth, consoling herself instead.

"Don't rock so hard," Hannah ordered. "You'll wear a hole in the floor."

Janice kept rocking. With Alzheimer's ahead, Hannah would only forget about it.

One by one the heads of the others appeared. First up the narrow stairs was Kate. Then came the tall redhead she had seen leaving De Suikerhof early on opening night, the one who'd played Fish. A moment later she was followed by the comfortably round, motherly woman who'd played Dusa. *Good casting to type*, thought Janice. Then came the butch woman who'd done the sound for the show. Finally came the skinny girl who'd played Vi, the anorexic punk. *Typecasting again.* Janice wiped her hands on her jeans, dithering between standing up to greet the newcomers or staying in the rocker. Hannah was no help, as she had her head buried in a script and was ignoring the arrivals.

Kate decided for Janice by curling up on the sofa. "Hiya," she said. "Nice to see you again. Met the others yet?" When Janice shook her head, she called, "Say hello to Janice." It was an invitation, not an order, and the others responded with welcoming smiles.

The round motherly one came over and held out her hand. "Hello, I'm Netty."

Then the tall redhead approached, and Kate said, "This is Silly."

Janice frowned in confusion. "What's silly?"

"*Nee.*" The redhead laughed. "I'm Sylvia, but everyone calls me Silly."

Janice couldn't resist. "Isn't 'Silly' demeaning? Sounds like being called a fool."

Sylvia shrugged. "*Nee*, it doesn't bother me. It's a Dutch thing, I suppose, just a name. Anyway, it matches my mother's. Her name is spelled J-O-K-E, say Yoke-uh in Dutch, so if you put Moo and me together, we make a silly joke."

Moo? Was Silly calling her mother a cow? Janice decided not to ask what "moo" meant in Dutch and just smiled. "Bet that's not the first time you've had to explain that."

"Anyway," Kate said before Sylvia could agree, "Silly by name but not by brain. You're the smartest one of us all in TT, I reckon. You did a degree in physics, didn't you?"

"I got a master's in the history of physics at Groningen but switched when I moved here. Now I'm doing a research master's in philosophy at the University of Amsterdam."

Janice's jaw dropped in awe. "Wow, physics and philosophy. That sounds heavy."

Sylvia shrugged again. "It's not such a strange combination. Both deal with the same sorts of questions, in their own way. I find it quite interesting really."

Janice compared Sylvia's study to her own effort. She'd dropped out of a boring bachelor's in English in only her second year at the University of Auckland. As soon as she'd saved enough for the one-way ticket, she couldn't wait to get to London and start seeing real actors on the West End stage. And look where she was now. In Amsterdam, about to audition for a role on stage herself.

"Hi, I'm Sanne, short for Susanne." The butch one pulled up a chair and straddled it as if riding a motorbike. "Nice meeting you. Been here long? Where are you from? What acting have you done?"

What a chatterbox. Janice was about to go into her spiel when the skinny one intervened. "Hello, Janice darling," she drawled in a posh Oxford accent. "I'm Fern Mastiff. Yes, like the plant, yes, like the dog. Blame my parents, not me. Delighted." Fern placed a possessive hand on Sanne's shoulder. Her body language said plainly, Keep off, she's mine.

Fern, sweetie darling, Mastiff, thought Janice, amused by the woman's theatrical drawl. *There's no need to worry. I have absolutely no interest in your mousy-brown butch,* and she looked past Sanne and Fern at her Wonder Woman. The others followed her glance.

Hannah was standing in the middle of the room. "Are you all done?" She didn't wait for a reply. "Okay then, let's get on with the reading."

Sylvia and Fern took chairs opposite the sofa. Hannah handed everyone a copy of the script, then nudged Kate to move over, pulled Janice out of the rocker, and sat her down beside her on the sofa.

"Okay," she said. "First reading of *Romy & Jools—Do or Dyke*. Turn to page two and you'll see there are seven parts for women. Silly, I want you to begin with Jools. Kate, you do Romy. Netty, you can do the double role of Nana the nurse and Cousin Tabitha, and Fern, you double up as Linda the witch and Macutie, Romy's best friend. Sanne, you can be the storyteller, the Duchess of Derry. Okay. You all know what you're doing? Let's get going."

Janice held her breath. What about her? Hannah hadn't given her a role. As if sensing her tension, Hannah gave Janice's knee a reassuring pat. "Look and learn, for starters. Later on, you can have a go at Jools. Okay?" She cast a warm smile around the group. "Now, I'll start us off with the synopsis. Here goes."

Chapter 34

It was awful. Janice was mortified by how badly she read the part of Jools. When it was her turn to take over from Sylvia, she couldn't do the Irish accent, and she stumbled horribly over the lines. Hannah made her try the balcony scene and she hadn't been able to say "Romy, Romy, why aren't you here?" without stammering the "here" so badly it sounded like "ha-ha-ear."

But to her utter astonishment, Hannah seemed enthralled by her audition. At the end of the scene, she gave Janice a huge smile, cupped her chin briefly, and planted a quick kiss on her lips. The others pretended not to notice, but Janice was aware of Fern's suspicious glance. Janice had to do her best not to reveal what the little kiss had done to her. She was thrumming and stayed thrumming while the others continued reading the play up to its saccharine end.

"So tell me, what do you think of the play?" Hannah invited, opening the discussion.

"It's a bit polemical," complained Fern. "You know I'm all for women's lib and gay lib and I know we do women's theater and all that, and forgive me for being blunt, darling Hannah, but it's too preachy. It's hitting the audience on the head with a mallet."

"The message is strong," agreed Netty mildly. "I wonder if it might put people off."

"Well, it might put the straights off," said Kate. "The ones who might bother turning up to see it in the first place." She looked at Hannah carefully. "I mean, 'Do or Dyke,' the subtitle is a bit on the nose." She smiled to soften her words. "It's a pun, okay, but too in-your-face, as it were. If I were straight"—she glanced at Netty—"I might not want to see something that was so far from my bed, as the Dutch would say."

"Perhaps the end could be a little more realistic," said Sylvia. "That could make the play more convincing. I know you're sending an important message. I get how your reworking of *Romeo and Juliet* is countering the depressing image of lesbianism. I mean, think of that horrid book by Radclyffe Hall and the very few films that get made nowadays about lesbians. All that doom and destruction. Romy Schneider in *Mädchen in Uniform*, Sandy Dennis in *The Fox*, Audrey Hepburn in *The Children's Hour*, Beryl Reid in *The Killing of Sister George*—all those dykes always die in the end or come to a bad ending. Yes, I understand that you're trying to revise that dire destiny." Sylvia trailed off, not finishing the thought, as if she had realized she was making an unwelcome speech.

Hannah made sure that all, except Janice, had had their say. "Okay, fine. Thanks, everyone, but don't worry. Once we start rehearsing, you'll see there's more to the play than you might think. First impressions are not always right. Trust me, we'll make a great show out of *Romy & Jools*. It will be one of TT's best." She spoke so confidently, she won them all over.

Still, Janice wondered how Hannah planned to make this fairy tale work. She must have a clever solution up her sleeve. Janice wanted to be around to find out what it would be. If only Hannah could ignore how badly she had read and give her the juicy part of Jools. If she got it, she'd do her utter best to make Jools real.

The play reading was over. Hannah dismissed the actors. As Janice went to the stairs, Hannah said, "No, not you. Don't go. We need to talk about your audition."

Kate was the last to file downstairs. When only her head was in sight, she caught Janice's eye and gave her the thumbs up, then ducked down to follow the rest.

When they were alone, Janice said, "Yes, Hannah. What do you want?"

"You."

Janice felt her heart leap. Hannah wanted her. Not just as Jools, she could tell, but as her sweet little (tall) self as well. Hannah was going to make ravishing love to her right now, right here in the attic. Right on.

Hannah pulled Janice over to the sofa and fell back onto it, her momentum forcing Janice to fall on top of her. Not wanting to swamp the compact woman with her weight, Janice put out an arm to support herself. But Hannah tugged at the arm, rattling her bracelets, making Janice collapse onto her breast. Janice crouched half on and half off the woman, thighs splayed, and knees pressed into the floorboards. How romantic can you get? Ignoring how uncomfortable Janice was, Hannah brushed Janice's hair out of the way and stared into her eyes.

"You"—big breath—"were"—big breath—"perfect as Jools." Janice needed to swing her legs around, but Hannah held her in place. "You were so brilliant, I must"—big breath—"have you"—long pause—"now."

One part of Janice was falling for this unsubtle seduction. It was arousing, the way Hannah was looking at her through half-closed eyes. The light touch of Hannah's fingers zapped through to her core, demanding gratification.

But another, more critical part of Janice was sitting back on her heels, observing what was happening. Hannah was coming on to her so strongly simply in exchange for the role of Jools. It was a queer take on the casting couch cliché, a lascivious lesbian scene starring the dual-role dykes, Hannah as femme fatale/director and Janice as juicy Jools/contender.

Oh Hannah. So alluring, bewitching, and captivating, so all the rest of the alphabet. So Janice threw out her scruples and let herself be seduced. Willingly, thrillingly, she made love to Hannah. And taking that passionate love as her due, Hannah gave none of it back.

Chapter 35

Next Friday, Janice was on her way to join Colin in the lunchroom on the ground floor when she saw Kate hurrying up the stairs. "Wow, who let you out?"

Kate laughed. "My boss does let me have lunch. Even admin assistants have to eat."

"You've had lunch? What a pity, we could have eaten together. Have a coffee."

Kate glanced at her watch. "That'd be nice but another time. I've got to get back." She passed Janice and then turned. Now their heads were level. "Are you coming out tonight?"

Janice looked into Kate's tawny-green eyes. Those honest eyes, the golden mane that she was always brushing off her forehead, and the proud way she held herself reminded Janice of a lion. Kate could roar like a lion too, especially with raucous laughter. But Kate was not raucous now, simply waiting for Janice to answer. "Han didn't say?"

Janice shook her head.

"She probably forgot to mention it. Silly's new show, it's starting tonight. Late. We're all going. Han, me, and the other Thespians. You're one of us—nearly. You should come along too."

Janice was thrown into a dithering turmoil of indecision. Sylvia was in a late-night show. What kind? Some sort of cabaret? Was this why she'd left De Suikerhof early? Did she have to get to this other show as well? Janice was curious. She wanted to come along. But Hannah hadn't said anything about it. Hadn't invited her. On the contrary, yesterday, when Janice had asked if she could come to her place tonight, Hannah had said playfully, "Sorry, no, my sweetie darling. Not tonight." She didn't want Janice around.

And, as Kate had hinted, she wasn't one of the Thespians, yet. She didn't belong, she hadn't passed the audition. Yet. Whenever Janice demanded an answer, a definite yes or no, Hannah would string her along. "I'd love you to be Jools, my precious darling, but you'll find out for sure when we start rehearsals. Till then you'll have to possess your sexy soul in patience." And plastering Janice with little kisses, she refused to say anything more.

Kate was watching Janice wrestle with the confusion. There was no hiding from her kind eyes. "I'd like to come," Janice said, "but I don't think I should. Hannah wouldn't want me there."

"Come off it." Kate smiled to soften her words. "Han is not your boss or anyone else's lord and master, for that matter. If you want to see Silly, come with us. It'll be Fern and Sanne and Netty too. We're all going. It's not like you're gate-crashing a date."

Janice felt a surge of relief turn up the corners of her mouth. "Oh, that's all right."

"Would you mind if I said something about Han?" Kate hesitated, waiting for Janice to give some sign that she was open to hearing what she had to say.

Janice just stood there. The relief was draining away into the cold emptiness of fear.

"I know it's not the time and place to tell you this—" Kate broke off, checking her watch. "I need to get back. Before I go, let me say this. Han likes flirting with you, doesn't she?"

"Oh, really? I hadn't noticed." Sarcasm was a great shield.

"She's just flirting. She flirts with everyone, all the time. Especially the newbies in data entry. But she's just having fun. Don't take her seriously." Kate hesitated. "I mean, don't take her flirting to heart. It's not clever to get emotionally involved."

Janice interrupted. "Are you warning me off her?"

Kate reached out but Janice shook her off. Kate said, "Sorry. I know it's not my place to say this, but I can see you've fallen for her. Hard. I know Han and what she gets up to."

"The only thing she's getting up to now is me. I thought you broke up years ago."

Kate looked away. "I'm not jealous," she said quietly. "Don't get me wrong. Han's my ex, yes, but still my friend. She can be wonderful. She's a great director and fun to be around if you stand up to her. Don't let her walk over you. To get to the point"—Kate took a breath—"I really think you should come to Silly's show, even if you feel that Han doesn't want you there. It's your right to decide what you want to do, not hers. Okay?"

Janice felt the wave of fear drain away as fast as it had risen. She could see that Kate meant well. There was nothing insincere in her eyes, only kind concern. "Okay. Don't worry about me. I can look after myself." Janice nearly believed it herself. "Tell me when and where, and I'll be there."

Chapter 36

Well, well, well. This was not what Janice had expected. She was waiting for the others on the narrow canal that formed the spine of the red-light district. And as usual, she was early.

Hannah strolled up alone and did a double take on recognizing Janice standing in the shadows. "What are you doing here?" she demanded, not unpleasantly, just surprised.

Janice played it cool. "I've come to see Silly's new show. Kate said I should."

"Did she really? Well, I'm glad she did." And to prove her point, Hannah stood on tiptoes and gave Janice a quick but luscious kiss.

The others arrived soon after. Fern and Sanne pulled up on a silver-and-black monstrosity of a motorbike, and to Janice's astonishment at the reversal of stereotypical roles, the slightly built Fern was riding in front, not her butch partner. Once they'd dismounted, Fern asked Sanne to put the massive bike up on its stand, adding, "Do you think Miss Honey will be safe if we leave it here?"

Sanne nodded, unraveled a heavy chain out of the case mounted behind the saddle, and locked it around the front wheel. She took Fern's helmet off her hands and placed it in the case, along with her own helmet. Locking the case too, Sanne said, "Don't worry, Miss Honey will be as safe as a house, I reckon." She checked the padlock on the chain anyway.

Kate and Netty arrived together, and their group was complete. This was Janice's first time in this notorious district. Colin knew it well, but she had been put off by what he'd told her about the rabid throngs of tourists perving at sex workers in their red-lit windows.

Now here she was, standing outside a building emblazoned in neon with "Randy Andy's Live Sex On Stage, All Peepers Welcome." The others were acting as if it were normal for a group of women to go to a live sex show, but Janice was astounded. "Is this Silly's late-night show? Is she doing this sex thing on stage?" she muttered to Hannah.

"I knew you'd be shocked, little Miss Innocent." Hannah led the way to the ticket booth inside. "Come on, it's time to get rid of your naive prejudices."

"I'm not naive or prejudiced. I just didn't expect this."

The entrance price was an unpleasant surprise for Janice. It was just before payday, and her funds were running low. She hoped that Hannah would offer to pay for her, but that didn't happen. The woman just bought her own ticket and walked breezily inside. One crude assumption corrected.

A porn film was on as the Thespians groped their way into the back row of the theater. As her eyes grew accustomed to the gloom, Janice noted the sparse audience. A few men sat by themselves, spread well out from one another. They ignored the women, leaning away from them in their seats.

Janice settled to watch a straight couple do the porno thing. Kate, beside her, seemed as amused as she was by the length of the woman's nails, nearly as long as the man's spindly penis. Their giggles distanced them from involvement. Did Kate feel as uneasy as she did? She was glad when the film ended. The screen rose like a curtain to reveal a shallow stage.

In a subdued red spotlight, Sylvia pranced on to the repetitive beat of Donna Summer oozing "Love to love you, baby." Sylvia was wearing a leather bra and miniskirt that left her midriff bare. She hauled an object out from the wings that looked like a wooden ship's wheel mounted on a low trolley. It was a moment before Janice realized the handholds were dildos. Hitching her skirt to reveal she was not wearing anything underneath, Sylvia straddled the wheel and made it spin so that each dildo caressed her in passing. Janice wanted to laugh. How could anyone find this mechanical act erotic? She looked for a response, but everyone near her, Kate and Hannah included, was sitting self-consciously still.

With a discordant jump, the music changed to another Donna Summer number and a stocky man strode onstage. He wore leather trousers with nothing on top and had a whip draped around his neck. Sylvia was spinning the dildos as he approached, cracking the whip with macho flourish, and he scored a point from Janice for cracking in time with the beat. He pulled Sylvia off the wheel, and they danced, stripping their clothes off piece by piece until both were in the nude. Sylvia had a good body and showed it off enthusiastically.

The man lay down. Sylvia knelt between his legs, shaking her long red hair down so that it hid his pelvis. Her bobbing head suggested she was giving him a blow job. But was she really? Janice spotted one man in the front row of seats thrusting his head forward, as if he wanted to check if there was an erection. Kate stirred slightly in her seat and her elbow nudged Janice in the waist. Accidentally on purpose? Janice glanced over, wondering if Kate felt as disconnected as she did by what was happening before them. But Kate's face was a neutral mask, unreadable in the gloom. The man gasped dramatically, grabbed Sylvia's head, and stopped her bobbing. In unison the pair rolled over. Now Sylvia lay on her back with her face turned to the audience and spread her legs to accommodate the man. He mounted her, flexing his back, his mouth contorted in a ridiculous rictus of pleasure. Sylvia seemed oblivious to him, and the audience. She kept her eyes half closed and a saintly smile pasted to her face. The smile looked weird and incongruous to Janice, as fake as the sex being enacted. But Sylvia seemed to be enjoying herself as she and the man humped in unison until with another theatrical sigh, the man collapsed onto Sylvia and a blackout signified the end of the show. The screen descended and a new porn film began.

The Thespians filed out of the theater and waited for Sylvia in a nearby bar. Walking past the red-lit windows and sex workers negotiating deals with their clients, it struck Janice that it would be far simpler for someone to go straight to a window and fuck for real, instead of watching a fake.

Sylvia found them gathered around a table at the back of the bar. Sitting down beside Janice, she nodded hello. "So, ladies, how'd you like it? Do I get an Oscar for my acting?"

The others outdid each other in offering compliments. Janice wanted to join them in pleasing Sylvia. It should be easy enough to say, Yes, I enjoyed the show. But she couldn't. Instead, she sat there wondering how this highly intelligent woman could lower herself to this moronic level.

Sylvia noticed her struggle and quietly took the time to explain. "It's just a job, nothing more than that. It earns me the money to keep studying. I make more in fifteen minutes faking sex in public than I would working full time for a month in some office."

Janice thought of her own ill-paid job and knew Sylvia was right. She'd always thought that only prostitutes performed in live sex shows. Another assumption corrected. She felt Hannah's possessive eyes fixed upon her. She was huddling too close to Sylvia. Sitting up straight, she smiled reassuringly at Wonder Woman, bursting to say, Don't worry my darling, I'm all yours.

Hannah rewarded her by ever so subtly twitching her fingers around the top button of her blouse, lips curling in that teasing smile of hers. Oh Hannah. She was going to cast Janice as Jools, wasn't she? Despite her bad acting. She was going to make her be an official member of Thalia Thespians, let her belong to the group, just the way Janice desperately wanted. Wasn't she? Or was that yet another assumption that needed correcting?

Chapter 37

Colin and Janice were having their usual breakfast. Dalida was standing guard over the smorgasbord, silent as usual. It was Saturday. There was no hurry to get to work.

Negy stood in the doorway, his sturdy legs splayed like goalposts. "You two. Here."

Colin looked up to see Negy pointing at them. "How rude. Take no notice," he said, refusing to budge, taking a sip of coffee instead and giving Janice a wink.

Mouth full of gooey peanut butter and chocolate sprinkles, she could only nod.

Negy stepped aside to let a couple of nervous Italians pass and, seeing that Colin and Janice were not going to obey, gave in and marched over to their table.

Janice found Negy hard to ignore. "What is it?" The hostel owner peered down his nose, trying to intimidate her. That annoyed Janice and she stood, forcing him to look up.

"You must go," he said, eyes flashing. "Both leave the hostel. Today."

Janice was aghast. "But why? What have we done wrong?"

"Today is June the first. You are living here since March sixteen. Two and a half months already. That's too long. Hostel is not for permanents. Just overnight stays, one week at most. And you two take up too much space."

To be fair, that was true. They did use lots of space in the dorm. Their territory was clearly defined. Her rucksack and Colin's bag walled off their corner from the next four bunks, the one next to Colin's and the next three in the middle row. Other guests never dared to occupy these adjacent bunks, which meant that Janice and Colin were enjoying more than double the space they paid for.

"But, Negy, what does it matter that we're long term?" Janice protested. "We always pay on time, in advance. You know you have money coming in every week."

"Busy season is starting. I lose money on bunks not slept on. You go."

Colin stood too. "Now look here, I get your point," he began reasonably. "We can fix the issue of space if we really must. If you'll let us stay. But if you won't, you can't just throw us out today." He gave Negy a hard look. "We've paid up to Monday. You can't expect us to leave before then. Not without a full refund."

Negy looked from the angry face to the upset one and acquiesced. Turning on his heel to leave the room, he called over his shoulder, "Check out before ten o'clock Monday morning. I need those bunks." He couldn't resist rubbing it in. "All six bunks."

Janice sagged into her chair and smudged up the leftover chocolate sprinkles dotting her plate. Licking her finger, she said, "What are we going to do? Where shall we go?"

Colin sat too. "Let me think. There must be something cheap we can do." He gave a questioning look. "Any chance of us moving in with Hannah, temporary-like? Didn't you say she had a spare bed up in her attic? Couldn't I sleep there while you cuddle up with your darling diva in the master bedroom, or should I say mistress bedroom?"

"No way." Janice was adamant. "There's no chance that she will let us stay in the apartment. I'll tell you that for nothing. She's such a hardheaded woman—"

"Cue Cat Stevens," interrupted Colin.

Janice ignored him. "She'd never agree to having us stay. Even for a short while. Anyway, she uses the attic for TT rehearsals, so you'd only get in the way."

"Don't get your knickers in a twist. It was just an idea. Back to the drawing board."

In silence they walked back to the dorm, Colin leading the way. *At least I'm not in this alone*, thought Janice as she sat on her bunk. She was glad Colin was her friend. He never demanded more of her than she was willing to give, just accepted her as she was. He was kind and cared about her, even if he always wrapped his concern in a cloak of camp bitchiness. He was resourceful too. Look how he'd managed to find them a job. He'd find a way to get them out of this mess. But how? Janice didn't have a clue where to start. If only Ariel were here to help them out.

Colin was pulling on his denim jacket, getting ready to go out, but stopped when he saw her expression. "What's with the long face?"

"Can't you tell? We have to leave here, and I don't know where to go."

Colin leaned over and squeezed her hand. "No," he said slowly. "I don't mean that. You'll cope, I'll cope, the way we do in a crisis. I mean, what's really wrong with you?"

Damn Colin. He was always perceptive. Janice shook her hair over her face, trying to hide from his sharp eyes, knowing it was fruitless.

Colin went on, serious for once. "You talk in your sleep, did you know?"

Janice's jaw dropped. "I do not talk in my sleep. No way."

"Oh, but you do, lassie. I can hear you mumbling at night. What on earth traumatized you about your trip? What happened to make you so worried about missing the Magic Bus?"

Janice gave him a blank look. What was he on about now?

"I can't make it out, but it sounds like you're saying, "Bus, no." You get quite upset about missing that damn bus." He grinned. "All the noise you make, you'll wake the dead."

Colin waited for her answer, but Janice was mulling over what he'd said. *Bus, no, bus, no, bus.* What on earth did that mean? Then her eyes widened as the realization hit her. No bus. It was nothing to do with Magic Bus. It was Kobus. She was saying his name in her sleep. In her dreams—no, her nightmares—about what she'd done. No way she could tell anyone the truth about that. Not even Colin, her best friend. She couldn't look at him. She lay on her bunk and turned her back.

Colin waited for her to respond. When she didn't, he patted her shoulder and left.

Chapter 38

Later that Saturday morning, Janice went up to the newsagent on the Haarlemmerdijk to buy the *Daily Mail*. Sitting with the paper in a nearby coffee shop reminded her of how she used to do the crossword in London. Her thoughts turned to Kobus. How could she find out if a man had been found murdered in the front hall of a north London bedsit? She hadn't been brave enough to check the English papers for news when she'd arrived in Amsterdam and didn't know. Was he alive? Or dead? No wonder she was having nightmares. Was she a killer or not? How could she find out? Should she write Mrs. Palmer? There was no way she could do that. No way.

Janice treated herself to a toasted cheese-and-ham sandwich, to go with her cappuccino for lunch. On a tight budget, she didn't order more, even if she could easily have finished a second. The twelve hundred guilders she earned each month didn't stretch far. Oh, in guilders it sounded a lot, far more than it did in English or American money, but you had to realize that one-pound sterling was worth about four and a half guilders, which, if you had to think about it, meant that one US dollar was worth nearly two guilders. Dutch prices reflected the difference. Everything sounded five times more expensive than it was in London. Soon after she'd arrived, Janice stopped trying to convert prices. It was too complicated. She simply switched over to thinking in guilders. She kept track of how much money she had in her wallet and knew how much would be left if she spent any. The bunk cost ten guilders a night, and that was a big slice of salary (280 guilders to be precise). On top of that was four guilders for the smorgasbord breakfast (another 112 guilders). It all added up to quite a chunk.

Besides this necessary expenditure, she was trying to save as much as she could. Not just for the proverbial rainy day. She knew she was going to settle in Amsterdam, and one day she'd have to pay rent for a proper room or a flat, not to mention the deposit. Not being allowed to use the kitchen meant she had to eat out a lot. And that cost a lot. If Janice had her way, she would have subsisted on fatty takeaways. A Febo snack bar was just around the corner from the hostel. It kept the food warm in a long barrage of glass-fronted vending machines. Her favorite dish was the *frikandel*, a long thin sausage made from processed chicken and pork and flavored with spices she had never tasted before. It was delicious and cost only fifty cents a pop.

But Colin wouldn't let her indulge in fast food on a daily basis. He'd stretch to the occasional cheap meal at the pizzeria down on the Nieuwezijds Voorburgwal, but he was more into making healthy salads they could eat in the dorm. After a couple of months on Colin's salad regime, Janice had noticed a difference. She'd lost so much weight, she'd had to go out and buy a new pair of jeans.

That afternoon, trying on a horrendously expensive pair in a boutique with Colin fussing at her feet, checking that the hems were "Goldilocks length: not too long, not too short, just right," Janice recalled the extravagant shopping expeditions Kobus had taken her on. And quickly buried the guilty thought.

Distracted by her reflection in a mirror, she was amazed by the change in her appearance. Her hair fell over her shoulders and gleamed with good health. The store lighting made her face look tanned. The jeans flattened her belly, emphasized her narrow hips, and made her look like a tall and tanned Brazilian beach babe. Janice spun around in delight, knocking Colin onto his bottom.

"Watch out, you great lumbering fool."

She didn't care, she was "The girl from Ipanema." Now she understood what Hannah saw in her. She was ah … tractive.

Colin grabbed her hand to haul himself up to his feet. "You eejit." He would have gone on castigating but then he saw Janice grinning at herself. "Mirror, mirror on the wall. Who's the fairest one of all? Believe what you see, lassie. You really are a looker."

Janice smiled back. She was seeing herself as she really was, for the very first time, and Colin could tell. "Thanks, Your Royal Bitchness."

He did a theatrical double take. "But not half as good-looking as me."

Colin always had to have the last word. Like Hannah. What would her last word be on who'd get to play Jools? She had to wait till Sunday afternoon to find out.

Chapter 39

Janice had three good reasons to worry. From first to worst: She was worried about talking in her sleep. She was worried about leaving the hostel. And, she was worried about Wonder Woman. To Janice's tortured way of thinking, being cast in *Romy & Jools* was the only way she could stay close enough to Hannah to make their dream romance come true. She had to belong, to Wonder Woman, to Hannah, to someone. Or else.

Colin had only added to the tension. Last night he'd come back late, when the dorm was quiet, and Janice was already tucked in bed. She'd put away the new Inspector Wexford novel, switched off her flashlight, and flicked on the transistor. Listening vaguely to the John Holden show on pirate station Radio Decibel, she was fruitlessly trying to get to sleep.

"Hey, lassie," Colin whispered, seeing she was still awake. "I've got terrific news."

Janice gasped. "You've found somewhere for us to stay. Where is it, tell me."

Colin took off his jacket and hung it over his rucksack before answering. Slowly he sat on his bunk, making the springs creak under his weight. "Well," he began. "Not exactly."

Janice's heart plunged. "What do you mean, not exactly? How expensive is it?"

"Not that expensive. It's just not in Amsterdam."

Janice was puzzled. "Not in Amsterdam? Then where?"

Colin took his time before answering. "It's in West Berlin. I've found us a hostel near the Potsdamer Platz. We can get there on the Magic Bus that leaves Monday morning."

"Monday? This Monday? No, I've got to stay. I'm hearing about the audition this afternoon." Janice was aghast. She couldn't leave Wonder Woman now, not when she'd just found her. She turned a stricken face to Colin. "I can't leave Amsterdam. Not now."

"I want to go. I was always planning to go on to West Berlin and now's the time."

"But you can't just leave—" Janice wanted to say, You can't just leave *me*, but thought better of it. They weren't together. They were just friends so she turned it into, "You can't just leave. Mrs. Bekkema will kill you if you take off without giving proper notice."

Colin grinned. "Yes, I can. We're still on our probation period. That means we're free to leave without notice. Anyway, how can Mrs. Bekkema kill me if I don't turn up? She won't even notice I'm gone. Data entry will survive without me, don't worry."

"But what about your pay?"

"Payday, shmayday. They can dock me for all I care."

But where do I go? Janice wanted to ask but stopped herself. It wasn't Colin's job to look after her. She could and would find somewhere to live on her own. *But how will I survive without him?* Janice was intensely aware of how much she'd grown to depend on his friendship, his camp good cheer. His Royal Bitchness would be a hard act to follow.

"'But me no buts,' as the good Bard says." Colin reached over and took her hand. "I'll miss you too, but it's for the best. I'm off and away on Monday."

And that was that. Colin went to the shower room to brush his teeth and get himself ready for bed, leaving Janice adrift on her bunk, abandoned on a tsunami of anxiety.

Chapter 40

Sunday afternoon, Janice turned up late to the first rehearsal of *Romy & Jools—Do or Dyke.* She did so on purpose, not daring to be alone with Hannah before the others arrived. In the end it was Kate, waiting on the landing, who unlatched the street door for her by pulling the cord that stretched in loops up the long, steep staircase to Hannah's apartment. She gave an encouraging smile as Janice stumbled up the steps, clumsily falling over her feet.

Hannah shot a dark glance at Janice as her head emerged into the attic but, apart from this frosty greeting, acted as if Janice's tardy arrival was nothing momentous. She waited in silence for Janice and Kate to pull up chairs and sit near the others. Netty and Sylvia were spread out on the sofa. Sanne was astride a chair, and Fern was beside her in the rocker.

Taking her time to survey the women, Hannah said, "Welcome. Glad to see you all made it. Now, before we get on with the unmasking, I'd like to talk about the staging. Some of you seemed to doubt the quality of the play when we did the first reading." She gave Fern and Sylvia pointed looks. "When you know what I've got planned for the staging, you'll feel more confident." She disappeared behind the curtained section of the attic and came back carrying a flip chart on a stand. Sanne dismounted from her chair and helped Hannah set up the flip chart in front of the sofa.

Janice's ears had pricked up at "unmasking." What on earth was that? Kate noticed her expression and whispered, "It's a TT tradition, stems from the way our namesake, Thalia, the muse of comedy, is often depicted holding a comedy mask. We call the presentation of the cast of the forthcoming show the unmasking. Hannah doesn't just tell us. She always prints out the list and pins it onto Thalia's mask." Kate indicated a corkboard cut in the shape of a theatrical mask that was glued to the sloping ceiling above the head of the attic staircase. Janice hadn't noticed it before. Kate added, "It's supposed to bring us luck."

Well, good luck with that, thought Janice, nodding her thanks for the explanation but thinking that the tradition sounded like a foolish superstition. Then again, wasn't it typical of Hannah to make a game out of the ordinary? She might be an irritating tease at times, but she knew how to have fun and sweep others up in her fun. Janice looked at Hannah and, despite the churning in her stomach, couldn't help admiring the charismatic woman, all flashing eyes and wicked smiles, with all those bracelets shivering and tinkling on her wrists, a vibrant accompaniment to her energy.

"You may recall," Hannah said, "the play begins with our Romy and Jools meeting at a party. With only four of you on stage throughout the play, how do we suggest the cast of thousands at the party and in the background of the dueling-dyke scene in act one?" She turned over the first page of the flip chart to reveal the words "Multimedia Extravaganza." Hannah paused, waiting for comprehension to sink in.

Sylvia and Kate nodded first, then Fern and Netty, but Sanne said, "Multimedia?"

Hannah was generous in her patient explanation for Sanne, reminding Janice of how kind and professional the woman had been to the newbies on their first day in data entry. That was yet another wonderful thing about Hannah, if ever Janice needed justification for her crush.

Hannah continued. "We're using slides to suggest the settings, coupled with a prerecorded soundtrack of party and crowd noises."

Kate ventured a remark. "I don't want to throw soot in your food, as the Dutch would say, but won't this multimedia extravaganza cost a hell of a lot of money? Can TT afford it?"

That's exactly what Janice was thinking too, but she wasn't surprised to hear Hannah's answer. "Yes, we can afford it because it won't cost a cent. A friend of mine, Harriet Bouwen, is a sound technician for the English service of Radio Nederland. Harriet will do the recording for the price of free tickets to TT plays for the next ten years." She laughed. "That translates to a couple of beers before and after this show. Don't worry, it won't be much. Anyway, it'll pay to have a professional recording done because I've decided to record the part of the Duchess of Derry too. Her stuff is all narration, no interaction, so her lines will work fine on the soundtrack. And we'll illustrate her narrative bits with proper slides, of course. Any other questions?"

"Well, yes," said Sylvia. "Who's going to put this slideshow together?"

Hannah's lips curled in the teasing smile familiar to Janice. "Thanks, Silly, for volunteering. I'm sure Kate will appreciate your help." And she smiled at Kate too.

Kate smiled back. "Sounds like you've got all bases covered."

"But not the equipment," said Sanne. "De Suikerhof's got a good sound system. But do they have the projection system we need for the slideshow? I have never seen it there."

"Right. We have to hire a slide projector but there's enough in the TT coffers to pay for it. All systems go, this audiovisual strategy will enhance the show. Don't you agree?"

Sanne clapped her hands, Netty and Sylvia exchanged a huge grin, while Fern and Kate seemed subdued yet happy enough with Hannah's plan for the staging. Janice kept quiet in her chair, fighting not to show how overcome she felt by the nerves churning her stomach.

As if Hannah could tell what Janice was feeling, she said, "And now for the unmasking. I won't keep you in suspense any longer." With a shimmering rattle of her bangles, she crossed to the table, picked up a sheet of paper, and pinned it to the corkboard on the sloping ceiling.

Janice hung back, wiping her sweaty palms on her new jeans, waiting for the others to finish looking at the list and move back to their seats. None of them looked at her. Finally, she plucked up her courage and took her turn at the corkboard. She read:

> *Romy & Jools—Do or Dyke*
> A Play in Two Acts Directed by Hannah Remkes
> By Henka Sherman and William Shakespeare
> CAST
>
> | | |
> |---|---|
> | Jools | Sylvia Smit |
> | Romy | Kate Hynder |
> | Nana/Tabitha | Netty van der Voort |
> | Linda/Macutie | Fern Mastiff |

CREW

Slideshow	Kate Hynder/Sylvia Smit
Soundtrack	Hannah Remkes/Harriet Bouwen
Set/Program	Kate Hynder
Costumes	Netty van der Voort
Props	Fern Mastiff
Lighting	Sanne Schippers (prompt)
Sound	Hannah Remkes

Janice felt a wave of icy dread flow up from her toes to engulf her entire body. She stood frozen before the corkboard, not finding her name in print, no matter how often she read through the list. No Jools, no other part, not even listed for lighting or sound. Hannah had left her out entirely. There was no place for her in Thalia Thespians, none whatsoever.

Turning slowly, she saw Hannah smiling at her as if nothing were wrong. As if the audition had all been a big joke. As if she had not just dropped a bombshell of crushing disappointment on Janice and betrayed her trust in the most hurtful way possible. In public.

The others had the grace to look shocked by Hannah's cruelty. Netty was in tears. Frowning heavily, Sanne moved in front of Fern. Sylvia gave Hannah a beseeching look, as if she couldn't believe what the woman had done. Kate was clenching her fists.

Janice floated adrift on a cloud of confusion. It didn't make sense. Didn't Hannah adore her, lust after her? For weeks she'd done nothing else but let Janice know how much she wanted her to play Jools. And now this? Just in case, she turned back to reread the sheet of paper, but no, there was definitely no Janice de Vetter listed anywhere in the cast or crew. Rejection crushed Janice, squeezing the breath out of her. Hannah didn't want her. Not really, not truly. Not ever. Hannah had led her on. She'd merely toyed with her for her own selfish pleasure. For the sake of a few one-way fucks.

Janice was devastated by the duplicity of the woman. Hannah had used and abused her, far worse than Kobus had ever done. He at least had been sincerely in love with her. But Hannah, it seemed, had been insincere. She'd taken advantage of Janice, of her irrational crush, of her desperate need to belong, to find the Wonder Woman who would make her life complete. Hannah had dangled the promise of belonging to Thalia Thespians but had never intended to keep that promise for one wayward moment. One-Way Woman had taken Janice for a fraudulent ride, rattling her bangles all the fucking way.

Well, Janice was getting off the ride right here, right now. Regret was snaking around her chest, constricting her lungs, crushing her breath. She was suffocating. Out. She had to get out. Escape. Not looking at treacherous Hannah, ignoring the others, she fled the attic. She stormed headlong down the stairs to the street and ran nonstop all the way to the hostel.

Chapter 41

Colin wasn't in the dorm. Janice half expected to find a note saying something like "Sorry I can't wait. Have taken off now, am hitching a ride to West Berlin." But there was no note because that wouldn't happen. Colin liked his comfort and convenience too much and, anyway, his seat would still be waiting for him on the Magic Bus. His Royal Bitchness wouldn't be dethroned easily. Oh god, how she would miss him. Janice needed a friend now, someone she could trust, someone she could talk to through the flood of tears streaming down her face. Someone like Colin, but he wasn't there. He was out, in a gay sauna somewhere, taking his last chance to have fun before leaving Amsterdam early in the morning.

She, too, would have to leave the hostel tomorrow. Janice sat heavily on her bunk. She needed to think. But there was no room for rational thought. Thank goodness it was a quiet Sunday and no one was in the dorm to see her blubbering like this. She buried her face in her hands, not caring about the snot smearing on her fingers.

The mean look on Hannah's face when she saw Janice realizing that she wasn't on the list. What she had done to Janice was not harmless teasing. It was manipulative mind-fuckery of the highest order and she, little Miss Innocent, had fallen for it, all that egotistical casting-couch crap. Hannah had toyed with her feelings. She'd played Janice for a fool.

But no more. Janice punched the pillow. "Fool me once." She punched again, harder. "Shame on you." She punched again, even harder, beating the disappointment out of her body. "You won't fool me twice." She wasn't just furious at Hannah, but at herself for believing that Hannah was her long-awaited Wonder Woman. No way. Janice was done with her. Long may she rot in hell.

A slight movement caught Janice's eye. It was Dalida, quietly mopping the floor at the end of the dorm. Janice had thought she was alone, but Dalida must have been here all the time. Silent Dalida, who always kept her eyes turned down whenever Janice passed her.

Besides looking after the breakfast room, Dalida was the hostel's chambermaid. Janice had often seen her moving through the dorm and, on her way to the showers upstairs, had spotted her going from room to room, laden down with bucket and mop and a trolley full of cleaning materials. The job took her all day, Monday to Saturday. Working today, on a Sunday, was a first. It gave Janice an idea. She jammed her fists into her eyes, scrubbing away the tears, and walked over to Dalida.

"Hello," she said, sitting on a bunk so that she wouldn't loom over the small woman. "Do you mind if I ask you something?" Dalida wouldn't look at her, but Janice could tell she was listening. She went on. "Why are you working on Sunday? And so late in the afternoon?"

Dalida swirled the mop in its bucket, pressed out the excess water, and slopped it under the next bunk. Janice waited patiently, not pushing for an answer. Finally, in a small voice, Dalida said, "It is not day of rest in Islam. I work. *Gewoon*." She said the throaty Dutch "g" in the strong English way: green for go.

"But you never do the dorm this late on a Sunday afternoon. That's not normal, that's not *gewoon*." Janice knew this word, went for the Dutch pronunciation, and succeeded.

"Hostel is busy. Negy say many guests come tomorrow. Dormitory must be ready."

"Can I give you a hand?"

Dalida finally looked at her. "Why? I have two hands."

"No, I meant, shall I help? I can help you get the dorm done."

"No, not allowed. You must tell Negy if you want to help."

"I will ask if I can help." And with a parting smile, Janice rushed down to reception.

Chapter 42

As soon as Negy saw Janice approach, he began fiddling with pieces of paper. He tried to ignore her when she placed her hands on the counter and demanded, "Can I talk to you?"

"I'm busy." Negy turned away.

"Yes, I can see you're busy. So is Dalida. That's what I want to talk to you about."

Negy looked up. "What is it?"

"I have a proposal."

"No thanks. I am already married. Dalida is my wife."

Janice couldn't help smiling. "No, I want to suggest something." She didn't know how to put it gracefully so came straight to the point. "Give me a job." Negy raised a surprised eyebrow. "I want to work here. I can help Dalida with the beds and the cleaning."

"No. I don't need you."

Negy's rejection made Janice see red. "You do need me. Dalida needs me. You've got her working seven days a week. That's too much. Let me help her. You must give me a job."

Negy staggered as if he didn't know what had hit him. He looked down and shuffled his pile of receipts. It was make-work, anything to convince Janice he had no time for her.

Janice knew she was taking out her anger at Hannah's rejection on Negy. She took a breath, forcing herself to calm down. Her mind raced to find an approach that would reach him. Then came the brainwave. "You don't need to pay me. No money. I'll work for free."

"For free? No money?"

"Just let me sleep here for free and have a free breakfast every day. I'll work for my board. That's what they call it in English. From breakfast till midday. How does that sound?"

"And you get no money at all?"

"No, you don't need to pay a cent." She could see that Negy was interested. Now it took all her self-control to keep her mouth shut and wait.

"Can you make a bed?"

Yes! She'd got him. "Of course, I can make a bed. My mother was a nurse and taught me how to do hospital corners."

"Show me. If you make a good bed, I let you have the room on the landing."

She followed Negy to the first-floor landing. He opened the door and ushered Janice inside. The room was dark and cramped, with barely enough space for the little double bed, called a *twijfelaar* in Dutch, so small it doubted it was a real double bed. No wardrobe, just a row of hooks with a wide plank mounted above them, alongside the back of the door. A narrow window looked out on the courtyard below. Under it was a small square Formica table, like the ones in the breakfast room, and two hard chairs. There was lovely crown molding, lining the top of the walls, which must have dated back to the glory days of the house, and a decorative plaster medallion, now dingy and gray, in the center of the ceiling. Judging by its forlorn state, the room was seldom occupied.

Negy drew the flimsy curtain, letting in a flood of late-afternoon sunlight speckled with motes of dust, moved the lumpy pillows onto a chair, and pulled the blanket and sheets off the bed. He thrust the bundle at Janice and said, "Show me how you make bed."

Janice did, working efficiently, pulling the sheets tight, getting the blanket centered exactly right, and folding the bottom corners neatly in the professional way her mother had taught her. It took her all of a minute to get the job done. "What do you think? Happy with the result?"

"Okay, bed good. You work here, stay in this room, no wages."

Janice felt an enormous wave of relief surge through her body. "Oh, thank you. You won't be disappointed. I won't let you down."

"You sleep in here, move in after work tomorrow. But if guests come and want a double, you go back to dorm and stay on bunk for as long as guests have room. Okay?"

"It's a deal." Janice stuck out a triumphant hand. "Thank you, Negy." Now she could leave data entry without a qualm. She wouldn't have to fear bumping into Hannah at work.

Shaking hands, Negy said, "I tell Dalida you start with her tomorrow, Monday morning at six. Be on time. Help set up breakfast. At nine you do dishes. Then mop the dorm. And at ten, go to the rooms of guests who check out and make beds and clean and be done by four o'clock. That is check-in time for new room guests."

"Not four. I'm already up and at it by six. I won't be working a ten-hour day. You've still got Dalida doing her bit. Cleaning my share won't take me all day. I work fast. I'm efficient. I can be done by midday. I'll work six hours maximum. No more than that. Okay?"

"Don't work so fast you don't do a good job."

"That won't happen, I promise."

Chapter 43

Janice walked to the dorm with a spring in her step. What a lark! Free board and breakfast! And real privacy again, in her very own room. But when she got back to her bunk, she began having second thoughts. What on earth had she done? The lodging bit was fine, but what was she going to do for money? She still had to buy an evening meal, though she reckoned she could eke out the breakfast deal to include a free sandwich lunch. She'd have to find a part-time job somewhere, something she could do in the afternoons or evenings that paid cash in hand. Otherwise, when her savings ran out, she'd be stuck. *I'll think about that tomorrow.*

For now, all she wanted to do was enjoy the knowledge that she had solved her problem of where to stay without needing Colin to ride to the rescue. Ariel would be proud of her. Noisy students were filling the dorm. Janice rubbed her forehead, felt the creases of a frown, and realized that despite the excitement she felt simmering inside, she must be scowling. Well, there was no way she was going to ask these intruders to pipe down. *At least I won't have to put up with the crowd much longer. Tomorrow I'm in my own room.*

"What are you smirking at, wee lassie? You look fit to burst." Colin had come back without Janice noticing. His hair was damp, and he looked relaxed.

Janice smiled, peering at his mouth. "What's that on your lip?"

Colin touched the spot. "Just a cold sore, nothing to worry about. What about you? Last time I saw you, you were down in the dumps. You look as if you've won the lottery."

Janice startled, fighting to repress the memory of Kobus triggered by the word "lottery." But she wasn't going to be deflected. "That spot looks like more than just a cold sore. Isn't it herpes? Very contagious that." She broke off, knowing that Colin realized the implication.

He sighed. "Well, I have been having a rather gay time in Amsterdam." He gave her a look. "But who isn't? Anyway, Berlin's the gay capital of the world, next to New York."

"West Berlin. And don't you think you should slow down on having a gay time once you get there? Throw up your own wall for a change."

Colin gave her a long look. They sat in silence. Janice was astounded to realize she felt far removed from Colin, even though he was sitting just opposite her on his own bunk. The way they had sat chatting so often before. How strange, this sudden distance between them. They'd met in March. They'd known each other less than three full months, and how quickly they'd become close friends. But now she felt this enormous gulf widening between them. It was as if she'd already switched off, to protect herself from missing Colin when he'd really be gone.

He broke the silence. "Have you found somewhere? Is that why you're pleased?"

"I'm staying here. I've made a deal with Negy, free bed and breakfast in exchange for helping Dalida every day with a couple of hours' worth of chambermaiding."

"You brilliant lassie." Colin's eyebrows shot up in amazement and he gave a shout of delighted laughter. "I knew you'd land on your feet. How on earth did you convince Negy?" He paused to think. "But if you're working here all morning, what are you going to do about data entry? It's a full-time job. Will you ask Mrs. Bekkema if you can work afternoons?"

Janice shook her head. "No way. I'm leaving data entry too. Resigning tomorrow before the probation period runs out. Like you are." Abruptly her heart missed a beat. "I don't ever want to see Hannah again." She tapped her pillow for emphasis.

Colin gave a drawn-out sigh, serious for once. "Oh, you didn't get the part?"

Janice shook her hair over her face, needing to hide how overcome she was by Hannah's betrayal welling up in her again. Her feelings were often volatile, it was like riding a careening rollercoaster, and she couldn't even keep up with herself at times. Unable to express what was happening to her now, she looked away.

Colin stood, mumbled something about going to the loo, and tactfully left her alone.

* * *

That evening in the dorm they did the good-bye thing, knowing that in the morning Janice had to start work at sparrow's fart and Colin would have to leave by seven thirty, to allow himself time to walk to the bus station.

Colin fastened the last buckle on his rucksack. The only things he hadn't packed were his sleeping bag, the clothes he wore now and would put on again in the morning, and his fat volume of Noel Coward plays. "Here, lassie, a wee farewell gift. A little something to remember me by."

Janice felt a tear prick the corner of her eye. "You royal bastard. Don't make me wait a year to see you again." She sniffed. "Thanks for the plays. I hadn't finished them all yet." She put the collection beside her own books. The shelf looked depleted without Colin's books.

Colin patted her shoulder. "I'm not sure how long I'll be staying in Berlin."

"West Berlin."

He ignored the interruption. "But it won't be long. I've got to be back in Edinburgh before the end of August to get ready for the new term at St. Andrews."

"Oh, you're going to start doing your art history degree this year after all?"

"I may as well. I'd like to see Copenhagen too, before I have to get back. Then I'd have done my A, B, C at least." He answered Janice's look. "Amsterdam, Berlin, Copenhagen."

"West Berlin. That doesn't scan."

Colin just smiled. "Let's keep in touch. Write to me in Berlin."

"West Berl—"

"Yes, I get it, lassie. West Berlin. Write to me care of the post office on Potsdamer Platz. Here's the address." He handed over a scrap of paper. "And I'll write back to you at the main post office behind Dam Square. Okay?"

"But you can write to me here. I'm staying here."

Colin gave her a look. "For as long as it lasts. You never know, you might move out and, knowing Negy, he might not hold any letters for you once you're gone."

Janice could see the sense in that. "Okay, I'll keep you posted via the post office."

And that was that. They gave each other a hug without clinging, and then Colin turned his back, stripped down to his underpants, and slid into his sleeping bag. Janice went up to the shower room to freshen up before going to bed herself. Colin was snoring when she got back. She stood a long moment, absorbing the sight of him, reminded of how angelic she'd found him the first time she'd watched him sleep. Innocence personified. If only he didn't have that little scaly sore at the corner of his mouth. It looked ominous. If only Colin would look after himself better. Stifling worry, she went to bed. Early start tomorrow.

Chapter 44

Monday morning, between washing up the breakfast dishes under Dalida's watchful eye and helping to mop the dorm, Janice went to use the telephone in reception. Negy gave her a filthy look as she approached and barely moved out of the way so that she had to stretch across the counter to pull the telephone toward her. Ignoring Negy, she dialed the number printed on her salary slip. It was the first time she'd phoned the office. And it would be the last time too. She turned her back, waiting to be put through, pressing the receiver hard against her ear until it hurt.

Someone picked up. "*Goede morgen, met Ineke Bekkema.*"

"Um, hello, good morning, Mrs. Bekkema."

Mrs. Bekkema switched to her heavily accented English. "Is that you, Janice? Why are you and Colin not at your desks working? It is extremely late."

"Um, yes, that's what I'm calling you about. Colin and I won't be in—"

"Today? Why not? You cannot take a free day without asking. It is not allowed."

"No, Mrs. Bekkema, listen. Let me explain. Colin and I won't be in at all, ever again."

"Never again? You are stopping data entry? You are leaving the firm?"

"Yes, we are. Our probation period runs out in two weeks,, and we can resign before it ends." Mrs. Bekkema would have interrupted, but Janice kept on. "We're both very sorry, but it hasn't worked out for us, and we have to leave straightaway."

"B-but you cannot do this."

Janice sounded firmer than she felt. "We checked the contract, and it says we can resign without notice. Thanks for putting up with us." And she hung up without a good-bye.

Negy gave her a grumpy look, which Janice countered with an impervious smile. She slid the phone back across the counter, strode down the corridor and went upstairs to the first floor, looking for Dalida to help her clean the next empty room. Whatever had got Negy's knickers in such a twist had nothing to do with her using his phone. Colin had probably annoyed him by checking out without warning, even though Colin was only following Negy's own command to leave.

Oh, but bad Colin for putting her through the ordeal of the call to Mrs. Bekkema. Janice hadn't expected him to be such a coward about phoning in to resign for himself. His Royal Bitchness had charmed her last night into doing it for him.

* * *

As arranged, Janice finished making beds and mopping floors by twelve o'clock. Holding out her hand in a stop sign, Dalida made her wait while she fetched Negy to check her work. He came quickly, cast a cursory glance around the spotless room with its six perfectly made beds, and let her go. *No word of praise or thanks for a job well done, but who cares?*

She smiled at Dalida, mouthed a thank-you that didn't demand a reply, and ran down to the dorm. Ignoring the one or two tourists hanging around the table, she crossed to her corner, shouldered her rucksack, and went up to her new room on the first-floor landing. Unpacking the rucksack, she arranged her foldables on the plank alongside the door and, on the hooks beneath the plank, hung up her leather jacket, brown pants, and new jeans, the one pair too baggy, the other a precise fit. She set her small library of picture books with Colin's collection of Noel Coward plays in pride of place on the little table under the window and moved one of the hard chairs to the right-hand side of the bed, closest to the door, to act as a nightstand. She shoved the rucksack out of the way in the corner and straightened to survey her domain.

The sun wouldn't reach her window until late afternoon, so the room was dim. She'd have to buy a reading lamp, secondhand if she could find one. But it was a good start. And clean. This morning she'd wiped the surfaces, changed the bed, and mopped up a warren of dust bunnies from under the bed. Despite its simple furniture, it was her own private palace.

Unhooking her jacket, patting its inner pocket to make sure she had her wallet and passport, Janice left the hostel for a walk. What a pleasant change to be outside on a sunny Monday afternoon. She crossed the bridge and ducked down a narrow lane to reach her favorite coffee shop.

She knew better than to wait for service and went inside to buy a cappuccino. She considered sitting inside, but two seedy-looking tourists were blatantly smoking joints at their table and the insidious stink of marijuana put her off. The seat she'd had her eye on was taken when she brought her coffee outside, so she had to sit on the street side of the terrace. She leaned back in the chair, stretched her legs into the gutter, and took a sip of delicious coffee. The sun was shining. She had a job (unpaid) and bed and breakfast (free). A room of one's own. Yes, Virginia, what more could a woman want? Janice closed her eyes to enjoy the sun.

Janice opened her eyes to see a stranger sidling up to her, pushing an old bicycle with a padlock and chain draped over the handlebar. The man was unnaturally thin, with greasy hair and a straggly beard fuzzing his jaw. His clothes looked as worn and unkempt as he was. "*Fiets te koop.*"

Janice sat up and pulled in her legs. "Sorry, I don't speak Dutch. What do you want?"

The stranger switched instantly over to English. "This bike is for sale. Want to buy my bike? Real cheap. Only fifty guilders. You look nice, I make it twenty-five guilders for you." He smiled, revealing the gaps in his yellowing teeth.

Restraining a shudder at the sight of the teeth, Janice looked over the rusty bike. It had a high, old-fashioned handlebar and a worn leather saddle. No cross bar and an extremely low instep. Reaching for her wallet, Janice said, "I'll have it for two tens if you throw in that chain and padlock." She held out the notes enticingly. "And don't forget the key."

The stranger accepted with a shrug. Cash smothered in his fist, he sidled away as silently as he had approached, and Janice was the owner of a secondhand bike. A stolen secondhand bike, and that guy was going to buy dope with the money she'd given him. Not a lot she could do about that.

Chapter 45

To her dismay, Janice discovered that the saddle was too low for her long legs. Pedaling at this height forced her knees to bend more than was comfortable. But at least the handlebar was high enough and set at an easy distance. She took off carefully, glad there was no traffic coming up to meet her on the narrow lane so that she had a moment to get used to the thing. She wobbled along the bumpy cobbles of the canal. This was nothing like riding her bike in Auckland. She had to keep on reminding herself to stick to the right-hand gutter. It was nerve-racking the first time a car overtook her, passing so close she nearly lost her balance.

At the corner of the main road, she turned gratefully onto a broad bike lane. Smooth riding at last, even if she felt as if her widespread knees were brushing her ears as she pedaled. She'd have to do something about that. She rode down the busy road, thankful that the bike lane was keeping her out of range of the lethal trams and unceasing flow of cars.

And then, miracle of miracles, she spotted a shop with its windows crammed full of cycling gear and bicycles of all sizes and types parked on either side of the door. She stopped without warning, earning a yell from a cyclist who'd had to swerve to avoid crashing into her.

"Oh, sorry," she called, but he ignored her.

Janice pushed her bike into the shop and looked around for someone to help her. An old man in neat brown overalls appeared from the back room. "*Dag mijnheer.*"

"Sorry, no Dutch. Do you have a wrench I can borrow to lift the saddle? It's too low."

"*Nee.*" The man regarded her, slowly taking in her face and the length of her legs and the condition of the bike.

Janice shook her head in disbelief. Had this old bloke refused her perfectly ordinary, polite request? For no particular reason? She was about to protest when the man continued.

"No, lady, I do it for you. Bring the bike here." And he shyly produced a wrench.

Adjusting the saddle took no time at all. Janice thanked the old man and offered to pay for the service. He shook his head. "*Gratis, geen probleem.*"

Well, the Dutch could be blunt, all right, but like this old bloke, they could be kind enough to help a damsel in distress. Mounting the bike, Janice had to laugh at casting herself as a damsel. There was nothing frilly or damsel-like about her. But what about the distress? She remembered Hannah standing too close to her at work, holding her hand in Saarein, pushing her away that first night in bed. Leading her on about Jools, always accompanied by the ominous rattle of her bangles. Sinuous Hannah-the-Hex snaking in for the kill.

Janice stomped hard on the pedals, pushing the heartbreak away with each turn. She pedaled steadily, stopping only for the lights, beginning to relax (*forget the Hex*) and to look around. By the time she reached the Roelof Hartplein, she'd had it. Her bum was sore, her hands were cramped, and her calves were protesting. She'd been pushing those pedals for an hour. It was time for a rest before she went home.

Janice knew that *plein* meant "open square" in Dutch, but the Roelof Hartplein wasn't square-shaped. It was more of a triangle, leaning to the right. The base of the triangle was taken up by a grand art deco café. Its curved terrace looked out on a tree-filled patch of grass, too small to be a park. Janice dismounted by a bookshop. Glancing in the window, she noticed many English titles on display. She'd pop in there after she had a coffee.

Keeping half an eye on her bike chained to a tree on the edge of the pavement, Janice sat on the terrace and waited for her coffee. The sun was lovely and warm, and she relaxed, easing the cramp out of her calf muscles and idly watching the traffic. Then her heart missed a beat. What was this person doing here? Janice hid behind her hair, hoping not to be noticed, but it was no use. There were too few people on the terrace at this time of day. She was the only one sitting alone. She stood out. She'd been spotted.

Part 3: Kate

Amsterdam, June 1980

Chapter 46

"Mind if I join you?" Kate stood before Janice's table. Carrying a neatly wrapped parcel, she was not dressed for work but in a cool-looking blouse and comfy old jeans.

Janice turned to look anywhere but directly at Kate. "If you must. Go ahead."

The waiter arrived, set down Janice's coffee, and poked a slip of paper under the saucer. Peering down at it, Janice was shocked to see that her cappuccino cost three guilders. What a rip-off. She'd have to be careful with cash until she got herself a paying job.

"*Alstublieft, mijnheer*," said the waiter.

Wrong! She was not a *mijnheer*, but Janice couldn't be bothered correcting him.

The waiter looked at Kate. With her golden hair swept off her wide brow, her patrician nose and bow lips, there was no mistaking her femininity. Despite the circumstances, Janice couldn't help noticing how attractive she was.

Kate smiled at the waiter, ordered "a cup of tea, *graag*," and sat facing the little park.

The waiter withdrew, deftly negotiating the scramble of tables and chairs on the terrace. As he went, he gave the pair a bold look that said he had realized that Janice was a woman and thought they were a butch-femme couple. Wrong again.

Janice sat in uneasy silence, staring at the lime trees in the patch of grass across from the café. Kate seemed content to stay quiet and enjoy the silence, but the constriction in Janice's chest forced her to speak. She wanted to ask, What are you doing here when you should be at work? But turned it into, "What's with the '*graag*' and '*alstublieft*'? They both mean 'please,' don't they? Why did the waiter say the one and you the other?"

"Do you really want a Dutch lesson?" Janice merely nodded, not trusting herself to say more. A hint of a smile curled Kate's lips. "Well, yes, they both mean 'please' but *alstublieft* also means 'at your service.' That's the sense the waiter was using it in. More formal than *graag*, which can also mean 'you're welcome' when you say *graag gedaan*."

"Good god, I'll never get the hang of this language."

"Oh, don't worry, you'll pick it up in time if you stick around. Even I did."

"Sounds like it." Janice plucked up the courage to add, "What are you doing here?"

Kate angled her chair to make it easier to see Janice. "I live up the road. This café is my local, *mijn stamkroeg*, as the Dutch would say, and I've just been into the store across the road to pick up some books I ordered."

Oh? Kate was a reader too. Janice wanted to ask, What have you bought? What do you like reading best? Instead, she said, "It's Monday, shouldn't you be at work?"

"It's my day off." Kate smiled again, not condescendingly, just being friendly. She hesitated. "Shouldn't you be at work?"

Janice hid behind her hair. "I've left the firm, resigned this morning. I don't work in data entry anymore"—her voice trailed off—"for obvious reasons."

Kate digested this in silence. The waiter arrived with her glass of hot water and a wooden box of tea bags and withdrew discreetly. Finally, Kate said, "Janice, I'm sorry about what happened at the unmasking yesterday."

"What's there to be sorry about?" Defiance was the best defense. No way was she going to reveal to Kate how she felt about Hannah's treachery. Kate was Hannah's ex and still her best friend. No doubt she'd share any beans that Janice spilled on the subject. She'd run straight to Hannah and compliment her on how clever she'd been, destroying Janice with disappointment. Could she trust Kate? Janice decided to play it safe and assume she couldn't.

But Kate wouldn't be put off. After a moment she tried again. "Hannah shouldn't have done what she did. Lead you on like that, let you believe that you'd be in the play when everyone knows that newcomers never act in their first show with TT."

Janice jumped in her seat, hitting the rickety table and spilling her coffee. "You mean you all knew what was happening and kept quiet, didn't say a thing? How could you?"

"Well, I did try to warn you."

"Not to get emotionally involved."

"Not to take Han's flirting seriously. That always ends in tears."

"And now I suppose you're going to say, I told you so." Janice was on the brink of angry tears. She'd had enough. Enough of Hannah and of Kate. She took a hasty swallow of her coffee, slopping dregs into the saucer, and bumped the table as she stood. She went to turn away but then remembered she hadn't paid. Hauling out her wallet, she fished in it for her last five-guilder note and threw it on the table. The waiter could keep the bloody change.

"Please, don't go." Kate put out a restraining hand. "Han always puts newcomers to TT on trial, to see if they fit in. She should have told you about her audition process."

To be fair, Janice remembered Hannah did say something about having to do a proper audition when she'd given Janice the script but, at the time, hadn't explained the process. She'd just said a tantalizing, "You'll see."

"Failing Han," Kate added, "at least one of us Thespians could have let you know."

"Then why didn't you?" Janice was rigid.

Kate spoke intensely, choosing not to answer the direct question. "I'm furious that Han didn't explain things properly. Believe me, you're not the only one to be put on trial. Look at Sanne. She's with Fern, who's been with TT for years now, but just because they're lovers is no guarantee that Han is going to let Sanne go on stage. Han let her read for the Duchess, you saw that. But now Han herself is going to record the part. Don't you think that's a disappointment for Sanne? She's on to her second show with us and Han is still only letting her do the sound, well, the lighting this time around. That's Han for you."

"I don't understand. Why do you Thespians let her get away with this crap?"

Kate swept her hair off her brow. Finally, she said, "Perhaps you're only seeing one side of her. She's not all crap, you know, not by a long shot."

"Oh yeah, what are her non-crappy sides? Tell me."

"Besides being stinking rich and generous with it? She funds the Thespians totally on her own, you know. The rest of us never have to fork out a cent on theater hire or anything. She's brimming with passion for TT and that's contagious. Besides that, haven't you felt her warmth? There's nothing fake about that. Han likes people. Okay, she's a tease, but that's just part of her loving life to the fullest. There's more to Han than just that selfish flirty side."

"All this sexpot stuff with me, are you saying it's an act? Just a game?"

"No, not an act, but yes, it is a game to Han. You've got to realize that." Kate paused, looked away for a moment. "If you must know, it's why we broke up. I couldn't handle Han being an incorrigible flirt. She's a serial flirt, flirts with everyone, especially the newcomers in data entry. Only with you her game's been more of a power play than usual. She doesn't normally race her flirts off to bed the way she did with you. But I can see why." Kate took a breath. "You're gorgeous."

Chapter 47

Janice looked hard at Kate, not believing that the woman found her attractive.

"Anyway," Kate added, "I tried to warn you about Hannah's flirting."

Suspicion was eating at Janice. "I still don't understand why you stick around. She's your ex, for god's sake. You couldn't put up with her flirting. That hurt you. What are you doing with someone whose games only hurt others? Whose side are you on?"

Kate reached out to Janice. "I don't take sides, but I'm on yours, if you insist."

"Oh, spare me the soft touch." Janice shook off Kate's hand.

"I'm not insincere and I'm not trying to seduce you." Kate's eyes flashed, then cleared just as quickly. "I'm not like that."

"What are you like, then?"

"I'm not the kind of person who plays with people. I don't like it when people get hurt." Kate stood, tossed some coins on the table beside her unfinished tea, picked up her parcel, and followed Janice to the bike. "Is this *stalen ros* yours?"

Janice was seething but couldn't be rude. "What's a 'stah-len ross'?"

"A steel horse, the old term for bike. But the Dutch would call this an *oma fiets*, a granny bike. High handlebar, low instep, made for women wearing long skirts. It suits you."

Ignoring the compliment, Janice said, "Bought it this morning. It's my first spin."

"I wondered what you were doing all the way out here. You and that Colin chap live in the center, don't you? You're both at the same address on the Keizersgracht?"

"Colin's resigned too. He took off for Berlin, West Berlin, this morning. He's gone." Janice stopped a moment. "How do you know where I live?"

"I happened to see your address at work."

"Just happened to see it. Not checking on me, were you? On behalf of Hannah."

"Oh, come off it." Kate's eyes were fiery again. "There's no need to be paranoid. I work in personnel, as you know. It makes sense that I help process the new hires. Of course I'd get to see your details. I'll have to process your resignation when I get back tomorrow. There's nothing more to it than that." She swept the hair off her forehead, eyes still flashing, then relaxed. Speaking calmly again, she said, "What was it like biking through Amsterdam for the first time? Where did you go?"

Kate was volatile, blowing hot and cold so fast, Janice could barely keep up. Still simmering with suspicion, she said, "The traffic was hairy at times. Followed my nose all the way here. No destination, just kept going till I'd had enough."

"Is that what you're like? You don't stop till you get enough?"

Janice recognized the Michael Jackson song and despite herself had to smile. "Something like that. But not when it comes to hurting people."

"Me neither." Kate gave her a look. There was no hidden message, no manipulation.

Janice wasn't wearing her chunky-heeled Brazilian boots. Kate's head was nearly level with hers. She didn't want to look in her honest eyes and hid by bending down to unlock the chain attaching the bike to the tree. As she straightened, Kate was gazing at her. "What?"

"Look, I don't know how to say this without giving the wrong idea. But I'll try anyway. It would be nice to see you again. Sometime, someplace."

"Oh yeah?" Janice was dubious. The erratic pounding of her heart was warning her not to make amends too quickly. She was not ready to make friends with the enemy.

"No hassle, I promise. Let me give you my number." Kate felt in her pocket for her wallet and took out a business card. "My home number's on the back. Take it, please. Give me a ring when you like. Maybe one day you'd like to come around to mine for a cup of tea."

"Strong English tea? Not this pig's piss they serve over here."

"Proper tea. My mum sends me teabags, so I never run out."

Real tea. Janice was hooked but tried to play it cool. "I might think about it," she said, pocketing the card anyway. Mounting the bike, she nearly added, See you later, but changed it to "Good-bye."

Kate was no longer paying attention to her. Instead, she was focused on a middle-aged woman, laden down by shopping bags, crossing the road from the tram stop on the far side of the Roelof Hartplein. Not bothering to say good-bye, Kate walked to the woman, calling out something that sounded like "Ahoy, Coby." Clearly, she offered help because the stranger handed over the heavy bags with a grateful smile.

The two made a comical sight as they left the terrace, tall Kate bending down to listen to the small woman talking her head off. Something about this cuddly person reminded Janice of someone, but she didn't know who. Then she got it. This person had come to the office to bring Kate her lunch box. It must be the nice neighbor. Come to think of it, yes, Coby was her name. In a funny way this Coby looked a bit like Mrs. Palmer in London. Janice shrugged. Couldn't be. But looking at how she was rabbiting away at Kate, this person was just as chatty as Mrs. P. That could be the only resemblance.

Dismissing the thought, Janice weaved carefully down the bike path. *I'll see you again.* That stupid old Noel Coward song was pounding through her head in time with her pedaling.

Again? Well, Kate, we'll see.

Chapter 48

Janice dated the letter she was writing in the dim light of her room: June 15, 1980. She'd pulled aside the dusty curtain and opened the window to let in as much light as possible. It was two o'clock in the afternoon, but even so, dark shadows filled the room. Still, she refused to switch on the overhead light. It reminded her of the harsh light in her London bedsit. She'd have to buy a reading lamp. Soon. When she could afford it.

She signed the letter and put down her Waterman ballpoint, a glossy black thing with golden rings that Kobus had bought on one of the shopping sprees. When she'd first arrived in Amsterdam, it had hurt to use it because it evoked guilty memories. But, as with the jacket, the boots, the toothbrush, and all the other expensive presents Kobus had splurged on for her, the pain had faded, and now the pen was merely an object, something practical she could enjoy using with no strings attached.

Or so she told herself now. It was a different matter in the middle of the night. Last night she'd woken up gasping from another nightmare. She'd dreamed she was a helpless morsel of prey bound in luxuriant threads of silk. A monster spider was about to devour her. It had the compact body of Hannah and the unshaven face of Kobus. Talk about strings attached. Ha. No prizes for interpreting this blatant message from her subconscious.

Janice shook her head to dispel the horrid memory and folded the letter into an airmail envelope. She didn't have a stamp. No problem, she'd buy one at the main post office behind Dam Square and send her letter from there.

It was hot out on the canal today. She decided a walk would do her good and left her bike locked to the railing outside the hostel. A stroll would shake off the worries of the night. She was getting to know the center of Amsterdam well, all the little shortcuts to Dam Square in the heart of the city. Playing it safe, following the long curves of the canals down to a main thoroughfare was always the long way around. Now, with the tower of the Westerkerk in sight, she went down the canal, turned left, crossed two bridges, and nipped into a tiny alley.

Too narrow for cars, these alleys were open only to cyclists and foot traffic. Janice had learned fast that only tourists walked down the middle. After a couple of irate Amsterdammers had yelled at her, she'd learned to keep out of the way and stuck to the footpath wherever possible. She was glad she'd left her leather jacket behind. It was only June, but Amsterdam was already hot and sticky, much hotter than London had ever been, too hot even for her favorite flannel shirt. She was wearing the tunic Kobus had bought her, with the sleeves rolled up. The material hugged her breasts a little too snugly for comfort, although she stretched it out every time she hand-washed it. But what the hell? She knew the crimson shade went well with her coloring. Tucked into her jeans and set off by her favorite leather belt, she knew the top made her look good. Lengthening her stride on purpose, she didn't mind the admiring glances she was catching from passers-by, men and women both.

Ha. Vanity, thy name is Janice.

* * *

Janice pushed the massive revolving door and entered a cavernous hall. Spacious was not the word for it. It was the grandest public building she had ever seen, let alone been in. Even the outside was imposing. The architecture was a mishmash of styles, combining neo-Gothic with neo-Renaissance into something you could call Post Office Gothic. If ghastly Gothic could ever be as decorative as this intricate brickwork in the walls and all the fussy dormers ranging along the roofline. The pear-shaped turrets made the majestic edifice look more like the Kremlin than an ordinary post office. Most un-Dutch. The inside was just as fanciful, with sweeping rows of arches on pillared galleries richly decorated with carved animal motifs on the walls. And high, high above, a splendid glass canopy shed mellow light onto it all.

Ahead of her, across the vast expanse of tiled floor, was a long, polished counter with numbered cubicles sectioned off by gratings. Several cubicles were closed, and there were long queues in front of the remaining open ones. All the signposting was in Dutch. Which queue should she join to buy a stamp? Janice didn't have clue, so she tagged on to the shortest, fastest-moving line. The people in front were French, a couple on their honeymoon, judging by the way they couldn't keep their hands off each other's bums.

She was soon hemmed in from behind by three German boys, shoving each other playfully. Janice gave them a fierce look when one bumped into her by accident, but she didn't really mind. The sound of their German made her think of Colin and wonder how much of the language he'd picked up by now. With his propensity for pillow talk, he'd know all the dirty words at least. Overhearing the lively chatter in French and German, she thought, *I'm the English-speaking Kiwi filling in a European sandwich. How cosmopolitan Amsterdam is, and how glad I am I got out of parochial New Zealand to experience this.*

Ah, New Zealand and thoughts of faraway home. Janice felt into her back pocket and pulled out the letter she'd written to her parents. It was long overdue. She'd written it purely out of duty and hadn't put much into it. Nothing about Kobus and why she had left London. Just that she was here and having a fun time. They could write back to her care of this post office in Amsterdam. If they ever bothered. Janice didn't care a hoot whether they did or not.

At last, the French couple moved aside, and it was her turn. The official sat behind the grating, waiting for her to say what she wanted. For some mad reason, Janice decided to try speaking Dutch. It couldn't be that hard. She only wanted an airmail stamp for New Zealand. Waving her letter at the man and clearing her throat, she said "*Graag, een zegel voor New Zealand, alstublieft.*" She tossed in both "pleases," just in case, but didn't know the word for "airmail" so left that bit out.

The man looked puzzled. Janice guessed he couldn't understand what she wanted because of her Kiwi accent. She tried again. "*Een zegel voor New Zealand. Wat is de kost?*"

"Ah," said the man as comprehension dawned. He opened a drawer exposing several big rolls of stamps and ripped off a small blue one. He placed it in a little tray and pushed that through a slot under the grating. Janice had no idea what the man had babbled, but she could read the amount printed on the stamp. Forty-five cents. Not even half a guilder. Gosh, that was cheap for airmail all the way to New Zealand. How generous of the Dutch. She placed the right change in the tray. The man pulled the tray back and swept her coins into the cash drawer. Janice wanted to ask where the letterbox was, but the man indicated that she should attach the stamp and pass the letter through to him. She did so gratefully and was about to thank him for posting the letter when he looked past her saying, "*De volgende.*"

But Janice wasn't finished. "*Graag, mijn post restante, alstublieft.*"

"Ah," said the official, dismissing her. "*U moet naar een ander loket, daarginds.*"

Janice gathered what he was saying because he was pointing to a section of the counter at the far end of the hall. Fuming, she went down there and waited in line for what felt like another eternity before she could ask if there were any letters for her. This time she spoke English. The official asked to see her passport, compared her face with the photo, and then checked the box labeled "V."

"It's De Vetter. Won't you find my post under the letter 'D'?"

The man ignored her, came back, and said curtly, "Nothing for you. *De volgende. Der Nächste. Le suivant.* Next."

Nothing from Colin yet. Not even a postcard, the royal bastard. Probably having too much of a gay time to bother writing to her. She stepped out of the way of the person next in line, a smartly dressed, preppy American by the sound of his accent. Turning, she spotted someone who just had to be his girlfriend waiting for him by the long bank of telephone booths lining the front wall. The girl shifted from foot to foot as she waited, clutching her shoulder bag so tightly her knuckles had turned white. Janice imagined the pair had run out of money and had wired Daddy-dear for more funds. She hoped for their sake that it would turn up in time to bail them out of whatever cashless mess they'd got themselves into.

As for her own lack of funds, there was no use asking her parents to bail her out. They wouldn't lend her a single cent, not that she'd ever ask them for money. It wouldn't even occur to her parents that they might give anything more than what they had already given. They'd fed and clothed her, supplied a bed and a desk for her homework, but when she'd begun university, that was it. Their job was done. Janice had left home as soon as she could. Long ago she had reached the conclusion that she could not depend on her parents. They couldn't care less about her, not even that she was lesbian. Their child was beyond disappointment. She didn't belong to them, and they didn't belong to her. She was a loner.

A broke loner if she didn't watch out. Janice hovered by a telephone booth, turning her back on the crowd to check the meager contents of her wallet. It was time to swing into action. She had to find a paying job.

The smart American boy ran up and hugged his jubilant girlfriend. Oh goody. Daddy must have forked out. She wished the young couple luck, hoping that some of their luck would rub off on her. Oh god, she was starting to sound like Kobus. She hugged herself as a cold wave of dread swept over her. Kobus was dead. He'd pushed her too far. She'd pushed him back and now he was dead. She hadn't meant to kill him, but it was her fault that he had died. Just like it had been her fault that Ariel had died. She had to accept what she'd done.

She marched back to the hostel chanting, "Kobus is dead, Kobus is dead, Kobus is dead, and I killed him."

Chapter 49

Janice swallowed the last morsel of *frikandel*, wiped her fingers on a paper napkin, threw it neatly into the bin, and left the snack bar. She was on that narrow boutique-filled pedestrian lane that goes up from the Dam and curves around at the top to meet the road to Haarlem. It was her part of town, close to the hostel. The lane was packed with ordinary shoppers and office workers, some nipping into boutiques for a dose of retail therapy on their way home. Janice was in no hurry to go home. July was hot and humid in Amsterdam. The heat made her room far too muggy for comfort, even with the window open. Far better out here.

Automatically, she merged in with the flow of people streaming toward the Dam. Understandably, Dutch pedestrians followed their road rules and kept to the right, which was something you had to get used to if you came from a country that stuck to the left. There was no point in trying to go against the flow. You'd only face a barrage of filthy looks from Amsterdammers annoyed by the inconvenience you represented. It made Janice smile, the way they refused to budge from their path. She had quickly discovered that many, if not most, Dutch pedestrians seldom gave way to anyone coming toward them. They walked straight on, obdurately expecting the person opposite to move out of their way. Janice wondered if this stubborn attitude had anything to do with the fact that most of the country was below sea level. The implacable builders of dikes that held back the force of the sea would never let anything as slight as a dyke stand in the way of survival. Could it be as simple as that?

If Colin were here, she'd tell him what she was thinking, making a joke of it. He'd find it funny too, adding his own crack about dikes and the putting of fingers therein. Or something like that. She missed his charming vulgarity, his camp observations of life that often amused her. She missed Colin. Full stop.

Janice stopped midstride, earning an irate "*stomme trut*" from the man behind. Ha. She knew what that meant. She was neither stupid nor a bitch. Colin was His Royal Bitchness, not her. And stupid? Hm. She was stupid, she conceded, thinking of her foolish crush on Hannah. As for Kobus, she'd stupidly let him treat her dreadfully and now he was dreadfully dead.

"Sorry, I'm dreadfully sorry!" Janice yelled at the man's fast retreating back. He shrugged, waved his briefcase at her, and hurried on toward the tram stop on the Dam.

Janice joined the throng on the vast square. How on earth had the English cops not tracked her down? It couldn't be that hard, but here she was, months later, alive and well and living in Amsterdam and no one seemed keen to find her. Then Janice thought again. How could anyone in London know where she was? Back in the middle of March, when she'd run away from the bedsit, she hadn't said where she was going in her note to Mrs. Palmer, her old landlady. Nor had she told Mrs. Brockett, her old boss at Willing Workers employment agency, when she'd resigned her job without notice. And when her Magic Bus reached the Hook of Holland and she'd had to pass through customs, the official took one look at her Dutch passport and waved her through. They'd assumed she was a Dutch citizen coming back from holiday. Not a foreigner visiting her birthplace for the first time since her parents had taken her off to New Zealand. There was no need for concern. Was there?

Janice crossed the narrow road on the edge of the Dam and was instantly surrounded by a pack of tourists feeding the pigeons. She was facing the Royal Palace, a building so huge it took up a whole side of the vast square. *I bet Kobus could tell me about it*, Janice thought, stabbed by a sudden pang in her chest. *If only he were alive.* She'd have to do something about his death. Could she face the consequences? Turn herself in, or what? That was a huge decision, and she couldn't handle making it. Not yet.

Janice sidestepped a ravenous pigeon. It flurried off with the rest of the flock, circled the tourists' heads and divebombed onto the cobbles to squabble over crumbs. She turned her back on the circus and jaywalked dangerously across the Damrak, the avenue that intersected the square, heading for the cenotaph.

Standing sentinel before the Hotel Krasnapolsky, the conical pillar of the war memorial was a famous symbol of peace and liberty. Several punks were lazing around it, enjoying the afternoon sun. All safety pins and torn jeans, the punks were honoring their hippie forerunners, smoking marijuana by the pungent stink of it. Janice was not interested in trying it. Colin had told her he enjoyed a toke when offered but Janice couldn't see why. She had no wish to turn herself into a giggling ninny. If she wanted to get high, she'd stick to the warm buzz a good whiskey could give her, thank you very much for asking.

Oh god, she had to stop talking to herself like this. She'd be talking out loud to strangers in a minute and then she'd really be in trouble. She circled the cenotaph, avoiding wafts of secondhand smoke, increasingly aware of an empty pit of longing in her stomach. This was no ordinary hunger. *Frikandel* could never fill this gap. Analyzing the sensation, Janice realized she was hungry for someone to talk to, someone warm and intelligent who wanted to listen. Someone articulate to discuss ideas and experiences with. Someone to be her friend and make her feel she belonged.

She sighed deeply. Enough of these maudlin thoughts. She'd go home and treat herself to a Noel Coward play. She'd been rationing herself, not finishing Colin's present in one binge, wanting to draw out the pleasure. She was looking forward to reading *Design for Living*. This raging hit of the 1930s was about the lascivious Gilda, Otto, and Leo and their shocking ménage à trois. How carnal, how amoral. How what she needed now.

Hang on. Janice edged back from the pedestrian crossing. In the crowd on the far side stood Kate, patiently waiting for the lights to change. She was wearing a tailored blazer and pants. She'd come from work. Janice slid behind a tree near the Bijenkorf, the deluxe department store that claimed to be the Dutch Harrods. She didn't want to meet Kate when she was in this fragile mood. Turning her back as Kate passed, Janice snatched a glance over her shoulder and saw Kate push through the revolving door of the Bijenkorf. She dithered, not knowing whether to go home or go after Kate.

Impulse won. Janice sneaked in, skulked behind a pillar, and peered around carefully. Ah. There was Kate, at the perfume counter, looking at the Yves Saint Laurent collection and rows of Rive Gauche. Bloody hell. What was Kate doing, looking at Janice's favorite scent?

Hiding behind the pillar, Janice watched Kate buy a Rive Gauche atomizer. Kate turned down the assistant's offer of gift wrapping and slid the slender bottle and its receipt in her blazer pocket. Ah. It wasn't an expensive present for someone else. Kate must earn a mint if she could afford Bijenkorf prices. She was way out of a hostel cleaner's league.

What was Janice thinking? As if comparing her earnings with Kate's could be relevant. Janice leaned on the pillar. Her brow was hot and sweaty. What the hell was she doing? Stalking the best friend of Hannah-the-Hex. If Kate caught her snooping, no doubt she'd run straight back to Attila-the-Han and tell on her. What a good laugh they'd have about her, the Besotted Buffoon. Cringing at the image, Janice shook her hair. How stupid could she get? She had to get out before Kate noticed her. As stealthily as she'd entered, Janice pushed through the door, leaving the willowy woman behind in the Bijenkorf.

Chapter 50

Next Saturday night was too hot again. Janice couldn't sleep in this ferocious heat. She kicked the blanket onto the floor and draped a corner of the sheet over her pubes to expose the rest of her body to whatever fresh air could seep through the open window. That damn mosquito was buzzing frenetically around her head again. She reached over to switch on the lamp clipped to the back of the chair she used as a nightstand. It shone a cone of light over her shoulder, not strong enough to illuminate the space above the bed so that she could track down the insect. Bane of her bedroom, an infestation of mosquitos was the price you paid for living on a canal.

The insect had feasted on the ball of her thumb and the bite itched like hell. Janice scratched, wishing it had chosen her right hand instead. Itchy right palm meant good luck, like getting an unexpected gift or winning money. Itchy left palm meant bad luck. It's what her superstitious mother said, and come to think of it, Kobus had believed in it too.

That's all she needed, to lose more money. She'd spent too much on the lamp, bought new in the HEMA department store on the Nieuwendijk. It had cost twelve guilders that she shouldn't have spent. But she'd had to splurge on it. There was no way she could read by candlelight the way she had in London, because Negy had a key to her room. Janice suspected he opened her door once in a while. Not that he came in and poked through her belongings, but she didn't feel that she could trust him not to peek through the door when she was out, just checking. Negy would never let her do something so dangerous as burn candles in bed.

Now she was down to her last guilders. Two tens and change in her wallet and fifty stashed in the bank. Even if she restricted herself to *frikandel* meals only, what was left wouldn't last much longer. She needed to find a job that paid money. Soon, sooner, soonest.

Janice sucked at the bite, hoping saliva would soothe the itch. Served her damn right (left) to be burdened with bad luck. Isn't that what murderers deserved? Her just deserts for killing Kobus, even inadvertently. The word "deserts" made her think of the after-meal treat and conjured up an image of her lying pinned to the floor by a giant chocolate pudding, round and dark and heavy as lead, with her arms and legs flailing wildly like some helpless cartoon character.

Oh, stop it. This was not a joke. Forget the money worries. Under the circumstances, having no money to live on was the least of her concerns. Kobus was dead. She'd killed him. There, she fully admitted it. Now she had caused not one but two deaths. Ariel and Kobus. She was only twenty-two, alone and friendless in a foreign country. There was no one to help her get out of the guilty mess she'd created for herself. There was only one thing to do.

Janice sat up and swatted at the invisible tormentor, sending the high-pitched buzzing away. It returned a moment later to plague her as insistently as the cold ball of guilt settled deep inside her. That horrid weighed-down feeling wouldn't go away. It was Sunday tomorrow. Were police stations open on Sundays? She'd find out soon enough. She had to do the right thing. Tomorrow she'd go to the police station across the road from the bus station, and turn herself in. She'd confess to the killing of Jacobus Boer, late of London. Janice glanced at her watch. Two in the morning. Tomorrow, my foot. It was already today.

Three hours later Janice was still awake, watching the dark fade into soft dawn through her window. Mosquito strikes were on her thigh and upper arm, but she'd managed to smear the one biting her arm to bloody death. Her blood, its death. Oh god, she didn't want to think about death. Not now, not again. She hadn't closed her eyes all night and was desperate to sleep. She slid down in the bed, pulling up the sheet to cover her whole body. Her skin felt clammy with sweat. It was no use. She couldn't get to sleep. It was too darn hot.

Ha. Too darn hot. Wasn't that a song from *Kiss Me Kate*? She'd seen the show on TV, during her final year at school when she and Ariel had discovered Broadway musicals. They'd read whatever they could find about Broadway in the library and watched whatever turned up on TV. Their butch bull dyke of an English teacher, Miss Torrence (El Torro), encouraged their obsession and always warned the class whenever a Broadway classic was due to appear on TV. When *Kiss Me Kate* was coming, El Torro told the class that it was a thinly disguised rendition of Shakespeare's *The Taming of the Shrew* and advised them to read the original. Then she'd asked, "What other famous musical is also based on a Shakespeare play?"

Janice and Ariel had exchanged smug glances when no one gave the right answer.

"Miss, we know," said Janice. "It's *West Side Story* based on *Romeo and Juliet.*"

Another hot show. But not as hot as the torrid Ann Miller tapping her toes to the ferocious beat of the bongo drums, singing her feral heart out in *Kiss Me Kate*. Kate, kiss me.

No. Janice sat up with a start, shocked by her train of thought. In her mind's eye she'd replaced the seductive dancing star with the kissable Kate, hot Kate Hynder, star of Thalia Thespians. Janice wondered what would happen if she really did ask Kate to kiss her. Ha. As if she ever would.

Chapter 51

Later that Sunday morning, after breakfast, a bleary-eyed Janice was dusting the counter in reception when the phone rang. Negy picked up. "Kay-Gay Youth Hostel."

Negy's English often made Janice smile. Not that she'd ever show that it did, of course. That'd be rude. She guessed no one had ever put him right on the pronunciation of "KG" for Keizersgracht. Negy often said, "Ka-Gay," not realizing he sounded as if he were giving the okay to all in the gay community to come and stay here. Other times it sounded like "Kah-Gah," as if he were gagging on something.. He never said it the way an English speaker would. On second thought, if he did say K-G normally, potential guests might get the wrong idea, that there was something cagey about the hostel and stay away in droves. Instead, they were staying in droves. This weekend the hostel was full to bursting. All the bunks were taken in the dorm. Luckily, no one wanted a double and Janice was able to keep her room.

She was about to leave reception when Negy spoke. "Wait, for you." She turned and saw him holding out the receiver. He was livid. "Not allowed for guests. That means you."

"No, it doesn't. I'm more than a guest. I work here." Janice grabbed the receiver and mouthed, "sorry" to pacify Negy before speaking her name. Who could be calling her?

"Oh, hi. Hello, you, glad I caught you. Sorry to ring you at home but—"

Oh god, it was Kate. Janice's heart did a flip-flop. "How did you get this number?" What a dumb question. Of course, Kate knew her number. It would be on her personnel record. But how dare she? Janice had never said that she could. "What do you want?"

"Is this a bad time?" Kate was conciliatory, as if she wanted to soften Janice's tone.

"No, it's just that the hostel guests, I mean residents, we're not supposed to use the phone. You're getting me into trouble with the owner."

"Sorry. I'll be quick. Have you seen *Een Vrouw Als Eva*? It's on at the *bioscoop*, as the Dutch would say, close to where you are. There's a matinee this afternoon and I wondered if you'd like to see it with me. Starts at two, if you can make it."

Janice was stunned. Was Kate asking her out? On a date? To see a lesbian love story starring that Dutch actor, Monique somebody, and the notorious Maria Schneider from *Last Tango in Paris*. Janice had read about *A Woman Like Eve*, and yes, she was keen to see a film that showed lesbians in a positive light. But with Kate? This very afternoon? When she would be on her way to the police station to turn herself in for killing Kobus?

She dithered, feeling torn. Negy tugging at the phone cord and hissing at her to hang up made up her mind. "Look, I've got to go. I've got your card. I'll call back from a phone box." And she hung up without saying good-bye.

Janice knew there were telephone boxes on the Dam, in the main post office, and at Central Station, but the nearest one to the hostel was a coin phone in her local coffee shop. The only thing was, the café was in the opposite direction from the police station, where she had to be if she was going to confess to the crime of murder. What to do? After work, unlocking her bike from the railing in front of the hostel steps and slinging the chain over the handlebar, she pondered. She had to turn herself in. No question about that. But when? Was the timing important? The police had already waited months to find her. Would it matter if they waited another half hour or so? She made up her mind. She'd call Kate and turn down the invitation because, let's face it, what murderer should be allowed time off to see a movie before making a true confession?

Janice hopped on the bike and rode the short distance to the café. Locking the bike to a "No Parking" post, Janice realized that she was just up the road from The Movies, where *Een Vrouw Als Eva* was showing. That did it. She couldn't phone Kate without inspecting the cinema first. A moment later, she was peering at the display of publicity stills. It looked good. That film star was Monique Van de Ven. Not bad looking, if you were into blondes. Maria Schneider was gorgeous, with her long dark ringlets, sultry eyes, and sensual mouth. The poster showed the two women in a clinch. There could be no doubting that the film was a passionate lesbian romance. Now there was no doubt that Janice wanted to see it.

She dawdled on the way to the café, tummy in turmoil. Inside, she nodded at the bar staff, ordered "*een cappuccino, graag*" and headed straight to the phone mounted on the rear wall. Kate's business card was where she'd left it in her wallet. She memorized the number and dialed. The receiver felt clammy in her hand and—*oh god, no*, Kate picked up at once, before Janice had time to think what she was going to say.

"Oh, hi. Janice, wow. Terrific, you called. Thanks for getting back to me. My apologies for disturbing you at the hostel. Hope I didn't get you into trouble."

Colin would say that Kate was blethering like a manic hen. Could she be nervous too? Janice tried to play it cool. "It's okay. No hassle. I was going to phone you anyway." She hadn't meant to say that. She backtracked. "One day." She stopped. "Sooner or later."

Silence. Then Kate jumped in. "Well, I'm glad I gave you my card. I didn't want to be pushy then, and I don't want to nag you now, but how about seeing this film? It's fabulous."

"You've already seen it?"

"I went to the opening, along with most of lesbian Amsterdam. It was terrific. The cinema was packed to the rafters with dykes. We all cheered at the good bits. You'll love it."

"But it's in Dutch. I won't be able to follow it."

"Not a problem. The Maria Schneider scenes aren't in Dutch. She plays Liliane, a French girl, and all her bits are in English. I can help you with the Dutch if you need translation. But you won't. I mean, it's a film, visual by definition so you should be able to get by—"

"Looking at the pictures."

Kate laughed. "Exactly. How about it? Are you ready for some quality lesbian culture? Do say yes." She waited. "If you haven't got anything better to do this afternoon."

Janice did have something better to do. But she was sorely tempted. The police had waited this long, let them wait a while longer. What damage could it do to see one last film before she turned herself in? She gripped the receiver so hard her nails bit into her skin and made her palm itch. Her right palm, to be precise. It was an omen.

"Okay, you've convinced me. I'll come."

"I'm glad you said that. Terrific!" Kate roared so loudly Janice had to pull the receiver away from her ear. Calming down, Kate added, "You won't regret it, that's a promise."

Janice's heart was doing flip-flops. "Don't make promises you can't keep."

Chapter 52

When the film started, Janice was aware of Kate close beside her in the nearly empty auditorium. Kate's legs were nearly as long as her own. The cramped space between their seats and the row in front forced them to angle their legs to one side. But instead of bending away from Janice, Kate slanted toward her so that their knees met. Janice didn't move. It felt friendly. No sparks, nothing like Hannah's electric touch. Just warm and accommodating.

It was stuffy in the cinema. To begin with, Janice tried to watch the film, but after fretting all night and fighting off mosquitos, her eyes felt dry and heavy. It was an effort to follow the opening scenes. Judging by all the yelling going on, the husband wasn't happy with his wife, and Eve wasn't happy with her hubby, kids, or life. No marital bliss for this couple. Janice got that, without the need for translation, but where the hell was Liliane? When would the lezzie bits start? In easy-to-understand English. Trying to follow this Dutch was so tiring it was boring. Janice shut her eyes, only for a second, mind. Just an extended blink to lubricate her eyeballs. She settled deep in her comfortable seat, leaning on Kate's shoulder, inhaling a trace of familiar scent. Rive Gauche. How lovely. How good that Kate didn't move away.

A sharp nudge in the waist. Oh god. Janice's mouth was parched, her cheeks burned hot. She had no idea how much time had passed. Kate had poked her awake. Janice was glad Kate couldn't see how embarrassed she felt. "Sorry. Was I snoring?"

"Not quite," Kate replied, gently detaching herself. "You won't want to miss this."

Kate was right. Janice sat up straight, collecting herself. Now Eve was in what must be a women's commune, somewhere hot and dry and Mediterranean by the looks of it, and there was the lovely Liliane, dressed in light muslin, slicing bell peppers at an outdoor table, seducing Eve with her sultry eyes while a choir of earnest women warbled backup vocals.

Oh goodie, the lezzie bits at last. The rest of the film flew past without Janice falling asleep again, but truth to tell, she wasn't impressed. She found the extended custody battle at the end especially tedious. Major trauma (Eve), minor lovemaking (Liliane), sex too chaste by far. Janice knew she wasn't being fair to the film, or to Kate, for that matter. Even when they were back on the street unlocking their bikes, Kate was still raving about how groundbreaking the film was in treating sensitive lesbian issues seriously, how good the performances were, especially Van de Ven's, what a convincing lesbian she was when everyone knew she was straight. Janice let her talk on and kept her own views to herself.

Finally, Kate wound down. "I do go on rather, don't I? Hope I'm not boring you … to sleep." Her eyes were laughing. "Do you always fall asleep on a first date?"

Janice shook her hair down, needing to hide the heat in her cheeks. "You must think me awful, dropping off on the dyke hit of the century. I feel embarrassed."

"I know how tiresome it is when you don't understand the lingo. I once fell asleep in the middle of a birthday party. A living room full of people, sitting around in a circle the way the Dutch always do, eating cake and nattering away nonstop. I found it overwhelming. I had to switch off, and before I knew it, I'd dozed off. Couldn't keep my eyes open."

"Really? Then it's not just me?"

"It happens to lots of people when they first arrive. Don't worry, you're forgiven."

"That's a relief," said Janice, adding impulsively, "You know, it wasn't just the film that put me to sleep. I was already tired, didn't sleep a wink last night." She wanted to explain further but stopped herself in time. How much of the truth could she tell Kate? She'd told no one about Kobus, not Hannah—perish the thought—not even Colin. What would Kate think of her if she knew Janice was a murderer? That did it. She couldn't tell Kate a thing. She glanced at her watch. Nearly five. Would the police station still be open? Janice didn't have a clue. She'd have to go there and find out. Now.

Kate noticed Janice checking her watch and her face fell. Leaning on the handlebar of her bike she asked, "What now? Shall we go down to Saarein, have a coffee or a drink?"

Janice picked up her bike, slung her leg over the saddle, mounting the bike like a horse instead of using the low instep. She called over her shoulder, "Sorry, got to go." And she rode off without saying good-bye, leaving Kate behind on the pavement, mouth agape.

Chapter 53

Janice fully intended to ride straight to the police station and turn herself in when a tug of sticky pain stopped her in her tracks. Oh god, her period. She wasn't expecting it until Tuesday. She was bleeding into her underpants. No doubt the cops would want to strip-search her before locking her up in a cell. She'd have to undress if the procedure went anything like she'd seen in crime series on TV. Oh no. She couldn't stand the humiliation of revealing her blood-stained knickers to some butch cop.

She turned the bike around and went back to the hostel, shoved open the door, and without acknowledging Negy, stationed as usual in reception, ran up to her room. Janice kept her tampons in the top pocket of her rucksack. She looked for the little package, worried that there'd be no tampons left from last month. Thank goodness, she still had three, enough to keep her going till she could buy a new supply in the morning.

This early on a Sunday evening no one else was using the showers. Stepping into the largest cubicle, Janice was glad to have the place to herself. Soaping between her legs, washing her hair, rinsing the blood out of her cotton knickers, she let the tepid water stream over her body and wash all the tiredness away. Reaching down to rinse off her knees, Janice remembered the feel of Kate's long legs against her own. She hadn't minded the touch, had welcomed it in a way. It felt easy, strangely familiar, not something her body needed to guard against. It was as if her body trusted Kate enough to let Janice relax in the dark, lean against a warm shoulder, and fall deep into vulnerable sleep. But at the same time, her mind was filled with doubt. The question of Hannah hadn't arisen before, during, or after the film. Janice wasn't going to mention her, and it seemed as if Kate was happy to avoid all reference to her ex, Thalia Thespians, and the play.

Janice stepped out of the shower and dried herself with her towel, a present from Kobus, bought with the Egyptian cotton sheets and pillowcases from Liberty's on Regent Street.

"I'll turn myself in tomorrow." She spoke out loud, her strong voice bouncing off the tiles in the shower room. "And that's a promise." A tiny echo of what she'd said to Kate earlier today played back in her mind. Don't make promises you can't keep.

* * *

Next morning, she should have gone straight to the station to turn herself in, but after cleaning the hostel and quickly visiting the nearest pharmacy to pick up tampons, Janice couldn't resist making one last detour to the main post office. When she'd finished in the hostel, fully intending to do the right thing, she realized she couldn't let herself be arrested without checking if Colin had written to her yet. And if he had, the least she could do was take the time to write back, tell him what was going on, and explain why he would not see her again. Well, not if he couldn't get down from Edinburgh to visit her in prison.

Now, finally, it was her turn in the queue. Giving her name, handing over her passport, and waiting for the clerk to delve into the compartment marked "V," Janice didn't feel hopeful. His Royal Bitchness would be having too much of a fun time in West Berlin to want the bother of writing to her. But her heart lifted when the man slid a chunky envelope and her passport across the counter and, leering at her, said, "*Uw brief, mijnheer.*"

Janice gave him an evil look but didn't bother correcting him. Instead, she flashed a brilliant smile and left him to intimidate the next in line. Clutching the treasured letter with its German postage stamp in the top-right corner, she fled the cavernous hall of the main post office, heading for the bike rack just outside. On the pavement, she stood there confused. She'd left her *stalen ros* here, securely locked with the chain threaded through the front wheel. Where the hell was her bike? Janice looked up and down the row of parked bicycles and checked the crowded railings in front the post office for good measure. But her bike had gone. Disappeared. She hadn't double-checked the padlock in her haste to get inside the post office. The lock couldn't have been shut properly. And, stupidly, she must have left the key in the lock. More than likely the bike had been stolen, lock, stock, and saddle, by some sleazy punk who wouldn't wait to sell it for drug money to the next innocent tourist. And it was her own fault for not securing the lock.

Slapping her thigh, Janice knew there would be no point in reporting the theft. Given the vast number of bikes stolen in Amsterdam every day, the cops would laugh in her face and tell her to fork out the cash to buy an expensive new one. Or get a secondhand bike, stolen, like hers had been. Another lesson learned, the hard way. What the hell, there was nothing else to do but walk to the police station. It would take far longer than the bike ride, but look on the bright side, a leisurely stroll across the canals would be a lovely way to say good-bye to this ancient part of town Janice had grown to love. But first she had a last treat in store.

Chapter 54

Why did the chicken cross the road? Janice gave herself the silly answer: to read Colin's letter in the seclusion of their favorite pizzeria. She used the pedestrian crossing by the tram stop outside the post office building, waiting obediently for the lights to change along with the usual gang of tourists. But instead of following the crowd past an ancient church and on to the Dam, Janice headed up to the pizzeria on the next corner, run by Marcello and his wife, Marcella. On learning their names, Colin had instantly dubbed the place M&M's.

Marcella was small and gaunt, as lean as her well-padded husband was fat. Stationed in the open kitchen, Marcello was always showing off how high he could throw wheels of pizza dough, making the tourists laugh by pretending to drop the dough on the floor. Often he warbled an aria in a reedy tenor, playing up the "O Sole Mio" stereotype for all it was worth, but his performance went down well with the captive audience, so where was the harm? Marcella served the meals. Watching her work, Janice was amazed by how she could balance four fully loaded pizzas in her spindly arms at once, sliding the plates onto the recipients' table with a graceful flourish. If Janice tried to do the same, no doubt she'd dump a sizzling hot pizza in some poor person's lap.

Janice had often been to M&M's with Colin and headed straight to their usual secluded table. She liked coming here, not only because the food was cheap and tasty but because of the welcoming atmosphere. This time of day, Marcello and Marcella were arranging the terrace for the lunchtime crowd, and Janice let them get on with it. They registered her arrival with friendly nods. Marcella would bring her coffee when she had a spare moment. Janice sat with her back to the wall, ripped open the envelope, and withdrew six densely filled pages of neat handwriting.

Meine Liebe Lassie

At last, a long overdue letter has landed in your grubby little hands. Will it be worth the wait? Read on, Macduff. Yrs Trly is writing this missive ensconced in the salubrious surroundings of the Schöneberg, W-Berlin's gayest village. Mine hostelry is around the corner from U Bahnhof Nollendorfplatz (that's the N Underground Station for plebs like you), and tho cheap tis not nasty at all, considering the tasty quality of the clientele, of which I am one of the more favored, well in demand quality-wise if not often enough quantity-wise.

But seriously, Liebling Lassiechen, I am having the time of my life (nearly wrote wife, must be slipping). To continue. Last night my latest Leckermaul (look it up) took me out to the ever so hammer Dschungel aka the Jungle, W-Berlin's answer to Studio 54 and the haunting ground of the uber in-crowd aka VIGs (Very Important Gays). We disco'd the night away to Marianne Rosenberg's "Ich Bin Wie Du" and then … across the crowded room … I saw David Bowie, looking gorgeously wasted. Yea, verily, some enchanted evening. Nearly fainted at his feet but couldn't get close enough. Aber Jetz. Tho I got nowhere near HIM (His Incredible Majesty), my Lassie-Liebling, I can honestly say I have inhaled the same … air as Ziggy Stardust aka the Thin Breit Duke.

The letter continued in this vein for another five pages. Turning to the last, Janice read that despite having the royal time he'd promised himself, Colin was leaving sooner than later. A shot of joy surged through her heart as she continued reading.

I'm not staying till mid-August as planned but coming home a month early. My Magic Bus gets to

Amsterdam next Friday (July 11), arriving at five in the Pee Emma (pardon). If you know what's good for you, wee lassie, you'll do me a meet & greet at the station and—if you promise to be VERY GOOD—I'll let you carry my bag to Negy's for a small but perfectly formed reward. You'll never guess what it is. I'll stay the night, naturellement so please book me a bunk.

Colin signed off with "Be queer and be there." That did it. Janice couldn't turn herself in until she'd seen him again. The police would just have to wait. What would another few days matter?

Marcella brought over Janice's cappuccino and, since no other customers needed service, stayed to chat. "Hello, stranger." She spoke English with a charming lilt. "We have not seen you in a while. Where's Colin? Are you waiting for him before you order lunch?"

Janice shook her head. "Just coffee today, thanks. And I'm not waiting for Colin. He took off for West Berlin three weeks ago. He's coming back briefly on Friday. Just a quick stopover on his way home to Edinburgh."

"West-Berlin, eh? So that's why he hasn't been in. What's kept you away? We miss you."

Janice didn't want to tell the truth. She wouldn't admit that she couldn't afford to eat here the way she and Colin had done when they were working in data entry. Avoiding Marcella's curious gaze, she couldn't confess that she was broke. This coffee was a luxury. Janice stirred in her seat and gave a sigh of relief when Marcella noticed a group of tourists and slipped away to serve them.

Janice took her time finishing her coffee, rereading Colin's letter. How wonderful it was that she could see him before she had to go to prison. She definitely couldn't report to the police today, not after this news. She'd have to wait until after Colin had been and gone. Another five days of freedom, hooray.

Waiting by the kitchen counter to pay Marcella for her coffee, Janice's eye fell on a card pasted to the back of the cash register. She nodded at the card. "Does that say what I think it says? Are you guys looking for somebody to wash dishes?"

Marcella smiled. "We need a helper in the kitchen for the afternoon. Rosaria, my pregnant sister, you know? She does this shift but now she's too far gone. Her baby comes in a few days. Tommaso, our son, you know him? He does the dishes in the evenings, but in the day he is studying. That's why we need a replacement for a couple of months, while Rosaria looks after her bambino. Twelve thirty to five thirty, Monday to Saturday. Do you know anyone who can help us?"

"Me."

"You? No, seriously."

"Yes, me. Seriously. I can wash dishes, no problem. And the hours suit perfectly. I work in the mornings, but I'm free in the afternoon. I can start tomorrow if you want."

Marcella looked dubious. "This is not fun. We don't want someone to stay a few days and then give up. Washing dishes is not exciting work. It is not easy."

Janice perched on the corner of the nearest table so that Marcella wouldn't have to strain her neck looking up at her. She tried to speak calmly, but eagerness threatened to take over and the words spilled out. "You can count on me to do a decent job. I've done it before. I washed dishes part time in a café in my first year at university. I know what a drudge it can be. It's messy, I know that, but I don't mind getting my hands dirty. Give me a chance, please. I really need a regular paying job."

Marcello slid a pizza into the hot oven and came over to lean on the counter. He'd overheard the conversation. "Seven fifty an hour. Cash in hand. You work black?"

"Oh, you think I have to work black. No need for that. I'm born Dutch, you see, and don't need a work permit. Let me show you my passport, see?"

Marcello wiped his floury hands on his apron. "Put it away, we don't need to see your passport. You work black for us. You get the full amount of pay, okay? Cash, every week."

Working black meant no pension or health insurance for Janice. But who cared about that? She was young and always fit—that is, when she wasn't having her period. But other than a day or two of inconvenient cramps every month, she was always bursting with health. More to the point, M&M wanted to keep her off the books because it would save them from having to pay tax on her salary. Janice was working black in the hostel. She was sure that Negy hadn't put their deal on his books, so he wasn't paying taxes on her cleaning job either. Suited her fine.

Janice did the mental arithmetic, five hours a day, six days a week. "Gee. Seven fifty an hour is two hundred and twenty-five a week. I can get by on that, no problem. But only if you throw in a free meal every day." She held her breath in agony, regretting her audacity.

Marcello exchanged a searching glance with his wife. She nodded. He nodded.

Janice was jubilant. "Thank you, Marcella, Marcello. You won't regret taking me."

Marcello beamed at her. "Don't worry. You start washing dishes tomorrow, and for sure, you work hard for every slice of pizza you eat."

And that settled that. Or did it? Janice stopped a moment. What on earth had she done? Pushing for this paying job when she knew she could only do it this one week, while she was waiting for Colin to arrive. If she turned herself in as planned, after Colin had gone, she'd be letting M&M down. Leaving them in the lurch. After she'd sworn that they could count on her. Could she do that to these kind people? She didn't want to think about it. For now, at least. She thrust her concern away.

Chapter 55

Janice didn't want to waste her last free afternoon before starting at M&M's. She decided to go and explore Xantippe, the women's bookshop. For some time now she'd been meaning to visit Amsterdam's famous lesbian-feminist enclave, named Xantippe after Socrates's argumentative wife, to check out the stock, but somehow something had always gotten in the way. The sad fact that she hadn't had any money to splurge on new books might have had something to do with her managing to avoid the temptation. But *hah-lay-loo-yah*, as Colin would say, thanks to the benevolence of M&M, she had a paying job, and she could reward the achievement by treating herself to a brand-new book. Just the one. She hadn't been paid yet. Never mind. She'd enjoy a leisurely stroll across the canals and, anyway, in a couple of weeks she'd be able to buy a new bicycle. Only a secondhand one, to be clear, but soon she'd have wheels again. Funnily enough, all thoughts of turning herself in to the police had disappeared.

Waving a cheerful farewell to Marcella, now busily taking orders from a new bunch of tourists, Janice set off on the most direct route to her destination. Sunlight drenched the broad canals, making ripples in the murky water gleam like pewter. The way the light played on the water and bounced off the windows of houseboats moored to the canal walls was mesmerizing. Janice lingered on a bridge to relish the sight, noticing the tall Westerkerk tower peeking out from behind the lime trees. Not that Janice ever needed signposts to find her way around the inner-city canals, but it never hurt to note a famous landmark.

On the other side of the bridge, she stopped in her tracks. Kate stood on the top step of the bookshop, on her way out, pausing to talk to a woman about to go in. She looked up and saw Janice. Giving a delighted yelp of recognition, she roared, "Hey, you! Hi, Janice."

Janice wasn't ready to see Kate again. Her heart lurched. Watching *Een Vrouw Als Eva* with her felt as if it had happened ages ago, but in fact it was only yesterday afternoon. She owed Kate an apology for taking off rudely in that mad rush to turn herself in. She looked around, searching for an escape. But there was no avoiding this confrontation.

Holding a book-shaped paper bag, not checking for traffic, Kate impulsively closed the short distance between them. "Fancy running into you. How nice."

Not knowing what to say, Janice blurted, "We've got to stop meeting like this."

"Meeting like this? Outside Xantippe? Nah. It's more a case of great minds thinking alike." Smiling irrepressibly, Kate seemed inordinately pleased to see Janice.

Janice watched her sweep a thick lock of hair off her brow. Her golden mane shone in the sunlight. And what about that gorgeous mouth, those luscious kiss-me lips? Janice couldn't help noticing how good the graceful woman looked in her navy polo shirt with the collar turned up to just the right angle, her tailored blazer and sleek black pants. A work outfit.

Janice registered that her body was turned on, maybe because of the pesky hormones raging through her system, but her rational head wasn't ready to deal with that. She didn't want to find Kate attractive, not yet, not now, not while she was processing the damage Hannah had done. A whole string of nots. Janice exhaled, covering her bewilderment.

Kate went on unwittingly, "I mean, you're on your way into Xantippe, I take it?"

"And you've just come out." Oh god, what a dumb thing to say. Janice hid her mortification by turning to check the clock mounted on the Westerkerk tower. "What are you doing away from the office? Is this another one of your days off?"

"Nah, I've been for a checkup at the dentist. When the appointment is this late in the day, you don't have to go back to work." She paused, noting Janice's reluctance to look her in the eye, and changed the subject. "I've just bought the new Rendell."

Despite herself, Janice was intrigued. Kate liked crime fiction too. Especially written by the fabulous Ruth Rendell. Snap-snappety-snap. Hang on, Xantippe was a feminist bookshop. "How come you got a book by the queen of detectives here? I didn't think the women's collective that runs Xantippe would stoop to selling crime."

"You haven't been inside? Then you'll be surprised by the range. Xantippe covers all tastes in reading, from academic dissertations to lesbian pulp. It may be a women-only space, but that doesn't mean the stock is limited to boring old feminist tomes, otherwise known as Clit Lit."

Janice had to laugh. "Dry Clit Lit." Oh god, such a crass remark was worthy of His Royal Bitchness. But Kate didn't seem put off. Instead, she laughed with Janice, roaring huge guffaws. It was all a bit over the top. Janice stopped the noise by asking, "What did you get? Is it the next Inspector Wexford?"

"Nope." Kate collected herself. "It's a stand-alone called *The Lake of Darkness*. About a naive chap who wins a fortune on the football pools and decides to share his good luck with those who need it. But his generosity backfires and there are devastating consequences, not just for him but for all concerned." Kate brandished the book under Janice's nose.

Janice swayed as the blood drained from her face. To stop herself from collapsing, she clutched at the iron railing of the bridge. What was that old cliché? Truth is stranger than fiction. How could Rendell's fiction mimic the truth of her experience? A coincidence? It didn't bear thinking about. She needed to slam the lid on the memories before they could overcome her.

Kate noticed Janice's struggle. Reaching out to support her elbow, she was full of concern. "Hey, are you okay? You look as if you're going to faint. What's the matter?"

Janice shook herself free. "It's my period. Feeling lightheaded, that's all. It'll pass."

"You need to sit. Saarein's around the corner. Come on, let's get you a cup of—"

"Don't you dare say tea. I'll never have another glass of that pig's piss."

Kate laughed. "How about a coffee then? I was about to go there. Come on, join me." And as if it were the most natural thing in the world, she slung her arm through the crook of Janice's elbow and led her off the bridge and down the quiet lane to the women's café.

Chapter 56

In Saarein, Sanne and Fern were in Janice's old hiding place, up in the mezzanine, nearly hidden behind the round table. As Kate pushed open the door, Sanne waved down at Janice. "Yoo-hoo. We're up here."

Janice turned a mystified glance to Kate. "How did they know I was coming?"

"They didn't. They only knew I was meeting them here for a drink after work. You're a bonus." She gave Janice an endearing grin. "For me too. How about that coffee?"

"Cappuccino, please, if they've got it."

"Go on up. I'll bring it to you."

Janice returned the smile briefly and used the banister to hoist herself up the steep stairs. Sanne sprang up in greeting, her belly brushing the magazines on the edge of the table onto the floor. "Oops. Clumsy again. I am always knocking things off when I am not looking. But don't worry, I pick it up later. Hello good-looking, how good to see you."

Such ebullience. Janice didn't know how to take Sanne's enthusiasm. It felt like an onslaught. She was regretting coming to the café, having to be social with people she hardly knew instead of spending her last free afternoon quietly browsing the stacks at Xantippe.

Fern put out a restraining arm, gently but firmly drawing Sanne back into her seat. She took in Janice's wan face and seemed to understand that Janice couldn't cope with Sanne's elation. "Hi there," she said quietly. "How are you?"

Janice sat opposite Sanne. "Oh, good, thanks. Ran into Kate outside Xantippe and, lo and behold, here I am. How about you? How are you doing?"

Before Fern could reply, Sanne leaned across the table and grabbed Janice's hand. "Fern and me, we are happy to see you. How can three weeks be gone after the unmasking? Nearly a month, too long for no contact with a new friend. We are so worried about you. The unmasking. It was extremely horrible for you?"

Sanne's palm was hot and clammy. As soon as she tactfully could, Janice pulled her fingers out of the sticky grasp. The last thing she wanted to discuss was how she felt about the unmasking. Or anything else to do with Thalia Thespians. Or Hannah.

Fern noticed her reticence, but Sanne forged ahead. "Are you let down by the casting, like me? I want so much to be Duchess of Derry, but Hannah wants me only for the lighting."

Fern covered her lover's hand with her own and murmured a string of urgent sentences in Dutch, not bothering to translate for Janice. Sanne's eyes widened, and her cheeks flushed. She turned to Janice. "Oh, I have a mouth full of teeth, how you say? I always put my teeth in my mouth. I am too brutal, too direct. Again, I say the wrong thing at the wrong time." Earnestly she added, "But I don't want to hurt. Or be offending. Okay?"

Janice hid a smile. "I think you mean you're always putting your foot in your mouth."

Sanne smiled. "Fern is telling me to shut up my face. I should listen to her, no?"

Janice was saved the burden of responding by Kate arriving with the cappuccinos. She slid one over to Janice and sat beside her. Winking conspiratorially at her, she addressed Fern and Sanne, "Hello, girlies. We've got to stop meeting like this."

A second round of coffee and beers for the girlies later, Sanne had calmed down enough for Janice to relax. She felt better after she'd visited the tiny loo in the basement, even if it had been a hassle inserting a fresh tampon without bashing her elbow on the walls. Amazing how confined Dutch toilets were. It was as if the architects (men) never considered that women needed more than standing room only. Some toilets in cafés were so tiny, her bent knees pressed tight against the door. Perhaps Dutch women were clever contortionists and found it easy to negotiate the narrow space. Not Janice, though she'd quickly learned that going in backward saved the effort of turning.

Never mind about that. Janice was enjoying herself. The company was convivial. The Dutch had a good word for this cozy atmosphere: *gezellig*. Sanne had stopped her interrogation and, like Kate and Janice, was laughing at Fern's droll jokes.

Fern loved the laughs her jokes were getting. "Did you hear the one about the new running shoe for lesbians?" The others shook their heads, grinning in anticipation. "It's called the Dyke-y. Has an extra-long tongue and only takes one finger to get off."

Janice realized she had formed a wrong impression of Fern the first time they'd met. That snooty attitude of Fern's, thinking that she had to protect Sanne against the threat of the single lesbian. Unnecessary in Janice's case. But she'd been more put off by Fern's accent, as hoity-toity as the voice of the famous English actor Joyce Grenfell elocuting her comic monologues. Now she realized that Fern wasn't a snob. The contrast between her crude remarks and cut-glass English accent was funny enough on its own.

"Enough already," said Kate.

"Just one more," Fern protested. "This one's for you, Janice. Did you hear about the lesbian who was having an affair behind her lover's back?" Janice shook her head obediently. "She soon learned you can't have your Kate and Edith too."

Keeping a straight face, Janice pretended to be confused. "Who's Edith?"

Kate roared with laughter and rested her arm possessively on Janice's shoulder. Janice leaned into the arm without thinking, enjoying its comfortable weight. She felt good in this *gezellig* company. Sanne, Fern, and especially Kate treated her as if she belonged.

Fern proved the point. "Janice, come to the *Vrouwendansfeest* with us."

"What? A dance party for women? Is that right?"

Fern nodded. "*Feest*, yes, it's nearly the same word as our 'festivity.' July twelfth is women's night. COC dances are always fun. You must come."

"Next Saturday?"

Kate nodded. "Do come. We'll dance the night away."

Janice smiled, thinking of the Michael Jackson track. "You want to rock with me?"

Kate played along, "And not stop till we get enough? Sounds good to me." Taking her arm back, she added lightly, "How about it? The three of us are going. It's not as if you won't know anyone there. Do you know the COC? It's quite near here."

"What does COC stand for?"

"Dutch lesson?" Kate was teasing. "It stands for *Cultuur en Ontspanningscentrum*, means Center for Culture and Leisure. It's the oldest gay association in the world. The organizers are right-on political and do lots for our community, but COC discos are always fun. How about it, are you coming or not?"

Janice took her time answering. This Friday afternoon she was meeting Colin off the bus from West Berlin. He'd stay at Negy's and take off for London and Edinburgh early next morning. That meant she'd be free, as usual, on Saturday evening. Going to this dance sounded like it could supply the distraction she'd need from the pain of having to say good-bye to Colin. One last night of freedom because, of course, she reminded herself with a guilty tremor, she had to turn herself in the morning after.

Or would she? Maybe. She thought of M&M, grinning hugely, delighted that she was going to be their dishwasher. Oh god, let's not forget them. She couldn't let M&M down. She had to tell them about Kobus. It was different with Negy. He didn't care a hoot, wouldn't lose a moment's sleep if she never came back to the hostel. Poor Dalida would have to shoulder the burden of housekeeping on her own again. He wouldn't care.

But M&M would care if she didn't turn up. If she left without saying why she had to go. She'd have to give them a reason. But Janice realized for the nth time, she couldn't. If she told M&M the truth, that she was a killer, they'd be shocked. She'd have to postpone turning herself in. Yet again. There. Decision made. She had to stay free, at least until she'd sorted M&M out. That meant she would be free to go to the dance, no strings attached.

Chapter 57

Oh goddess, this was grubby work. Janice had forgotten how messy restaurant dishwashing was and didn't like it. But she couldn't complain. She'd fought for this job, and it was going to pay hard cash, enough to get by on if she was careful. How clever she was to arrange work that not only included a free bed but, thanks to the kindness of M&M, free dinners from Monday to Saturday too. She'd still get breakfast on Sundays because she had to do the hostel dishes, but that left only one meal to buy in a whole week. How good was that?

It was cramped in the dishwashing area at the end of the kitchen, a narrow galley set behind a half wall that kept her out of sight of the diners. The long steel counter held three sinks, the smallest for hosing leftovers and two bigger ones for washing and rinsing. Beside the sinks was space enough for her drying rack and stacks of clean plates, and Marcella's ever-growing pile of dirty dishes.

Following the first day of trial, error, and discovery, Janice had developed a routine. She worked efficiently, and judging by M&M's expressions, they were pleased with how fast she was. Janice didn't like washing dishes, but she was good at it. By Friday afternoon, she could do the job blind, leaving her free to think about Colin (not Kate).

* * *

M&M let her go early that afternoon so that Janice could get to Marnixstraat on time to meet the bus. Colin made her wait, as usual. His Royal Bitchness did like making a grand entrance, so what else was new? Now he made sure that he was the last passenger to disembark. He stepped carefully to the ground, gripping the door rail and clutching his commodious travel bag. Janice sensed something was wrong. Colin was wearing a baseball cap, of all touristy things. The brim hid his face, and instead of looking out for her, he kept his head bowed. Colin acting the coy damsel? Now that did make a change.

Janice brushed past a couple of straggling passengers. "Your Royal Bitchness, I presume." She was about to add to add another bright cliché but stopped herself when Colin raised his head. The sight of his face made Janice stagger. Those crusty sores Colin had near his mouth when he'd left Amsterdam had grown into a great lump that nearly covered his cheek. The rest of his face was dotted by nasty little red spots. This couldn't be measles, surely?

In the time he'd been away, he'd managed to lose weight. Chiseled cheekbones, thinner lips, longer chin. The knuckles looked huge in his hands. He'd never been fat but now he was gaunt. His jeans sagged off his hips and his coat drooped off his shoulders. He'd gone down two sizes at least. Colin was ill. Badly ill. How could he have lost so much form in only four weeks? Full of concern, Janice reached out to hold his shoulder.

Colin shuddered at her touch. "Lassie," he whispered. "Now you know."

"Know what?" Janice didn't understand. What had made him unwell?

"This." He waved a hand at his face.

At the gesture, his coat sleeve pulled up and Janice noticed a browny-pink blotch smudging the inside of his wrist. "Colin, you're speaking in riddles. Stop it. What is it?"

"It?" He smiled bravely. "Just a tiresome little something." He gave a dismissive cough. "A bit of fever and a sore throat. A spot of flu, that's all, and then this funny rash popped up."

Janice caught sight of a flash of the old Colin, but it faded quickly.

"It's nothing to worry about," he said, unconvincingly. "But just in case, I'm going home to see my family doctor. Once I get on a course of antibiotics, I'll be as right as the rain on that plain in Spain, and before you know it, I'll be back on track to finish my Grand Tour, calling in on my way to Copenhagen just to annoy you, wee lassie."

Colin was playing up his Scottish accent. Trying to distract her, Janice supposed. She gave him a dispassionate look. There was no point in interrogating him. He looked exhausted. Too tired to manage the twenty-minute hike to the hostel, even if she carried his bag for him.

"Wait here." Janice left him leaning against the bus and strode to the taxi stand on one side of the terminal. She had to get Colin to the hostel fast, to rest in her bed. She'd give up her room for him, spend the night on a bunk, no problem. She pulled open the passenger door of the first cab and told the driver to wait. Then she went back to Colin, slung an arm around his shoulder, grabbed his bag, and led him to the taxi.

"Come on, your chariot awaits."

"But no, lassie, no. This is ridiculous. It's only a wee way to the hostel. I can walk."

Ignoring his insincere protest, Janice pushed Colin onto the backseat and took her place beside the driver. Seven minutes later the taxi deposited them in front of the hostel. Janice paid the driver a ten-guilder note. "Keep the change." Judging by the sour look on the driver's face, she'd overestimated the value of the change. Tough tippy. She had more important things to worry about.

Colin refused the arm she offered to help him up the hostel steps. "Stop fussing, ye blathering hen. I may be a wee bit fatigued, but I'm not a fucking disabled person."

Janice put up her hands, backing off. Colin was proud, she knew, and he wouldn't want a show of weakness in front of Negy. Carrying his bag for him, she followed him in and then stood aside in silence while he dealt with Negy and paid for his bunk for the night. Only when they were walking down the hall did she speak. "You're not sleeping in the dorm."

"What?" Colin's eyes were dark hollows in his haggard face. "Where else?"

"My room, so you can rest in peace." Colin raised an eyebrow at her word choice, which Janice ignored. "You'll need a proper sleep if you're going to catch the bus in the morning."

Colin objected, but Janice refused to give in. Leading him, she said, "Walk this way."

"Walk this way?" Colin hunched his back and put on an exaggerated limp, imitating the silly walk Marty Feldman did in the film *Young Frankenstein.*

"You eejit." Janice had to laugh. His Royal Bitchness wasn't totally gone. She hoped.

Chapter 58

"Was your letter total bullshit or what?" Janice leaned forward on her desk chair, caught in a late beam of sunlight spilling through the window. Colin lay in her bed, his thin limbs barely making an impression on the sheet pulled up to his chin. With his wispy hair combed flat, his high forehead, big eyes, and huge hands clutching the sheet, he looked like the Tenniel drawing of Humpty Dumpty before the great fall, all head and no body.

"Total bullshit?" Colin raised his eyebrow in theatrical shock. "Now come on, lassie. Don't you believe I met David Bowie?" He turned his head from her piercing eyes. "Well, nearly. I did see him across a crowded room in the disco."

He stretched uneasily and the sheet slid down, revealing a scattering of bright red bumps on his bare chest. He caught Janice staring, pulled up the sheet, and sighed heavily. "My letter wasn't total rubbish. It all happened the way I said it did, but I did shuffle the timing." Janice gave an inquiring look. "The first week I had such a gay time with those Ger-mans"—he put a corny emphasis on the second syllable—"and their ever so tasty bratwurst. I tell you. A diet of sausage was never so good. Fabulous. But then, silly me, I caught this strange flu that's doing the rounds and got really tired. Spent the rest of the time in bed."

Janice was horrified. "You mean you've been sick all this time? All alone in Berlin?"

"West Berlin. And don't get your knickers in a twist. I wasn't on my own in the hostel. I was sharing a room with three noble men, all English and gay-gay-gay. They looked after me, got me takeaways, cough drops, and skin cream when this silly rash started, that sort of thing. Come off it, lassie. I wasn't doing a Mimi, warbling a glorious aria while dying of tuberculosis in a bohemian garret. There was nothing Puccini about it. Au contraire, I was in good company. Gays are good at sticking together." He smiled. "As you and I know well."

Janice didn't know what to say. Her mind was racing with indignant thoughts. How promiscuous Colin was. Doing it with strangers night after night. All those visits to gay saunas and public toilets on the beat, "going cottaging" they called it. How often had he put himself at risk of catching a disease? That so-called cold sore on his face just had to be contagious herpes, and more than likely he'd have sores on his genitals as well. What a foolish person Colin was. Janice was furious at him, so she kept her mouth shut, afraid she'd sound judgmental if she spoke.

Colin went on, as if he knew what she was thinking but chose to ignore it. "I would have come back sooner, but all the Amsterdam buses were full, so I had to wait to get here."

Janice stood. "Well, you're here now." She checked her watch. "It's getting close to seven. Time for munchies. What do you feel like eating? Shall I nip down to M&M's and bring us back a pizza with extra salami and olives on top? They give personnel a discount, you know." Colin raised a questioning eyebrow. "Oh, didn't I tell you? I work afternoons washing dishes at M&M's, and lookee here"—she pulled her wallet out of her pocket and withdrew a wad of notes—"they pay me in cash. It's my treat."

Colin slid down in the bed. "*Liebchen*, you've made me an offer I canna refuse. I'll just have a wee nap till you get back. Okay?" He yawned deeply.

* * *

That night the air in the dorm was stifling. There was no window to open. Besides that, the snores and smells of the other users did nothing to lighten Janice's mood. She was not used to the dorm, no longer able to trust strangers with the vulnerability, the little death of sleep. She'd been spoiled by the weeks of privacy she'd enjoyed in her room. No doubt His Royal Bitchness was relishing the peace of her private space while she lay awake here on this public bunk, stuck between a couple of middle-aged New Zealanders and a young man from Leeds.

Kate came from Leeds. Janice wasn't going to think about her now as she tossed on the sagging mattress. She felt confined by the tight sleeping bag after the luxury of being able to spread her legs under cool sheets. She was worried sick about Colin, about how ill he was, and how well he would manage the rest of the long journey back home. The bus ride to London was only half the distance. There was still the long train journey to Edinburgh.

Janice hoped that someone from his family would come to meet him at the station. Did he have a family? He never talked about his parents or siblings, or anyone you could call family, apart from the family doctor he'd mentioned when he got off the bus. All at once, Janice realized she knew nothing about Colin, besides the name of the suburb where he'd grown up, and even that she'd forgotten as soon as he'd told her. After they'd met and introduced themselves, they'd never dwelled on their pasts, choosing to live in the here and now. Not interested in talking about her own parents and not keen to tell Colin about Kobus, it had suited Janice not to divulge her background. It suited Colin too, but now Janice regretted not knowing more about him.

Well, there was a simple answer to that. She'd just have to get to know him better. She would visit him at St. Andrews, where he'd get on with his art history degree as soon as he recovered from this flu. She'd save the pennies she earned at M&M's and invest in a ticket to Edinburgh. One-way for starters. Scotland belonged to the European Community, and with her Dutch passport she'd have no problem with visas or work permits. It would be easy to find a job. Janice thrummed with excitement. A future in bonny Scotland beckoned. She would make a new life there, near Colin. They would look after each other again, the wee lassie and His Royal Bitchness. What a great pair.

Janice pulled herself back from this fantasy. Kobus and all that. She couldn't ignore the evil niggles of guilt that always reminded her that she had to turn herself in. Colin would just have to visit her, locked up in prison. No doubt after conviction at the Old Bailey, she'd be carted off to Holloway, the prison for women. Wasn't it somewhere in London? Colin wouldn't mind coming down to see her in midterm breaks. He'd love to see her, she knew, even in prison. She could look forward to his visits. She was getting ahead of herself. First, she had to see him off to London. Rubbing her eyes, Janice wished frantically for sleep and hoped just as badly that she would wake early enough to get him to the station on time.

Chapter 59

They'd agreed to leave her door unlocked so that Janice could come in unhindered to wake him. Colin was feverish when she entered. A lock of strawberry-blond hair flopped over his eyes. It was as greasy as the sweat filming the livid bumps on his naked chest. Janice felt her throat constrict. Colin's body was limp, as inert as Ariel lying dead on the road and Kobus lying dead at the foot of the stairs. Colin, the living dead. She closed the door gently, but the squeak of the hinge woke him.

"Rise-and-shine time?" Colin sounded frail. He stretched gingerly. "I've been tossing all night. Thought tomorrow would never come."

"Oh, it's all the same day." Fear tightened Janice's voice, raising the pitch to chipmunk level. She tried to be cool. "Just get up, you lazy bugger."

Still sleepy, Colin made no remark at her weird voice. He heaved himself up to perch on the edge of the bed, casually draping the sheet over himself.

Janice couldn't help noticing a bulge tenting his crotch. Gracious me, he was sick as hell yet still managed to get a hard-on. Morning wood. She turned discreetly away. The last thing she wanted was to embarrass him. "I'll leave you to get dressed." She glanced at her watch. "Not quite six. You'll have the showers to yourself."

"Don't think I'll bother, lassie. I'll only be stinky poo again by the time I get to London, but if I'm lucky, anyone forced to sit beside me on the bus will have a cold and can't smell."

"Who nose?" quipped Janice. "You might be lucky. No, they would be the lucky ones. Okay, whatever. I'm going down to reception to phone a taxi to take you to the station."

"What do you mean, taxi? You're not coming with me? No fluttering farewells, no lingering good-byes? No ever so poignant, brief encounter on the station platform, with the wee lassie left waving sadly behind as the Magic Bus drives me off into the sunrise?"

"Yeah sorry, no extended exit." Janice didn't want to offend if she could avoid it. She couldn't tell Colin that he wouldn't manage the walk. He was still exhausted, even after this night's rest in her bed. "You know I can't get away from the hostel. I've got to do the breakfast shift and I can't be late. We'll have to take our leave downstairs." Her voice trailed off. "I'm so sorry. I've got to work."

"How could I forget? *Arbeit uber alles*, aye? Work comes before friendship."

Janice ignored the sarcasm. His Royal Bitchness was pulling out all the manipulative stops, and it wasn't fair. But she understood why he was lashing out. She'd be upset too if she were as sick as he seemed to be. She was letting Colin down.

Thirty minutes later, with the taxi's diesel engine rumbling beside them, they exchanged a last hug. Janice couldn't bear to say good-bye. "See you," she said, shaking her hair over eyes that threatened to spill tears. Janice mumbled into his shoulder, "Better get better, you eejit."

Colin stepped out of her grasp. "What do you mean, better? I'm already the best."

Janice grinned. The Royal Bitchness may be down, but he wasn't out. She stood motionless on the stoop long after the taxi had driven across the bridge and disappeared down the other side of the Keizersgracht.

Later that morning, Janice did her work on autopilot, ignoring Dalida, wrapped in a cocoon of silence, closing herself off from the pain of losing another friend. First Ariel. Then Kobus. Now Colin. At least she wasn't responsible for him getting sick. That was all his own damn stupid fault. Before heading over to the pizzeria, she nipped up to her room and stripped the bed. She bundled the sheets in a pillowcase and dropped that off at the nearest laundromat. She'd pick up the pressed results at the end of her shift at M&M's. Striding along the canals, not giving in to the weights in her legs doing their best to slow her down, Janice swore. "No offense, Your Royal Bitchness, but I must have clean sheets. I won't risk catching your flu or the rash that goes with it. Simple hygiene." She stopped on the next bridge, turned around to look up at the eggshell-blue canopy of the Westerkerk tower, and sent a prayer up to the heavens. "Please, please let Colin get well soon." *Who knows? Someone might be listening.*

* * *

That Saturday evening, out with the girls in the COC, Janice used her sleeve to smudge the sheen of sweat off her forehead. Dancing to disco music in synchrony with energetic Kate was fun, moving in time with the relentless rhythm of Patti Labelle and her soul sisters chanting, "Lady Marmalade." Janice had been far better at English than French at school, but even she knew what the chorus line meant. The idea was not without its appeal, especially with this sexy partner strutting before her.

In the crowded gloom of the *danszaal*, the huge, high-ceilinged room the COC used for parties, Kate stood out. She had on a cool white outfit, muslin tunic and flared pants, a bit old-fashioned these days, but who cared about that? As she danced, her golden hair caught splinters of light reflected by the mirror ball above their heads. The flickering light and white clothing made her look angelic. Heaven on a stick.

Finally, Lady Marmalade served her last cup of milky coffee, and the song ended. Kate twirled with a flourish and clasped Janice in a stylish ballroom finish. Janice was acutely aware of a fluid pull of magnetism drawing her deeper into the snug embrace. She was drowning in desire. Too much. She pulled away, wiping her forehead as an excuse. "Sorry, don't want to sweat all over you," she mumbled in the brief silence before the DJ turned up the volume on the next track.

Kate released her. "You mean glow." She smiled but Janice frowned, so Kate went on to explain. "Horses sweat, men perspire, and women merely glow. Isn't that the old saying?"

Janice laughed. "Don't tell me, you're a horse in the Chinese horoscope."

"No way. I'm a tiger."

"Oh. That explains why you roar when you laugh."

Now Errol Brown was warbling, "You Sexy Thing." Janice realized that Kate couldn't hear her over the music. It was too damn loud in here. Hot Chocolate was all she needed. Not. She was flushed and needed a break from so many people in the dark. Bringing her mouth close to Kate's ear, she asked something.

Instead of answering, Kate took Janice's hand and led her out of the *danszaal*, forging an erratic path between gyrating dancers, past Fern and Sanne grinding in a clinch, through the quieter bar area, and out into the foyer. It was cooler here and Janice flapped the lapels of her shirt gratefully. A line of women snaked along the wall, heading toward the restroom. Janice and Kate joined the end of the queue and shuffled patiently along until it was their turn. Janice used the toilet and then joined Kate at the washbasins. Ignoring the chattering of the women behind them, they washed their hands and Janice splashed water over her face. Ah, that was better.

Looking up, Janice met Kate's eyes in the mirror. Kate was smiling warmly, but in that never-ending instant, Janice felt pinned to the spot by the searching gaze, pried open and vulnerable. She didn't know if she wanted to be revealed as honestly as Kate was seeing her now. It felt as if Kate could suss her out, detect her secret soul, and know exactly what she was thinking and feeling, just the way Colin always could. Her face fell.

Kate noticed at once. "What's wrong?"

Janice tried to smile but didn't succeed. Kate took her hand again as if it were the most natural thing in the world and led Janice to a corner of the bar in the room beside the disco, as far away as possible from the din. There was space for them on a sofa, beside two Dutch women. Smiling politely, the couple shuffled over, and Janice collapsed onto soft cushions, easing her legs under a low coffee table. Kate remained standing, acknowledged the couple with a nod, and asked, "What can I get you?"

"Can you stretch to a whiskey? Ballantine's, if they have it. Neat, please, no ice."

"Oh, you're on the hard stuff?"

Janice was embarrassed. "Sorry, I don't like beer. Or wine. I know French wine is delicious, but I'm not used to drinking it. It was too expensive for me to buy in New Zealand. The crappy bull's blood I could afford to drink is just awful. Sour hangover stuff. I know it's different these days. Kiwi wine is supposed to be getting really good, but I haven't developed a taste for it. Someone introduced me to whiskey in London. I know it's expensive, but I like it. Sorry." Janice was blethering, as Colin would put it, and snapped her mouth shut.

"No problem. Neat Ballantine's coming up, not shaken or stirred, my lady."

"Am I your lady now?"

"Just a figure of speech." Kate flashed a smile and headed off to the bar.

Janice leaned against the comfortable arm of the sofa, creating more space between herself and the Dutch pair. Room enough for Kate, for when she came back with the drinks.

Chapter 60

Kate hummed along with Rod Stewart's raspy voice grating away in the *danszaal* on "Da Ya Think I'm Sexy?" Smiling flirtatiously, she handed Janice a tall glass full of ice cubes drowning a shallow layer of liquid. Janice had specifically said, no ice. Kobus always said that ice bruised good whiskey. It wouldn't do the Ballantine's any favors.

Kate noticed her downturned mouth and guessed why. "The woman behind the bar filled the glass with ice before I could stop her. Just habit, I suppose. No one drinks hard stuff without ice."

"Okay." Janice took a polite sip of watery whiskey. It was too cold but tasted good.

"My pleasure, sugar." Smiling at the Dutch couple, Kate squeezed into the space beside Janice and draped her free arm across the back of the sofa so that her fingertips rested on Janice's shoulder. She tapped Janice in time with Rod Stewart wailing in the background, still asking the world if he was sexy. "It's true what Stewart says about blondes." Janice was mystified by the allusion. "This song," Kate explained. "It's from his hit album *Blondes Have More Fun*, and being a sexy blonde myself, I couldn't agree more."

Colin had strawberry-blond hair. He wasn't having any fun.

Kate noticed Janice's mournful face and instantly turned serious. "What's the matter? You look too glum for words. What's up?" She stopped tapping and drew Janice close.

Janice relaxed into the hug, relishing the softness of Kate's breast. She loved the way Kate's Yorkshire accent stretched the vowel in "glum" and made it sound more like "gloom." Recovered after a while, Janice leaned on the arm of the sofa. She looked into eyes brimming with concern and knew she could trust this kind woman. "I had to say good-bye to my best friend this morning and I don't know if I'll ever see him again."

"The gay guy from work, the one who lives with you in the hostel?"

"Colin." Janice nodded. "He went off to West-Berlin and stayed here last night on his way home to Edinburgh. It was horrible seeing how he looks now. Terribly ill. Caught some strange flu that's tired him out and covered his whole body in a rash. Looks contagious. I don't know for sure, but I think it's something he got from cottaging. Doing the gay scene. You know queens, they're always so bloody promiscuous. Stupid bastard." Scalding tears ran down her face. "I had to work in the hostel this morning and couldn't take him to the bus station. I couldn't see him off. I wasn't there for him. I let him down."

Kate plucked the glass from Janice's grasp before she could spill whiskey and set it on the coffee table. Gathering Janice in her arms, she murmured soothing sounds that told Janice she was safe with a person secure enough to let her be sad and not try to cheer her up. *Oh, how kind she is.*

"That's enough." Kate untangled herself and massaged her own shoulder.

Janice couldn't keep up with the sudden switch. What made Kate cut off so radically? She'd felt comforted by the embrace and wasn't ready for it to end. She was mourning Colin. He was ill, for god's sake. But before she could protest, Kate put her thoughts into words.

"Listen, you. I'm not being cruel or anything. I mean, I don't mean to be. There's nothing you can do about Colin. Be realistic. You say he's sick. More than likely, he hasn't got health insurance in Berlin, Amsterdam, whatever, so he has to go home to Scotland to get treated. He's looking after himself. And you're going to miss him—" Janice wanted to interrupt. She missed him already. Badly. "—while he's away, but that's no reason to wallow in misery. Come on now, cheer up, chum. Colin will recover. You'll see him again as soon as he gets better. He'll be back here in a jiffy, no doubt. Put him out of your mind. For us, for now, it's still early. And remember your promise? We're gonna rock the night away."

Kate sprang from the sofa and hauled a stunned Janice up beside her. Making her leave her drink behind, Kate led her back into the disco, threading a path through the crowd of dancers to the dark corner where Sanne and Fern were still locked in a passionate clinch.

Kate patted them on their shoulders and the couple jumped apart. "Only us!" yelled Kate into their startled faces over the sound of Michael Jackson crooning "Rock With You." Recognizing the track, Kate roared with laughter. "That DJ's got perfect timing. Come on, dance with me."

Janice gave in to the music, rocking the night away with Kate, with Sanne and Fern prancing beside them. The two couples danced in a circle, facing inward, doing their best to outdo each other's moves. Janice held her own, showing off how well she could dance.

* * *

Goodness gracious, Jones. Talk about extended exits. The closing note of "La Vie en rose" held on forever. By the time Grace Jones ended her final ah-gasm, Janice wanted to escape.

Kate leaned in close. "Can't take the good life, huh?"

Janice shook her head. She was enjoying herself with Kate, and Sanne and Fern, but enough was enough and she'd had it. She glanced at her wrist, frowning to read her watch in the dark. "What's the time?"

"Time to come home with me."

Kate's voice was loud in her ear. Janice stepped out of range of the magnetic force drawing her inexorably closer. The whole evening had been building up to this moment and now it had come. It was true, she had to admit it. Janice would like nothing better than to go home with Kate. Janice wanted Kate as much as Kate wanted her. There was just one teensy problem. Waving at Sanne and Fern to gain their attention, Janice pointed at the door to show she was leaving. They blew kisses at her before merging in a clinch again. Donna Summer sang it for them: "Love to love you, baby."

"Answer my question." Kate smiled, reached out, and tapped Janice's nose.

Janice quivered at the touch. "Didn't think you were asking, sounded more like an order. Here's your answer: I can't come home with you. I've got to make the hostel breakfast. It starts at sparrow's fart, even on Sunday, and Negy will sack me if I don't turn up. What time is it?"

Kate pressed a little button and her digital watch lit up. "Only twelve thirty. Past your pumpkin time, Cinderella. Don't tell me the hostel has a curfew. You must have a key."

"Well, there is a curfew. Negy locks up at one and, no, I don't have a key. He won't let me have one." Janice sighed. "I need to leave now if I'm to get back before he locks the door. I've got to walk because some fool stole my bike last Monday. I've got to go."

"If a girl's gotta go … let me go with you. I'll give you a lift."

"Seriously? You want to come with me to the hostel?"

Kate put on a serious face. "If the mountain won't come to Muhammad."

Chapter 61

Half asleep on his feet, Negy was on guard as usual. As Janice pushed open the hostel door, he looked up from whatever he was playing with on the counter and spotted Kate. "You're not a guest. Too late to check in tonight. Sorry."

He wasn't sorry at all, the bastard. Janice stepped aside so that he could see Kate properly and realize she wasn't a tourist. "You've got it wrong," she said. "Kate's given me a lift home. She's not looking to stay the night." Janice hesitated, not knowing what else to say.

Smiling confidently, Kate took over. Whatever she rattled off in perfect Dutch charmed Negy. He leered back at her. "*Ik sluit af in vijf minuten.*" Noting the confusion on Janice's face, he translated. "I lock up in five minutes."

Gathering that Kate had told Negy they were going to her room, Janice took off down the corridor before he could stop them. Kate kept up with her easily, even when she strode up the flight of stairs two steps at a time. Pausing to catch her breath before she turned the key in her door, Janice mumbled, "Come on in. Ain't much to look at, but it's home sweet home."

Closing the door, avoiding the harsh overhead light, Janice switched on the bedside lamp. In its soft glow, Kate looked around, registering the small room. Pointing at the pillows on the bed, she said, "What's that teddy doing here? Didn't think you'd be into fluffy toys."

"Well, I'm not." Janice tried not to sound defensive. Picking up the little bear, she said, "This is His Royal Bitchness, Sir Camp Bell the Bearest—Bitchy Bear for short. A small but perfectly formed souvenir Colin brought back for me from Berlin. Apparently, it's the city mascot." She tucked it carefully in the pocket of her rucksack. She didn't want any witnesses to what was going to happen next, least of all any painful reminders of Colin. Stepping toward Kate, she said shyly, "*Voulez-vous* kisser *avec moi?*"

"*T'embrasser? Mais bien sûr.* Thought you'd never ask."

"Shut up and kiss me." At once bold, Janice didn't mind Kate correcting her French. Janice didn't mind anything about this woman. Not in this mindless moment. Nothing in her life had ever felt so right as standing here kissing Kate, at last. Janice tasted the salt on Kate's lips and knew her own lips tasted salty.

Kate sighed, breaking off the kiss. "That tastes like more, as the Dutch would say."

Janice cupped Kate's face, looked deeply into her tawny eyes. This tall woman was the perfect height. Ariel had been tiny, Hannah was small too, and Kobus? Well, he didn't count. But Kate was only half a forehead shorter. Janice wasn't used to being able to stand and look across at a (dare she say it?) lover eye-to-eye like this.

Observing how Janice was studying her, Kate said softly, "We're equal, but different."

It was as if Kate could read her mind. Janice shook her head. "Kiss me some more." And she dove in for a second taste of heaven.

But Kate stepped aside, thwarting the kiss before it could start. "No more, more, more. We can't get carried away now, much as I'd like us to." She held Janice at arm's length. "I told that Negy chap we'd be straight back down with my book." Her eyes danced at Janice's confusion. "I said you'd borrowed one of my books and I was only coming up to get it. Have you got one spare that I can wave in his face on the way out?" She looked around the room again. "Now I've seen where you sleep, I'd better go."

Janice was desperate to hide her disappointment. Her legs were trembling from the first thrilling kiss, and lightning strikes of desire were flashing through her veins. How on earth was she supposed to think in this aroused condition? How could Kate be rational and regain composure so quickly? It was beyond Janice. Kate was unpredictable. She could change gear in an instant and Janice couldn't keep up. Now she could only obey. Shaking her hair over her face, she went to the desk and grabbed a paperback at random. "Here, take this."

Kate read the spine. "Oh, you're a Ruth Rendell fan too?"

In silence, hand in hand, they walked downstairs. Janice was acutely aware of the click of their heels on the marble floor of the hall and tried to tread softly. The reception area was in darkness. Only the low-wattage exit sign above the front door shone in the gloom. At the end of the counter was the door to Negy and Dalida's private quarters. A line of light flared from under the door. Before Janice could decide what to do, the light snapped off.

"Negy's gone to bed." Janice whispered the obvious. She tugged at the handle of the front door. It refused to open. "Bloody buggery, he's damn well locked us in for the night."

Kate rattled the door handle herself. "That's a fire hazard." She sizzled. "Hotels can lock people out, but they're not allowed to lock people in at night. It's dangerous. It must be against the law." She turned the handle the other way and pulled hard. The door shifted. It wasn't locked after all. Janice felt the door budge against her palm. She didn't want Kate to leave and pushed the door shut.

"Oh no, you're trapped." She leaned against the door to keep it shut. "Negy must have forgotten all about you. And your book I'm supposed to have borrowed."

Kate's eyes gleamed in the low light. Her dawning smile told Janice that she chose to play along. "Dearie me. I'm locked in. What next?"

"Do you want me to get Negy to let you out? He'll be furious if we disturb him."

Kate leaned against the door too, turned her head to whisper, "He'd be angry if you did. I wouldn't dare get him out of bed if I were you."

"You're so right. I wouldn't dare either if I were you."

Kate gave Janice a long, slow look. "Well, what would you dare, if you were me?"

Janice sighed deeply, intensely aware of her thudding heart. So loud. Surely Kate could hear her heartbeat. "If I were you," she said deliberately, "I'd dare go back upstairs."

"And stay the night?" Kate's wild smile lit the dark. "Your dare is my command."

Chapter 62

Soft light streamed through the open window and fell in a swath over the long-limbed women stretched across the bed. Kate took up most of the space, lying near the middle of the bed, with Janice curved around her on the window side. No blanket, only the sheet that lay tangled under their feet. Half awake, beginning to feel the dawn chill raise goosebumps on her skin, Janice carefully retrieved her arm from under Kate's neck. Drowsily scratching a mosquito bite on her left breast, she was about to pull the sheet up when the door slammed open.

Negy stood in the doorway, sturdy legs splayed like goalposts. His jaw dropped abruptly at the sight of two naked women on the small double bed. Oblivious to the intrusion, Kate snuffled a breathy little snore, turned onto her back, and opened her legs wide. Negy could see right up her crotch. His mouth formed a huge O of indignation. His chest heaved as he searched for words to express his shock. Janice pulled at the tangled sheet, trying but not succeeding to cover Kate and herself up from the horrified gaze.

The jerky movement woke Kate. Rubbing her eyes, she saw Negy standing in the doorway and instantly registered the situation. Sitting up, giving Janice a confident pat on the thigh, she addressed Negy in Dutch. After babbling cheerfully, she turned to Janice. "I just asked your boss if he slept well. Like we did after making luscious lady love all night long. Lovely, wasn't it, my lady?" And she planted a big kiss on Janice's unprepared lips.

Negy was apoplectic, mouth groping for breath like a fish drowning in air. Shooting him a livid glance of her own, Janice reached down and, with a violent tug, released the sheet to fully cover Kate and herself. How dare he perve on Kate like this? How dare he perve on her? Janice was shaking, not just with surprise at receiving Kate's shameless kiss, but with anger at Negy. Her thoughts raced. Seeing the key in his hairy fist confirmed her impression. Janice had long suspected that he used his passkey to check her room behind her back, whenever he felt like it. Now she knew for sure. How dare he spy on her? How dare he burst in. It would have been normal good manners for him to knock first. He'd stormed inside as if he owned the place.

Oops. Negy did own the place. He was her boss and … Janice grabbed Kate's wrist to check the time. It was after seven. Janice had slept in when she should have been up and at 'em an hour ago to help Dalida prepare the breakfasts. No wonder Negy had come to fetch her. Seeing his purpling face, she knew he was angry with her for not turning up on time. She'd let him down. She'd let Dalida down. She'd not kept her side of their bargain.

But added to his righteous anger was his obvious embarrassment at catching her with Kate in her (his) bed. Kate had just kissed her. How daring could you get? The kiss had hauled her out of the hostel closet in one giant step for lesbian-kind. There was no turning back.

Act two of the drama began in ominous silence. Instead of ear-bashing them, Negy spoke in a savage whisper. "Disgusting. Perverts," he seethed. "Shameless whores of Lesbos. Get. Out. Of. My. Hostel. Now." For good measure he added, "You filthy, dirty lesbians." Turning on his heel, jabbing his index finger at Janice, he ordered, "Pack your things. Leave my house this instant!" And he left the door wide open behind him.

Janice reached for Kate's hand under the sheet and took comfort from a reassuring squeeze. Kate's palm was cool and dry in her slithery grip. Now Janice felt as if her veins were on fire. She was boiling, frozen, engulfed in icy flames trapping her in the chasm between fight or flight. Kate's clasp told her there was no point in calling Negy back and trying to fight. No use demanding an apology for his insults, for invading their privacy. There was only flight left. She had to do what she was told and leave his hostel. Get out of here and go, go, go. But where?

Kate seemed unaffected by what had just happened. "Well, I guess that's that," she said calmly. "You're leaving." Giving Janice a brief kiss on the nose, she crossed to the door in one stride, slammed it shut, didn't bother turning the key, and came back to where Janice was now sitting, frowning, on the edge of the bed.

"Come on, chook, don't be glum. It's not the end of the world. If you ask me, you're well rid of the homophobic bastard. Now, let's get you packed and out of here."

Kate's matter-of-fact response upset Janice. She wailed piteously, overwhelmed by a wave of anxiety, "Where can I go? I've got nowhere to go."

"Don't you start imitating Negy." Kate grinned, but the smile didn't reach her eyes. "How melodramatic can you get? Shades of Big Daddy telling daughter dearest, 'Never darken my doorstep again.'" She gathered Janice in a firm hug. Letting go quickly, she added, "Come on, chook, buck up. This is no time to wallow in the dumps. You're not a damsel in distress. You're a strong woman with options. And the first is to stay at my place until you get yourself sorted."

Packing didn't take long, because Janice had few possessions. Or so she thought when they started going through her stuff. She'd forgotten that, when she'd arrived in Amsterdam five months ago, she'd had few books and no reading lamp. Not all of her books would fit into the rucksack now. She had to discard some.

Kate helped make the choice. Casting an eye over the row of secondhand paperbacks lined up on the desk, she picked out six. "You can leave these by Ruth Rendell and P. L. Travers. They're in my bookcase if you want to reread them."

"Whatever." Janice was subdued after Negy's high drama. She stopped folding clothes and made sure that Colin's complete works of Noel Coward went in the rucksack, along with Kobus's picture books and her clothes squashed higgledy-piggledy inside. She kept Bitchy Bear on top so that he could breathe. Waiting for Kate to look away, she gave the toy a little stroke. How could she even think of leaving him behind?

At last, it was done. A few worn out T-shirts and the discarded paperbacks were left to languish on the desk. The hostel's pillows and unfolded blanket lay where they'd landed after she'd stripped the bed. The room looked gaunt, hollow. Unoccupied.

Kate went ahead, taking the lamp. Janice strapped her rolled-up sleeping bag onto the rucksack, heaved it onto her shoulders, and turned for a last look. The dusty curtain billowed in the breeze wafting through the open window. She'd never got around to washing it.

"Bye-bye, room," she said. It had been fine while it lasted. She wouldn't miss the nightly torture of mosquitos, but there were worse things than having a canal address in downtown Amsterdam. Catching up with Kate in reception, Janice sighed with a mixture of relief and regret. Negy was conspicuously absent. Given the chance, Janice would have thanked him for having her (not). Which reminded her of something. She asked Kate, "Do you have one of your business cards on you?"

Kate fossicked in her wallet. "You're in luck. Why do you want it? Forwarding address?"

Janice nodded, took the offered card, reached over the counter for a ballpoint, and crossed out Kate's name and the firm's logo and address on the front. Scribbling her own name on the back, above Kate's home address, she left the card and her room key on the countertop. "You never know," she said bleakly. "Colin might write to me here, and Negy might need to know where I am. Chances are, he won't throw the card out, not straightaway."

Kate looked at her impassively and made no comment.

Out on the street, Kate unlocked her bicycle. Janice waited, laden down by the rucksack and cradling the lamp in one arm. With everything she was carrying, she'd never fit, sitting sideways on the carrier of Kate's bike.

"We'll walk," said Kate, slinging the lamp over the handlebar. "Dump your gear on the carrier. Don't lug it yourself."

Looking ahead, no turning back, the women set off on the two-mile trek to the Roelof Hartplein, walking on either side of the bike, balancing Janice's world between them.

Chapter 63

"Welcome to my humble abode." Kate stopped the bike a block up from the café on Roelof Hartplein and pointed to one of two identical doors in a shallow tiled portico of a terraced house. Like all the other doors in the row, these were painted a glossy dark green. The houses were a uniform height, five-stories tall, and all had attic windows topped by solid beams.

Kate noticed Janice looking up. "That beam is for a pulley contraption. People use them to hoist furniture upstairs," she explained. "The stairwells in these old terrace houses are too narrow and steep for moving furniture easily. This row of houses was built in 1900 and, believe me, the ceilings and walls are paper-thin. So bloody thin I can hear Coby coughing her head off." Kate's eyebrows lifted in surprise. "Talk of the devil, here she comes now."

Janice turned to see a woman walking toward them. There was something familiar about her. Janice knew she'd seen her before. Then she remembered. This was Kate's nice neighbor, the one who'd brought her lunch in to work. A real chatterbox. The same woman she'd seen nattering away at Kate after their meeting in the café down the road. Good old Coby, yes. Talkative as hell.

Stopping alongside them, Coby burst into a garrulous stream of Dutch, as if she knew what Janice was thinking and wanted to prove her right, all the while grinning from Kate to Janice and back at Kate again as if she were mightily pleased to see them together.

Kate held up a palm to halt the flow of verbiage and said something in Dutch. She turned to Janice. "I told her to shut up because you don't understand a word. Coby lives next door. She's the neighborhood watch, talks the hind leg off a donkey. Don't worry, she's harmless."

Kate had forgotten that Janice had seen Coby before. Whatever. Janice put a smile on her face. She was tired after the long trudge from the Keizersgracht, hot in her leather jacket and not in the mood to meet a talkative stranger. But her rucksack was still on the carrier of the bike, and on home territory, Kate was in charge.

For some foolish reason, Janice tried out her limited range of Dutch on Coby. "*Goede morgen, ik ben Janice.*" She held out her hand. "*Aangeraam u te ontmoesten.*"

Kate stifled a giggle. "Um, I suspect you meant to say, 'Pleased to meet you,' but you said, 'Charmed to discomfort you,' actually." She swapped a warm glance with Coby.

Janice felt her cheeks flush and shook her hair over her face.

Coby beamed up at Janice, unoffended. "Good morning, Janice." She pronounced the name Jan-ease. "Sorry, my English is evil. Not like my sister in London. She speak like a mother." Groping for the word, Coby trailed off.

Kate helped. "She means her sister speaks English like it's her mother tongue."

Janice took Coby's hand and gave it a firm shake. Coby wouldn't let go. Instead, she grabbed Kate's hand as well and let fly with another round of voluble Dutch. As she spoke, her gaze flitted from one woman to the other, and onto the rucksack perched on the bike.

Janice's mind drifted. The only word she recognized in the entire tirade was *pot*. Although she still wasn't sure what it meant, she did know it meant something entirely different in Dutch than the thing you cooked with in English. Words that sounded alike could be false friends, liable to turn and bite you on the bum with embarrassment if you didn't watch out.

When Coby finally wound down, Kate disconnected her hand from Coby's and helped Janice retrieve her own. Giving Coby a wink, she said to Janice, "Gracious me, she does go on a bit, doesn't she? I won't bother translating every word. Boils down to how glad she is to see I've found myself a girlfriend. She likes the look of you, thinks you'll be good for me. She thinks it's really time I settled down. I should be a good dyke and do that with you."

Janice's mouth dropped. "She knows you're a lesbian?" What she really meant to ask was did Coby know that Janice was a lesbian. Janice didn't think she looked butch or gave off dyke-ish vibes. She conveniently glossed over all the times people mistook her for a man. Strangers only called her "sir" because she was so damn tall, that's all. No doubt Coby assumed she was a lesbian by her association with Kate. *Hm. Being out of the closet to everyone on the street will take some getting used to.*

Kate smiled, as if she could guess what Janice was thinking. "Of course, she knows I'm a *pot*. We're *potten*." Registering Janice's mystified expression, she explained, "*Potten* is the plural of *pot*, which is Dutch slang for dyke. Coby's not using it in a negative sense. She's not putting us down, don't worry. She's not homophobic, and in fact, I suspect her son might be gay too."

"She's got a boy?" Janice wasn't interested, wanted only to end this encounter.

"A grown man. Left home, lives in London now." Kate gave Coby a friendly wave.

The woman took the hint, opened the door to her house, and disappeared inside. Janice unloaded her rucksack and took the lamp off the handlebar. Kate finished locking her bike, unlocked her own front door, and ushered Janice inside.

Chapter 64

Dragging the rucksack, with the lamp in the crook of her arm, Janice entered a corridor lit by a small skylight above the front door. Kate squeezed past in the narrow space and opened the door to her living room. Janice stepped inside and marveled at the height of the ceiling. With the tall windows, the high ceiling made the oblong room light and spacious. A wide sofa, strewn with cushions, squatted with its back to the windows. Between it and an ancient wingback chair was a standard lamp with an old-fashioned tasseled shade. A stack of paperbacks toppled across the low coffee table, nearly hiding a coil of soft white rope. Janice had seen one like this before. Kobus had a rope just like this one, which he used to practice his sailor's knots on. What did Kate do with hers? No time to wonder now.

"What a lovely room. You've got great taste."

"Glad you like it. I love it. I was lucky to get this place when I moved to Amsterdam. Garden flats are hen's teeth in the free sector." Janice was tired and didn't follow what Kate was saying. It must have shown. "Most Dutch people live in subsidized social housing with government-controlled rents. You have to qualify to get in, and the waiting list is as long as your legs." Kate smiled. "It's different on the open housing market, where foreigners working for the big corporations, multinationals like mine, usually end up living. Rents are not controlled in the free sector, a misnomer if ever there was one, and bloody property owners can and do demand astronomical rents. Mine is cheap compared to places closer to the city center, but I still pay a small fortune for the privilege of living here."

Janice thought of Colin reading about the squatters' riot that took place the day Queen Beatrix was crowned. "Yes, I hear that property owners are holding downtown housing to ransom, the mercenary bastards. That's why squatting is such a thing in Amsterdam."

"And in all the other big cities," Kate agreed. "Here, give me those." She took the lamp and rucksack and dumped them beside an oak cupboard standing across from the dining table at the other end of the room.

Janice took off her jacket and slung it over a chair. Kate was so kind, taking the time to explain things. Janice would have lost patience ages ago. "Hope you don't mind me asking all these questions. I'm such an ignorant idiot. I'll never get the hang of the Dutch."

Kate shrugged. "No, I don't, and yes, you will." She picked up the jacket and turned to the bedroom door, flanked on either side by bookshelves. "Now then, enough chitchat and on to practical matters. Are you feeling as mucky as I am after our long walk? How about we freshen up with a shower? And then we can have a nice hot pot of tea."

"A proper Yorkshire brew? Yes please." Janice couldn't imagine anything nicer than a hot pot of tea. Or any *pot* hotter than Kate.

Kate's bedroom had plush carpet that felt indulgently soft underfoot. The back wall was one expanse of glass—a huge sliding door that opened onto a small patio. A king-sized bed was pushed nearly up to the glass, leaving just enough space for a floor-to-ceiling curtain. Janice spied an optimistic patch of lawn in the garden. The high wooden fences on either side of the lawn were draped with lavish spreads of silver lace vine.

Kate dove across the bed to draw the curtain. It was velvet, the same rich royal blue as the duvet. Flopping onto her back, she smiled. "Only the one bed, so we'll have to share. If you don't mind." Without waiting for a laugh, she sprang up. "Come, I'll show you the rest."

Across the narrow hallway that connected the bedroom to the kitchen was the bathroom. It turned out to be a tiled cubby hole under the stairs to the second- and third-floor apartments above, holding a toilet, miniature wash basin, and tiny shower. Noting Janice's surprise, Kate said, "You'll get used to it. The Dutch had to put bathrooms in somewhere and don't waste space. All these terrace houses were built before the days of indoor plumbing, when people washed in a bathhouse up the road. It's now the Zuiderbad, a lovely pool with gorgeous mosaics. Do you like to swim? I go there once in a while."

"I'm not into indoor pools. All that nasty chlorinated water. Besides, the only thing I'm good at is breaststroke"—Janice gave a wicked grin—"and you don't need water for that."

"Naughty, naughty." Kate tapped Janice on the nose and led her back to the bedroom. "I'll let you get wet while I put on the water for tea. Towels are in there. Help yourself." She pointed to a cupboard, then ducked into the kitchen. Just as fast, her head popped back around the bedroom door. "Oh yeah, you'd better leave your clothes in here. They'll get drenched if you put them on the loo. Reminds me, lift the seat so that it stays dry. You have been warned."

Following Kate's instructions, Janice had a quick shower, enjoying the piping-hot water pounding on her back. This pressure was wonderful, stronger than what you got in the hostel.

The velvet curtain didn't let in a dot of light. As her eyes adjusted, Janice dried herself, dithering by the bed. She wanted to put on fresh clothes, but her rucksack was in the living room. Winding the wet towel around herself, she was about to fetch the bag when Kate walked in from the shower. Naked, leaving a trail of droplets on the carpet, Kate strolled to the cupboard and picked up a towel from the bottom shelf. Patting her face, she turned to peer at Janice. "You're all dry and I'm still wet."

"You're all wet and so am I," Janice added foolishly.

Kate dropped her towel and took a stride to close the space between them. Janice let her towel fall and joined Kate in the kiss. Then it was the most natural thing in the world for Kate to nudge her onto the bed. Janice spread her legs for the welcome jut of Kate's hip.

Kate was making love to her. First. She didn't have to lift a single finger, just lie back and love what this skillful lover was doing to her. Holding her breath in delicious anticipation, she loved submitting to Kate. And then she came, in a generous wave that swirled down her legs and ebbed slowly up again. Janice exhaled in a rush. Clasping Kate tightly so that their slender bodies melded into one, she felt replete. At last. Kate was the other half who filled the aching void that Ariel had left behind. Finally, Janice had found the real Wonder Woman. At long, exceedingly long last.

Chapter 65

Next morning, dressed for work, Wonder Woman took a final slurp of tea and set her mug in the kitchen sink. Nudging Janice out of the way, Kate opened a drawer and rummaged inside until she found a spare key. Handing it over, she said, "Here, make yourself at home."

"Oh, thank you." Janice clutched the key to her breast. "Are you having just tea for breakfast? Most important meal of the day, you know."

"No time." Kate smiled. "Make some toast if you feel like it."

Janice didn't want breakfast. "Not after all the munching we did early this morning."

Kate tapped her on the nose. "Naughty, naughty."

Janice grabbed Kate's hand and gave it a kiss. "You're so kind to me. Have I told you how grateful I am that you've taken me in like this?"

"Better here than living on the street." Kate shrugged, wiping her hand on her blazer pocket. "Being practical. That's all there is to it. There's no need to get soppy about it."

Kate was smiling, but the smile didn't reach her eyes. Janice had seen Kate cut off before, the way she had at the COC when she'd been sad about Colin. Was this something Kate did to shield herself? Some sort of defense mechanism to stop people finding out what a big softie she was underneath. Well, Janice wasn't going to let her get away with it.

"Can't take a compliment, aye? Well, here's one I won't let you brush off easily. You are a genuinely nice person. It's truly kind of you to let me stay here and you know it." Janice stepped in to give Kate a warm hug.

"So sue me." Kate relented, accepting the embrace. "I just happen to like looking after people. Just as well, given that it's my profession." Indicating the dishes crowding the sink, she added, "You're a professional dishwasher. You can look after those if you like." And blowing Janice a final kiss, she turned and left for work.

Walked right into that, Janice thought. Never mind. Looking after this flat was the least she could do to repay this kindness. How lucky she was to have met Wonder Woman.

* * *

What a wonderful world. What a wonderful sun was warming her bare legs. A week after moving in with Kate, Janice was sitting on the patio with a second cup of strong Yorkshire tea. It was nearly August and steaming hot. Janice was wearing a pair of Bermudas she hadn't worn since New Zealand. London had always been too cold for shorts. The waistband was tighter than it used to be. She popped the top button, quickly looking up to check if anyone on the other side of the block could see what she had done. No one was out on their back balcony, as far as she could see. Everyone must be at work.

Which reminded her, she had to go to work this afternoon. Thank goodness she still had that job at M&M's. The cash was handy, but on just the afternoon shift, she couldn't earn enough to afford a fair share of the cost of staying here. Kate had let her know how expensive the rent was. Janice couldn't take advantage of her generosity. She wanted to pay her own way. She had to find a full-time job. She'd look for one soon. Just not today.

Janice took a last swig of tea. It was strong and milky, the way she liked it. Kobus would have hated it. He had taken his tea the bland Dutch way, tepid water tinted with a homeo-pathetic trace of tannin. *Oh, Kobus.* How could she forget him? How could she forget what she still had to do? If it were any excuse, things had been happening too fast in just over one week: Colin coming and going, Janice coming with Kate for the first time (and the second and the third), and Negy making her go from the hostel in his not-so mellow drama. No wonder her resolve to turn herself in for Kobus had slipped her mind.

What mind? Janice thought again. Who would mind if she postponed the inevitable yet again? Call it a stay of execution. She owed people an explanation. She couldn't disappear from Kate's life, love her and leave her without saying why. She couldn't leave M&M

in the lurch. Janice had to sort out her life before she could deal with the death she had caused.

It was settled then. She'd get herself sorted today. The afternoons always started off slow in the pizzeria. She'd find a moment to sit with M&M and tell them why she had to go. They'd be saddened but would understand that she had to do the right thing. And tonight she'd tell Kate what had happened in London. Janice knew it would destroy Kate to discover she was a killer. It would ruin any chance of their relationship developing into something lasting. Janice hated the idea of killing Kate's love. She would lose Wonder Woman just as soon as she'd found her.

A cloud passed over the sun. Janice shivered, feeling the dread of loss drop into her belly. She couldn't tell Kate about Kobus. Not yet. It was too soon to break them up. Please let them have just one teensy month of heaven first. She'd put it off till August thirteenth. Then she'd really and truly turn herself in. *And that's a promise.*

Promise, my foot. Who am I fooling? This was the umpteenth stay of execution Janice had contrived for herself. Just another in a lengthy line of cowardly excuses for not facing the consequences of her actions. This habit of creating delays had to stop. Sooner. Or later.

Chapter 66

Janice had never lived with anyone besides her parents, and they didn't count. She'd shared a house before, but that had been different. Still grieving for Ariel, she'd graduated from high school (goodness knows how she'd managed to pass her exams) and used the scholarship she'd earned to leave home. She moved to a cheap student flat in Ponsonby for her first year at Auckland University. She couldn't stand her roommates, three blokes sitting med school finals who never seemed to study and were only into having a fun time. They had taken her on for her share of the rent and couldn't have made it clearer that they had no patience for a gangly, inhibited eighteen-year-old who didn't share their tastes (soapy beer and bimbos) or interests (more beer and blondes).

No matter. Janice kept to her room, skipping lectures and reading plays and biographies of actors instead of writing essays. On her nights off from washing dishes in that grungy café, she went out on her own to see the plays the professionals put on at Mercury Theater, around the corner from the flat, and Central Theater out in Remuera. She saved all she could and dreamed of escaping Auckland, living in London, and waltzing down Shaftesbury Avenue in homage to the famous actors of the West End. She may have shared living space, but it wasn't the same as living with Kate.

Kate had cleared a plank in the wardrobe for Janice's clothes and let her put her books on the living room shelves to make her feel at home. Mind you, Janice kept Bitchy Bear hidden in the rucksack because she knew Kate found the souvenir childish. Even if it were sentimental tat, the toy reminded her of Colin, and she loved it. And him.

But not as much as she loved Kate. Or Kate loved her. They'd said the magic words two weeks ago last Wednesday, on their third (time lucky) night in a row of making ardent love. Pillow talk murmured while they were recovering from a bout of wild reciprocal love that left Janice exhilarated.

When Kate had said the L word back, Janice felt her brain explode. She was flying, soaring through clouds of oxytocin contentment. "You're so good in bed. You're so kind—"

"Don't tell me," Kate interrupted lightly, shifting a bit to see Janice better, "no one's ever made you come the way I do."

"Never. And I love you for it." Janice raised her face for a kiss to seal the moment.

Kate brought her lips close, then teased away at the last moment. Sitting up, stroking Janice's long waist, she sighed. "Oh, please, I hate to have to ask this, but please, let's not get started again. You know I can't keep my hands off you, and I really wish we could keep on rabbiting the whole night through, but"—she raised her arm to look at her watch—"shit, it's way past two. I hope you understand that I must get me some shut-eye, darling, otherwise I'll be no good for work tomorrow."

"Tomorrow never comes."

"Not as hard and fast as you do, that's for sure." Kate laughed, slid down in bed, and landed a kiss on the tip of Janice's nose. "Now, my little Kumquat, let's go to sleep, okay?" She reached over and switched off the bedside lamp.

Janice burst into laughter. "Kumquat? Rhymes with? Calling me a come-twat?"

"You got it." Kate grinned and snuggled her head into the pillow. "Ever tasted one?"

"A kumquat? Those tiny golden fruity things? I didn't know you can eat them."

"Bite-sized bursts of citrus. Sweet on the surface and tart underneath. Like me." Kate tapped Janice on the nose. "Like you too." She yawned. "Kumquat, let me sleep."

"Your wish is my come-and." Still giggling, Janice let her lover go to sleep.

* * *

Two Wednesdays later, Janice was in the garden arranging wayward tendrils of silver lace vine before getting ready for work. She heard a thump on next door's balcony. She looked up to see Coby waving a cloth duster at her. Hang on. What was Coby doing up on the second floor? Janice thought she lived beside Kate. Her home must have an upstairs as well.

Coby seemed wan, her face was drawn. Seeing her through the slats of the banister, Janice thought Coby had lost weight since she had seen her last. She didn't have time to wonder why because now the woman was leaning over the banister and trilling down at her.

"Yoo-hoo, Jan-ease. How is it going with you? And with Kate? Do you find it *gezellig*, how you say, *samenwonen*?"

Oh god. Janice guessed Coby was asking if she liked living together with Kate. She tried to reply in Dutch. "*Samenwonen* is…" She faltered, wanting to say that she and Kate were a perfect match and loved each other very much.

Coby laughed as if she understood the intention and let fly with a torrent of Dutch. Janice nodded and shook her head where she thought was proper, according to Coby's inflection. At last, the woman slowed down. Shaking the duster, Coby said, "I have free from my work."

Janice remembered that Coby worked for a dry cleaners and tailoring service near the Albert Cuyp market. She was a good mender apparently and did all the small repairs.

Coby went on. "I have to start making the house clean for my son. He comes from London in over two weeks. All must be in order for him by then. *Ja*."

"Your son is coming home? How nice. You must be looking forward to seeing him."

For some reason Coby looked doubtful. "Oh, *ja*, I am lucky to see him back."

Lucky. Funnily enough, Kobus used to make the very same mistake. He'd once explained that the confusion came about because the Dutch word *gelukkig* meant both happy and lucky. Oh well, Janice knew what Coby meant. But now she'd had enough. "Good luck with the *grote schoenmaat*." And with a friendly little wave, Janice went inside.

A moment later, rinsing her hands in the bathroom, Janice slapped her forehead. What an idiot she was. She'd said *schoenmaat* instead of *schoonmaak*. She'd wished Coby a big shoe size, not the spring cleaning she'd meant to say. She'd never get the hang of Dutch.

Chapter 67

At knocking-off time the next afternoon, Janice hooked her apron onto the partition that hid the dishwashing galley from the rest of the kitchen at M&M's. The bib of the apron was splotched wet, and no wonder. No matter how careful she tried to be, when Janice was rinsing the dirty plates, she could never avoid hosing herself at least once every shift. Never mind, she was clumsy at times. That was a fact, and she was used to getting wet. Which reminded her. Kate was coming to pick her up from work today. She'd be bringing a surprise. She'd said so this morning when she was getting ready to leave for the office. Janice thrummed with anticipation.

Marcello saw Janice step out from behind the partition. Clapping dusty flour off his hands, he took her by the elbow and guided her to the cash register. He pinged it open and slid out a twenty-five-guilder note. "Marcella and me"—he nodded at his wife in the dining area, serving coffees to a pair of tourists—"we talked this over last night. You are a good worker, turn up on time, work fast and never complain. Here, today we give a little extra." He crumpled the note into Janice's hand.

Thrown off balance by the gesture, Janice automatically clutched the money. Dutch currency was beautiful, far more colorful than dull New Zealand dollars. Brilliant designs too. The Dutch slang for this particular note was a *geeltje*, but anyone could see that it was nowhere near a "little yellow" but rather a vivid mix of scarlet and shocking pink. Kate would know the reason behind the misnomer. Probably something historical. Janice must ask her one day. But now all she could do was snap her surprised mouth shut.

"But, Marcello," Janice turned to include Marcella, who joined them at the counter. "But why? Really, I don't deserve this."

"Yes, you do." Marcella put away the tray she was carrying and smiled up at Janice. "We show our appreciation. You are a good dishwasher."

Marcello agreed. "Don't worry, tip comes out your wages."

Janice's mouth drooped in disappointment. At the sight, Marcello burst into laughter.

Frowning at her husband, Marcella folded Janice's fingers over the note. "*Cara* Janice, don't listen to 'Cello. He is such a big bear. He teases. You know that, eh?"

To prove what a jovial bear he was, Marcello spread his arms and enveloped Janice and his wife in a huge embrace. Janice leaned into the hug, snuffling deep into Marcello's floury shoulder, inhaling his pleasant-smelling sweat. Taking care not to squeeze Marcella's fragile bones, Janice detected a trace of perfume, something sweet, woody, and old-fashioned, like the Tweed perfume her mother used on occasion. Janice took a deep breath. If only her mum were as lovable as Marcella. If only her dad were as cuddly as Marcello. Well, they weren't. Period. M&M were warmer, kinder, more loving than her parents had ever been. Janice was glad she had M&M in her life. If you could choose your own parents, she'd choose them. She snuggled deep into their comfortable embrace.

"Group grope." Kate stood in the doorway of the restaurant, smiling at the swaying trio. "Is this a private grope or can anyone join?"

Janice broke free, heart jolting with delicious shock. Wonder Woman looked gorgeous, standing there in her smart work blazer and tailored pants. A wave of possessive pride swept through her. This elegant woman loved her, actually wanted her. She held out an arm, inviting Kate over.

"This is Kate, she's my…" How should she introduce Kate? She wasn't used to being out of the closet, and admitting she was in a relationship with a woman didn't come naturally.

Kate smiled at Janice's timidity. "Hi, I'm Kate, her girlfriend."

M&M took Kate's confident hand and gave it a good shake, introducing themselves in turn. Janice was struck speechless by their friendly acceptance.

Marcella turned to Kate. "You are the reason why Janice is happy. She has been singing for weeks now. Not just washing the dishes but dancing at the sink."

Kate wrapped her arm around Janice. "Twinkle-toes here is a mighty fine dancer. I've seen all her moves, so I know."

Janice felt the heat rise in her cheeks. She'd never get used to being teased, even by these lovable fools. Marcella noticed her discomfort. Taking Janice and Kate by the hand, she ushered them to the quietest corner table. "Sit," she ordered. "I bring you coffee. Espresso? Cappuccino?" Noticing Kate's expression, she added, "Or you want wine? Yes, I have a fine soave for you, dry white, very refreshing. You like it. Wine is better, yes?" And before either Kate or Janice could stop her, Marcella darted behind the counter, opened the fridge, produced a bottle, and poured two glasses to the brim. Returning quickly, she set the wine down and said, "I'm happy for you, *cara* Janice. You love each other, yes?" She smiled at Kate. "Make sure you look after her." She waited for Kate's nod, then left them in peace.

Watching Marcella join her husband, Kate said, "What a lovely couple. I can see why you like working here." She raised her glass. "Here's to Marcello and Marcella."

"To M&M." Janice clinked her glass against Kate's. "Now tell me. What surprise?"

Kate took a long sip of wine and put down her glass. "I've magicked a bike for you, to replace your stolen one. It's parked outside, next to mine. Belongs to a colleague and you can have it for free, but don't lose it because one day you'll have to give it back."

"Oh wow, how did you manage that?"

"It pays to work in the personnel department. Or human resources as they're starting to call it these days. Anyway, you get to know lots of people. And someone owed me a favor, so there you have it." Kate pulled a sturdy key out of her pocket and dropped it on the table. "Don't lose this either. The lock it opens costs as much as the bike."

Janice swept up the key and her lover's hand. Giving the fingers a kiss, she said, "You're so good to me. I really don't deserve your kindness."

Kate shook her head, reached over the table to stroke Janice's cheek. "Stop it, Kumquat. No need to get soppy. I told you, I like helping people get what they want." She smiled. "Especially hopeless fools like you."

Later, after a shared pizza and two more glasses of delicious soave, they rode home, cycling side by side, holding hands. As they took off down the Nieuwezijds Voorburgwal, Janice wobbled at first. She wasn't just tipsy from the unfamiliar wine. This bike was strange too, and she needed to find her balance on the cobblestones. She quickly got the hang of it. It helped that the saddle was set at the right height. She sat up straight, boldly holding her lover's hand. Demonstrative dykes, they were, out of the closet and onto the street, proclaiming their lesbo-love to the world. Not that any jaded Amsterdammers lifted an eyelash when they passed. So gay, so what?

Because Kate knew all the shortcuts, their ride home was fast. Janice hadn't realized how humid Amsterdam was in August, and when they got home, glowing from the exertion of pedaling in this sticky heat, she was keen to freshen up. So was Kate, who squeezed behind Janice in the shower "just to soap your back." Fooling around in there inevitably led to a dose of bedroom delight that went on all evening. And all night. Nonstop.

Chapter 68

Janice couldn't be happier. Kate was so easy to live with, this final week of freedom had simply flown by. August twelfth already. One day of honeymoon left before she would turn herself in. They were lying in bed, floppy limbs spread, waiting for their breathing to calm down when Janice startled. Kate rolled over lazily. "What's wrong, Kumquat?"

Janice couldn't answer the question. She hadn't mentioned Kobus yet. Surely, she had to reveal something about him and what had happened so that Kate could understand why she had to go to the police tomorrow. Come to think of it, she hadn't got around to warning M&M either. Her heart sank. She really had to stop putting things off.

Kate settled her head close beside hers on the same pillow, but Janice had never felt so far away. If she told Kate now, before Sunday morning, she'd risk losing her. Knowing the truth, that Janice was a killer, would bring out the worst in Kate. The tough, unsentimental side. The human resources robot would reject her at once. She just knew. Janice sighed. She couldn't do it. Not yet.

Kate misunderstood. "No, don't tell me, I can guess. You've had enough of me."

Janice sat up to protest, but Kate pulled her back down and smeared a kiss over her lips. Drawing back, she said, "It's okay. You want us to slow down. That's okay with me. I mean, we've been fucking each other silly all month. Too much of a good thing and all that."

Janice giggled in relief. Kate didn't have a clue what was really bothering her. As if Janice could ever tire of sex with Kate. Unimaginable. "Too much of a good thing can be wonderful, to quote my favorite sapiosexualist."

"Sapio what?"

"Someone who finds intelligence a turn-on, like Mae West. It's one of her quotes."

"I don't know about intelligence, but we've had enough arousal to last a lifetime."

"Or a whole month, at least."

Get it while it lasts. Janice wasn't going to lose Wonder Woman. Yet.

* * *

Kate always bought fresh fruit and vegetables at the Albert Cuyp street market. It was just on the other side of the canal, but this Saturday the weekly shopping trip began with a detour. Arm in arm, Janice and Kate strolled up Hobbemakade to the fire station, crossed the bridge, and entered a typically narrow road. A moment later Janice exclaimed, "This is it! Here's where I was born." She pointed at a flat-fronted house identical with the others on the terrace.

"Doesn't look like much, aye?" Kate shrugged. "Your parents must have been glad to escape to New Zealand. Lots of tulip munchers fled there in the fifties."

"I'm glad I got to grow up in the wide open space of New Zealand."

"No regrets you came back and met me?" Kate gave Janice a kiss.

"None whatsoever." Janice flung her arms around Kate and returned the kiss.

Later, on their way home from the market, each carrying a loaded shopping bag, who should Kate and Janice catch up with but Coby. She was struggling to manage two hefty bags filled to the brim with fruit and vegetables. Without asking if Coby wanted help, Kate took her bags and passed one to Janice so that they shared the extra burden. The three continued, Janice and Kate on either side of Coby, both shortening their stride to match Coby's. The woman walked slower and slower until halfway across a bridge, she stopped completely.

Coby held on to the bridge railing. "Sorry," she began, which was the only word Janice understood in the deluge of Dutch that followed. Kate listened intently, her face showing nothing but sincere concern as Coby went on, her voice becoming thinner and rising in pitch until it was little more than a mouse-like squeak. When at last she paused for breath, Kate patted her shoulder and turned to Janice. "Did you get any of that?"

Janice shook her head. "What's the matter with Coby? Why is she sorry?"

Kate took her time preparing an answer. She gave Coby a long, questioning look. When Coby nodded permission, she spoke. "Coby's dying. She's got cancer of the throat and the doctors have told her there's nothing to be done. She hasn't got long to live. A month at most." Kate stopped abruptly, bent down, and gave Coby a hug.

Babbling something, Coby brushed away the tears sliding down Kate's cheek.

Kate turned to Janice. "I've got to stay strong for her. Coby needs my strength."

"Cancer. No wonder she looks poorly. I had no idea."

Coby smiled bravely. "It goes right, Jan-ease. My son comes home to care for me."

Janice wondered why this son wasn't here, right now, helping his mother with the shopping. As if she knew what Janice was thinking, Coby added, "Yesterday he come late, late, late in the night. His bus got a…" Giving up the effort to speak English, Coby let loose another burst of Dutch.

Janice looked to Kate for help. "Flat tire," Kate explained. "Coby says that the bus he was on blew a tire outside the Hook of Holland. Everyone had to get off and the bus had to be unloaded before the driver could change the wheel. Her son got home later than expected."

Coby smiled gratefully at Kate for the translation. To Janice she said, "I good mama for my boy. He is tired this morning. I let him sleep out. But from now he looks for me."

"We'll look after you too," Kate said. "You can count on us."

Coby smiled again, took Kate's hand, and went to take Janice's hand too. "*Ja*, I know. But please, dear girls, look after my boy when I go. I warn you, he go mad when I die. When I leave him alone, I warn you, he want to die too. Please. You girls do help him. Please."

What kind of son was this? Janice didn't think she was going to like this weakling. But she didn't have to wait long to meet this poor excuse for a caring son. As the three turned the corner, she saw a small man waiting by Coby's front door. There was something familiar about his mousy-brown hair, the slope of his shoulders, and the nervous way he jiggled from foot to foot.

Coby straightened. "*Lieverd, hier ben ik,*" she called.

The man gave a yelp of delight at the sound of his mother's voice and turned around. If he had a tail, he'd be wagging it, so pleased was he to see Coby.

"Mama!"

Chapter 69

She knew his voice. She knew his face. Janice nearly died. Her heart faltered, skipped a million beats. Coby's son was looking as shocked to see Janice as she felt to see him.

Kobus.

Her jaw dropped. She shook her head but had to believe her eyes. What a double whammy. Kobus was Coby's boy. He'd been her upstairs neighbor in London, and now, it turned out, he was Kate's next-door neighbor. The odds of this happening must be one in a zillion, but with her luck, it had. And, as if this coincidence weren't weird enough to take in, Kobus hadn't died in that fall. She hadn't killed him. He wasn't dead. He'd come home to look after his dying mother.

"What do you do here?" he barked, staring aghast at Janice.

Janice couldn't answer. There was too much to say. She wanted to run from the misery in his eyes, but there was no escape. Coby's and Kate's eyes were burning the skin off her face. Coby looked as if she didn't understand what was happening. She stumbled and Kobus grabbed her arm.

Kate was sizing Kobus up, looking at him, then at Janice. "My, my, my, what a small world. You two know each other." Her tone was flat, suppressing astonishment.

Ignoring Kate, Kobus whimpered, "You pushed me down the stairs."

"You pushed me too often. I pushed back and you fell. It was an accident."

Kobus and Janice glared at each other. Janice shook her hair over her face, fighting the urge to cry. All the agony, all the guilt she'd felt these past months, believing she had killed Kobus. The injustice of it all threatened to burst out in one fierce explosion. She couldn't afford to lose control. Not on the street. Not in front of the neighbors. She stepped past Kobus and Coby, turned her back, and waited impatiently in Kate's portico.

Kate stayed where she was, asked something in Dutch. Kobus answered, punctuating his guttural words with mournful yelps. Kate listened, not interrupting, letting Kobus finish in his own time. Coby chipped in, accusing her son of something. Kobus mumbled something apologetic. There was a pregnant silence, then Coby gave a hacking cough followed by a sorrowful sigh. Kobus hung his hangdog head and obediently followed his mother inside, shooting Janice an evil look on the way.

Kate unlocked her door, brushed past Janice, went to the kitchen, and put the kettle on.

Janice went into the living room and sagged onto the sofa. She was seething. Her fingers twitched, her knee wouldn't stop jerking. What a fucking relief. She wasn't a killer. It wasn't manslaughter. Kobus was alive. She didn't have to go to the police. Now she understood why no one had been looking for her. The English police, the Dutch police, Interpol, whatever, no one was interested in her. All this time she'd been fretting about killing Kobus, feeling guilty, believing she had murdered him, if only by accident, knowing she'd have to do the right thing and turn herself in but, terrified of prison, constantly putting it off. All for nothing. She was innocent. That was why she'd kept on procrastinating. Deep down, Janice knew she couldn't have been a killer.

From nowhere, the title of a musical, a wonderful compilation of Jacques Brel's inspiring songs popped into her head: Not *Jacques Brel* but Kobus Boer *is Alive and Well and Living in Amsterdam.* He'd be living with his mother, right next door, and Janice wouldn't be able to avoid him. They'd be neighbors. Again. She wasn't ready to deal with that, not yet. Not now. If she didn't watch out, she'd be overwhelmed by anger and grief and rage and despair, and goodness knows what else. She couldn't afford to lose it. She had to park all thoughts of Kobus and seek distraction. Ha! A useful diversion was right under her nose. Janice reached out and stirred the snake's nest of rope lying on the coffee table.

In their time together, Janice and Kate didn't bother much with television. Kate only switched it on for the news. Last night, when the news was on, Kate had stretched out on the sofa with her head in Janice's lap and played with this very rope. She'd tied a loose hangman's knot and, using the noose as a lasso, tried roping her feet. More often than not she missed. Tiring of the game, she'd coiled the supple length and worked the loose ends, practicing sailor's knots: a reef, a round turn, and two half hitches. Janice couldn't see why Kate found tying knots relaxing, but it was a harmless hobby and amusing to watch. She shared Kate's pleasure last night, when Kate managed a perfect bowline on her first attempt. "The king of sailor's knots," Kate had said triumphantly, "the *boeilijn*, as the Dutch would say." Her fingers were dexterous. She was good at tying. *And why knot*?

Janice smiled, remembering her joke.

"What are you laughing at?" Kate stood in the doorway holding mugs of piping-hot tea. Handing Janice hers, she sat in the wingback chair. "I should think you'd have nothing to laugh about after what you did to Kobus in London."

Janice put her tea on the coffee table. "What I did to him?" She was incredulous. "How dare he. What did he tell you?"

Kate angled in the chair to look at Janice. "I'm not going to give you what he said word for word, just what it boils down to. Here goes. You were his neighbor in his aunty's bedsit in London. Standoffish at first, but when he won the lottery, you came over all sugar and spice. You seduced him, forced him to spend his money on you, ripped him off for all you could get, and when the money was gone and he was broke, you pushed him down the stairs and left him for dead."

Kate turned away from Janice, picked up the coil of rope, and slid it through her long fingers. "Well, that's his side of the story. What's yours?"

Chapter 70

Janice couldn't move. Shards of ice stabbed the chambers of her heart and stilled her lungs. She couldn't believe that Kobus had told Kate this. She couldn't believe that Kate had believed him. Was Kate convinced his version was correct? By the looks of it, she was. How could Janice set the record straight? It'd be a losing battle. She stood stiffly. "Okay, if that's the way it is, I'll pack my bag and leave you to it."

Kate sat up. "What?" Her mouth gaped. "You're leaving? But why?"

"You believe that I seduced Kobus and tried to kill him on purpose!"

Kate rose from the chair. "No, Kumquat, darling, no. You've got it wrong. I was paraphrasing. If what I said sounded nasty, it was my fault. That's the spin I put on his words. Sorry, darling. I didn't say I believed him. I don't, not without hearing your side of the story."

Then the tears began. Wrapped in Kate's arms, Janice howled her freezing heart out, not caring that slobber was streaming down her face and soaking into her blouse. Kate pulled a clean tissue out of her pocket and wiped Janice's cheeks. One or two hiccups later, one wan smile and the brutal bout was over. Well, nearly. Still sniffing, Janice followed Kate to the sofa and curled up beside her.

"Tell me, what really happened to you in London?"

Janice buried her face in her lover's chest. Although Kate's breasts were soft, her ribcage was hard. Symbolic really. Underneath that surface warmth, Kate was a tough woman. Now, instead of telling her what had happened in London, Janice asked her own question. "Have you ever been to bed with a man?"

"That part is true." Kate cut to the chase. "You did fuck him."

Janice sat up. "It wasn't like that. I didn't go after Kobus. I'd never been with a man and was curious, so yes, I did let him fuck me, twice in fact, but only because he kept on begging, badgering me until I had to give in. I'd been honest with him from the start, told him I was gay and only wanted to be friends but that didn't stop the fucker from so-called falling in love with me, clinging to me, stalking me, never leaving me alone."

Kate said nothing, just held Janice close until a second bout of furious tears had run its course. Sitting up, mopping her eyes with the sodden tissue, Janice said, "Then the bastard won a big share of the lottery and blamed his fucking luck on me."

Kate raised an eyebrow. "Blamed?" She took her mug and swallowed some tea.

Janice nodded. "He was convinced I brought him luck." She hiccuped. "He's a gambler, bets on the horses, the pools, you name it. Made me his lucky charm because I'd drawn the winning ticket for him in a pub raffle. The pressure he put me under."

"And the gold digging he says you did? What about that?"

Janice sprang from the sofa in a burst of anger. "It wasn't like that. I didn't ask for a penny. He was the one who wanted to spend on me, buying me stuff whether I wanted it or not. In the end I couldn't look at a damn thing without him getting it for me."

Kate finished her tea and put down her mug. "You didn't have to take his presents."

Janice flinched at the look in Kate's eyes. "I defy you to resist the onslaught of extravagance Kobus forced on me. He wouldn't take no for an answer. It wasn't generosity. It was bribery. He was trying to buy me. That's all there was to it." Janice collapsed on the sofa. "And I was dumb enough to give him what he wanted. I felt guilty for taking all his presents. What else could I do but give myself in return? I did, until he slapped me."

Kate's hackles rose. "He fucking hit you. Is that why you left London?"

"I refused to let him do me again." Janice paused, recalling the awful scene on the staircase when she was terrified that Kobus would strike her again. "He kept pushing until one night I pushed back. Literally. He fell and knocked himself out. I thought I'd killed him." More tears now. "It was an accident. I didn't mean for it to happen. I was too scared. All I could do was run away."

Kate hugged Janice closely, then let go, slowly getting to her feet. "How about a nice cup of tea? Look, you haven't touched yours and it's gone cold."

Janice called after her retreating back, "Do you believe me?"

Kate stopped by the dining table. Turned slowly, she said, "Yes, I do believe you. I know Coby. I know Kobus. I know how much he depends on her. How attached he is to Coby, not in a good, healthy way. I don't know what fucked him up like this. Maybe his father's suicide when they lived in Urk."

"Suicide? Kobus told me his dad drowned in a storm."

"That's what Coby told him. He was nine at the time and she spared him the truth. She told me it was a dead-calm day, and his dad was out fishing as usual. When they dropped anchor to cast the net, he jumped overboard, grabbed the anchor chain, went down with it and didn't come up. The crew did their best to haul him out, but he'd drowned before they could."

Kate put the mugs on the table and came back. She sat on the edge of the coffee table with the rope coiled beside her. Her knees felt warm against Janice's thigh. Janice leaned onto the knees, letting their warmth ease her anxiety.

"Coby never knew why her husband drowned himself," said Kate. "Didn't know he was depressed, least of all suicidal. His death came right out of the blue for her."

"I suppose having lost her husband dramatically"—Janice was thinking aloud—"Coby wasn't about to lose her son and turned herself into a mummy dearest." Kate didn't get the reference. "Doing a Joan Crawford, she turned into an abusive, possessive, overprotective yet unreliable mother. Do you think that's what turned Kobus into such a clinger?"

"Maybe." Kate picked up the rope and slid the supple loops through her fingers. "I don't think we're in a position to judge. And tempting as it is, Kumquat, we shouldn't be making assumptions either. But I will say this. Coby is too nice to be abusive. On the contrary, she's the soul of patience. How she put up with Kobus for so long is beyond me."

Janice thought of her time with him in London. Despite what Kate said, she couldn't resist playing the analyst. "I guess losing his dad at such an early age made Kobus super insecure. It made him scared of losing his mum and that made him cling. And Coby, for her own broken reasons, clung to him. She didn't let go so that he could grow up like a normal person. It's all about attachment." Kate's look reminded Janice not to jump to conclusions. She changed tack. "Was Kobus into gambling before he went to London?"

Kate sat beside Janice on the sofa. "His gambling drove Coby bonkers. He never held a job for long and spent all his dole money on the horses. Coby never let him out of her sight if she could help it. But she had to go to work. I'd try to give her a breather. Invited him over and got him to teach me some knots, but he never stayed long. In the end, Coby had enough of him and sent him off to her sister, Corrie, in London."

Chapter 71

Life went on, and by the first week of September, Janice had become good at ignoring the neighbors. It was hard because the thin walls between Amsterdam houses constantly let in their noise. Coby's bouts of coughing were getting worse, especially in the mornings. The sound filled Janice with dread.

She hadn't seen or spoken to Kobus since he'd arrived a fortnight ago, and if Janice had her way, that's how it would stay. Another confrontation was the last thing she wanted, so she always checked the street before taking off for work in case he was there.

Early Friday morning, Janice was still in bed, watching Kate dress for the office. Kate always put on her clothes in the same order: underpants, bra, tights or socks, smart skirt or tailored pants, then high heels or stylish ankle boots, and only then, blouse and sweater or blazer. It amused Janice that Kate always dressed the bottom half before the top, slipping on shoes before buttoning blouse. Janice always laced her trainers last. *But hey, it takes all types.*

Shrugging into a bodywarmer, Kate crossed to the bed. "Bye, Kumquat, see you later."

Janice returned the fond kiss, reaching up to tug her lover down beside her.

Kate evaded her grasp. "Naughty, naughty." She laughed. "You'll have to possess your soul in patience, you ravishing creature. Till tonight." In the doorway, she turned. "Oh, that reminds me. I bumped into Coby yesterday and asked her and Kobus over for dinner. Tonight. It's your turn to cook, isn't it? If you don't feel like cooking for four, would you mind bringing home some of M&M's scrummy pasta? Or I can pick up some Chinese."

"You invited these people to dinner without asking me? How could you?"

"What do you mean, these people? We're talking about my neighbors, not any old people." Kate spoke lightly, as if it were no big deal. "No need to get your knickers in a twist. I'm sorry if it feels like I'm not considering you, how you feel about Kobus and all that. In a way I suppose I'm not, but you should know I don't feel the need to ask permission to invite people to my home."

Is this how Kate saw it? Janice's heart missed a beat. She hadn't expected this.

Kate went on, unperturbed by Janice glaring at her. "I'm not going to drop my friendship with Coby just because you had a run-in with her son in London. That's your problem, not mine, and you're going to have to sort it out with him, sooner or later. But leave me out of it, please. We're different people, we have other relationships with other people."

"But you're my lover. What we have ranks higher than other relationships. We don't have an ordinary friendship. We're closer, more intimate."

"More intimate," Kate agreed, "but not exclusive. Just because we're lovers doesn't mean we should cut ourselves off from the rest of humanity. I'm with you, yes. You're the most important person in my life at the moment, but that doesn't mean we're joined at the hip. I won't let you, or anything that happened to you in your past, cut me off from my friends."

So—Janice's heart cramped in pain—she was important only for the moment? Blood was pounding loudly in her temples. She could hardly hear. Didn't Kate realize how distressed she was by Kobus's return? After all she'd gone through with him in London, after all she'd endured because of him in Amsterdam, it made sense that she wouldn't be able to cope with him on her own. She needed support, a big dose of kindness and consideration. And it wasn't just a matter of wanting Kate's tender loving care. It had to do with loyalty, surely. As her lover, Kate owed her loyalty.

Janice reached out. "Whose side are you on?"

Kate sighed, standing by the door. "I've told you, I don't take sides, and if I did then I'd have to be honest and say I'd choose myself. Selfish or not, Jan-ease," she said, putting on Coby's accent. "I think it's my job to look after myself. And it's yours to look after yourself."

"But no, it's reasonable for lovers to want empathy and consideration from each other. Lovers look after each other. Well, they should do. It's what we do."

Kate relented. "Yeah, okay, we look after each other in physical terms, in material terms. And empathy and consideration rule, okay, in general. But in terms of emotions, on this deeper level of feelings, I reckon we're all—even lovers—we're all on our own." She crossed to the bed, forcing Janice to move over to let her sit. "Listen, Kumquat, you must have learned from your experience with Kobus. He tried to make you responsible for the way he felt, didn't he?"

"He said it was my job to make him happy."

"It isn't," said Kate, tapping Janice's nose for emphasis. "It's not your job to make other people happy. And it's the same the other way around. It's no one else's job to make you happy. You are responsible for your own happiness, your own life. That's your job. Sure, we all get affected by what happens around us. But how you look at it, what you feel about it is in your own hands. You're in charge of what you feel, all by yourself."

Janice had to nod. Damn it, Kate's words hurt, but she was right.

Chapter 72

So the neighbors came to dinner, a meal that Janice prepared despite her objections. Kate answered the knock at the door, accepted the glorious bunch of peonies Coby offered, and ushered her into the living room, followed obediently by Kobus. Leaving the visitors to find their own seats, Kate nipped down to the kitchen to dump the flowers in Janice's arms and pick up a tray of drinks: cold pils in the bottle for Kobus, a tiny glass of sour sherry for Coby, and a big fat wine for herself.

Janice stayed in the kitchen, glad that she had an excuse to keep out of the way. She'd promised Kate that for Coby's sake she'd be on her best behavior tonight and not make a scene with Kobus. Waiting for the pasta water to boil, she entered the bedroom and peeked into the living room through the jamb of the bedroom door. Coby didn't look well. Perched on the edge of the sofa, she looked slight and insignificant beside her son. In only this past week she'd lost more weight. Her face was ashen. There were dark hollows under her eyes and the cords in her neck stood out. Fucking throat cancer. Poor Coby. But to see her chattering away to Kate in her guttural Dutch, eyes flashing with humor, Coby made it seem as if nothing was wrong. By the looks of it, she was good at putting on a front—to reassure Kobus, Janice supposed. Coby was pretty damn convincing, right up until she had to stop talking mid-word, overcome by a bout of hacking coughs.

Kate flew into the kitchen. Nudging Janice out of the way in the narrow galley, she grabbed a glass off the shelf and filled it with chilly water. Spotting the simmering water, she asked, "Everything under control?" Without waiting for a reply, she rushed back to the living room, taking the short cut through the bedroom, to give Coby the water.

Following Kate into the bedroom, Janice peeked through the door jamb and saw Coby wave the glass away. Kobus was patting her back while she cleared her throat. His screwed-up face mirrored Coby's pain.

"*Is goed*," Coby gasped finally, pushing aside her son.

Kate put the water down on the coffee table. "We're worried about you, Coby. It's only natural. Kobus is concerned, I'm concerned, and Janice is too." Glancing at the bedroom door, as if she knew Janice was hiding behind it, she called, "Aren't you, darling?"

Sprung. Janice swung the door open. Fixing a smile on her face to show that she agreed with Kate, she entered. "Hi, Coby. Hello, Kobus. Nice to see you. We're having pasta carbonara tonight."

Kobus hunched into the sofa, making himself as small as possible, nodding hello.

"Hey, Jan-ease." Coby laughed off the bout of coughing, sitting up straight and smiling brightly. "Tonight, you are the *keukenprinses*." Looking to Kate for confirmation, she added, "You say that in English?"

"Kitchen princess," Kate agreed, adding for Janice, "Pretty sexist, aye?"

Darling Kate and her helpful translations. In return, Janice did her best to be nice. Smiling back at Coby, she said, "I don't know if you can call me a good cook. I have to admit I didn't make the sauce. It comes from M&M's, the pizzeria where I work. It's delicious. Their carbonara is our favorite. I'm just boiling the penne that goes with it and that'll be done in a minute. But I've made a nice green salad. That I did cook if you can call dicing cucumber and slicing tomatoes cooking. Oh well. You know what I mean. Hope you're hungry."

Janice realized she was blathering and snapped her mouth shut. Wiping her sticky palms on the tea towel tucked into the waistband of her jeans, thrumming with nerves, she went to the table and pretended to check the settings.

Kobus was keeping his head bowed, trying to hide his watery eyes. His shoulders slumped in that familiar hangdog attitude. He took a long pull of his beer and clattered the bottle down on the coffee table, nearly knocking over his mother's untouched sherry.

Janice was unable to meet his mournful gaze and escaped back to the kitchen. "Must check the pasta. Won't do to let the water boil dry."

As she left the room, she heard Kate break the strained silence, asking a question that Kobus answered in Dutch.

Kate was amazing at dispelling tension. During the meal she kept up the flow of conversation, asking lots of questions and listening properly to the answers. Initially the chat stumbled along, half in English to favor Janice and half in Dutch to favor Coby. But within minutes, Kate had Coby laughing out loud and even Kobus cracked a snigger or two. Mind you, the flow of wine helped ease the situation and soon Kobus, Janice, and Kate were well onto the next bottle of soave. Coby stuck to her water, which she sipped more often than she touched the food on her plate.

Janice had arranged the seating so that Coby faced her, and Kobus was across from Kate. No way did Janice want to sit opposite him. It would have been too confrontational. While they were eating the main course, their glances did cross several times, but somehow, both Kobus and Janice managed to avoid speaking directly to each other. Not until Janice brought in the tiramisu for dessert (thanks to M&M) did Kobus finally look her in the eye.

Putting down his wine, he held out his hand for his plate. "*Ach*, my favorite."

Janice smiled politely and handed it over. She was about to set the second plate in front of his mother when Coby suppressed a cough.

"*Nee*, Jan-ease, let Kobus eat it for me." She slumped in her chair and made a show of patting her flat stomach. "The pasta was *heel lekker*. I am too full."

Rubbish. Coby hadn't eaten a morsel, merely moved the food about with her fork. Janice chose not to insist, not when the reason for Coby's lack of appetite was staring her in the face. Instead, she gave Kobus the second plate and darted back to the kitchen to pick up Kate's dessert and her own.

Janice liked to linger over food she enjoyed eating, stretching out the pleasure for as long as possible, and was still nibbling the edges of her tiramisu by the time Kobus had finished gulping down both portions. He gave a huge sigh of contentment and, for the first time, smiled at Janice. "Thank you. That was nice."

His English accent had improved since she'd gone away. Janice had to repay his good manners. "Glad you liked it, but all thanks should go to M&M. I'm not much of a cook but I do know how to heat things up." She added, "And take cold puddings out of the fridge."

Kate gave Janice a smile and caressed her thigh. Janice took comfort from the warm touch. She could do it. Be nice to Kobus. Not for Kate's sake, for Coby's sake.

Chapter 73

Now the delirious days of bedroom delight were truly over. For some mad reason, the firm was reorganizing the Amsterdam office, which meant Kate's department was involved. Kate had to work lots of overtime and came home too tired to play in bed.

Janice had asked for more hours at the pizzeria so that she could pay her share of the household expenses. M&M were happy to oblige a good dishwasher. Now her one day off was Saturday and she worked all day Sunday. That made sense because Kate's Sundays were going to be busy too. Hannah had finished the rewrite of *Romy & Jools—Do or Dyke*. The Thespians were happy with the results, and rehearsals were about to begin.

Janice was putting away the dishes when Kate said she was going to do the play.

"How can you choose Hannah over me?" Janice was staggered by the betrayal.

"What are you on about?" Kate's eyes were hooded. "What have I said about taking sides? Didn't that sink in?" Kate sighed. "I'm not choosing Hannah. I'm choosing to play Romy. I like acting with the Thespians and I'm not going to stop just to please you, just because the director's your ex."

"But she's your ex too. Or is she?"

"Dammit, Janice. I've told you, Hannah's a friend. We've known each other for years. I like her nice bits and gloss over the rest. Yes, she can be selfish, and she did treat you badly. But that's your business. What happened between you has nothing to do with me. It's your past, Janice. Deal with it."

Kate hardly ever called her by her name. This was serious. Janice repaid the favor. "Kate darling, you're with me now. That means anything to do with me is now your business. Besides that, you're Wonder Woman. The real one. I used to think that Hannah was Wonder Woman, until her betrayal put me right. I've been looking for you all my life. Ever since…"

Janice stopped. She hadn't told Kate about Ariel. They'd never discussed their past loves, mainly because Janice didn't want to hear about Hannah. "You're my other half. You make me complete."

Kate shook the suds off her fingers and turned on Janice. "I can't believe you actually said that." And she roared, not in anger, which was what Janice expected, but in laughter.

Janice folded her arms over the hurt. "Are you making fun of me?"

"Oh, Kumquat, I'm not Wonder Woman, not your other half. That's wishful thinking, a fantasy. You're making us stars of a soppy rom-com. Stop it. We're not lovey-dovey dykes joined at the hip. We're separate, complete in our own right. Stop this bullshit. Get real, girl."

Janice stood in stunned silence, needing time to absorb what Kate said, knowing deep in her heart she was hearing the cutting edge of truth. The sharp tone gave Janice the shock she needed to realize she had to accept Kate as she was, as her own person. And to understand that she was complete on her own.

Check, check—reality check. She got it, this flash of insight, and exhaled in relief. She'd been holding her breath and felt lightheaded. "Any minute now I'll be doing a Kobus." She smiled at her honest lover. "We're equal but different."

* * *

On September thirteenth, the ninth Saturday of her life together with Kate (not that Janice was counting), Sanne and Fern came around in their wonky little car to pick them up for a drive. It was a Citroën 2CV. Janice couldn't resist making fun of Kate's habit of using Dutch expressions. "As the French would say, a *deux chevaux*," she said. The Dutch called it a duck, and you could see why. Painted a daffy yellow, the little car had a retractable canvas roof and cute little windows that clamped open. With their long legs, Janice and Kate found the backseat confined but nestled on it quite happily.

Fern sat behind the wheel with Sanne beside her, appointed official navigator. On their way out of town, heading south, Fern drove fast, zipping through traffic and shifting down a gear at the lights to nip through before they turned red.

Sanne took her task seriously. Speaking over her shoulder, she said, "The tank is full, girlies. Where to? Someplace special? Or we give you lover-birds a magic mystery tour?"

"Magical mystery tour," said Kate at the exact moment Janice asked, "Can we go to Urk?" They both laughed.

"Urk." Fern giggled. "Why would you want to go to Urk?"

Janice couldn't explain why. She'd have to mention Kobus. Kate noticed her hesitance and filled in. "Our neighbors come from Urk. They say the seafood is great down on the harbor. Why not? Let's have lunch in Urk."

"Urk it is." Sanne added for Fern, "*Schatje*, we go to the A1 and turn off to Lelystad."

Since coming to Amsterdam, Janice hadn't left the city. Now she wasn't impressed by the flat Dutch landscape. The highway went on and on in a straight line, and the fields on either side were equally flat and ever flatter. She cuddled into Kate and let the monotony of the ride lull her to sleep. Kate nudged her awake as they drew into Urk.

Fern drove straight through the village, cutting down a narrow road the wrong way. "Don't worry," she called over her shoulder. "I'm prepared to say, 'But officer, I am going one way' if we get caught." She parked behind a lighthouse that loomed over the headland. Piling out of the car, Kate and Janice stretched their cramped legs.

The women meandered down to the harbor. Rounding the corner, Janice recognized the picturesque view. The quay, seawall, and sleepy beach were in the postcard. So were the bobbing fishing boats and gray-brown nets slung over lines to dry. The scene hadn't changed a pixel since the photographer had snapped the boy walking his dog twenty-five years ago. Urk harbor was as fixed in time as young Kobus was fixed in the postcard, as fixed in the past as adult Kobus was today. A rush of sympathy choked her throat. Janice knew how Kobus must have felt when his father had abandoned him in death. Four years ago, she'd felt abandoned by Ariel's death. Kobus was still suffering from his loss, while Janice had recovered from hers. If only Kobus had his own Kate to help him move on.

Chapter 74

The following Monday, when Janice was preparing to go to work, a letter clattered through the mail slot in the front door. Assuming it was something for Kate, she didn't bother going to see what the postman had brought. But on the way out, she saw that the letter was for her. Postmarked Edinburgh. Judging by the crossed-out hostel address, Negy had forwarded it. Surprise, surprise, he must have kept Kate's business card. Janice pocketed the letter and went outside. Letting their front door slam shut, she quickly checked if Kobus was out in the street. Not today, thank goodness. She unlocked her bike and pedaled around the corner, out of range, before dismounting to read.

> Dearest Lassie (woof)
>
> Hope this missive* finds you well. Having the time of my life being pricked (pardon) into a veritable sieve by a witless ward of doctors who don't know what the hell they're doing. And that's putting it wildly. Serious now, they can't find what's behind this strange wee blemish that's gone all Sextra-Large on me. I mean, the wee spots have grown together and turned into fetching purply pink carnations.
>
> Did you notice I said "ward"? Yrs Trly is in HorsePiddle, a private room no less, paid for by Mummy, who is vaaaiiry relieved to see me. Must say I am glad, verily, not to be stuck on the open ward with the lousy addicts who seem to have caught the same affliction. One suffers in solitude. Not complaining. Don't know your plans, but if you can, why not drop in on Edinburgh? If compelled, I might let you in to see me. No rush.
>
> *Copy of letter sent to main post office. Just In Case.

Colin signed off with "be queer, not square" and put in his room number and the address of the hospital. Janice reread his letter twice before crumpling it in the envelope. Colin wanted to see her. Thanks to the extra hours at M&M's, she could afford a trip to Edinburgh. Ordinarily, she would go in a flash, but there was no rush. Life with Kate was so full. Truth to tell, she didn't know if she wanted to go if it meant leaving Kate behind, even for a few days.

Continuing down the busy road, Janice found the decision too hard to make. Forced to stop for the lights, she was struck by a new thought. Colin needed her. Aloud, she said, "I've got to stop this habit of putting things off. If I want to see Colin, I've got to act. Now."

When she arrived at M&M's, she used their phone to call Magic Bus and book a seat on the next bus to London. But it was full. The first available seat was a fortnight away. She'd have to be patient. Anyway, the delay gave her the chance to tell Kate and arrange things with M&M. Meanwhile, she'd write and tell Colin she was on her way. Soon.

Later, Janice arrived home from work first, as was usual these days. Kate was still working long hours, helping to manage the reorganization at the firm. Besides that, it was Janice's turn to cook and on her way home she was going to nip into their local supermarket to pick up the groceries she needed for dinner.

Now that M&M had given her more hours, Janice could afford to pay her half of the kitty. Agreeing to the practical aspects of living together was still a novelty, but one Janice enjoyed. Sharing the drudgery of food shopping, cooking, and cleaning the house was a fair exchange, the upside to having Kate in her life. Sharing Kate's home was wonderful even if the heady days of honeymoon were over. Their life had settled down, and it might have been perfect if not for the niggling unease Janice felt at the thought of the neighbors.

Speak of the devil. Janice was unraveling the chain on her bike when Coby popped her head around her portico. "*Dag*, Jan-ease," she called, holding on to the door and restraining a cough. She looked dreadful. Face gaunter than ever, purple shadows underlining her eyes. "Kate not home yet?"

As sick as she was, the woman still kept watch on the street and knew all the goings-on. Just like Mrs. Palmer, her sister, always did in London. *Must run in the family.*

"Jan-ease, you have coffee with us, *ja*? Kobus make a good cup."

Janice couldn't refuse, not with Coby entreating her like this. Her heart sank. *Please let there be no hassle with Kobus. Not in his own home, not in front of his fragile mother.* Summoning a smile, she called back, "Okay, I'll come in for a minute. Just let me finish locking my bike first."

Coby stood aside to let her in. This was the first time Janice had been inside the neighbors' house. The layout was identical to Kate's. Same long corridor down to the kitchen, same lofty ceiling in the oblong living room, but there the similarity ended. Unlike Kate's airy place, this was a cave. Broad venetian blinds and dusty net curtains cloaked the tall windows, blocking the light. Hideous orange-and-brown-patterned wallpaper, a relic of the early seventies, lowered the nicotine-tinted ceiling, and a muddy-green carpet oozed over the floor. The furniture wouldn't have been out of place in one of Amsterdam's brown cafés: masses of fussy potted plants, miraculously flourishing in the dim light, a heavy dining table with too many extra chairs shoved tight against the walls. There were too many little side tables as well, most of them holding plants. Finally, there were two worn armchairs and a stiff, tatty couch with flat wooden arms. The armchair near the window was angled so that whoever sat in it could peer through the blinds and spy outside. Coby's lookout.

"Jan-ease *is hier.*" Coby raised her voice with visible effort. "Kobus," she ordered abruptly. "*Kom eens beneden en maak ons een kopje koffie.*" She pointed at the second armchair and waved at Janice to sit. "I tell him to come down and make us a *lekker* cup coffee. He make real Douwe Egberts."

Silence. Janice sat awkwardly in the armchair. The seat was too low for her long legs. Bet she'd have trouble getting up later. Looking around the gloomy room, she asked, "Is Kobus upstairs?" Coby gave her a blank stare. "Hope you don't mind me asking."

"*Nee*, I try to think the English." In her broad accent, "think" sounded more like "sink." Coby shook her head in frustration. "Sorry,

Jan-ease. My boy must tell for me." She went to the door and screeched, "*Kobus, kom hier! Nu!*"

Kobus yelled from above and followed his voice downstairs, stomping on the steps.

Coby sank into her armchair, choking on a suppressed cough. Before Janice could offer help, Kobus sidled into the room and saw his mother. "*Zal ik je een glas water halen?*"

Coby rejected his offer with a fierce look. "*Nee, idioot.*" She gasped a breath, pointed at him, and said curtly, "Make coffee for Jan-ease." It was an order and must be obeyed.

Janice pulled up the neck of her T-shirt to cover her mouth, hiding amazement. This was a side to Coby she hadn't seen before. Not the chatterbox she knew on the street, nor the endearing version she presented whenever Kate was around. This little Coby was an awful tyrant, talking to her son as if he were a naughty infant, not an autonomous adult.

Coby must have known she'd dropped her mask of niceness in front of Janice. Was this awful person her real self? Why had she chosen to reveal it? Was it because she didn't care what Janice thought of her? Was it because, unlike Kate, Janice didn't count? Coby had no need to impress her or keep in her good books the way she did with Kate, to maintain their friendship. But if Janice didn't carry the same weight of friendship as Kate, why had Coby invited her into her domain? The dragon's den. Janice turned her eyes away before Coby's piercing gaze could detect her confusion.

Yes, Mama. No, Mama. Three bags full, Mama. Kobus bowed his head and obediently left the room, shooting a mournful glance at Janice on the way. His eyes beseeched: *Rescue me.*

Chapter 75

Janice stirred in her chair. Poor Kobus. Okay, in London his whining had often annoyed the hell out of her, but he had his bright and cheerful side, and he'd often swept her up in excitement. Here his hangdog stance was more than clear. Slumped shoulders, bowed head, he looked beaten, totally collared by Coby. His only form of protest at the punishing way his mother treated him was the slothful speed of his response. *Passive resistance rules okay.*

Kobus made them wait ages. Janice put a strained smile on her face, not knowing what to say. Coby looked at ease in the silence, ruling her little roost. Finally, Kobus appeared with a tray holding three fine porcelain cups of rich black coffee, a little jug of milk, and a bowl of sugar. He approached to serve his mother. Before he could reach her, Coby waved him away. "*Nee, idioot,*" she commanded. "You give Jan-ease first. She is guest."

Kobus deliberately turned on his heel and held the tray so Janice could take a cup. He offered the milk. Janice peered into the jug and saw that it was that dreadful condensed milk that the Dutch always put in their coffee: *koffiemelk.* Janice hated its slimy texture.

"No thanks." She smiled politely at Kobus. "I'll have it black today." She took a large swallow of bitter coffee and, rivaling Coby, coughed it straight back up again. Yuk. Way too strong. If this were unadulterated Douwe Egberts coffee, the Dutch could have it. She'd take M&M's delicious milky cappuccino over this vile muck, any day.

Kobus produced a tissue from his back pocket. "Here, take it. It's clean."

Janice accepted the tissue with a grateful glance and mopped her chin. Damn it, she'd spluttered droplets of coffee onto the carpet, and worse, down her favorite T-shirt.

Coby sat in rigid silence while this happened. She spoke only to order Kobus into the kitchen, to fetch salt to sprinkle onto the carpet. She made no move to help clean up the mess, but her irritation at Janice's clumsiness showed in the ceaseless drumming of her fingers on her armrest. Her face was drained. She looked exhausted, in sullen agony.

Ordinarily, Janice would have tried to comfort the ill woman, do something, anything, to ease her pain. But Coby's irrational fury scared her off. Janice wondered if the effort of fueling all that anger was draining Coby more than the cancer was.

Janice couldn't finish the coffee fast enough. At last, she could put down her cup on a side table and heaved herself out of the armchair. "Thank you," she said to Coby, who was sitting in obdurate silence. "It's been lovely, but I must go. Sorry for ruining your carpet. If the salt doesn't get the stains out, let me know. I can get you some carpet cleaner."

Coby didn't respond to the offer, merely waved angrily at Kobus to show Janice out. He did so in silence, ready to close the door behind her when she stopped him with a whisper. "What's got into your mother? Is she always this nasty to you?"

Kobus jiggled from foot to foot. At last, he whispered back. "It is her cancer. It is such a cruel illness, the cancer makes her cruel too. Underneath she still loves me very much. My mama…" His eyes filled with tears. "I don't want to lose her, the way I lost my papa."

"The way you lost me," Janice interrupted, filled with sudden empathy for Kobus. It must be the season of insights. Check, check—double reality check. Finally, Janice realized that what had happened between them in London hadn't been Kobus's fault alone. On the one hand, she'd wanted to keep things platonic, and the way he kept pushing that boundary was inexcusable. On the other hand, she was as much to blame, accepting all his gifts as her due, shamelessly flirting with him whenever she felt like it. She had played her own role in the disaster, as selfishly as Kobus had played his. She hadn't meant to hurt him. But he hadn't meant to hurt her either.

Now Kobus wanted to shut the door. Triggered by this insight, Janice said, "Please, wait a moment, I have to tell you something."

He waited unwillingly, jiggling from foot to foot in the anxious way she knew so well. She wouldn't let his nerves annoy her. People acted according to their own ability. Kobus was being his nervous, helpless self. But she could help herself. It was time to stop passively reacting to things that happened to her. Recalling what Kate had said, Janice took charge of how she felt about what she had done to Kobus.

"Listen, I'm sorry. I treated you badly in London. It was wrong of me to accept all your presents. I shouldn't have let you spend all that money on me."

Kobus went to interrupt but Janice wouldn't let him. She continued. "It was wrong of me to give you the wrong impression. I was sending confusing signals, I know. Out of loneliness, I suppose. I don't blame you for believing that I fancied you as much as you fancied me. Well, I did, Kobus, a bit. You're a nice guy and I did fancy you a bit. But not enough to keep on wanting to go to bed with you. I just wanted to find out what it was like being with a man and, yes, I used you for that. I wanted us to be friends. We were going to have a platonic friendship. Remember?"

This had turned into a sermon, but Janice wasn't finished. "I wasn't fair to you. I should have been consistent, stuck to my guns, and made it absolutely clear what my boundaries were. I did try. I did tell you, I'm a lesbian. Like Kate."

She would have gone on, but Kobus put out a hand and stopped her. "You love Kate."

"Yes, I love Kate. And she loves me."

"I thought you were my Kate. I wish I had a Kate." And Kobus slowly and carefully shut his door in Janice's face.

Chapter 76

The last Sunday in September, the day before Janice's twenty-third birthday, Kate and Janice lingered in bed, enjoying the first lie-in they'd had in ages. They took their time making love, Janice on top, relishing the power she had to satisfy Kate. Janice marveled at their lovemaking, both giving and taking in equal (but different) measure. So distinct from the selfish demands of a certain One-Way Woman whose name wouldn't be mentioned here. Definitely not now, with Kate quivering in delicious agony under her touch.

Kate stiffened, clamped Janice as hard as she could, then let go completely, flopping her arms wide on the bed. Janice waited a long moment, holding her lover close, feeling their hearts beat as one, feeling their limbs fit together as if they belonged to the same body. Finally, she rolled off and buried her nose in Kate's neck, snuffling a trace of Rive Gauche.

A comfortable silence enveloped them, punctuated by the soft sound of Kate regaining her breath. Janice inhaled when Kate exhaled. The peaceful synchrony of their breathing reminded Janice of her first kiss, with Ariel, so very long ago.

The buildup began in class. They'd been pretending to pay attention to their geography teacher, Mrs. Dalloway (not yours, Virginia), ranting about the undulating peaks of the English Pennines. Underneath the desk they'd been playing their game: Ariel grabbing Janice's hand, "Lez be friends," and Janice pretending to pull away, "Homo you don't!"

That first kiss happened by accident. After school. They'd stayed behind on purpose, making sure they were the last to fetch their bikes for the ride home. Ariel had a flat tire. Janice reached down to unhook the pump from her bike, and as she straightened, Ariel bent down, and their faces collided. Their lips met. And. The. World. Stood. Still. Janice lifted Ariel onto tiptoes, hauling her deep into her arms, inhaling Ariel's peppermint breath.

Janice remembered thinking at the time: *This is us. This is how we're meant to be.* Now it was exactly the same with Kate. They were meant to be. Despite all her ranting about being separate people, in love for now and not forever, Janice felt utterly at one with her lover.

Unexpectedly, Kate sat up, dislodging Janice and disrupting her reverie. "Kumquat, when did you last see Coby?"

Janice wanted to ignore the stark pounding of her heart. Slowly, she sat up beside Kate. "Um, let me think. A week ago, last Monday, when I got home from work. She asked me in for a coffee."

"Coby had you inside her house? Wow. She must like you a lot."

"I don't know about that. And I don't know why she bothered inviting me in. She wasn't nice to me, and she was really cruel to Kobus. He reckons the cancer has brought out her nasty side."

"I can't imagine Coby being nasty. She's a sweetie."

"Well, she was awful. She looked in pain. Maybe her throat was making her have an off day. Her nastiness seemed out of character. That's why I didn't mention it."

"When did you last hear Coby coughing? Any time after that Monday?"

Janice realized she hadn't heard a trace of a cough coming through the wall all week, nor the week before. "Not a peep." As she spoke, she felt a wave of dread wash over her.

"Neither have I." Kate put Janice's fear into words. "I think Coby's dead."

Janice tumbled out of bed in blind panic. "Oh no, Kate, what shall we do? Come on, quick! We've got to do something!"

"What's the rush?"

Janice stopped pacing up and down beside the bed and stared at Kate, aghast. Kate was level-headed, sure, but this calm reaction was beyond understandable. "You've just said Coby's dead. You're just as worried as I am. Come on, the least we can do is check up on Kobus. We have to make sure. Now!"

Kate slid out of bed and pulled on her jeans and sweater. "Oh, Kumquat, stop running about like a headless chicken. It's not like someone drowning. A dead person stays dead no matter how fast you move."

Janice wrapped Kate's dressing gown around herself. "Shall I phone the cops?"

"Let's see what's happening first. Keep still. Wait here," Kate ordered, and left.

Janice didn't recognize her lover. Her face was a mask. Did Kate put this mask on to distance herself from people at work? The staff she had to fire in the firm's reorganization. Janice had never seen that mask turned on her before.

She went through to the living room and could hear Kate pounding on Coby's door, calling on Kobus to open up. Janice couldn't keep still. She paced up and down the room in an agony of obedience. Rushing back to the bedroom, she hauled open the heavy patio door and strode onto the patch of lawn, gulping air in an effort to calm herself.

There was a scurry on Coby's balcony. Janice looked up at the sound and saw Kobus cowering in the far corner. She heard him crooning his mother's name repeatedly.

Janice stormed through the house and onto the street. Kate was still knocking on Coby's door. "Come quick. It's Kobus. He's out on their balcony, gibbering like a madman."

Kate came back inside and called the police. When they arrived, they listened to her explain the situation and then, without bothering to knock, simply battered down Coby's door. Without waiting for the police to give her permission, Kate followed them inside.

Janice stayed in the living room, hovering by the window. She saw a van arrive and double-park in front of Coby's house. After a while, Janice watched two uniformed men slide a small black body bag into the back of the van. It looked to be of no weight at all. Kobus rushed outside, thrusting a police officer out of his way, and tried to throw himself into the van. Kate bustled him back into his house, away from the prying eyes of the crowd gathering in the street. Janice waited in silence for Kate to come home.

Finally, Kate returned. She leaned against the living room door. Answering Janice's unspoken question, she said, "We found Coby upstairs, lying in bed, bathed in sunshine and stinking to high heaven.

The whole house was full of stink." Shivering, Kate sat beside Janice on the sofa. "It was awful. Coby's sheets were rumpled where Kobus had lain beside her."

Janice was horrified. "Was Kobus sleeping beside his dead mother?"

Kate nodded. "Could be he slept there for days, a week at least. They can't tell when Coby actually died. The cops said they'll have to wait for the autopsy to know for sure."

"Can't Kobus tell them?"

"He's useless." Kate shook her head. "Totally rabid with grief. He's beyond telling."

"Who's with him now? He can't be left alone, surely?"

"What, are you offering to go over and look after him?"

Janice had to look away, ashamed of the panicky fear that froze her to the spot.

"I didn't think so." Kate smiled briefly, more a grimace than a real smile. "But you don't have to worry. The cops have left a social worker to stay with him for now. She won't leave until she's got him sorted. And they'll notify the next of kin." Seeing Janice's blank look, she gave an exasperated sigh. "Coby's sister, Corrie someone, in London. Your old landlady."

Oh god, yes. There would be no escaping Corrie Palmer. She'd probably blame Janice for Kobus's deranged state all over again.

Kate had brought home the stench of death in her hair and on her clothes. She plucked at her sweater. "Might as well throw this away. I'll never get rid of the stink. Come on, I need a shower. You can help me wash my hair."

Janice followed meekly, stunned by Coby's death and even more shocked by Kate's callous response to it. That night she lay awake long after Kate had dozed off into an easy sleep, mulling over what had happened. Her rational mind said she wasn't responsible for how Kobus felt. Still, irrationally, she felt responsible for him not coping with his mother's death. Hearing the muffled dongs of the local church chiming midnight, she thought, *What an awful way to begin my birthday.*

Chapter 77

Coby had warned them what would happen. She'd told them Kobus would go mad if she died, and he did go mad with grief. He wanted to join his mother in death. Luckily, he was as bad at dying as he was at living. The day after they'd taken Coby away, he made his first attempt. He got up on his roof. Teetering near the gutter, he was about to jump when a neighbor noticed him and called the police. They came, talked him down, then went away and left him to it.

Janice was at work, but Kate had the day off and had been home when it happened. She saw the flashing lights of the police car and went to see what was wrong. The neighbor filled her in. Kate waited until they were in bed that night before she told Janice about it.

"Why didn't you tell me sooner?" Janice ripped off the headphones of the little Walkman Kate had given her for her birthday. She'd been listening to Kate's second present, a tape of the Au Pairs.

"Oh, Kumquat, I didn't want this bad news to spoil your birthday."

"Well, you've spoiled it now." Janice was incredulous. "Are you telling me the cops stopped Kobus from jumping but didn't do anything else to protect him from himself?" Kate had to nod. "So they don't give a damn if you kill yourself. They only care if you kill someone else in the process, by accident, by falling on them. As if that could happen. For fuck's sake, he's suicidal. He needs help to get over Coby. When is Mrs. Palmer getting here, do you know?"

"Tuesday evening, apparently. He's on his own until then."

"We can't wait till tomorrow. Coby warned us he'd go mad if she died. We must get him onto a psych ward tonight. Get him committed, now, straightaway!"

It sounded right to Janice, but Kate shook her head. "When the cops left, I spoke to Kobus, told him we could help him check into the Valerius Clinic. He said no. He was very definite. He does not want psychiatric help. Hard as it sounds, we can't force him. You can't commit people against their will, not even to protect themselves. That's the way it is here."

Janice thrust her new Walkman and the headphones under her pillow and slid down the bed, fuming with anger. It wasn't right. Given therapy, Kobus could get over Coby's death. He was only thirty-six, healthy, with a long life ahead. "I don't care, we must get him the therapy he needs."

Kate took Janice into her arms. "I know it stinks, Kumquat, but you have to accept it. Therapy might be what Kobus needs, but it is not what he wants."

* * *

The evening before Janice was due to leave for her visit to Edinburgh, she arrived home from M&M's expecting to find Kate preparing dinner. Strangely enough the house was empty. She slid open the patio door and wandered into the garden to enjoy the orangey-gold beams of the long-evening sun. About to go back inside, she heard a dull thump. She looked up. Kobus and Kate were out on his balcony. Kobus had climbed over the banister and was perched on the ledge.

Kate was crouched down, holding out the end of a long white rope. Its other end was bound firmly around the banister. Janice recognized the rope. It was Kate's lasso, the one she used to tie the knots Kobus had taught her. Kobus reached out and took the lasso from Kate's outstretched hand. He slung the supple noose over his head and drew it around his neck.

"You can do it," Kate insisted, her face enclosed in that hard mask. "Jump, Kobus, jump!"

Janice reached up her arms, appalled by what she was hearing Kate say, desperate to stop what was going to happen.

Gripping the banister with his free hand, Kobus slowly turned to face the garden.

"You can," urged Kate gently, again and again. "Jump, Kobus, jump. Go on, Kobus, you can do it. Jump!"

Kobus squeezed his eyes and leaned forward. Janice screamed "No!"

Kobus let go and stepped into space. The rope twanged a deep, dark note as it took the falling weight and left Kobus choking a meter above the ground. His head flopped, his hands twitched, once, twice, and were still. A pitiful stream of wet dribbled down his right leg.

Janice howled, clenching her useless fists, horrified by what she had seen. She was outraged. It was wrong, wrong, wrong.

Kate eased herself to her feet and held on to the banister. She stared at the swinging corpse then turned her glare on Janice. "Coby asked us to help Kobus, and I did. I gave him what he wanted." Then the mask slid from her face and her voice was sad and small. "Didn't I?"

Janice glared back at Kate, too angry to answer the question out loud: *Yes you did. But was it the right thing to do?*

Chapter 78

Long into the night, Janice lay seething in bed, crammed against the window, as far away from Kate as she could get. The dusty scent of velvet filled her nostrils. Janice clenched and unclenched her fists, pointed and relaxed her toes, thrumming tight energy. She was aware that Kate was also awake.

"Oh, Kumquat," Kate turned over and reached out cold fingers to stroke her face. "Go to sleep, for god's sake. You know you've got to get up early or you'll miss the Magic Bus."

Janice sat up, throwing the duvet off her clammy skin. "Do you really think I'm still going off to Edinburgh after what happened today? Just like that?"

Kate sat up too. "Why not? Just because Kobus jumped doesn't mean you need to change your plans. Colin is expecting you. You want to see him, so go."

Kate's slender body was a shadow in the dark. Janice tugged on the chord of the reading lamp above their heads, making Kate blink in the burst of light. Janice mumbled something.

Kate frowned. "If you've got something to say, say it!"

Janice turned from the challenge in Kate's eyes. Summoning courage, she said, "Kobus is … he was someone we knew well, yet besides that moment straight after he jumped, you don't seem to care that he's dead. All this time I've loved you for how kind you are to me, to Coby, to Kobus too, but underneath that soft façade you're a hardheaded, coldhearted bitch."

Kate smiled without mirth. "Sprung, at last!" She took in Janice's horrified expression. "Gallows humor, get it?" When Janice didn't respond to her scathing tone, she said, "Of course I give a damn, but what's the point of dwelling on death? Kobus is gone. Coby's gone. Corrie's here now. She's arranging Coby's funeral. Now she can arrange his as well."

How callous could Kate get? The irony of the situation was killing. All those wasted months of agony, believing she had murdered Kobus when she hadn't. Kate, the so-called love of her life, her one and only Wonder Woman, had managed to do that. When the police turned up, the same pair who had attended Coby's death, Kate led them to Kobus, still hanging from the balcony but now hidden by the sheet she had draped over his body. After giving Kobus a cursory examination, checking if he was truly dead, and talking briefly with Kate, the police had cut the corpse down and carted it away in the same black van.

Hovering in the background, Janice heard Kate tell them that she and Janice had found him strung up when they'd come home from work. Janice kept her mouth shut, silenced by the fierce looks Kate was sending. She debated telling the cops what had happened but didn't. It was not her story to tell.

Bullshit. Janice had seen Kate help Kobus kill himself. Assisted suicide was against the law. That made Kate a criminal and Janice complicit, if only as a passive witness, unable to stop the lethal act. Still, that made it her story to tell too. Janice might not be responsible for what Kate had done, but she was responsible for her own reaction to the crime.

Now she said slowly, "Are you going to give yourself up?"

Kate folded her arms. "You cannot be serious. Of course not. What difference would it make? Kobus was determined to die. He would have, eventually, with or without my help." She reached above Janice's head to switch off the lamp. Bringing her face close to Janice, she whispered, "If I admitted anything I'd lose my good job, my whole life in Amsterdam. I'd go to prison, and what good would that do? It won't bring Kobus back. Be sensible. What's done is done. Don't look back, look forward to seeing your friend Colin again." Kate slid down on the bed and turned her back on Janice. "Let me get to sleep. You're not the only one with an early start in the morning."

Janice didn't say a word. She couldn't express how angry she was as the claws of fury clamped onto her heart. But now she knew what she had to do.

Chapter 79

Janice was on the number two tram on her way to the Magic Bus and Colin, as planned. The bus would take her to London, ferry crossing and all, arriving at Victoria Station early next morning. That meant hanging about for hours before she could catch the train to Edinburgh.

Getting off at the Leidseplein tram stop, heading down the long stretch of road to the bus station, Janice recalled her arrival in Amsterdam, seven full months ago. How surprised she'd been by all the black lambs frolicking in the fields. She remembered thinking, *The Dutch let the black sheep live, while in New Zealand they let them die.* She sighed. The Dutch let them die too. Kobus had been a black sheep, led to death before his time.

Talking of sheep, she mulled, *what about Hannah, that devious wolf in sheep's clothing?* Hannah's teasing had shorn a coat of naivety off Janice's back and, she realized now, that wasn't such a terrible thing. The betrayal had hurt but it had taught her an important life lesson. Don't always take people (read: selfish narcissists) at face value.

Janice sidestepped into the gutter to avoid a nasty dog turd. It paid to watch your step walking the streets of Amsterdam. If only she'd known enough to watch her step with Hannah. Now she realized her crush on One-Way Woman and urgent desire to join Thalia Thespians had been driven by her foolish belief that she needed others to make her complete.

With Ariel she'd felt whole. Losing Ariel in that accident had sliced her fragile soul in half. Ever since, Janice had felt helpless. Sure, on the surface she had agency. She could look after herself on a practical level. Hadn't she managed the flight to Europe? Hadn't she found a job and a place to stay in London, double that here in Amsterdam? But underneath, on the secret level, she'd felt like a vulnerable wreck, unable to protect herself. Losing Ariel had turned Janice into a people pleaser, easy prey for needy users, like Kobus.

And greedy users, like Hannah. It had driven the futile search for Wonder Woman, a fantasy femme who could wave her magic wand and make Janice whole again. Just like that. Just like Kate.

How stupid to believe she was incomplete. Janice was her own person, in charge of her own feelings and actions. Kate and her callous contradictions had taught her that. Was Kate's pretending to care a way for her to feel good about herself? Janice wasn't sticking around to find out. On getting up this morning she'd told a stunned Kate she was leaving and not coming back. "Our so-called love affair is over," Janice had said. "You destroyed whatever I felt for you the moment you kindly helped Kobus destroy himself."

Halfway to the corner, Janice looked up and saw the Magic Bus pulling into the station. It was early, not due to leave for another half hour. She might have time to get on before it left. But if she didn't, no worries. She'd catch the next bus that had a seat for her, leaving tomorrow morning with any luck.

What to do tonight, in case she had to miss this bus? No way would she go back to Kate. And no way could she go back to the hostel. Negy wouldn't let her in, she knew that for a fact. It would be different with M&M. They'd put her up for a couple of nights. They'd let her sleep on a sofa, something like that. On her way to the restaurant, she could pop into the post office, send Colin a telegram saying she'd been delayed. He'd understand.

Reaching the corner, Janice ignored the bus and crossed the road to the police station. Pausing at the front door, she let the rucksack slide down her arm. She had packed only the possessions she wanted to keep. She'd left Kate's expensive birthday gift, the Walkman, lying demonstratively on the dining table. Tucked behind her transistor radio, Bitchy Bear peeked out of the top pocket. She gave the toy a stroke on his cute little head. This was going to be hard, but telling the police what she had witnessed was the right thing to do. For Kobus, it was too late, but for Janice, it was not too late to act.

Yet, she dithered. Telling on Kate would be a betrayal, far worse than anything the arch mistress of betrayal (read: Hannah) had ever done to Janice. Could she do it? Destroy Kate's comfortable life in

Amsterdam? Janice couldn't be that cruel, not to someone who had cared for her as much as Ariel had done. All the love Kate had given her, asking nothing in return, all the wisdom she'd shared, that couldn't be ignored. Surely her kindness couldn't all be a pretense. Despite her surface callousness, underneath, Kate was okay. She had only done what she felt was best for Kobus. Given him what he wanted. If you looked at it that way, it was the kindest gesture a caring person could make.

But, well-intentioned or not, Kate had done wrong. Impulsively, Janice reached out to pull open the station door—why were Dutch doors always so heavy?—when she heard the clatter of an arriving bicycle. Distracted, she turned to see who it was and—oh no! Kate had dismounted and was chaining her bike to the rack. She was dressed for work, looking as cool as she usually did. Except for the terror in her eyes when she straightened and saw Janice. Aware of the taut muscles stretching her own face, Janice froze in speechless shock.

Poles apart, the startled women stood for what felt like eternity in silence. Then, seeing Kate's mask slip into place, Janice broke the gaze. Kate came a step closer, impelling Janice to give way. There was too much to say. And no point in saying it. With a niggle of relief, Janice realized there was no longer a need for betrayal. Kate had taken the decision out of her hands. Clearly, she agreed with Janice's unspoken criticism and was going to give herself up. She was facing the consequences of her act head on, voluntarily. Good for her.

Shouldering the rucksack, Janice gave a sad smile, acknowledging the brave step her ex was taking. Then, without a backward glance, she crossed the road and boarded the Magic Bus. She went down the dusty aisle to the back, dumped the rucksack, and knelt on the seat to squint through the rear window. Kate was standing immobile by the station door. What was she waiting for? A young cop arrived, gave her a curious glance, and hauled open the door. Politely he motioned for Kate to enter, but she shook her head, stepped aside, and let him go in without her. She was still standing outside the station a quarter hour later when the Magic Bus coughed to life and, blasting fumes of diesel, took Janice and a horde of hippies away.

Settling into the middle of the backseat, glad that no one had sat beside her, Janice stretched her long legs and tried to switch her mind off Kate. But she couldn't ignore the familiar shards of guilt piercing her heart. Leaving Kate behind to cope with the aftermath of Kobus felt as if Janice were abandoning her. Janice knew how much that hurt, remembering how bereft she'd felt when Ariel had left her behind. Then realization dawned (we're equal, but different), melting the pinpricks of guilt, and Janice thought, *I've come full circle, only now I know it's not my fault. I'm not responsible for either one of their deaths.*

So be it. Kate would cope alone and so would Janice, on her own. As the bus trundled down the road to Haarlem, en route to the Hook of Holland and the ferry to Harwich, Janice stared at the tidy landscape. No wilderness here, just ranks of perfectly oblong fields lined with precise rows of willow. Even the cows seemed well behaved, cropping the grass in unison. Lulled by the rumbling wheels, Janice drifted away in thought. *This trip to Edinburgh is not like my reckless ride from London. Now I'm not running away but moving on to a new beginning. With Colin, the start of a new life.*

Poor thing, he was probably far more ill than he'd made out in his letter. That awful rash had been livid enough to land him in hospital. It must be serious. Janice gulped, knowing she didn't want to lose Colin. Not her best friend (after Ariel). He couldn't possibly die. He had to get better, and Janice would make sure that he did. Then His Royal Bitchness and the enlightened lassie would love and laugh and look after each other and be gay, gay, gay all the long way to their happily ever afters.

Please.

Acknowledgements

Becoming Janice took its time coming to life. Writers write what they know (as you know) and the plot was sparked by events that happened *very* long ago. I didn't start working on it till years later, eventually producing a novella called *Janice in Action*. Alas, life got in the way and the story languished for so long I began calling it *Janice Inaction*. Finally, with the encouragement of my developmental editor, Corina Onderstijn, prize-winning author of *Vanbinnen en vanbuiten*, I managed to write a book-length draft.

A rough draft, mind you, which my team of readers helped me hone into a publishable story. Humble thanks to Lindi Belfield, Marijke Brandsma, Alberto Cortés Navarette, Alexandra van den Doel, Amelia Fendell, Megan Paxman, Annie Perkins, Jill Ripley Hughes, and Stephanie Wheatfield for your terrific feedback.

Huge thanks to the professionals at Iguana Books: Greg Ioannou (CEO) and Cheryl Hawley (publisher) for your calm management of the publishing process, and to three expert editors, Paula Chiarcos, Amanda Feeney, and Julia Rhebergen for your meticulous improvements to the quality of my book. Any remaining mistakes are all mine. Finally, my heartfelt thanks go to Chris Houston (TheIdeaShop.ca), whose marketing skills have ensured that you—dear Reader—are holding *Becoming Janice* in your hands.

www.ingramcontent.com/pod-product-compliance
Lightning Source LLC
Chambersburg PA
CBHW030618030726
47497CB00006B/1542